imPERFECT DEMONS

C.N. ROWAN

VINCI
BOOKS

By C.N. Rowan

The imPerfect Cathar

imPerfect Magic

imPerfect Curse

imPerfect Fae

imPerfect Bones

imPerfect Hunt

imPerfect Gods

imPerfect Blood

imPerfect Blades

imPerfect Demons

To all the readers, to the imPs, who've come with me this far.

There is never such a thing as The End.
It is only ever an opportunity for new beginnings.

Vinci Books

vinci-books.com

Published by Vinci Books Ltd in 2026

1

A CIP catalogue record for this book is available from the British Library.
Paperback ISBN: 9781036710828
The EU GPSR authorised representative is Logos Europe, 9 rue Nicolas Poussion, 17000 La Rochelle, France contact@logoseurope.eu

Chapter One

Cry Havoc and let slip the dogs of war. Though I'm ready to put a leash on the bastard demon mutt who stole my city.

Don't fuck with Toulouse.

Seriously, don't do it.

There are some simple rules in the Talented world.

One. Don't bring the big cojones if you don't have the power to back them up. Otherwise, you might not take them away with you again afterwards. Or if you do, it'll be in a little wooden box wrapped up in a vas deferens bow.

Two. Don't make deals with the fae, and if you do, count your fingers, toes, and all your organs again afterwards. Also, make sure your offspring's teeth haven't got inexplicably sharp all of a sudden. And if the baby in the cot starts asking you for a dram of whisky, you might be in trouble.

And three. If you mess with another Talented's territory, you better be ready for war.

It happens so rarely. No one wants to risk exposing the Talented to the Talentless. It'll happen sooner or later and probably be the end of the species – if humanity hasn't made the world explode by then, which also looks highly probable. But whoever actually becomes responsible for blowing our cover, for outing all the magic users and weird creatures living behind carefully crafted illusions and *don't look here* spells?

Well, they won't be Mr or Ms or Being Of Unidentified Gender Popular, put it that way. The likelihood of them getting invited to parties is going to reduce dramatically. Unless said party involves red-hot pokers and the rest of magical society waiting patiently in line for their turn to do interesting things with them to the poor unfortunate soul who brought us out of the shadows and into the spotlight.

So magical squabbles tend to be more the equivalent of the Cold War, only with curses instead of polonium-tipped umbrellas. Because if two major Powers throw down, it's going to get messy. And no one wants that.

Except, apparently, Caacrinolaas. President of Hell.

The griffin-winged arsehole has stolen my city and is threatening to spread mayhem through the unTalented population of Europe, starting there. He doesn't give a fuck if that blows the cover on the whole Talented secret society.

And right at this moment, neither do I. Because I'm ready to go and start blowing things up to get my city back. Starting with his cojones.

Caacrinolaas is about to get neutered. Ideally by me tearing them clean out of his ball sack with my bare hands. I'll need to sterilize my mitts in bleach for a couple of days afterwards, but by the Good God, it'll be worth it.

My friends? They're trying to calm me down enough so

I don't just walk straight into what is –quite clearly– an obvious trap.

'Did you not hear the bit where the Karnabo told us none of us would leave again if we go back to Toulouse?' The bear of a man-mountain that is Johannes Faust quirks an eyebrow that is almost as bushy as his beard at me. I'm not sure if that's supposed to be a prompt for me to remember how to use my brain or exasperation at my lack of one. Possibly a bit of both. I try to ignore the quirked eyebrow. Mainly because if I look at him, I'm liable to do something like trip over my own feet and erase half of my cheek on the stone path I'm hurrying down at high speed, aiming for mountain goat in my leaping descent but probably looking more like a deranged ape. Which is a fair description of me much of the time.

'Yep. I heard him. Easy solution to that. I'm going to shove his trunk up his posterior, pull it back out of his throat, and then play him like a church organ with hammer blows to his midriff.' I'm quite proud of that one. I think Aicha would like that. What I'd like is for this whole fuckery with elephant-faced, turn-you-to-stone-with-a-glance magical beings and their equally fucking irritating demonic masters to all fuck right back off to where they came from so that we can get back on with trying to find Aicha, along with Jakob and his angelic companion, Nanael – our missing companions.

'That's not a plan, lad; that's a vague threat.' Isaac tuts in frustration. Which is funny because you'd think after eight hundred years of being my mentor, he'd have worn out his tut-box.

'It wasn't vague at all, 'Zac. I thought it was pretty bloody detailed.' That wasn't the point he was making, but, hey, it's the one I feel like answering, so let's go with that, shall we?

'I think you're quite right, mano. Let's go!' Fucking hell. Mephistopheles has been absolutely on one, furiously riled up since he saw Caacrinolaas. I'm not sure what part of him's been triggered. Whether he hates the fucker from his time in the demon dimension or whether it's his doggy side kicking in, getting all possessive and basically wanting to piss on the entire mortal realm to mark it as his territory. Either way, the giant demonic Dobermann – and yes, I know all Dobermanns can look a bit demonic, but this one is *an actual demon*, so it's a different cup of tea entirely – is absolutely raring to go track down the *other* demon dog who's dared to step up into his domain.

'Not helpful, Mephy.' Faust absent-mindedly fusses the top of the creature's head, which considering Mephy's slavering foam everywhere and his eyes are literally glowing red like those creepy kids from *Village of the Damned*, would be a brave move on the part of most people. As they're soul-bonded –much as Isaac is with his angel, Nithael– it's perhaps less brave than if I were to perform that manoeuvre.

But one needs to be more than just *brave* for this fight. We need to get back onto home turf, back behind our wards, somewhere safe to recharge our magical batteries.

Except those wards don't exist anymore. The main ones anyhow. And I'm running through the seven stages of grief like a two-metre tall, hundred-and-twenty-kilo linebacker smashing through a whole opposing team. Anger, denial, bargaining. They've all taken up residence, squatting in my cerebellum and showing no intention of moving on despite my attempt to serve them with an eviction notice.

Because in all the times I've lived, all the mistakes I've made, all the plethora of fuck-ups I've made over the centuries?

I've never lost Toulouse. And it's like someone just tore my heart out. As someone who's had their heart torn out more than once –literally– I'm qualified to make that comparison, and it's surprisingly accurate, if less instantly fatal.

Right at this moment, it feels like it's killing me.

'It's not just you, my boy. I know how you feel.' Isaac pushes his glasses up his nose as he hurries along beside me. 'Believe you me, I want my home back too.'

I look over sharply at the tone. Damn. I'm a selfish bastard sometimes. I've been so focused on *my* loss, on *my* city that's been taken from me, that I've not even thought about how 'Zac must feel. All his treasures – his grimoires, his tomes, his research, his life's work – are inside that farmhouse that now lies bare and exposed and in enemy hands.

Isaac sees me staring at him and reads me like the open book I am to him, then waves down my concerns. 'Enough, lad. Your feelings are justified. I think there's enough of them swirling around in there that we don't need to add guilt into the mix, all right?'

We arrive at the car, my finger jabbing at the little oblong excuse for a car key, getting those doors unlocked so we can all go careening in. I'm still carrying momentum, slipping down the mountain scree, and I slam into the side of the Tesla with enough force that I might have scratched it, enough to make Isaac wince. *Sorry, 'Zac.* Fuck it, I'll buy him a new one once this is all over. Hell, I'll buy him a whole fleet of electric cars if we can just make it to the other side of this bullshit. If we can just get Toulouse back.

Gil, Faust, and Mephy scramble into the back, Mephy taking up position in the middle, his teeth still bared in that furious snarl. Anyone sensible would leave him well alone at a time like this.

I am not sensible. Plus there are questions I need answers to. 'So who exactly is your doggie demon pal, then, Meph? Cos I can't help noticing that the only two demons incarnate on this plane both have a penchant for canines. What's that about? And how the fuck, if you hate him so much, did you not spot it was him?'

Mephistopheles is my friend. He really is. I can tell that by how he doesn't lean over as I half-sprawl into the driver's seat and bite my face off. 'I'd tell you off for being a racist, mano –what, all demons that look like canines are related or something?– but you know you're being a prick, Paul.'

'Is he really the President of Hell?' Isaac's half-collapsed into the front passenger seat. He's looking better than he has done, certainly since I came back to Toulouse and found his arm infected with that demon gunk. Which brings up another question I want to ask, but Isaac has that gleam of intellectual curiosity in his eye, and I'll let him get his answer first. It's worth it, seeing that life back in his face even if he does still look wiped out.

'Well, yeah' –Mephy nods– 'but it wasn't like it was put to a vote or anything. I was Chief Party Animal Supreme. Like, I'm confident I'd have been elected if we did have to make it official, but we just picked titles we fancied. Hierarchy and bureaucracy aren't really a demonic go-to.'

Okay, sounds like it's a decorative title only. That's good. And it makes sense. I can't really see demons listening to one another. Or being prepared to sit through a presidential campaign. What would he offer them anyhow, considering they could create whatever they wanted from their dimensional plane on a whim? Bumper stickers?

Which brings my question back to the fore. 'Was that who sent you here, Mephy? To spy on us?' Maybe that's why the fucker turned up. He decided Meph wasn't doing a good enough job, so he came up here and decided to start fucking with us personally.

I've achieved something I never thought was possible. I've stunned Meph into silence. For about one second as I start up the car. 'Work for... *work for him?!* Paul, you absolute cockhead of an unevolved mano, I don't *work* for anybody. And certainly not that... that... that... *arm-fancier!*'

I guess that's as big an insult as Mephy can think of.

I spin up the Tesla's wheels, stones pinging off as I spin us around hard. I'll be doing the driving back to Toulouse. Firstly, because my heart can't handle Isaac's peculiar mixture of being both incredibly slow and yet simultaneously terrifying as a driver on top of what we've just witnessed, and secondly, because even when he's not bumbling along, he's never going to break the speed limit.

I'm about to see exactly how much you can get out of a Tesla Model S when you put your foot to the floor.

There're still questions that need answering too.

'So who were you working for then?' By the Good God, I feel like a cad in many ways. Mephy's just backed me up to the hilt in the fight with De Monteguard, came through in Home to save Isaac, even if indulging his appetite with the murder moles was more a lucky win than a calculated guess, and generally always been there for me. But there're too many of these half-answers, too many strands of information where we've been given little piecemeal crumbs but nowhere close to the full truth. Hard questions seem to be the only option.

'No one!' Mephy shakes his head, frustrated, giving Johannes and Gil on either side a small shower with his slobber in the process. 'It doesn't work like that, okay? We're not manos, eagerly waiting to march to the tune of some other mano who's offering us the great honour of dying dressed in his particular choice of colours against some other mano's dickheads in a different set. We're demonicos. Happy little individualists. All doing our own thing.'

'So why are you here?' I have to press. Have to. Getting my head around this feels essential. I trust Meph, I really do. But there's no space left for doubt in the mess we've found ourselves in.

'The way opened. Faust opened it.' Mephy rubs his head against Johannes' shoulder, nuzzling slightly. Faust rubs him back, scratching between his ears, an affectionate smile on his face when I risk a look in the rearview mirror, in between terrifyingly sharp bends down the mountain path. 'I took it. Knew the angelicos were here, didn't I? And I could feel the mano on the other end. Felt his qualities. While the angelicos were here on their own, everything was out of whack. All sorts of risks for you bumbling simpletons. We decided that if I came, it might help maintain the balance. Stop some other shitstain like Muttley back there from sliding over instead.'

Fuck. So Mephistopheles left his home, his own personal form of paradise, to try to keep us all safe. Giving up a place he considered perfection to slum it up on our plane to keep anyone or anything nastier from coming through. It's worked – up until now at least.

Perhaps I should stop giving him such a hard time. But...

'You said *we* decided you should come down here? Who was we?

8

'I… have a friend.' The way Meph says *friend* makes me suspect that might be underselling the depth of their relationship. Although I don't get the impression demons are big into monogamy, this is clearly someone important to him. 'We… we could see the possibility. That if an opportunity arose, then one of us might be able to travel up, to stay for a while. It wasn't a job! Wasn't like someone *told* me to do it!' I can hear the horror and disdain in his voice at the very idea.

'So did you think you would be staying here forever?'

'Flipping heck, no!' If the demon dog sounded horrified before, now he's aghast, practically beside himself. 'But you manos and your civilisations are so short-lived. Sooner or later you'd pop your clogs, or your angelico'd get bored and sod off back to strum his harp solo-style again, if you get what I'm saying. Then the thought was I'd bounce off home. A few millennia, max. Blink of a gnat's arse, basically.'

I don't point out he means gnat's eye. Mainly because he'll probably explain exactly why he doesn't. In great detail.

We fall into a short silence, but Isaac frowns in pensive thought beside me. It's Gil, though, who raises the big question. The one I'm sure is driving us all mad, that has been since the Karnabo called us.

'Why did they tip us off?'

Faust supplies the first, most obvious part of the answer. 'Because it's a trap.'

Problem is, that's not the tricky part. That's the real question itself. 'The thing is, we all know perfectly bloody well this is a trap, and a trap they feel so confident about as to put up a flashing neon sign saying, "This is a trap; walk in here and die". Why?' Isaac asks.

I don't want to answer that. Sadly, Faust is more than willing. 'Because Paul here has a habit of doing just that and then dying – like with the shizzard.'

'Exactly!' Isaac twists around to jab at the demonologist with his finger. 'So basically, let's not do that, okay?'

'Quite.' Faust nods wisely. The two academics are in full agreement. Mind you, so are Mephy and I. Just our agreement is to go fuck shit up instead.

Faust and Isaac's viewpoint is all well and good – believe you me, just because I do go rushing into traps and get killed regularly because of it doesn't mean I *want to*, just that I'm incapable of coming up with a better plan. But it doesn't provide us with any more information, with anything that's going to allow us to counter whatever's waiting for us in Toulouse. The Tesla's eating up the mountain roads, screaming round the corners, but as fast as we're going, my heart's beating faster. It's hammering in my chest. Forcing me to pay attention to the fact that I'm on the edge of a panic attack. Because we've been behind so far. Playing catch up. Racing around chasing our tails, following whereever we got sent, while this demon cuntbubble has been able to do whatever he wants. Fuck, look at what happened in Auch. The whole town evacuated, leaving it as a killing zone for us to run through, packed with possessed, murderous apes. Then once we survived that, everyone just happily accepted some utterly bullshit excuse about a gas leak, no questions asked. Caacrinolaas is packing major influence, both magically and politically, to have pulled that off.

Then a thought strikes me like a bucket of water hurled at high velocity at my face. After it's been completely frozen.

What's he doing to the people in Toulouse right now?

I can't believe I didn't think of this earlier. Auch was one thing, but it's still small fry compared to the sprawling expanse of my home city. There're a lot of people, innocent people, now inside the demon's area of influence, with us having received a gold-gilded invite to come there for a royal rumble.

What's happened to all of them?

'Isaac.' My voice is strained, the sound pulled tight, the ligaments in my neck are straining as though against the very idea running through my head itself. 'The news. About Toulouse. Check the news about Toulouse.'

I don't look at him deliberately, avoid the temptation of watching over his shoulder while I drive round steep drop bends, but I can see him pale out of the corner of my eye as realisation strikes him too. He fumbles his phone out, and I force my eyes to stay fixed on the twists and turns ahead, to not think about what he might be discovering on the tiny glowing screen in his hand.

'Paul.' Oh fuck. Isaac only sounds that controlled, that monotone flat and careful in his words when something's gone disastrously badly. 'Stop the car.'

'Really, 'Zac?' That's the last thing I want to do. Whatever he's seen is *bad*, like capital B Bad. In fact, throw in capitals the whole way through. B-A-D. Taking time out to pull over isn't even close to part of the plan.

But Isaac insists. 'Lad, trust me. You need to see this, and you need to not be driving when you do.'

Fuck. I trust him though. Plus, I'd really rather not kill us all when my willpower cracks, and I sneak a peek at whatever horrors he's currently watching. There's a passing point on the left, a shallow enclave into the rocks where you can let a faster vehicle scream past you if they're not content you're driving suicidally fast enough down the winding narrow roads. I bring the car to a screeching halt while half-snatching the phone out of Isaac's hand. I think he'll forgive me for not standing on niceties right now.

He was watching a news report. National news at that too, though you'd be forgiven for thinking it was something out of a horror film instead.

I've no idea where the news channel got the video from. It's definitely not a professional camera team. On the screen is a scene that looks like it's been pulled from some sort of found-footage shaky-cam film set in a war zone. Whoever's filming it is running, their hand whipping around as they hold their phone. Buildings are on fire; screams penetrate the chaotic din carrying through. People are yelling, cursing, crying, and there's a second where it looks like a scene straight out of a shadow puppet retelling of *A Clockwork Orange*. It's impossible to make out details; all I can see are blurry, shade-like humanesque shapes, but the way they're hunched over a prone form, the way their 'arms' (or perhaps they're pieces of wood or piping) rise and fall over and over again... We don't need to be able to see the spilled insides, the leaking fluids as the skull caves in to know this is where the phrase "having their brains beaten out" comes from. Then the camera's owner breaks into a run again, and that moment of clarity dissolves back into the general carnage and chaos.

The clipped professional tone of the reporter kicks in over the top. 'Once again, these are the scenes this evening from Toulouse. You are seeing here the only footage anyone has been able to access. A military cordon is currently in place, blocking all access in and out of the city, and all attempts to reach family or colleagues within the restricted zone have been unsuccessful. Speculation is rife as to what might have caused this, with suggestions running from drugs in the water supply to leaked bio weapons, but there hasn't been any official statement from the authorities at this time. The media blackout continues, but the questions will not be silenced. We will be staying with this story…'

By the Good God, I thought it would be bad. It's even worse than I could have imagined.

Toulouse is bleeding. She needs us. Now.

Chapter Two

So much Toulouse. So little to win.

There's no time for sitting about. If I was pushing the Tesla and my luck with the sheer drop verges before, now I take it to a whole 'nother level. Isaac's knuckles are white, pressed hard against the dashboard, which is probably unnecessary considering I'm almost generating G's, the pressure pushing us into our seats, locking us in place. I wonder how long before he asks us to switch places.

Not going to happen.

'We've got about two hours the way I'm going to drive it *—Isaac, put your hand down—* before we get to Toulouse, and neither of you have managed to find a way to trap a demon.'

That's enough to make both the two scholars in the car hang their heads, even against gravity trying to lock them in place against the headrests. They both put in place a

14

sporting wager with academic pride on the line as to who might find a solution to trapping the demon first. Neither has succeeded in the challenge. That life has been a non-stop shitshow since that second doesn't stop them from feeling like they've failed. On a personal level, I may feel bad for causing their expressions to droop, but I know perfectly well it's going to be a motivating kick up the arse for them. Right now I need top form geniuses in the game. I'll worry about hurting their egos once Toulouse stops screaming.

'Any ideas, now is the time to thrash them till they bleed.' My teeth are gritted so damn tightly I can feel my jaw locking up, the muscles seizing into place from the pressure.

Movement in the rearview mirror grabs my attention for a moment, although only briefly as taking your eyes off sinuous roads at speeds considerably faster than those required to travel back to the future is guaranteed to ensure your future is only measurable in milliseconds. Mephy is turning round and round in the middle seat, searching for a comfortable position while Gil –sitting behind me– and Faust –behind 'Zac– duck and weave like boxers in the golden ring to avoid his tail and head each time he spins. The back seats are comparatively roomy, but an oversized Dobermann isn't a small beast, and he's not exactly respecting the others' personal space. He settles into a position where he's half-sprawled across Johannes' lap, with his legs hanging out into the legroom of Gil in a way that looks like he must have abs of steel to maintain. Serious core strength.

I shake the mental image of the demon dog doing abdominal crunches from my mind, even though no one has leapt on my suggestion and started throwing out dazzling insights to allow us to outwit the fucker who's taken my city. Silence reigns.

Looks like it's on me. 'Okay, first, why did he want the sword?'

Nothing. Crickets. This is ridiculous. I have the two finest academic minds I've ever encountered – masters of esoteric knowledge – an actual demon, and a kid who's survived shit nobody should be able to and stabbed a demi-goddess in the neck, and there's a whole load of zilch being tossed my way.

Isaac eventually chimes in, 'I've not got a bloody clue, lad. It doesn't make any sense.'

I'd normally come back with some sort of sarcastic riposte about that being why we're having this fucking conversation in the first place, but the frustration is clear in his voice. Taking the piss is only going to make him feel worse, and it's not going to get the ideas pouring forth. Best to change tack.

'Right, okay. Let's come back to the sword. Bigger picture stuff. We know that De Montfort somehow managed to summon this Carcinoma –'

'Caacrinolaas.'

'Carcinoma. I know his real name, thanks, Jo. I just think this is more appropriate considering what a total cock-tumour he is. Anyway, somehow De Montfort got him over and persuaded him to stick about, giving him a plan B option for magic if we killed his current body –'

'And a way to neutralise Nith and Nan,' Isaac adds grimly. I know that one still stings. Without the demon essence having nullified the Bene Brothers, we might have managed to stop De Montfort and Nicetas up on Mount Bugarach without losing the best of us nearly five months ago: Aicha, Jakob, and Nanael.

'Right. Which we still don't understand, correct?' I take the resultant silence as a resounding yes. 'Okay. So three main mysteries at the moment. Why Crapnoselass –'

'That one's rubbish, mano.'

'I'm just trying out a few, see what works best.' Damn it, there are many times and many reasons why I miss Aicha, but this sort of wordplay brings her absence home every time. 'Anyway, why the dickhead waiting in Toulouse came to our plane of existence and stuck about, why the demon essence nullifies the angels, and why they want the sword.' I flick my eyes to the rearview mirror. 'What about you, Mephy? What can you tell us? You didn't seem to be his biggest fan, to say the least.'

Mephy shakes his huge black head from side to side as he chuffs air out through his nostrils. 'I'm not really supposed to say.'

Oh. Brilliant. 'Well, good. That's fine then. It's not as though it's anything important like *we're on our way to our potential deaths or anything*.'

'Look, mano, it's not that simple, is it? Matters beyond the mortal ken and all that.' And now he's pulling the "bless your little cotton socks, you wouldn't understand; leave it to the grown-ups" card. I think he can tell from the Paddington Bear Hard Stare I give him in the rearview mirror exactly how impressed I am by that.

The dog demon chuffs again and drops his eyes, unable to meet mine. I let him take a minute to think about it. We all know there are weird conditions and compacts in place on all magical beings, and there's no reason demons should be any different, I guess. I'll only give him a minute though. Time is of the essence.

Eventually, he nods and raises his eyes again. 'Isaac, can you pass me your hand please?'

'Sure, Meph.' Without even thinking, Isaac swings his arm behind him, fully confident in whatever our friend wants.

Which is when Mephistopheles bares his lips, growls, and then latches onto his hand, sinking his teeth in deep.

If there were ever a doubt as to my capabilities as a driver, let them now be expunged eternally from the annals of time. Because despite the whole car erupting into a level of batshit cacophony – Gil's yells, Isaac's howl, Johannes' shocked hollers – and also every single person simultaneously shifting position, I don't cross the centre line and smash headlong into the oncoming articulated lorry. I may well give the driver a minor heart attack when I suddenly veer wildly in his direction, but I manage to yank the wheel back across in the opposite sense and pull us back to something like normal driving. Straddling two lanes, yes. And with the blaring horns of the traffic in both directions simply adding to the mind-meltingly atonal noise-fest.

And of course this all feels like it's been going on for about half an hour but has actually only been happening for about five seconds. Once again, I'm reminded that even if I don't end up getting stabbed in the pineal gland or decapitated with the little circular blade from a rusty tin opener, the chances of me surviving to old age in this body are minimal. Heart failure seems like a sure and certain promise in my future.

Mephy releases the hand he was slavering over, his jaw locked down like he was given the juiciest T-bone steak in the butcher's shop and every dog in the neighbourhood was sizing him up for a mugging. He swings his head back and forth, looking at us all.

'What are you manos making so much noise about?'

The confusion in his voice is clear. Guess I better explain it equally clearly.

'Because you just tried to amputate Isaac's hand for a road trip snack, you leg-humping fucktoboggan!' I'm not sure if that was crystal in its clarity, but I'm confident I got the message across.

'Are you absolutely bloody stupid, mano?' Mephy drags a back paw round to scratch behind his ear. Gil dodges hard left to avoid losing an eye to him. 'He's got an angel inside him. Do you really think I'd be able to just bite his hand off?'

'I don't know!' I'm slightly less shouty now. My heartbeat has calmed down enough that it's only feeling as though I've run a few marathons as opposed to being pinned down by enemy gunfire next to a primed nuclear warhead. 'You are a demon, and he's not been having much luck with demons as of late.'

'I'm fine, lad.' Isaac sounds as shaky as I feel, but when I risk a glance across —having re-established us properly in a single lane– he's showing me his hand, the skin pristine, unbroken. 'Hurt like hell for a moment when he latched on, but it's okay now. Nith's been explaining to me.'

'Look, I needed to chat with the old angelico, private-like, and it's not as though I can ask you to stick your fingers in your ears and turn your backs, is it? Sometimes the old ways are best.'

Okay. Apparently the extra-dimensional beings needed to have a secret pow-wow to which we weren't invited, and the only way to manage that was by taking a bite out of Isaac's hand.

'What was so important that you couldn't just talk about it? We're all friends here.' Johannes' voice doesn't hold the same level of worry. There's something else there though.

It's like when you find out all your friends had a party on your day off, but somehow none of them let you know.

Mephy sighs. It's an odd noise off the Dobermann. There's a weight in it that makes it clear the creature sitting in the middle of the backseat is ancient – and not just in dog years. There's millennia in that exhalation, a breathing out of accrued experience loaded with knowledge and pain.

'Faust, mano, it's not about you, but you're not going to be all that happy. You neither, 'Zac, would be my guess. Don't think either of you like not knowing things.'

Oof. If there's one thing absolutely certain in this life, it's that neither of those two appreciate holes in their knowledge. Isaac swivels himself round, his eyes narrowing in suspicion. 'You're right. I don't. Now. What do I not know?'

And there, once again, is Isaac the Blind, magical powerhouse, creator of a whole Talented discipline, and a man with a mind sharper than one of Aicha's blades. I shake that thought from my head. Need to concentrate on the here and now. Save the world. Then save Aicha.

Mephy shrinks back into the seat, trying – and failing – to make himself seem smaller. Even a demon doesn't want to be subjected to Isaac's piercing stare. He whines slightly and puts both his paws over his nose, muffling his voice. As such – and because I am also trying not to cause a multi-vehicle pile-up on the motorway, I almost miss what he says. I have to replay it several times in my head before I'm sure.

Yep. He did say what I think he said.

He said, 'The truth about the relationship between angelicos and demonicos.'

Oh, shit. This should be good.

Chapter Three

I sometimes wonder if forbidden knowledge might be forbidden for a reason. Especially when I see academics at work.

Predictably, after a moment's peace when everyone focused in on trying to hear what Mephy was saying, the car once more erupts into furious chatter as both Isaac and Johannes try simultaneously to demand answers.

'What do you mean –'

'– thought you'd told –'

'– there's never been any –'

Gil, sensibly, is keeping his mouth shut, trying to avoid stepping into the firing line. Risking a rightwards look, I see Isaac's turned a mottled red and is waving his hands around like Stan from the *Monkey Island* series. I'm amazed he's not whipped the rearview mirror off with an accidental blow, but it's surely only a matter of time. Glancing in it, I can see Faust hammering the side of one hand down onto the palm of his other, emphasising every syllable of the outrage he's trying to get out. Mephy's sliding his paws up higher, covering his eyes as well now. Honestly? I don't blame him. Having two furious, magically-superpowered beings shouting at you is bad enough. When they're academics finding out they've had information withheld from them? You've just added a whole other layer of pissed-offness and danger to the equation.

Problem is, we're not getting any answers, just chaos. Time for me to take on a diplomatic role.

'*Shut the fuck up, everybody.*'

There. That was diplomatic, right?

Either way, it worked. Silence descends. Isaac slowly lowers his hands, and Johannes stops trying to karate chop his own palm in half. It's a start.

'Right. I get the general outrage – *yes, that includes you, 'Zac* – but it's not getting us anywhere apart from closer and closer to a war zone with promised sure and certain death waiting for us. Mephy, why don't you explain what the fuck you mean before one or both of them either die of apoplexy or dissect you to try to see if the answer's written through your core like a stick of candy rock?'

The demon dog shakes his head. I'm not sure if it's in despair at me, at them, or because he really doesn't want to talk about this. 'Well, manos, there're some things that haven't been told to you about the angelicos and us.'

'We picked that much up, Meph. What we want to know is what it is that we don't know.' Johannes is straining to maintain his calm politeness, but you can hear it's wearing at his last remaining nerve.

'It's nothing personal, Faust. Nor from the angelico you're all tied pretty with, Isaac. The agreements put in place were always there to protect you people, and we're not supposed to break them.'

I think I can understand. 'Except Caacrinolaas already has.'

Mephy looks at me in the rearview and gives me a doggy wink. 'Got it in one, mano. That's it exactly. I needed to check that the angelico was in agreement. He is, so I'm going to give you the true and factual tale of how them and us came to be long ago.'

This is going to be fascinating, but I can only hope he keeps the long to the ago. We're limited for time, and this sounds like it could be quite the complicated tale he's about to tell.

'Once upon a time…'

Shit. That doesn't bode well for us getting this done before we drive smack-bang into a war zone.

Chapter Four

Looks like Mephy thinks it's story time. 'Are you sitting
comfortably?' Because I bloody well am not. I'm not so
much antsy as having a whole ants' nest crawling about
under my skin.

'Okay, Mephy, I know I've not been giving you the easiest
time so far this drive.' My eyes flick to his in the rearview
mirror, and the demon hound gives me an approving nod, a
gracious little *right-you-are-you-silly-mano* expression on his
face. 'But time is pressing, okay?' My eyes flick to the
speedometer, which is tattling on me as a law-breaking
rebel, eating up the distance back towards Toulouse.

'What's your point?' I'm not sure if Mephy's being
deliberately obtuse here.

'Skip to the end, basically. Keep it tight.'

'Okay, fine.' There's a sullen tone to his voice. Guess
he's a bit miffed at me spoiling his Mephy-Storytime
moment. Particularly as it's apparently a forbidden tale.

'Look, you know how the angelico and I have always told you how the whole "celestial war" malarkey in the various religious texts didn't actually happen?'

Oh, for fuck's sake. I don't need him to spell this part out further. Based on the other hurt expressions in the car, neither do Isaac and Faust. 'You're saying it actually did?'

'Well, yes. Kind of.' There's a truculent whine to Mephy's tone. I guess he's picking up the frosty vibe of disbelief permeating the vehicle. 'Look, we made an agreement, okay? When we made peace, we agreed to keep it from the manos. Don't tell 'em the truth. So whenever there's been contact with you since, we've always denied it. On both sides. Seems like it stuck about in your collective memories though. Mind you, it was *horrific*. And you lot were the front line troops for both sides. It wasn't pretty. Trauma does tend to linger. Awful enough trauma inflicted on the whole species? Really sticks around through the millennia.'

Fuck me. This does not sound pretty. 'But why did you go to war at all? Why not just go your separate ways?'

'Because we weren't that powerful. Weren't as evolved as we are now. Plus, we weren't the only sentient species on the planet, not by a long shot, but none of the others were anywhere close to reaching the required evolutionary point. The closest to us were still little better than hopped up monkeys, over-excited because we showed them how to rub two sticks together to help keep them safe and warm.'

That's a pretty dismissive evaluation of humanity, and I'm about to say so.

Mephy isn't done, though. 'People like the jentilaks and their worldwide equivalents. Oh, and manos, too, scrabbling about in the muck, I suppose. Point is we needed to decide. Some of us wanted to travel higher up the vibrational ladder, to seek the purity of spirit that could be found from understanding and thought distilled.' Meph blows air out through his nose, a powerful push as though trying to clear a bad smell. 'Some of us thought that sounded about as much fun as chopping your balls off in order to sing a particularly high note well.'

Oof. Interesting metaphor. And effective. 'Did you just call the angels eunuchs, Meph?'

'Well, lets put it this way. I'm not talking about their rapidity at weaving magic when I talk about cast rate.'

Zing. Killer burn for the feathered ones from the demon dog.

I'm not that easily distracted though. For once. 'Still doesn't explain why you went to war.'

'Because changing the vibrational frequency of a whole population in each direction without tearing the rest of the planet apart is no easy matter, mano.' There's no humour to Mephy's tone now. It's totally serious, all business. 'And there were plenty – on both sides, let me add – who were quite happy to say, "Fuck 'em", concerning all the manos and other animalos and flora on the planet at the same time. Others didn't want that to happen, but realised it'd be far easier to keep this place intact and still fuck off if we only headed in one direction. That maybe we should either force the others to come with us…'

His words trail off, and he doesn't need to say the rest. Apparently, working out how to reach an alternative vibrational frequency doesn't mean you're all peace and love. Plenty of these super-powerful beings were ready to potentially kill off a fuckload of their fellows if it meant they could catch the next train to Heavensville. *Plus ça change*, and all that.

'So how was it managed then?' Ah, Faust. I can hear it.

The inquisitive nature winning out against the choleric fury. He wants to know these hidden truths more than he wants to remain angry, despite himself.

'A smaller group on each side worked together. Sorted out the required *talent*, dotted the i's and crossed the t's of all the workings, if you will. Found a way for us to shake hands, say toodle-pip, and toddle off in each direction. No harm, no foul. But there was something else they realised.'

Ah. Now we're getting to the meat of the matter if I'm not mistaken. Gil and Faust lean in closer, and Isaac's apparently trying to disconnect his spine from his hips with how far he's attempting to twist round.

Mephy nods sagely. 'They realised it needed to be a one-way trip. We couldn't go traipsing back and forth up the dimensional ladder. It'd risk fucking things up too much.'

'What about the war on Faerie?' A valid point from Isaac. The puzzle of the mysteries being resolved is winning out against his hurt anger too.

'That's more sideways than up or down, ain't it?' Mephy gives a doggy shrug as if that explains it. Perhaps it does. That's not the main point right now. 'Thing is, once we put everything in place, angelicos and demonicos were divorced from each other. Locked away on either end of the dimensional ladder. At least until you pulled those bird-brains down here, mano' –he nods at Isaac– 'and fucked everything up.'

Isaac flushes. The change of colour – the fact his face has any colour at all – makes me think of something else. 'What about the demon essence? You said you all shouldn't be able to affect each other. So what the hell is that?'

Mephy's lip curls back as though the question leaves a bad taste in his mouth. 'I still don't really know, mano. That's the other reason I bit Isaac. Wanted to check there was none left, make sure he was all clear. But also see if I could taste anything to it, knowing now it's Caacrinolaas. See, it didn't smell of him. Never did.'

'What does that mean?' It's hard to keep the frustration under control.

'It means it isn't his essence.' Mephy's tone matches my own. 'I don't know what it is, but it isn't a part of him that he infected Isaac with. It's something separate. A working of some sort. A weapon he came up with to allow him to start a scrap with the angels all over again. A brawl that the blithering idiot was never happy about stopping in the first place, back all those bloody years ago.'

Fuck me. So this whole thing has just been a way for Caacrinolaas to get his grudge match with the angels back into action. All of this misery and suffering, all these humans used and abused just so he can get a chance to have a crack at Nithael.

'But he didn't need to do this in the first place, did he?' Isaac sounds baffled by the whole thing.

'Because?' The demon dog's eyes are still narrowed, and there's the very slightest of growls to his voice now. I think he's getting frustrated with the whole thing.

'Well, if he wanted a throwdown with Nithael, we could have just organised that anyhow!' Isaac sounds bright and breezy, an absolute bundle of positive vibes. I think he reckons he's just clocked the way to solve the whole mess with zero confrontation.

'Organised it?'

'Yep. He could have just invited us to a brawl. Sent us a letter. Or an email.'

I groan. *Really, 'Zac?*

'You want Caacrinolaas, a warmongering demon warrior, to have sorted out a Confrontation' –the capital letter is clear in Mephy's voice– 'between ancient rivals, the reviving of a war that roared across the firmament and every form of reality when your species was still trying to work out which end of a thigh bone to hit each other with *by email?*'

'Well, yes.' There's still that brightness to Isaac's voice, but I can hear it's slightly strained. 'Or he could have knocked at the door.'

'*Knocked at the door?*' The disbelief is building in his words now. Even Faust is staring at the man I have to remind myself is the cleverest human I've ever met. Most of the time. Mephy mimes rapping on a door with his right paw. 'Knock, knock, hello? Can Nithael come out to wage war and see who can rend the other asunder, please? I promise he won't be back too late if he survives the obliteration I intend to rain down upon him?'

'Aye, precisely!' Isaac's face brightens up, showing once more both his naturally optimistic, sunny demeanour and his utter inability to grasp sarcasm. 'We could have planned it out properly. Chosen a suitable battleground. Drawn up the rules –'

'Rules? For a fight?' The chuffing from the back sounds like a helicopter going into a death spiral. 'That's not how fighting works, mano.'

'But it could've been! It still could be, couldn't it?' Now Isaac's getting excited. 'We could work out the rules, have a decision based on certain criteria. Get judges in! Then one of you could still emerge victorious. And no one would have to die either!'

'So what you're proposing,' Mephy rumbles out, 'is that we set up some sort of organised contest, with judges? Like a cross-dimensional MMA tournament? A points-based thing? No-holds barred –'

'Well, some holds barred!' Isaac's really in the swing of this now. I can see from his slightly dreamy expression that he's already drawing up tables for the qualification rounds, spreadsheets for who gets to enter despite the fact this is really supposed to be about one single battle between an angel and a demon. 'We wouldn't want anything *fatal*, after all!'

'Oh, no, of course!' Hmm. Call me a cynic, but there's the slightest hint of something that might be mockery creeping into Mephy's tone. 'Dimensions forbid that the angelico should get seriously hurt!'

'Well, quite!' That sarcastic edge has, of course, gone straight over Isaac's head. 'But it'd be to protect you demons too! It works both ways.'

'I see, I see.' Mephy sounds so thoughtful that I have no doubt he wishes he had a beard to stroke right now. And opposable digits with which to stroke it, of course.

'There's a lot of interesting proposals in there, mano. But there's only one theoretical problem I can see.'

Isaac is beaming. Problems and solutions, especially theoretical ones, are his forte. 'Go on!'

'It's utter bollocks.' Mephy turns back to me, dismissing Isaac, whose jaw hangs open, goldfish-mode activated. 'Anyhow, now you know why I bit this Forrest Gump wannabe, with the plus side of making sure he was clear of any traces of this peculiar fucking weapon that the stupid fucker somehow managed to come up with. Like, he still tastes of demonico, obviously, still has lingering traces of our vastly superior energy hanging about. But nothing that's going to turn his flesh all bubbly again.'

Which makes me realise something. 'What about Gil?'

Mephy frowns at me. 'What about him?'

'Can you make sure he's clear too?'

In the seat behind Isaac, I can see Gil turn that shade of white that's almost green, his horrified wide-staring eyes meeting mine in the mirror.

'Did you just ask the demon to bite me, Paul?'

Erm. 'Maybe?'

Chapter Five

EN ROUTE TO TOULOUSE,
30 OCTOBER, PRESENT DAY

Considering all his recent trauma, I'm not surprised that's set him quivering like Jello. Gil-o, if you will.

'Don't worry, mano!' Mephy turns his brightest smile in Gil's direction. Unfortunately, that just gives him front-row seats as to how shiny and large his teeth are. 'They're incredibly sharp!'

'I'm not sure that's helping, Meph!' I say. Gil looks on the point of hyperventilating, pressing himself back against the window.

'I meant in the sense they'll go in and out in a second!' Mephy turns back to Gil. 'You won't even feel it. A little nip, and we can make sure you've not got any of that weird shit hanging around inside you, looking to fuck you up when your back's turned. Plus, now we know who possessed you, I can make sure there's no lingering taste of Caacrinolaas' magic floating about in your system, ready to be triggered again.'

I can see the war going on in Gil's expression. He's terrified. That's clear and unsurprising, considering all his recent
trauma involving demons. But he also understands what
Mephy's saying, understands what's on offer. A clean bill of
health. Confirmation he's not about to be seized by the
demon's control all over again.

Slowly, carefully, he raises a trembling hand and slides it
in between the demon dog's razored teeth. Good God, the
kid's bravery knows no limits. Mephy meets his gaze, gives
him a nod – whether to reassure him or to acknowledge just
how courageous he is, I don't know, probably both – then
leans forward and nips. The demon dog's teeth break the
skin, and Gil bites his lip, his whole body shaking, but he
doesn't cry out. A second later, Meph breaks contact. Gil
stares down at his trembling hand, looking for the puncture
wounds, for the rivulets of blood pouring down around the
skin folds of his hand. But his hand is unmarked, whole,
though the kid doesn't look like he can convince himself it's
true.

Mephy chuffs. 'I was never going to hurt you, mano. Be
a pretty rubbish demonico if I couldn't do that without
wrecking your inferior little hand, wouldn't I?'

Gil shakes said inferior member disbelievingly, his eyes
narrowing, searching for the injury he's convinced must be
there. But then he must remember why Mephy did it, why
he agreed to it in the first place.

'Well?' The kid's on the edge of his seat, desperate to
know if he gets the all clear.

'Nothing.' Mephy's tone is soft, low. 'No sign of that
weird poison bullshit. No sign of Caacrinolaas either.'

Gil sinks back into the chair with a soft exhalation, a
half-oof, like the relief of it has taken the wind out of him,
all the nervous tension shooting out of his body in that

single breath. Or, maybe, like he can breathe properly again for the first time.

Meanwhile, I need to concentrate on driving. The traffic density is increasing as we're drawing closer to the city. Muret's up on our right-hand side, and it gives me the same shudders as it did the first time I headed to Hastingues to meet Lou Carcoilh. That we're heading into a war zone – one specifically created for us– and passing the site of the last battle where we might, truly, have turned the tide against the Albigensian Crusade feels like an ill omen. That we won last time we went this way against my once best friend Benedict in his Phone Dick-slash-Emperor Palpatine routine was due to three things. The interference of the Good God, a huge smattering of good luck, and the indomitable will of Aicha Kandicha. And we still nearly lost.

This time I feel like we don't have any of those on our side.

But we have Isaac and Nithael back in the game, even if they're not at a hundred percent. And we have an actual manifest demon as well as another magical genius. Still not, I suspect, as deadly as Aicha Kandicha, but they'll have to do. Especially if we're going to have any chance of ever getting this utter shitpile of a problem resolved so I can get back to trying to find her. And we have Gil. The kid might not be much use in the *talent* department – none at all, in fact– but he's still not a pushover. Ask Melusine if you don't believe me. If you can find her down in whatever infernal version of an afterlife her spirit might currently be squatting in. Plus, while I might not feel like we have much in the way of luck on our side, if we have any, it's manifest in him. He's like our good luck charm in the face of insurmountable odds. Let's hope he cancels out any bad juju coming from Muret.

We're getting closer to the tiny stretch of peage –toll road– that reaches in from the south towards the Toulouse ring road. Normally I would take a slightly longer route to avoid it on principle; I can afford it, but fuck it, I'd rather not. However, today speed is of the essence.

Except taking it this time isn't going to help me. Because all the peage barriers are shut. Plus, we'd have to get past the army barricade to start with.

'Fuck!' I slam my hands on the wheel to express my frustration almost as hard as I stamp on the brake. 'Ideas! Now!'

'Angelico?'

Isaac turns back to look at Mephy, and I guess he can read whatever he needs to in my mentor's expression without having to pull his very bitey equivalent of the Vulcan Mind-Meld because the gigantic Dobermann huffs air out of his nose. 'Fine. I'll do this one. Crack the window down, will you, Faust?'

His friend does as requested, bemusement bristling off him like his oversized beard, and Mephistopheles leaps through the now open window.

Let's just clarify a few things. Firstly, although I am decelerating rapidly, screeching towards a halt, we're not at a complete stop. Secondly, there is no way that Mephy should be able to clear that gap. Not without tearing a permanent hole in the side of the Tesla. Mephistopheles is not a small dog. Hell, he's not even a small Dobermann. A few mid-sized horses might start getting a bit edgy about winning a size-measuring competition with him, if size comparison competitions between smallish horses and extremely large dogs was an actual competitive sport. The backseat windows are almost an aesthetic thing. Sure, you can drop them if you really want to, but as with most things about the Tesla – and their frankly weird owner and over-lord Musk – it's about style over substance. For a moment, as I manage to drag the car towards a screaming halt without sending it careening sideways and flipping over the traffic in front like the cop cars that chased the Blues Brothers – I wonder how he manages it.

Then I remember he's a demon. Not bound to our earthly limits and all that.

He proves that even further as he gets even bigger. The biggest in fact. Enormous enough that Clifford the Big Red Dog would just insist everyone calls him Cliff and ix-nay with the needless itle-tay, okay? Mephistopheles does a bit of Jake The Dog stretching except without looking like a cutesy lovable acid trip made incarnate. Nope. Mephistopheles still looks like a ferocious, demon-possessed Dobermann. Just one big enough that he can now swing his bulldozer-sized head around and gently clamp his teeth onto the Tesla's roof. Then he turns, lifting us high into the air so we're now on a semi-diagonal tilt, the ground lurching away from us as we're plucked up like the gigantic hound's new favourite chew toy.

All I find myself thinking is, *I wonder what oversized demonic dog drool does to car paint work?* I really want to ask Isaac, but a quick glance sidewards where he's pressing himself hard against the door, an arm on both that and the dash tells me I really don't need to do anything that'll add to his stress level.

The now Tarrasque-sized Dobermann turns back towards the military barrier in front of us and starts pounding towards it.

Crikey, I think. *I really hope he's remembered to put up some form of* don't look here *because if not, there's a lot of bullets about to come flying our way any second.*

The world remains marvellously empty of the sound of deafening semi-automatic gunfire. Count your blessings, people.

What it doesn't remain is stationary. Instead, we're shaken around furiously as Mephy picks up speed. It makes me think of the kid from the *BFG* when the Big Fuckoff Giant really starts motoring to travel between the land of the Giants and the land of the Humans. How that kid didn't shit themselves the first time, I have no idea. Perhaps the inside of his pocket was completely covered in vomit by the time they arrived, and Roald Dahl decided to skip that bit. Although, it doesn't seem his style to miss out on a bit of gross bodily humour.

Looking at the two green-tinged faces in the rearview mirror, it may be that we're about to see what Mr Dahl left out first-hand any second. So when Mephy launches himself upwards like some sort of dog-powered scud missile straight into the sky, I'm sure it's about to all come up. I suspect the only reason it doesn't is that they're so terrified, they've gone past forgetting how to breathe, all the way up past forgetting how to vomit.

The pounding landing vibrates through the metal so hard I can taste it on my teeth, and the rearview mirror twangs, producing a *boing*-like noise. Instead of being even vaguely concerned by what has just happened – Mephy changing size, us leaping over a military barrier, et cetera – I've chosen to become absolutely obsessed with how that particular piece of plastic and glass can move so damned rapidly but not fall off. My eyes are locked on it. The oscillations settle down into a calmer pattern. It's actually quite soothing. And a fascinating example of how we, as a species of jumped-up monkeys, survive situations that should make us shut down into some form of catatonic shock. Possibly for the rest of our lives.

'Will you fucking drive, mano?' Mephy's barking tone breaks me from my reverie, bringing me back to the world outside my tunnel vision moment with the mirror. Apparently, while it's settled down, he's shrunk back to normal size and has rejoined us. 'I'm absolutely beat and in need of something to eat. Or fuck. Or both. Pronto.'

Right. Head back in the game. The accelerator pedal brings instant forward movement.

It's time to find out what Toulouse has in store for us.

Chapter Six

This isn't the homecoming I ever imagined. Except for that one time I daydreamed about a zombie flick called The Homecoming, of course.

It's unbelievably eerie driving along the peripherique, the ring road that circles Toulouse. It's not like the one round Paris, of course, where I have – and no word of a lie – hit a traffic jam at 1:30 am. Outside of rush hour, it's rarely heaving. But there's always *presence*. Other cars. Trucks hauling goods from Spain up towards the north, bringing fruit and veg to those less blessed with sunshine. Motorbikes and scooters apparently being driven by reincarnating immortals based on how they weave in and out with no concern as to whether they live or die.

People. There are always people.

Instead, I seem to have wandered into some sort of post-apocalyptic sci-fi film. The road is entirely deserted. The only thing stopping it feeling like *The Walking Dead* or

39

28 Days Later is the lack of abandoned cars blocking the way. It seems like everyone was considerate enough to vacate the main road before whatever happened actually kicked off.

Problem is, that leaves me wondering where they all went.

Thanks to the clear route, we make record time around to the Pont Jumeaux junction. The leafy greenery that runs down the side of the canal warms my heart. Those distinctive orange-red bricks that people constantly insist are pink –giving the city the nickname of the Pink City– are a balm to my tired soul.

But the fact that I'm not connected to the land? That I'm not recharging like Mario getting high on a whole bagload of mushrooms?

That breaks both my heart and soul just as quickly. Though it does, at least, bring my anger blazing back up.

Toulouse has always –*always*– been mine since I first claimed it. I don't know why there wasn't any other Talented, human or otherwise, holding the city before I took it. It was certainly large enough. Perhaps it was the result of the Crusade itself – wiser beings turning tail and running when the Church became entirely too interested in this little tract of land.

Whatever the reason, it was unclaimed when I came, my eyes now open to the Talented world, and I made it mine. Even when Franc snuck in and polluted the place with his shithead aura, he never took it from me. Toulouse still responded to my arrival, still fed me power. The streets still sang with the sigils I had walked into them over the centuries.

Not now. Now they're quiet. Silent. Just like the town itself.

'I don't get it, lad.' Isaac's voice trembles slightly. He's as unnerved as I am, I reckon. 'Where is everyone? It doesn't look like the scenes we saw on the telly, does it?'

It really doesn't. He doesn't need my confirmation of that though. He wants to know what the fuck is going on. That makes two of us.

'The manos aren't here. They're all inside the wards.' Mephy's voice is a subwoofer growl. He's really pissed at Caacrinolaas. 'I can smell 'em. He's taken all that work you did and remade it through the breaches, mano. Claimed it as his own.'

'But we should be well inside the wards now!' That's the bit that doesn't make sense. Even when Toulouse was a whole lot tinier, I kept the wards far enough out to sense trouble coming a literal country mile off. Now they're so tightly in that we're almost at my house and they still aren't...

'My house,' I say slowly. 'It must be my house that's forced him to reduce them.'

'Yes!' Faust looks up, a grin muscling his bushy beard aside to show his pearly whites. 'That must be it, Paul. The other wards were keyed to Isaac when he was infested with the demon energy. But your house –'

'Never was,' I finish, and the relief hits me like the first blast of a power shower on a sleepy morning. Until this moment, I didn't realise how worried I was, how much I was hurting. Losing Toulouse has been terrible, and I'm grieving underneath the rage. But taking my home from me would be another step, an additional violation. It's strange how even those of us who've walked far and wide and long enough to understand the pointlessness of material posses- sions can become so deeply invested in a pile of brick and mortar. We intermingle our roots in the foundation's cement somehow. And we can pull those up, choose another dwelling to make our own. But it carries a cost, and it has to be a choice. Having that taken from us is violating that single speck of safety we have in a cold, uncaring world. It's why people who get burgled are more scarred by the act than what they lose. It's the one place we should feel completely secure, but it's been ransacked. It's a wound driven deep into our psyche that takes a long time to heal.

And I've been preparing myself for that deep gash since I saw Toulouse was no longer mine. Now I can breathe again. A little, at least.

We park up, then get out of the car. Being the only vehicle moving on the roads is starting to feel way too conspicuous –a good way to draw bad attention to ourselves very quickly. Besides, we don't want to go smashing through any wards without seeing them.

'How far away are they, Mephy?' I could try to reach out myself, but this isn't my territory right now. Not till I kick the usurping demon wanker right in his pitchfork. Chances are I might trigger the alarms and give away our location. I mean, it's not like they don't know we're coming but even still. A tiny element of surprise – where we are, when we're coming – is better than none at all.

Mephy sniffs, scenting the air, then points like he's spotted a rabbit in the woods with his snout. 'About a ten-minute lope that way,' he says even though I know he's fully conversant with the idea of metres and kilometres. He's edgy, distracted, his fur bristling. Caacrinolaas' presence has really got to him. 'Can… smell him.' The words are half-gargled through lips baring back to show teeth coated in the first foam of his rage. Mephistopheles is seriously pissed off.

'Okay, well, before we go all "Lassie Come Home", and you take us to the poor demon trapped at the bottom of a well…' Mephy's head snaps around, with the emphasis on *snap.* He crunches his jaws together so hard I'm astounded I don't get lacerated by enamel shrapnel hammering out in a fifteen-metre spray radius. The glowing red eyes don't help either.

'Lassie's a punk!' Ooh, apparently I've touched a nerve. 'Helping all those manos, *bark, bark, woof,* pant. Who's a good girl? Fuck off, you doggo prick. Doggos used to be *wolves.* All this subservient tongue lolling crap is a bunch of bull. They're the doggo equivalent of an Uncle Tom.'

Okay. He's now comparing the domestication of a species with the collaboration of certain individuals during the days of slavery, and I don't even know where to begin with unravelling that particular bit of false equivalency. But, as he's actively slathering and looking like he's about to eat each finger I use to count off his fallacies, I decide to let it slide just this once.

'Mephistopheles, you must relax and stop this now! Plus, for the last time, having black fur does not mean you can equivalate to the struggles of the Afro-American community!'

Oh dear. Mephy has managed to raise Johannes' stern side. This is the equivalent of turning the Kindly Ones into the Erinyes, and Mephy knows it. 'It is unacceptably rude to take out your frustrations on our close friends.' The demon hound lowers his head and whines slightly. *Yeah! Eat that, Mephy!* 'Even if they are being exceptionally annoying.'

Now it's my turn to droop, a hangdog expression on my face even lower than the actual hound's.

'I was just trying to lighten the mood!' I try for explicatory but somehow miss the correct vocal tone register bus stop and end up at the whiny and petulant station instead.

'And I was only trying to sniff out our villain, mano.' Mephy sounds smug. But at least his eyes no longer look like red-hot coals. I'll take smug over murderous every time. 'And I was trying not to bite your hand off too, of course.'

Okay, so he's smug and murderous. Smurderous, if you will. Mind you, trying to resist biting my hand off makes a pleasant change from trying not to make sweet, sweet love to my lower limbs. Let's hope he's more successful at not killing me.

I decide that, having completely derailed the conversation, it's only fair I drag it back on track again. 'Right, point is that before The Littlest Murder Hobo over here goes all "Law Of Claw And Fang" on Caacrinolaas, which I am looking forward to ringside seats at, popcorn and all, I want to go home. Grab a few bits.'

I'm not an idiot despite what a lot of my enemies think. And a lot of my friends would say. Caacrinolaas hasn't taken my house yet because it's too much work. The wards around Toulouse were compromised. Easy pickings. Hammering down the ones I've worked into every nook and cranny of my home will be a lot harder.

But not impossible. Not for a demon incarnate on our plane.

So I need to go clean out a few things. Not many. Most magical items we stashed at Isaac's. Mainly because having an angel keeping watch has always seemed an impregnable defence. Up until now.

So there're only a few loose ends at mine. But anything that is there, I'd rather have on us. Plus, I need to replenish my *talent*. It won't be long enough for Isaac and Nith to get much of a recharge –they're my private wards, after all– but it'll make a difference for me. Give me the energy to die spectacularly instead of just fizzling out disappointingly in the first few seconds, like the dodgy fireworks your dad picked up from some back-alley merchant, confidently asserting they'll be just as good as the ones from the shops. I don't want to be the Wish-bought version of a powerful wizard, thanks very much.

Sadly, I'm not sure it matters how magically charged up I am. Now that we're in this eerie silence instead of the normal bustle of my home city, the anger's fading slightly. Dread's creeping in. Terror at what lies ahead of us. That I'm not capable. Not strong enough. That might seem ridiculous to you. After all, I basically went up against the Evil God Creator of our known world with no magic left and an intention just to try to kick him in the balls until he gave up. But that's the thing. Dogged determination and reincarnation have got me this far with a whole dollop of good luck thrown into the Bonhomme cake mix.

Right now, I'm not sure I have two of the three. And it's making maintaining the first one far more difficult.

Not that I'll let the others see that, of course. 'Right then,' I say in a breezy tone. 'Off we toddle then, shall we?'

So off we toddle indeed. As I start to re-attune to the city, even though it's no longer mine, I can feel the wards. It's not an impressive bit of *talent* on my part. They're packed with that same crackling demonic energy we've come to know and hate. The road splits off, a concrete underpass to the left and rising up to meet the bridge leading towards Saint Cyprien on the right. Call me paranoid, but I'm not about to go underneath tonnes and tonnes of concrete though. Not for that long anyhow.

We hop down onto the Canal De Brienne, the small spoke linking the Canal Du Midi to the wild running Garonne, and pass under the small red brick bridge. I'm confident if it gets collapsed that, low as it is, I can fling myself into the murky green waters beside me. I can't decide if they're safer or more dangerous now Franc isn't here. For one brief moment, I wish he wasn't dead. Wish he'd been here to at least try to hold Toulouse against the demon. Better the devil you know and all that. Then I remember what Gil and Aicha found in his mountain cold stores. And I only wish he wasn't dead so I could kill him all over again. And actually do it myself this time.

The next ten minutes are painful on my face muscles. I maintain a carefree grin by locking them in place until they ache. Short of whistling a jaunty tune, I couldn't come over as more nonchalant.

'There's a good tree over there, mano,' Mephy says, breaking the silence.

'What?'

'A tree. Over there.' Mephy cocks his snout towards one of the tall silvered and green birches leaning out over the water.

'Okay. Thanks. There's a building there, Mephy. A cloud in the sky just there. And –look!– a canal.' I shake my head. 'I, too, can point at random things for no apparent reason.'

Mephy chuffs disdainfully. 'For you, mano. For the massive shit you need to take. There's no need to keep holding it in. It looks like the effort is about to tear your bloody cheeks off.'

Okay. Based on the half-stifled sniggers that seconds later collapse into full-on belly laughs from all the crew behind me, I guess I haven't been doing as good of a job as looking nonchalant as I thought.

Mephy looks around, confused, whirling about like he's chasing his tail. 'What? Isn't that what he needs? I don't know; you're all bloody bizarre.' He goes to sniff at a park bench, muttering, 'Fucking manos,' as he goes.

The volume of the laughing dies down a little, but I

don't mind having been the butt of the joke. Firstly, because I'm used to it – hell, I almost miss it, although it's more I miss the person who usually does it – but secondly, because I can feel the difference it makes. The tension has ratcheted down a notch. Not a lot. Just enough to allow everyone to breathe a little more easily. Myself included.

We cross over by the ancient creche for tobacco workers. Toulouse used to be the centre of the French tobacco industry, and in typical Gallic style, free childcare was included for all the workers. The industry may be dead and buried (at least in France), but the title is still displayed, picked out in the pretty art-deco-style period tiling.

I quicken my step. There're a lot of children on the other side of those wards needing saving right now.

The last quiet roads take us to my house. And an awkward conversation.

'You'll all need to wait out here.' I smile sheepishly because I do feel like a bit of a prick.

'Why?' Gil raises his voice. He's been quiet for so long, it's almost easy to forget he's here. But looking at him, I can understand why he's asking. He looks absolutely shattered. Big black bruise-like bags hang under his eyes. He's had no chance to rest since all this kicked off, and I'd love to just put him inside, stash him there safe while we sort this out. But there're two problems with that. He wouldn't let me, of course. But that's not the main one.

'You've still got that residual demon energy on you. All of you have. Even Isaac.' I shrug apologetically, and 'Zac inclines his head. He gets it.

'So?' Gil looks puzzled.

'So I had to take the wards down the last time to get you all in. Considering what's going on' –I wave my hand in the vague direction of the city– 'over there, I don't want to do that even for a moment.'

Gil nods. 'Makes sense,' he says. He slumps down into a nearby doorway and closes his eyes. I try to silence that awfully shrill and insistent voice in the back of my head calling me a horrible person by pointing out he'll get as much rest there as he would if he came into the house. It doesn't work.

'I'll bring you all tea? Coffee?'

'My lad,' Isaac says, drawing out each letter, making sure my attention is entirely on what he has to say, hanging off each syllable like one of those crazy parkour guys, waving for a photograph from some impossible drop. 'If you go in there and return with anything less than the bottle of Kalavan port barrel, twenty-five-year whisky that I know full bloody well you've got stashed in the back of your drinks cabinet, hoping I hadn't seen it? When you're leaving us outside in the cold? To wait while you have a nice old time in your cosy little hobbit hole?' He raises an eyebrow at me, and his expression is mournful. 'I will be so, so very disappointed in you, my lad.'

Ouch. It's all I can do to not clutch at my chest. That one is a knife to the heart. Doesn't matter if we're five or fifty, if they're our parents by blood or by choice. Being told you've disappointed your parents? And not only disappointed but *really* disappointed them?

Well. It hurts. Even more than giving up my secret Kalavan stash will.

So with only the most minuscule of grumbling, I head inside and return with the bottle. Let it be noted, for the record, that I also bring them tumblers. And proper crystal ones at that. There're even a couple of ice cubes in each. They can toss them in the street to melt if they don't want them. I don't think anyone's about to complain about that, considering the state of Toulouse at the moment.

Of course, I'm not worried about them getting drunk. Even if they smash the whole bottle between the four of them – and they'd better not; they'd better leave me at least a mouthful of a drop to drain once I get back out, or we may spend the rest of this particular adventure in silence, with me sulking – the only one who'll be at any risk of getting even tipsy will be Gil. I've no idea what his alcohol tolerance level is like, but we're only bringing him along because we don't have a better place to stash him safely, so if he ends up a little worse for wear, I'm not too worried. He doesn't strike me as a loud drunk. Nor as one to let things get out of hand.

Once I have passed them the equivalent of a king's ransom in liquid gold, I head back in. Close the door. There's no need, really. No one is coming in without my specific invitation, and there's nobody about anyhow. But I want this moment. Need it. A second to myself.

The calm before the storm.

Chapter Seven

*Home, sweet home. It'd be a whole lot sweeter if I didn't
have to leave again. And if the Kavalan was still in here
with me.*

My house is still that. Mine. For a second, I can close my
eyes and breathe in the smell. There's a dry mustiness to the
place. I've been away too often and too long to air it out.
But underneath that are those scents you can't quite put a
label on. A touch of vanilla, perhaps, from when I knocked
a bottle over making pancakes when Aicha threw a baseball
at my head for giving her cheek. The faintest hint of spiced
almonds that might be the last lingering traces of whisky
and wine and song. From when times were good. When life
was simple, at least for a small window before the maelstrom
descended once more, and we girded our loins like knights
of old and stepped outside to fight the good fight.

I'm going. Soon. To do that all over again. To get done
what needs to be done so I can get back to finding my

missing friend. Bring back those good times. Reclaim what's mine both in terms of territory and the parts of my heart that went through that portal up on Bugarach.

But first, I drink in the sense of the place like a nightcap, that last dram that brings a sense of completion to the day. A job well done, when you can finally put your feet up and rest.

I can't, of course. But I wallow in the illusion for a moment still.

And being here is as good as a long rest for me. I'm recharging my spell slots, so to speak. Because I can pull on the energy here, draw *talent* from the very walls and floor. Drink it up like a sponge, pack my cells to the brim with power, and ready myself for what's to come. As far as possible, of course. In theory, we should have them outgunned. Caacrinolaas plus the Karnabo shouldn't be too much of an issue for the four of us, even not counting Gil.

But I'm still deeply worried. We're walking straight into a trap yet again. And I've no idea how it's going to spring.

Nor do we have Aicha with us. That swings the odds away from us. I can't lie to myself about that.

But hiding in here won't help either. Taking a moment to get my breath back is one thing. But I could easily linger here too long. Which would only make walking back out that front door all the harder. Plus, that'll increase the chances of them having finished the whisky before I can rejoin them. Which is a fate too horrible to even imagine, so feeling that I'm approaching fully charged, I get a move on about finding any items here that might help us in this fight.

It's slim pickings. As I said, Isaac's place is our magical storehouse normally. But there's a few bits and bobs. The Cailleach's wooden wand that she gifted me for my services and, ahem, my *services*. I might have avoided getting married to her –just– but she was still a good-looking lady. The wand, on the other hand, is nothing much to look at, little more than a stick. But there's a one-shot deal of death magic stored up in it. Nothing like what I worked when I fought against Papa Nicetas on Bugarach, but it's still enough to eat a soul away. Nasty stuff. I never even tried taking it to Isaac's. He'd have destroyed it in an instant. I should probably have done the same, but I held on to it, both as a last resort big gun and for sentimental reasons. The Cailleach was a black-hearted, evil old crone. But she honoured our deal and then some, and she was kind to me at a time when I needed a little of that.

I've no illusions it'll work against the demon incarnate. But the Karnabo? Perhaps. And I certainly don't want it being used against us if someone burgles the house, so into my inside pocket it goes.

I pick up the acorn from Aicha's and my battle with Le Guillaneu at the fairground museum in Paris. The thing's still absolutely packed with magic. Both the wyrd working of the hag herself, which whipped the fully grown tree back into its nascent form and my magic when I was wearing the body of a faerie queen. It's very different from the *talent* I'm packing now. But it's still mine. And so I'm connected to it. Enough that I can pull on it. Use it as a last gasp battery if my magic's getting low. Very handy when we're about to step onto enemy territory. Of course I can only pull on it if I'm in direct contact with it. And there's only one way I know of to ensure that's the case.

Because it's me, said method involves excruciating pain. I balance the acorn against my chest, then start to *push*. Just gently at first, then harder till I can feel the skin starting to bruise under the pressure. Then that top layer gives way, cracks, and the acorn starts to slip through each epidermis until I hit the fatty layer just between the ribs. Balanced above my heart. Symbolically, it links me directly into the magic, a back-up battery installed in my chest. It feels horrible. I doubt it'll be the most horrible thing I feel in the next few hours.

Last, I pick up the hilt of Clarent, the last remnant of King Arthur's Sword of Peace. Honestly? I'm not really sure why. It's nothing. An empty pommel, really. But there's still some magic swirling around on it. The last vestiges of ancient workings beyond my understanding. And with Joyeuse in the mix, it makes me feel better, thinking about having it in my hand rather than in the enemy's. The magic contained is light enough I can pop it into my etheric storage, so I stash it away for a later date. Just in case.

Then I'm done. I can't delay any longer. There's a strange feeling that settles on me as I look around. Like Bilbo closing up his scratch-marked front door, not knowing how long he will be gone. Every time I've ever left, there's always been the chance I might never return, but it feels stronger, a posed weight on my shoulders this time. Not a certainty, but if the Fates were shaking their Magic 8 Ball right now, I reckon it'd showing the "IT'S A STRONG POSSIBILITY" triangle. I give the place a last lingering gaze, letting my eyes rest on the sofa shaped perfectly to my posterior. The dust that glitters on the black TV screen, begging to be wiped off, for me to jump into the myriad films and series I've not even had time to consider catching up on over the last couple of years. The drinks cabinet packed full of tasty morsels.

But those are no fun when I'm on my own. And that's all the motivation I need to get my arse back out of the door and into the waiting cold.

'Pass us that then, will you?' I grab the bottle, which

gives a relieving slosh —they didn't finish it; I wasn't too late!— and take a swig. Fuck a glass. The time for niceties is done. Outside of the nicety of the delicious warmth blazing down my throat and setting every one of my internal pipes aglow with satisfaction, of course.

I raise the bottle. 'To Aich. To Jak. To getting them back. And fucking up anyone who stands in our path.'

Glasses lift, gleaming in the sunlight. Even Mephy manages to lift up the bowl I brought to put his dram in, and without spilling any, we all clink our drinking vessels, solemn, silent. No more needs to be said.

That's a toast —a plea? A promise?— that we'll all drink to.

Chapter Eight

It's like Damien Marley meets JRR Tolkein here. Out in the streets, they call it Mordor.

With the drink finished and the glasses and bowl deposited just inside the door along with the empty bottle because cleaning up and washing up is for Not-Dead-Later Paul rather than Facing-Death-Now Paul, I turn to Mephistopheles.

'What's the plan, dude? Can you still smell him?' I'm worried for a moment I might have pulled him too far off course, and my heart sinks when he shakes his head.

But it perks up again once he gives his answer. 'No, but I know which way he went. His stench was all over the road, mano. Follow me. Won't have any problem tracking him from there.'

So we head back up the Canal De Brienne, back under the small brick bridge. Mephy wheels left and leads us up the road that climbs level with the bridge. He nods towards the right, at the road heading towards another wide vehicular bridge that'll bring us back into where the slaughterhouses moved after the local authorities flooded the Garonnette. Where I last walked when coming back to find Franc from the shizzard's hideout.

It leads us straight to Saint Cyprien.

We start off down the road cautiously, our eyes peeled. Even Mephy, despite having got the scent back between his metaphorical teeth like a chew toy, isn't lost to his anger. Looks like a moment of reflection and a seriously good single malt has done us all the world of good. Or else the reality of what we're about to get into is finally hitting home.

As soon as the bridge is visible, I finally set eyes on them. The bastardised version of what was once mine.

The demon's wards.

I can still see crackling traces of grass-green and all-colour white, my magic and Isaac's combined. But it's shimmering, flickering like an illusion, a hologram hidden behind the tar-pitch magic that colours and covers it.

The wards won't welcome me. They're owned by another, wholly.

And that's not all we can see. Because on the other side of the wards, we finally see people.

And perhaps, just perhaps, we see their truths at the same time too.

'How are we ever going to get through there?' Gil's voice trembles, and I'd love to say it's because he's not magical. That unlike him, we can see an easy route thanks to all our centuries of experience and *talent*.

But it's not. And we can't. Because the streets are packed with humanity at its most basic.

And its most base.

It's hard to process really, to get our heads around what we're seeing. There's a lot of movement everywhere. Flesh packed against each other. Limbs flailing, in passion or fury or both at the same time. Skin visible through the rents in clothes. Underneath stamping feet. Pressed tight against another form. Willing or otherwise. Red liquid splashes like some gruesome version of 'Singin' In The Rain', a stomping dance of vicious death and lust written across the streets.

'Oh my. Paul, my lad…' Isaac breaks off. Lost for words. I've none to give him. Nothing I can tell him that will make this scene more palatable, less painful.

But Mephy does. 'No younglings, mano.'

I blink. Squint. Force myself to stare at the carnage up ahead. 'He's right. I don't see any kids, 'Zac.'

'Don't think he'd do that, mano. He's a prick all right, Caacrinolaas. But even he's got limits.' Mephy nods his snout decisively.

I notice the relief on Isaac's face, refrain from mentioning the possessed kids on the airplane that nearly crashed en route to Salzburg. If it brings peace to Isaac, I'll keep my mouth shut. And I don't think he's the only one. Perhaps Mephy needs to believe one of his own wouldn't do anything so horrendous either.

Demons might have a different idea of morality from us humans. But slaughtering children is wrong, whatever dimension you're from.

The people fucking, fighting, and dying are still horrific. Literally filled with horror. But we've all seen plenty of that. On battlefields. In torture chambers. Written in the faces and the hearts of men. It's a tragedy, a travesty even. But one we can deal with. The only way to save them is to get past and put a stop to the scumfucker who's making it happen.

Which raises an important question. One Gil's already asked us.

'How are we going to get through there?' I ask it again. Because even with my brain working now, recovering after having frozen in horror at the sight and the possibilities it might contain...

I can't see any way of getting through without slaughtering hundreds, thousands maybe of innocents.

Or getting torn to pieces, of course. Let's not forget Option Two.

Chapter Nine

Never in my life have I watched a zombie film and thought,
Oh, wouldn't it be fun if that happened in real life? In my
own city? So if reality could stop answering questions I
never even asked, that would be fucking great.

I look over at Mephy, who does that peculiar doggy shrug,
more ducking his head than raising his shoulders, but the
message is still clear. He doesn't have any specific idea about
how to counter this, how to stay under the radar without
killing everyone who moves in our general direction.

'Johannes?' He's been quiet through all of this, clearly
thinking. 'Can you do anything?'

Because let's not forget, Johannes is a force in and of
himself. In just the same way as Isaac can pull off miracles
with Kabbalah even without Nithael supercharging him,
Johannes Faust is the foremost demonologist to ever walk
this plane of existence, at least as far as we know. Yes, I

might ask the actual demon first, but when it comes to the workings themselves, Johannes is the man to ask.

He strokes at his wild beard as though trying to corral the hairs into heading in one single direction instead of all of them at the same time. For a while, we stand here, our breath bated, waiting to see what he has to say.

'Possibly.' It's a single word, the S sound stretched as he digests his thoughts, turning them over in his mind, tasting them, testing them. Then he looks at Isaac.

'But not on my own. Herr Isaac, I may need your help.' His eyes flick from Isaac to above him and back. 'Both your help.'

Interesting.

The two of them huddle together and start scratching things onto the sidewalk in luminous runes. Initially, it's fascinating to watch them work. Faust's runes are Enochian too – or at least close enough that I can make out the sense of them. It's like Chinese and Japanese. Close enough in written form to be almost distinguishable but still different enough to be a unique language.

'Why,' I say, pointing to them, 'did you never clock that angels and demons were from the same species, considering they speak the same language?'

Both men shrug. Both men also flush, the perennial response of intellectuals caught out by a simple bit of logical deduction.

'I just assumed,' Faust says, 'that this was how language became when it evolved.'

'Same!' Isaac's relief is almost palpable. 'That it was just how the ideas of the other dimensions became transcribed onto ours!'

Fascinating. And, of course, the obfuscations of their other-dimensional partners as to the truth would have helped lead them off down the wrong path entirely too. I decide not to point that out again though. Isaac and Nithael only seem to have just made up over that.

After approximately three and a half minutes of the two of them discussing intangible magical theory, my attention drifts away, and the second I'm not concentrating, I completely lose the gist of the conversation. So I head back over to where Gil is sitting.

'How are you holding up, man?' He's half-crouched, his back pressed to the start of the bridge's brickwork. Far enough away from the wards not to trigger them, but his eyes keep wandering back that way, staring at the carnage taking place just on the other side. I can't help wondering if he's seeing what's going on over there or if he's back on that table in Auch, with the demon worms ripping in and out of his body. Seeing so many others out of control from the wards woven overhead must take him back to when he, too, had lost control.

'Fine.' His breath carries that warm tang, notes of musk and orange that tell me he had a bit of that whisky. Some Dutch courage to keep him moving. I wonder how well it's doing in that task.

Sighing, I slide down next to him. There's a comfort to be taken in that scraping sensation, the rough edges of the brickwork tracing along the skin of my back even through my jumper. I knock his knee with mine. Shit as I am at these conversations, it still needs to be had.

'You're doing more than fine, Gil. You've done amaz-ingly. Holding it together. But this —' I wave my hands at the bloody mess waiting on the other side of the bridge. 'Is way more than you signed up for.'

I look up at the sky overhead. Think back to when it turned a putrescent green, when De Montfort triggered the

Grail's magic tied up in the bones he'd gathered, when he knocked down our wards in a heartbeat. At the prices we paid to bring that madness to an end.

'When we walk over there,' I say, 'the demons are going to be entirely focused on us. And one way or another, we'll bring it to an end. If we fail, someone else will take over. Pick up the mantle and try to stop them.'

I hope, at least. There's no certainty, especially seeing as how so many Talented creatures seem to have thrown their lot in with the demon. But there's no point telling Gil that. Nothing he can do about it.

Which is kind of the point. 'Their attention is going to be elsewhere from hereon in. You're unlikely to be a target again. If you want, you can walk away.'

I want him to in many ways. We're going to be heading into chaos, a bedlam the likes of which few have seen and survived. Only those who've suffered the worst of war in its most terrible of forms. But there's a key word in there. One that's haunting my mind.

One that Gil picks up on. 'Unlikely isn't certain.' His eyes drift back towards the war zone on the other side of the barrier. 'If we walk in there…' His voice falters, then comes back, strong and strengthened by will. 'When we go, can you keep me from becoming… like them?'

I nod, trying to project a certainty I've no right to have but which I fully believe nonetheless. 'Absolutely.' I know full well there's no chance Isaac or Johannes will let us cross that barrier if we're not able to remain in control.

'Then I'd rather go with you.' Gil sounds absolutely certain, entirely determined. 'I'd rather go there now, together, than end up like them.'

And what he means is clear.

He'd rather die by our side than be possessed again.

In my mind's eye, I see the fat white grubs burrowing in and out of his flesh all over again. The rot that coloured what remained of the boy now whole once more in front of me.

Physically, at least.

So thinking of that? I can't blame him. I won't deny him the chance to walk into battle by our side once again.

And to die doing so if needs be.

Chapter Ten

TOULOUSE, 30 OCTOBER, PRESENT DAY

This might be the only time I'm glad Aicha isn't with us. Zombies give her the heeby-jeebies, and the possessed on the other side are close enough to count. On the other hand, I also wish she was here so I could rip the piss out of her for it. It would make me feel a whole lot better.

Isaac and Johannes crack it, of course. I never doubted they would. Those two could solve the mysteries of the universe together.

But right now, I'll settle for them getting us through the carnage awaiting us in Saint Cyprien.

Isaac explains while Johannes walks down the line, sketching a strange sigil on each of us. It glows, and it's like a white light surrounded by umber, the white and black of their relative disciplines –as my eyes *see* them– mixing together.

'This is a rune based on the demonic form of Enochi-an,' he says, his hands crossed, his fingers fiddling with his sleeves. 'Basically a form of a *don't look here*. It will be powered by Nithael. The combination together should be enough to keep the people from noticing us and –' He stops fiddling and raises a finger. 'Should work even if we get separated.'

'Let's make sure that doesn't happen, shall we?' I've seen enough horror films to know how well it goes when the party gets split. 'Now what are you not mentioning, 'Zac? What's the downside?'

Isaac looks embarrassed, as guilty as a schoolboy caught red-handed with a smashed window, football in hand. 'Well, it has its limits.'

I groan. Of course it does. 'What are they?'

'Well, it should persuade them to not only leave us alone but to actively avoid us. But if they touch us, they'll see us. And at that point…'

'They'll attack?' I guess.

'Worse than that.' Johannes looks up from where he's marking Gil with the rune. 'They'll be drawn to us. The repulsion will turn to attraction. And if they draw the attention of others, it'll be the same too.'

Oh, fucksidaisy-do. If we bump into any of the possessed, we're going to be in a *28 Days Later* scenario before we know it, with hordes of the poor bastards hurtling down the street after us.

'Right. Don't touch them.' I nod grimly as I study Isaac's expression. He's studiously avoiding my gaze. 'And what else?'

'Well, that's it for me and Nith.' Isaac scuffs at the floor.

'Wait, *this will kill you?*' I screech, horrified. I'm about to leap at Johannes and knock his hand off Mephy's fur where he's started sketching the same rune, but Isaac waves both his at me, flapping them downwards, telling me to cool it.

'No, lad!' He smiles a real, warm grin, and I feel my chest ease. I was genuinely worried. It's exactly the sort of self-sacrificing bullshit Isaac would have pulled off. I had to learn it from somewhere, after all.

'All I meant is it's going to take all of our *talent* combined.' The smile disappears. Isaac's back in serious mode. 'We'll be able to maintain it, but we're on their home turf. We won't be able to pull off anything else, not while keeping us from their view.'

So it keeps us hidden, but takes two of us out of the game *talent* wise. Not ideal, but not like we have many choices other than wide-scale slaughter. Grimly, we start up once more, crossing over the bridge. The wards. And enter the demon's territory.

There's no way of being sure if he knows we're on our way. Odds are good he does, but then who knows the limits of demon magic? Keeping this many people contained – and possessed – isn't chump change on the *talented* spectrum, even for otherworldly beings. Mephy doesn't have a clue when I ask him, so we're just going to assume the worst.

The good news is, though, that he still has Caacrinolaas' scent. Small blessings.

We walk slowly, huddled together, pressed in tight.

It's utter chaos around us. Like a Roman orgy organised by the Droogs from *A Clockwork Orange*. Rapacious sex and ultra-violence. And not just men on women either. Each sex is running after their own interests. I see a woman striking a cowering man about the head with a piece of two by four. The sounds seem disconnected, a TV show overlaid by the wrong soundtrack. Contact with wood shouldn't squelch.

Then I see the nails driven into it. Turn my eyes away.

Not far after the bridge, Mephy tugs us as a group towards the park that nestles up the Abattoirs, the now-museum once more coated in rivers of blood. I don't think these will be so easy to sluice off though. These gigantic works of modern art – twisting three-dimensional shapes – seem more like climbing frames somehow, an aesthetically gorgeous playground for kids.

That childish image is shattered as a body hurls off the top. The contacting *crack* tells me something is broken. They move, so they aren't dead, but considering their breathless huffed growls of agony, they might wish they were. Seeing the carnal violence all around us? They probably will be soon. A woman stands on top of the structure, her right breast bared, scratched fingernail marks there bleeding profusely as she howls her victory to the sky. I wonder if they were fucking or fighting. Whether she defended herself or struck out in a moment of demented bliss.

Not that it matters. None of them are in their right minds. I don't blame any of them for their actions.

All my anger's focused on Caacrinolaas.

It helps. Keeps me moving. The temptation is so strong – to leap to someone's aid. To shield a head from a falling piece of piping being brought down over and over. But if I do, we'll have no choice but to kill them straight after. And how is that any more just?

I notice that Mephy's positioned himself strategically, flanking the other side of Faust and 'Zac. Making sure they can't suddenly move, to instinctively try to help as every fibre of their being will be crying out at them to do so. Both of them look shaky, shaken, but they keep moving forward.

Gil's head swivels from left to right, trying to take it all in, to comprehend, and he's so pale he looks washed out, a human faded by all of time's miseries. I loop my arm through his and pull him on.

'Don't look. I know –' I raise my hand to stem his forthcoming objection. 'It's like being told not to think about purple elephants, but you won't see anything here you want to see. And believe you me, we're all going to be seeing this in our nightmares for a long time to come. Right now, keep looking straight ahead.'

I drop us back a touch, positioning Gil behind Isaac and Faust while I keep enough to the side to block any of them from an ill-fated lunge to save one of these poor souls. Now he can concentrate on the backs of their heads. It gives him something to focus on rather than the sex and slaughter surrounding us on all sides.

Mephy leads us to the other side of the park, up some steps to the open concrete area where the *guinguette* – the pop-up restaurant bars so fashionable in France in the summer – are hosted during the warmer months.

It's going to take a hell of a clean up before anyone's going to want to enjoy a cool pint here again. If there's anyone left to even do so.

There's a small metal walkway leading along and down – the Vigurie Gateway. Neatly regular wooden planks are laid over the metal framework. Tubular supports allow maximum views of the river roaring through below. Steps descend to the side of the Garonne.

It's a tight space. Two people abreast at best.

'Shit,' Mephy mutters under his breath. I can't argue with that assessment. It's a properly shitty situation.

The only saving grace is that it's less packed than the main road, less even than the park. Probably because most people have either been hurled off the side already, based on the piles of broken bodies down below or because they didn't find enough bloodshed in this causeway between the two levels and went where the action was really happening. Down below, it's just as active as what we left behind; plenty of bodies are bobbing up and down in the Garonne's wild spume. As I watch, another one tumbles off Pont Neuf and cracks into the water hard enough that were they conscious on contact, I doubt they are now.

Gil looks away. I don't blame him. I wish I could.

'Down,' Mephy growls, making it clear where we're heading. Damn it.

Because sitting in the middle of the metal walkway is a huge man, his eyes the same colour as the ink dripping from them.

He's just a man, though that's almost hard to believe. I'd say he's about two metres tall. He's crouched, bent around a sword that looks like it belongs at a manga convention rather than out in the real world as it's almost the same size as him. He's built like the proverbial brick shithouse.

And looks about as easy to move.

But he's definitely a normal human, not Talented, although I reckon there has to be some ancient troll DNA mixed up in there a long way back to have produced someone his size.

He looks tough as nails, and he's swinging his head from side to side. Looking. Waiting.

It's worrying. We've not encountered anything like this yet.

'What do you reckon?' I ask.

'He's waiting for us, mano,' Mephy growls, and that guttural note is starting up again. He may not like what's happening around us, but it doesn't have the same impact on the demon dog as it does the rest of us. It isn't his species murdering each other, even if it's his species that has caused this. He wants to get back on the hunt, and that eye-stained giant is in our way. All he's bothered about is getting through him to get to Caacrinolaas.

For the rest of us, it isn't so simple.

'Can we find another way around?' It's a valid question from Johannes.

'Of course.' I nod. That's really the best plan of action. Don't go tangling with the man left looking for us. Sneak around him. Get out the other side.

Which is the exact moment that said man raises his head and looks straight at us. His lips peel back into a savage smile, and he raises his sword to the sky with one hand, which, let me tell you, should be impossible considering how heavy it must be.

He howls with glee. Somehow, he's seen through our *don't look here.*

And based on the swivelling heads all now pointing at us?

It looks like he isn't alone.

Chapter Eleven

Okay. Who let this dude out of Fist Of The North Star?
Although if he attacks, the Manga-nna die, all the same.

We don't have many options. Precisely two, actually. Run or
fight. And they both suck.

The giant man advances along the walkway, each step
making the metal *plink* like it's a piano wire stretched taut,
plucked and close to snapping. In a way, that'd be the ideal
solution. He'd be gone –injured or dead– but it wouldn't be
our fault. He could take it up with the Toulouse Town Planning Health Safety Department. If he survives. And if
Toulouse does, too, of course.

Sadly, we don't get that lucky, which is standard for me,
of course. We back up, aware that the numbers of heads
facing our way are in the tens. If we don't do something
soon, there's going to be noughts added to that at a rate of
knots.

I glance at the faces of my companions. Gil looks pretty

damn close to freaking out, but his fists are clenched and raised. He'll go down swinging, the Good God love him. Johannes has a hand resting on Mephistopheles' neck, although whether to take comfort or to hold him back, I can't tell.

Isaac looks back at me, a pleading expression on his face. 'Don't kill them, lad. Please. If you can help it, don't kill them.'

Fucksake, 'Zac. Why did you have to ask me that? Now I feel absolutely duty-bound to try to keep them alive.

Problem is, I don't know if I can keep us alive if I do.

The other park dwellers are starting to shuffle towards us, but only Meatboy is close enough yet to engage. So I swing myself towards him and, aiming for his midriff, unleash a series of devastating blows.

To my fists. Devastating to my fists.

Because apparently he's done the abs equivalent of Jaws from *James Bond* and replaced them with solid steel. Fuck. I was hoping he'd be a bit out of shape and relying on size, but apparently he does core work when he's not bench pressing a rabid hippopotamus to get his arms ready for the gun show. I didn't pack any magic into the punch because I didn't want to end up with my fist sticking out of his back. Now I'm kind of regretting it because I'm not sure I'm still able to wiggle my fingers after that impact.

I'm sure I did him some damage, of course. He's just not showing it because he's hyped up on some demonic possession. Otherwise, he'd be in a winded heap at my feet. Probably.

Sadly, it doesn't stop him from attempting to dismantle my head from my body without reading the instructions properly first. I see it coming –thank the Good God he isn't fast as well because that'd be *really* unfair– but only just. I hear the air, like a sudden localised gale whooshing past my ear. And then said ear explodes into a burning, raging agony because, while I did see it, I didn't see it soon enough to avoid it entirely. And just that clip to my ear has sent my nervous system into overload.

This guy is a serious brawler.

I duck back, sidestep, and then launch another one-two blow to his side. Dance back again as a sweeping arm comes perilously close to connecting. I duck once more and then launch myself up inside his grasp, connecting a hammering uppercut to his chin, ignoring the letter of furious complaint my knuckle committee is currently penning to my brain for having even considered such an action.

He doesn't go down. The Good God damn it, he doesn't even have a glass jaw. Absolutely fucking outrageous. It's enough to spin him back, to have him clutching his chin, but he's not out of action.

The other park dwellers are drawing nearer now, and they're picking up speed. Dropping down off structures, abandoning their individual battles. Focused on reaching us instead. A couple of them – a man who trails an arm that's either broken or battered out of use and a woman whose nudity is a threat, not an invitation – break into a loping run, and it's a signal for the rest to start as well.

I'm panicking now. The five of us draw closer, back to back, and I can see the park dwellers' shouts and screams are reaching the ears of those on the road. A few of them are heading in through the gates, and it won't be long till it's a throng. This has zombie movie disaster moment written all over it, and my heart is beating ten to the dozen. All I can think is, *Thank goodness Aich isn't here. She hates zombies.* The Good God knows why considering some of the horrors we've faced together, but apparently that's where she draws the line in terms of terrifying creatures. I blame George Romero.

But if your thoughts are ever frozen, if there's that one scratched record of an idea that just keeps skipping around and around in your head, then trying to fight it will never work. You can shout at your brain to think about something else all you want, but it won't matter. So the only answer in my opinion?

Lean into it.

I grab hold of that idea of Aicha. Of what she'd be telling me to do in this situation, as the bodies start pressing, their numbers thickening, as Meatboy shakes off the upper-cut, a quick back and forth that seems to dislodge what should have been a major concussion like a novice rodeo clown is thrown off the horns of a champion bull. Gone. Done. Dusted. He turns back towards us, hefts up that ridiculously impossible sword, and steps in our direction. We all group together even further. Threats are coming from every angle. We have mere seconds before they hit us.

So I grab hold of the Aich I carry in my mind all the time. The voice that tells me what a dickhead I am when I fuck up. Good God, I miss that voice in real life. Listening to my corrupted, imperfect heart-cloud copy of the Druze Queen, I think about what she'd tell me to do.

And I know. Deep down, I know.

Because what Isaac has asked me to do is impossible. I can't keep these people alive. All I'm doing by delaying the inevitable is increasing the numbers it's going to bring our way. Increasing how many will have to die. Or else accepting the death of me, my friends, possibly everyone in Toulouse at the hands of this sadistic demon fuck.

So I know what I have to do. 'Sorry, 'Zac', I murmur, soft enough to be private, loud enough that he definitely hears. I slide my hand between the nearest air particles and into my etheric storage.

My hand wraps around a pommel, forming to the contours of its grip. It isn't the one I planned on grabbing though. I was going for my sword. The classic hack'n'slash murder device I've been using since I left behind the path of non-violence during my time as a Perfect and learned how to use a noble's weapon. I may have lost a sword or two over the centuries —I keep a decent stash inside my storage with that in mind— but I know the feel of each of them in my grasp.

This isn't one of them.

It's hard to explain the difference, really. It's like when you wake up, still half-dozing, and you stick your hand out – maybe to grab your phone to check the time or your glasses to see what's going on. The moment your fingers brush the top of that bedside table, you know something is wrong. That you aren't where you thought you were, aren't home. Maybe you're at a hotel or a friend's house, but whatever it is, things aren't as they should be. It might be wood, might be the same sort of finish, lacquered just so as to be almost indistinguishable. But all the senses carry memories, and touch is no different.

So though I'm still holding a conveniently forged piece of metal, I know the instant I touch it that this isn't one of my swords. And that's weird because my etheric storage is keyed to my being. If I want something? My hand should find it straight away. This is my own pocket dimensional filing system. Everything is labelled and in its place.

Instinctively, I pull it out, and as it comes, it only confirms what I thought. Because there's no heft to it. Primarily because there's no blade on the other side of the cross-guard.

What I'm holding is the last part of Clarent, King Arthur's sword on the side, the one he dallied with behind Excalibur's back.

I'm completely disoriented. This has never happened to me, not since Al-Buni himself taught me how to manifest the storage. It's been a part of me for hundreds of years, and what I'm feeling now is like when you've had your arm numbed till it's nothing but dead meat swinging loosely around. Movable, attached but somehow not the normal appendage. Not connected in the way your brain insists it should be. Baffled, I raise the handle in front of me to peer at it, trying to understand how this could have happened...

Meanwhile, Meatboy, who's just started a lumbering run towards me, his sword dragging point down in the dust behind him like he thinks he's fucking Naruto or something —and who on Earth thinks that's an acceptable way to treat a bladed weapon?— stops.

Blinks.

For a moment, I think the spell's been broken. The black ink in his eyes clears, and I can see the white of the sclera again.

Then he turns and lumbers back towards the railing separating us from the Garonne. He flops down heavily enough I'm surprised he doesn't set off any nearby seismographs. He stares out over the river, apparently lost in thought.

I hear a half-cry, a small squeak of dismay from Isaac and wheel instantly. The first of the runners is almost upon him, and he's trying to pull farther back. Desperate for them not to touch him.

Without even thinking, I push through, muscling my way between him and Johannes. I raise the bladeless crossguard in front of my face like Van Helsing deep in the bowels of the count's castle, and I'll be damned if it doesn't work. The arriving runners skitter to an almost-halt, and their eyes, not ink-stained like Meatboy but clearly showing they're not in their right minds, skip over us, searching around, looking for whatever it was that grabbed their attention in the first place.

It doesn't stop there either. The effect – the magic, I guess – spills backwards out of them. Now I can see it, almost. A silvered light web, a single filigree that links from one to the next and stops the mad charge heading our way. It soothes the savage beasts the demon's wards have made of the Toulousains.

Well, blow me over with a gale force tornado and call me Dorothy. It looks like Clarent's name, the Sword of Peace, wasn't just hyperbole.

Chapter Twelve

He might have been an unpaying lodger in my house for decades. But right now? The Sword Of Peace has definitely paid its Cla-rent.

We stand here for a minute, getting our bearings.

'What was that, mano?' Mephy's head's turned to nip at his own coat; he's gnawing at his shoulder as if trying to remove something clinging to the hairs. 'Felt that. Didn't like it one little bit.'

'That? Oh, that was the remnants of Clarent,' I say carelessly and watch as Johannes' head swivels round.

'Did you say Clarent? As in the sword of King Arthur?' Oh, yes. The scholar has been triggered. He's in full-on discovery mode now, wanting all the details.

'Yes and yes, I promise to tell you the whole story later. When we're not out in the open, in the middle of what is basically Raccoon City.' I'm greeted by blank faces. 'Really? *Resident Evil?* No one? Not one of you?'

'Hard to play video games without opposable thumbs, mano.' The only argument I can put up against that is the films they made. But they were shit. So I keep silent and nod. I'll give him that one.

The possessed – or the, at least, heavily influenced (I'm not sure if they're all actually puppeteered by the demon, considering the difference between most of them and Meatboy) – that came close to us have all just sort of drifted off to the sides. They're not back to normal – not one of them is looking confused or screaming at the blood and body parts lying around, but neither are they trying to shove the nearest blunt instrument through the back of each other's heads, so I'll take that as a win. It's easy enough to scoot around them. Most of them are sitting now, cross-legged and staring at the sky. Those still upright scoot around us without noticing. The *don't look here* is definitely back in full working order.

Some good news. Finally.

'Still got the scent, Meph?' He nods. It would've been easy to have lost it among all the odours of bodily fluids of every kind being carried liberally by the chilled, crisp breeze. But Mephistopheles is on the case.

He leads us back to the metallic staircase. I pass Meatboy with a wary look, but he doesn't turn towards us. The staircase doesn't make any noise as we walk along it either. It's sturdy enough, apparently, as long as you aren't some sort of human equivalent of a Panzer tank. We make our way across, then down, following the path till we're standing by the side of the Garonne itself, with the Pont Neuf ahead of us.

It seems eerily quiet. I scan around, trying to work it out. Then I clock it. There aren't any screams of pain, any roars of rage, any ululations of primal, unbridled ecstasy, the fucking and fighting that have echoed off every surface of what was once my city. I feel a hand on my shoulder and look around to meet a grave expression on Isaac's face.

'There's no one else nearby. Nith is telling me it's empty up ahead, lad.'

Damn it. No wonder he's wearing that expression. I borrow it, hang it on my own face because that can only mean one thing. Our enemies have cleared the path ahead of us. And I doubt they've done it because they're concerned about casualties.

They know we're coming. And they're getting ready for us. Fan-fucking-tastic.

Mephy's oblivious to it all. He's focused once more on tracking down his demon dog rival or enemy or whatever the score is between the two of them. Maybe he mugged Mephy for his lunch money when he was little. Stole his favourite chew toy. I've no idea, but it's clear Mephy's out for revenge, whatever the reason behind it.

The pleasant, tended green strips that accompany the river, which are packed with picnickers in the summer, aren't strewn with discarded wrappers and wine bottles today. I try not to look too closely at what lies glistening across the grass blades. If I do, I'll be able to identify them too easily. They're all things I've either pulled out of other people's bodies or tried to stuff back into my own over the centuries. A high brick wall runs along our right, separating us from Saint Cyprien proper.

Ahead is the giant wheel, now an obligatory part of any touristic city. It's funny how fashions ebb and flow. I remember when the Big Wheel was the main attraction wherever it might be set up, a marvel to take you heaven-wards. Thankfully, it doesn't seem to be operating. Although, based on the bloody mess surrounding it, that hasn't stopped people from trying to climb it to run pitched battles on it before plunging, smashing down straight to hell.

We don't get that far. There's a break in the wall on our right – flung open metal gates, orange painted wrought iron, like rust-coloured metal trees imprisoned in rectangular boundaries, seemingly tiny comparative to the towering brickwork. Mephistopheles dashes through, bringing us back onto the main streets.

Empty. Desolate. Deeply unsettling.

I know where we are, of course. We're on the Rue Charles Vigurie. This whole area – the open Port Vigurie where the Wheel stands, the walkway we used, the road itself were named after an apparently brilliant nineteenth-century surgeon who operated in the nearby hospital. I don't know what he did to gain the honour. Our paths didn't cross, and I was otherwise occupied for much of that time.

But thinking of the hospital fills my heart with dread. There's no good memories for me in that place. It existed when I first lived, albeit in a much different setup and with far less chances of walking back out. Not that anyone walked out of there during the Plague times, doctors or patients. Except me, of course. There were always plenty of skins to pick up and wear when I died during those moments.

I can still see the scenes I woke up to when I whimper in the night.

The road narrows, and the pink-and-orange brickwork seems to loom over me. The ancient Hospital Hôtel-Dieu Saint-Jacques is not where I want to be headed, but it makes perfect sense as a hiding place for our demonic rival. No matter how much it's been modernised, it's still full of twisting corridors and a sprawl of outbuildings that could contain any number of horrors. The higher walls give way to concrete railings and an opened automatic gate that gives access to rear staff parking. I'm sure Mephy's going to dive into there. Instead, he carries on straight, ducking around a parasol obstructing the road, which was hurled from the wreckage of a bar café on our right, the grey and white of the umbrella part stained black. He's almost running now, and I avoid whistling him back, just. Mainly because I don't want him to bite off my testicles over treating him like a pet but also because I don't want to draw attention to us. This emptied area, only just previously thronged with violence, is giving me the heebie jeebies, and I'm sure we're marching straight into a trap.

'Mephy!' I hiss. To my amazement he slows, looks back.

'What, mano?' I can see that hint of fang again. He's ready to fight, ready for war, and he doesn't appreciate me checking him mid-stride.

'This is all too bloody easy, dude!' It's amazing just how much emotion you can inject into a hiss. There seems to be two volumes made for channelling frustration and incredulity. Ear-splitting, Brian Blessed-style bellowing or words expelled like super-heated compressed steam out between gritted teeth.

'Good?' Apparently Mephy doesn't get it. I don't know whether he's being deliberately obtuse, or if it's just the demon equivalent of the red mist settling over his vision. Either way, he's not picking up on the —pretty categorically obvious in my opinion— nuances of what I'm saying.

'So it's a fucking trap!' I can't quite believe I have to spell it out.

'He's right, my friend. We cannot go rushing in willy-nilly. It will not end well.' Johannes lays a comforting hand on his friend's ruff, smoothing down some of those raised hackles.

'But he's near!' The words are almost a whine. There's a petulant tone I know well. Mainly because it's normally coming out of my mouth. Oh, so this is how annoying I am for my friends when I want to go rushing off into danger. I'd say it's a lesson learned, except we all know that's a lie.

'All the more reason we need to slow down.' Isaac's voice is level, calm. If there's anyone adept at explaining things to the petulantly over-stimulated, it's him. He's had eight hundred years of experience doing so.

'Listen, Meph.' I try my hardest to mirror 'Zac's tone, to keep calm even though I'm about on the edge of panicking myself. 'He knows we're after him – knows you're after him. And, sure, he might have turned tail and fled last time –'

'Because he's a fucking cowardly custard.'

'– because, as you say, he's a cowardly custard, oh demon of the primary school playground. But he's had time to prepare since. And he's cleared the way for us. Laid out the fucking red carpet. He wants us to wander on into whatever he's got laid out to keep us entertained. And I can promise you it won't be prime rib steak and chihuahuas doing the Can-Can, my friend.'

Meph sinks down on his haunches and looks up at me. 'So what's the plan then, mano?'

'Well…' I stop. 'Um.' This is not my area of expertise. I'm normally the one sitting there asking what we do instead of rushing in like a bull with a bunch of discount coupons for fine white china that are about to expire.

Isaac rides in heroically to the rescue. Which goes about as well as one of his rescues normally does. 'We reconnoitre.' He nods proudly, with a smile on his face.

Mephy narrows his eyes. 'So what you're saying is, we

go there slowly and see what's happening because we've got no fucking clue instead of going there quickly, correct?'

Isaac's smile falters, weakens, watered down by the scorn Mephy's just poured all over it. 'Er, right?'

'Okay, brilliant. All the manos form a single file behind me, and we'll creep slowly towards our doom, okay?'

Well, when you put it like that, we're fucked.

Chapter Thirteen

Doom-creeping. Even worse than doom-scrolling. Just about.

I'm assuming we're heading over the Pont Neuf. That we'll spin left as we round the corner of the hospital and make our way into Toulouse proper.

Nope.

Mephy's been doing some exaggerated, Elmer-Fudd-hunting-Bugs "Shh be vewwy, vewwy quiet" style creeping forward, just to really make us all feel like dickheads. But he stops as we round the corner. The narrow road opens out into the main thoroughfare. He raises a paw, pointing straight across it.

'There.'

Well. That's a very strange choice for a demonic base of operations. Which means, in my opinion, it must be an excellent choice for a demonic trap.

Across the way is the Chateau D'Eau Photography

85

Museum. A Chateau D'Eau is a water tower rather than some sort of baroque undersea palace for merfolk as the name "water castle" conjures up. This one got transformed into a museum back in the seventies and is the oldest museum dedicated solely to photography in the whole of France.

It's a gorgeous construction. There is a round ground floor surrounding the tower itself, which extends towards the heavens, crowned by a dome and accompanying balustrade and finished off with a weathervane piercing the sky. All done in the orange-pink brickwork so beloved by the city.

'Look. The prick's hiding out in a prick.' Trust Mephy to soil the image. 'Looks like my rockin' red rocket, know what I mean, mano?'

'Yes, I think we all get that you think it looks phallic, Mephy.' Johannes sighs that weary exhalation of one who is well-used to their companion's coarse crudity.

'I mean, it's a bit small, comparatively, obviously...' Mephy breaks off with a bark of laughter. 'All right, Faust, I'll knock it off.' He bumps against his friend's leg. 'You manos always so worried about being proud of your penises. They must all be very, very small; that's all I'm saying.'

I'm not about to get into a dick measuring contest with a demon dog. But I'll admit, he's ratcheted down the tension a notch.

Now let's go kick the other demon dog square in the nuts. I'll happily have him singing falsetto for the rest of eternity.

We pick our way across the road carefully, cautiously. I feel ridiculous doing so. If he's sitting up in the tower watching us, then we must look like a bunch of prize plonkers, the five of us creeping across the deserted open space, standing out like a convention of sore thumbs. The metal gate is partially open. And, of course, when we push it wide enough to let us in, it shrieks nails-down-a-chalk-board style, a screaming doorbell to announce our arrival to whoever's inside.

'Well, I'm glad we decided to go slowly and creep on in,' Mephy says at a volume approximately loud enough to wake the dead and give them all a splitting headache in the process. 'Now Caacrinolaas will never see us coming.'

Nobody loves a smartarse –apart from everyone who's ever met me, of course– but I'm too on edge to think of a pithy put-down. So I let it go, and we slouch on into the tower itself.

The huge black front door –half my height again, I'd say– is precisely the same amount of conveniently ajar as the Spinal-Tap-volume gate wasn't. I look over at Johannes and get the nod back.

'Trap. Definitely.'

But I don't see anything to do with this particular mousetrap except to trigger it and hope it doesn't snap our spines.

Good God, I wish Aicha was here.

But she isn't. Not except in my thoughts. Yet, I can hear her. The advice she'd give. Be cautious. Stay alert. Look for ways to turn the trap to your advantage. Don't fuck it up, dickhead.

Don't fuck it up, Paul. Yeah. Easier said than done when you're me.

We creep into the building. The place is designed to not so much rattle my nerves as to shake them so hard their teeth fall out. We're in a narrow, round corridor that wraps around the tower. The same pink-orange brickwork as the outside makes up the inner walls, with the bricks exposed on both sides beneath the hanging photographs of the current exhibit. Something about South America based on the getup of the people in the photos. I'm not taking the time to read the signs or study the images too deeply.

The corridor's curve is sharp. It's fantastic for a gallery, each step bringing you a new surprise to *ooh* and *aah* at. But for me, in combat mode, it just means limited line of sight. Every footfall could be the one that puts us square underneath the trap's gleaming jaw. We're walking through a perfect kill zone. And I really don't want to die.

Fuck my life, this is horrible. I feel useless. My whole job has always been to charge in, trigger the tripwires, and get blown to smithereens. Rinse and repeat. Infinite-lives cheat mode engaged. And now I'm creeping forward, inching around what is effectively one long continuous corner, expecting that last death to come screaming at me in some unpredictable, unimaginably horrible way, and I can't do anything about it. Someone disabled all of my special options. Possibly. And I'm not about to take the risk that they didn't.

It takes us about five minutes to make a path that could be cleared in about thirty seconds. We find nothing. But as we approach the end of the round, the daylight an elongating rectangle painted on the grey concrete floor, Mephy stops. Sniffs. Wheels. Growls. And trots back.

To the dark metal steps leading into the basement.

'Down there?' I don't even know why I verbalise it. Of course it's down there. When was my doom ever waiting anywhere other than in the subterranean sections of buildings I really didn't want to walk into?

So we huddle at the top of the stairs for a moment, Faust resting his hand on Mephy's ruff to keep him from charging down the stairs, the bass rumble of his constant growl making it a clear and present danger.

'Any ideas?' I look around at a sea of blank faces. A veritable ocean of blankness, complete with tides of no ideas and rip currents of cluelessness.

'Walk down the stairs?' Isaac ventures, his voice rising on the end in that tone that's half-question and half-hope that someone might shoot it down with a better idea.

No one does. I can't think of anything better either.

So walk down the stairs we do.

Chapter Fourteen

TOULOUSE, 30 OCTOBER, PRESENT DAY

I could do with GIR deciding to sing the 'Doom Song'
round about now. Anything to lighten the mood.
Particularly as I'm more expecting to walk into Doom, the
video game.

The theme of curvature doesn't change. Neither in the movement of the stairs clinging to the wall, poured concrete and black-painted metal railings following their shape, nor in the room we find below, mirroring that above us.

Nor in the workings left behind from its previous days of utility: the massive paddled waterwheel we see on our left as we come down, the flywheel it once drove now visible through smoked glass flooring, grey pipe holes that look like a washed-out Mario might leap out of them at any second.

I feel like that. Washed out. Or washed up. Certainly not ready for whatever is waiting for us down here.

It's not immediately clear, the threat. Oh, we all know it's here. But this is a comparatively cramped space. The ring-like corridor around the central brickwork is so similar to upstairs, the only difference being the industrial remnants scattered about like a rich hipster's loft conversion. We edge around once more, our eyes darting about, straining to find the danger we know is lurking.

Nothing.

Not until we make our way to the doorway.

It's a simple archway, the same thin bricks following that endless repetition of curve around the top that makes up the entire building. No cornerstone. Nothing flashy in the design. Function over fashion. Through it, we see a carbon copy mirrored on the other side, another exit, but our eyes are drawn to what sits on squat haunches in the middle of the floor. Its fur bristling, its eyes staring madly, drool dribbling down its chubby little cheeks...

'Is that... a hamster?' Isaac asks as he steps forward, no doubt planning to stroke its adorably soft head and give it a cuddle.

I shoot a hand out, checking him mid-step. 'Stop, man.'

He turns to me, puzzlement clear on his face. 'What? It's just a little hamster, lad. Probably...'

Now his brow furrows as he tries to work out what strange happenstance might have led to a fuzzy little critter being here, in the basement of a photography museum during what's amounted to almost pitched warfare in the streets outside.

He tries again. 'Probably got left here by a visiting child? Before all this madness?'

'A visiting child who carried with them their beloved rodent, without question by parent or museum authorities?' Faust's tone is almost mild, but a slight hint of Germanic disapprobation at the very idea of such flagrant disrespect for an indisputable number of rules can't help but creep in.

'This has Holy Grail written all over it.' My words are an almost hiss as I stare at the wee beastie in front of us.

Isaac's really confused now. 'Holy Grail? You destroyed that long ago, lad. Is this linked to Nicetas or some such malarkey?'

'Not the actual Holy Grail.' I resist the urge to shake Isaac but only just. As I've been running on Grail Reincarnation Juice for the past few centuries, I guess it's an understandable mistake. 'The other Holy Grail. The funny one. Monty Python. This has "Beast of Caerbannog" written all over it. And I'm all out of Holy Hand Grenades too.'

I'd use one if I had one. I'd even count to precisely three if it got us out of this mess. Because if there's one thing I don't trust even more than get-rich-quick pyramid schemes and hand-wringing politicians, it's things that look innocuous when I'm expecting flaming death from every angle.

I point my sword, pulled clean from my etheric storage, straight at the hamster. 'That. That right there. Some sort of monster, I assume?'

And, of course, I assume correctly.

I feel the voice as it rumbles in my head. I've not heard it before, but I've felt its disdain about humanity. Its rage when I thwarted it. And its hunger. Its terrible, insatiable hunger. So when it speaks in my head, I know it. I've seen it, a vastness contained in a slender little thing before. Last time, it wasn't a tiny rodent though.

No. It was a glass wand.

'Well, manling. We meet again.' The syllables are echoing depths, reverberating around the inside of my skull like the slamming stone of a defiled crypt's entrance behind an unwary adventurer.

'Oh, fucking hell.' The others turn and look askance at

me. 'He's talking to me in my head. Is he talking to the rest of you in your heads?'

Small shakes give me the answer I half-expected. 'He talks?' Isaac quirks an eyebrow. 'Who is he? What's he saying?'

'It's the dickhead from the Matriarch's staff. The fuckhead from Lille.' I want to crack a joke, lighten the mood, but I can't. Because it's a punch to the jaw for Gil. Especially considering everything he's been through since then, and the price we had to pay to escape. All the colour drains from him, his legs bowing, wobbling as he half collapses against the wall, his Adam's apple bobbing back and forth as though trying to swallow down the impossibility of what he's facing.

But I'm not about to let this arsehole lead the conversation down the Villainous Monologue 101 path he's already set up. I switch back to inside my head.

What's with every evil twatfish I meet these days trying to talk like Darth Vader's ill-prepared understudy? Honestly, I'd almost rather run into an idiot who talks like Jar Jar Binks at this point. Almost.

Who is Darth Vader? Is he the power of the land now? A dark lord? There's an eagerness to the creature's demands. I reckon he's about ready to head off and try to join forces with the Sith.

A dark lord? Nah, that's Sauron. It's fantasy when he's a dark lord. It's sci-fi when he's a Sith commander.

'What are you saying to him, Paul?' Isaac's tone is insistent. I can tell he really hates being out of the loop on a chance to glean information.

'I'm explaining to him the difference between a Sith and a dark lord.' That should confuse him. Also, let them know

I'm dealing with the situation with my usual non-sequiturs to throw our opponents off-balance.

'Actually, mano, there isn't a difference.' Mephy's regarding the little creature with great interest. Great interest manifesting in great strings of drool forming along his rubbery lips. I reckon he's having flashbacks to his Trial in Home. 'The official title of the ruling Sith is Dark Lord of the Sith.'

Fuck. Not exactly helpful, Mephy. Less so than eating the furry fuckwit would be anyhow. Still, never let it be said I can't use it to my advantage.

'Apparently I stand corrected. Darth Vader is, in fact, a dark lord. He's also entirely made up. And not in a "check my beauty tutorials on YouTube" sense either.'

'Enough!' Apparently the creature has clocked on to the fact I'm basically taking the piss out of him. *'I shall destroy you all, now. Fear my doom, manling!'*

I shrug. *'Not really. I've had enough* Doom *of recent. Plus, you strike me as more original* Wolfenstein 3D *than* Doom.*'* I remember what Isaac asked, about who the being is. *'Out of interest, which old school shoot-'em-up should I say is calling? Before we wipe you from existence?'*

'Wipe me? Wipe me?' I very much doubt he recognises my references to the halcyon days of PC gaming, but he gets the gist nonetheless. *'It is you who shall be undone. Erased so as you will never be spoken of again. As for who I am? Nameless have I been for eons. The terrible horror in the eclipse. The unspoken ending that haunts the deepest night. Fear made form, the void in flesh.'*

'You could just say you don't have one, dude. Enough with the melodrama already.'

'I do! Now! My new master, he who freed me from that prison, he who has raised me up as his own, his loyal servant, to learn at his knee and do his bidding, has named me!' The pride in the creature's

tone is clear and present. '*The President of Hell himself, Lord Caacrinolaas, greatest of beings to stride atop this puny plane's undulations, has given me title and purpose. My name shall ring through the nightmares of those upon whom I feast. All shall know the name of* Mister Fuzzy Butt*!*'

Silence. You could hear a pin drop in the place as I swing my gaze from one to the other of my group, biting my trembling lip. The hamster – the dread lord Mister Fuzzy Butt – snarls squeaking defiance at us from in the middle.

'What? What is it, Paul?' Faust can see my effort, the trembling of my cheeks, the clenching and unclenching of my hands.

'He just. He...' I pause, gather myself, then start again. 'He just told me… told me his name. The one Caacrinolaas gave him.' I stop again, take a deep breath. 'Mister Fuzzy Butt.'

The silence lingers for a moment longer. Then everyone erupts into laughter. Tears roll down Isaac's cheeks as he chortles. Meph chuffs so loudly it echoes off the industrial ceiling, and even Faust shakes with laughter. Only Gil doesn't respond. Seeing that, seeing the look still on his face as he stares at the hamster brings back what this creature is to him. What it did to his brother. I stop laughing. Even his ridiculous name doesn't seem funny anymore.

'*Yes, yes!*' The creature's confusion was radiating off it, pouring into me, but now a triumphant edge returns. '*Now you know! Your mockery will not save you! For I shall eat you all one by one, just as I would have done in the witch's contraption. Just as I did to that pathetic specimen's broken excuse for a sibling.*'

Oh, fuck no. No, no, no. Not having that. My eyes narrow. '*That pathetic specimen*' –I sound the syllables out in my head slowly, deliberately– '*is a goddamn hero and a better man than you ever were, if you were ever even human once. Plus, he's killed bigger and badder than you and lived to walk away. Not that he'll have to this time because I'll do it.'*

'*Do you know...*' The creature's reply is just as deliberate, packed full of gloat and glee. '*What he tasted of? That one you sacrificed so you could walk away? Despair. Misery and despair. And potential. I so enjoyed consuming every drop of that. Just as I'll do to his ruined little brother too.*'

Okay, no. I just lost my taste for banter.

It's bloodshed I want to bring raining down on this little fucker. Right now.

Chapter Fifteen

Looking like a hamster won't save him from a Mister-Fuzzy-Butt-kicking.

Time swaddles us for a single second, as if aware it might be our last, that for some, it must be.

But then I launch myself towards the hamster.

Only to immediately regret it. Because the grin on the hamster's face widens. And widens.

The hamster's mouth cracks open, enlarging to an impossible degree, opening bigger and bigger. I can feel it's not just in the physical either. Magic crackles around the creature's maw. It looks huge, big enough to swallow me feet first. But magically?

It feels big enough to swallow the world.

The creature heaves a huge in-breath, and I'm sucked up into the air. This, let me tell you, is not the best position to find yourself in when a wind approaching gale force five suddenly starts pulling you towards an ominous mouth of doom that looks hungry for you as the first in a five-course buffet.

I manage to twist mid-air. Digging my fingers into the edge of the brickwork, I charge them with my *talent*, allowing me to push through the rough surface. Brick-dust crumbles to the ground as I lock in. My feet dangle horizontally, and my arm muscles start screaming at me that this is well above their pay grade and they'd like to speak to their union rep about working conditions. I'm too busy holding on for dear life to pay them much mind.

Looking around, I find my friends, who haven't just hurled themselves with reckless abandon at a complete unknown, are doing —unsurprisingly— slightly better. Isaac's positioned himself in front of Gil, and Nithael is anchoring them in place, his wings enfolding them both. Faust has fallen to one knee, his hand gripping the concrete floor, a mirror of what I'm doing but farther back and with a better hold. Still, Mephy's teeth are sunk into his leg, though there seems to be no blood, and the demon dog has sunk his claws in, his feet pressing deep into the solid material. Fuck, I've no idea what this creature really is, whether it's his freed form, or something Caacrinolaas has done, suping him up, but even Meph seems to be struggling; staying in place and keeping Faust safe is taking all his effort.

The brick beneath my hand crumbles. The grip I have is strong, but there's only so much time before it dissolves away to nothing.

And now that time is up.

And I go flying.

My body sails through the air, straight towards that impossible gullet, and surely this is it. An ending. Dissolving in a monster's stomach acid down in a dingy basement. Not an implausible ending for me – hell, not even the first time I'll have met this end – but this one may well be final, and I've failed. Failed my friends. Failed De Monteguard. Failed Toulouse. I'm going to die, and it'll mean nothing, not even buying the others any time, winning nothing but, at best, a bad case of indigestion and heartburn for the tiny monstrosity dragging me in.

Then neon feathers wrap around my waist and drag me back so my hands find purchase. I wrap them around the doorframe's brickwork as that sucking still drags at me, hauling me towards the creature.

Nithael saved me. His wingtips touch my midriff, and the pressure pulling on my legs eases a little. He's pushed forward, positioned as a shield, allowing Isaac to creep closer. My oldest friend rolls to the side, his back slumping against the ringed wall, clear of the immediate drag of Mister Fuzzy Butt's intake.

But I'm not. My feet aren't on the floor again, I'm not back to standing on my own two feet. The angel's positioning is keeping me from being swallowed whole but only for now. I've gained some time, that's all.

'What's going on?' I hiss. 'You've got an angel on your side, and that's a fucking hamster!'

'Not just a hamster, lad.' The worry in Isaac's tone isn't doing wonders for my blood pressure.

'Whatever the fuck he is, when he was in that staff, I had no problems overpowering him. Now you give him some fur and cheek pouches, and suddenly he's fucking Saruman of Many Colours? Seriously!?'

'When he was in the staff, he was restrained. Imprisoned. Limited.' His voice is strained. He's trying to work something, but I have to screw my eyes up, closed tight. Nithael's pushing into our world, and I can feel the urge to scream, 'Gloria In Excelsis,' into the air, can feel the first glistening drops forming from the ducts of my eyes, and I don't think they're tears. Not watery ones anyhow.

I'm trying desperately hard to keep my cool, but panic is starting to set in.

And then I hear it. Gil's voice. 'No!' There's a terror there, a primeval gut-wrench of inescapable fear grabbing hold. 'Not again! Please, no!'

Which is when I realise what he means by not again. What's happening to make him so afraid.

Because I feel it happening to me too.

The tethers, those bonds the creature formed with us back inside the Machine in the Matriarch's stronghold, have reactivated. Tendrils of energy run from the tiny power-house out to us, drawing and dragging in sustenance for his hungry maw. For me, it's just the first trickle of *talent*, though I notice this time I can't stop it. The speed's increasing so as in no time at all I'm sure it'll be a torrent rushing from me.

But Gil doesn't have any *talent*. The fucker's drawing on something else, the same thing he drank down from Gil's brother till he left him a desiccated corpse.

Mister Fuzzy Butt is swallowing Gil's life-force. Draining him dry.

'Tell me you can do something, Meph.' It's hard not to plead.

There's only one thing keeping me holding on to hope almost as tightly as I am the rapidly collapsing wall.

Last time we didn't have a demon on our side.

But it isn't Meph who does something; it's Nithael.

It's easy to feel when he leaves the immediate vicinity. That radiant neon glow of him entering our plane of existence was painting the insides of my eyelids an illuminated blue. It fades back to the normal reddish black, and I dare risk cracking my eyes open again. There's no sign of Nithael, but suddenly, the suction pulling at my feet cuts off, and I tumble to the floor. Rolling over, I push myself up from the sprawled heap. Raising my head, I look at where Nithael is.

Halfway down the throat of Mister Fuzzy Butt himself.

It's one of the most bizarre and impossible things I've ever seen. Mister Fuzzy Butt's head is distended like a snake, his jaw on the floor, his head tilted back, and he's half-choking, half-gulping, muffled gurgling noises emanating from deep in his throat. But it's no wonder his sucking got cut off. The angel's pinned his wings back along his body and has flown headfirst into the creature's mouth.

Not that Mister Fuzzy Butt is giving up. He's not trying to dislodge the angel from his mouth. The gulping *clucks* are to get him to go down.

Now it's not just the creature's jaw and throat that are distending. His furry little tummy swells, the hairs standing on end as it tries to accommodate something not even of our realm within whatever lies inside its – well, insides. For a moment, I think it'll pull a full-on Thunder God of Lo Pan and explode because it doesn't seem possible it'll succeed in swallowing Nithael. The stomach's so stretched now, it looks like a hairy balloon, stretch marks visible between individual strands of fur. The now proportionally tiny little head wobbles about on top as the last trace of Nithael vanishes down his throat.

But he doesn't pop. Instead, as that last crackle of neon vanishes into the black hole maw, the creature starts to shrink. A moment later, it's back down to its previous size, a little innocent, if somewhat bloated hamster once again.

He blinks, then opens his mouth as though to suck again but stops.

Then he gives the loudest earth-rumbler of a belch I've ever heard.

Mister Fuzzy Butt has swallowed Nithael whole.

Fuck.

Chapter Sixteen

When I said I wanted someone to do something, I didn't mean "serve yourself up as the amuse-bouche before the fucker eats us as the main course".

Silence sits heavy in the room. We should act, of course. Strike while he's suffering from angelic indigestion, unable to suck us down. Make Nithael's sacrifice mean something. But we're all too shocked. Isaac's chalk-faced, visibly shaken, close to keeling over. Gil puts his hand on my mentor's shoulder, steadying him as far as possible. Even Faust has stopped sketching, having paused mid-rune in some working he's attempting. None of us can quite comprehend what has happened.

The hamster ate our angel.

A second later, I regain my senses. Picking myself back up, I take a cautious step towards the creature, my sword pointed, ready for the suction to start up all over again. I've no idea what the hell I'll do if it does, but at least I'm going to go down swinging. Maybe I can cut his head off mid-air. Stop the suction that way.

But he doesn't start sucking again. Mister Fuzzy Butt just sits there. There's a peculiar look on his face. I'm not an expert on reading animalistic expressions. Most creatures I've met have been humanoid enough to be easier to understand or else like Mephistopheles – loud enough at expressing themselves. This just looks like a normal floof of a hamster. But if I had to put a word on it?

I'd say *uncomfortable*.

His eyes rove around, not looking at me or anything really as he puffs his cheeks in and out. He sways side to side, huffs a little, then gives a tiny whine.

Then it burps again. And if I thought the first one was loud, this one's on a whole other scale of decibels.

It's so loud it makes my teeth shake, so loud that all I can hear is that rumbling growl that grows, blocking out everything else, a sawtooth tinnitus that rings in my ears, in my rib cage, in my soul itself. All there is becomes lost in the loudness of the gap-toothed hamster's belching.

The creature's mouth widens too. In the depths of that pitch-black tunnel that seems to stretch on forever, I see something.

A tiny speck of crackling neon blue.

It grows, becoming larger and larger until I can pick up the sense of momentum. It's building up a head of speed, and I reverse, stumbling backwards, then throw myself to the floor.

Because Nithael is heading out like an angelic bullet train, and I really don't want to be in his path when he comes crashing back into our reality.

I land face down and bury my head in my arms, my eyes squeezed shut, but I can still see the crackling blue illumination that must be lighting up the room like a Bastille Day fireworks display. Part of me is hoping that Isaac has remembered to protect Gil's eyes in the same way, but I don't have time to worry about that because I'm too busy resisting the urge to babble Glossolalia, the non-language of speaking in tongues. I'm not convinced it's because of the holiness of the angels. More just that their unfiltered presence overloads our primitive simian brains to where we forget how to use our hard-won, slowly-evolved forms of speech entirely.

I sneak a peek, of course. Let a little nonsense slip out of my mouth. Accept the fingers I crack apart will get wet with bloody tears because I don't want to be caught off guard in case Mister Fuzzy Butt's just vomited his meal back up so he can have the delight of an angelic aperitif all over again.

Nithael is twisted slightly, an arm trailing behind him as he flies out of the hamster's mouth. As my eyes slip off his impossible presence, I realise that Mister Fuzzy Butt is disappearing up his own furred posterior. His legs vanish, retracting up into his body like he's caught the Dreaded Shrinks from Mr & Mrs Twit. He's suspended off the floor, shrinking rapidly. A moment later, I realise what's going on.

Nithael's grabbed some part of Mister Fuzzy Butt and is bringing him back out with him. From out of his own stomach.

He's turning the hamster monster inside-out.

My voice rises, threatening to burst into a nonsense chorus of Hallelujahs, so I'm forced to squeeze my eyes shut again.

Just in time. An angelic sonic boom claps like Zeus has hurled a thunderbolt into the middle of the room, and the shockwave smacks into me hard enough to make me very glad I'm lying down. Chances are it'd have sent me doing an amateur gymnastic tumbling routine into the nearest wall otherwise.

Then there's quiet. Silence. Enough to give me the confidence to risk another sneaky gander. Lo and behold, Nithael is once more almost invisible unless *looked* for, his presence subtly localised around Isaac. And where Mister Fuzzy Butt once sat, ready to swallow us all down, is what looks like someone's done origami with a slice of salami. Orisalami, if you will. A neatly folded package of pink meat-like material hovers just above the ground.

If I'm not mistaken, Nithael's turned Mister Fuzzy Butt into a flesh envelope.

Chapter Seventeen

I've just realised, even before his name, I was thinking of Mister Fuzzy Butt as male. Now? I think of him as mail.

The room feels unbelievably still now that the vortex in hamster form has been turned inside out. Crisis averted, creature everted. What was a terrible soul-chomping vampire is now reduced to a neatly folded pink parcel, sitting in the middle of the floor.

Either Nithael's done in after his incredible exploding hamster routine —and you'd better believe I'm going to be referring to him as MC Hamster for the foreseeable period, singing "Can't Touch This" whenever I can— or else he wants the safe haven of a flesh home he knows after diving down Fuzzy Butt's monstrous gullet. Either way he disappears back into Isaac, out of sight. I suspect he's going to do the angelic equivalent of a hazmat disinfection routine.

'What are we going to do with —' I start, hand gesturing towards the remnants of the ancient horror who came so close to swallowing us all whole, but that's as far as I get. Because by the time I've raised my finger to point, Mephy's bounced across the room and seized the handily packaged up flesh lump between his razored teeth. He flips his head back, sending it sailing up into the air, then chomps it down with a couple of quick snaps.

'Yes! Good bloody work, angelico!' Mephy's tongue lolls out the side of his wide-spread grin. 'Now that's a way to finish fights that I can get down with. Turn your enemies into a delicious snack to recharge the batteries after the hard work of kicking their arses. Hamsterlami! Fucking brilliant!'

Okay. Looks like the demon dog's answered that question before I could even ask it. I'd worry about what chomping down a trans-dimensional being might do to his digestive system. But I'm relying on the demon part dealing with it. Here's hoping it's not the equivalent of chocolate. I'm still not sure if he's forgiven me for offering him a pain au chocolat.

'You didn't actually do very much, Meph.' Maybe it's a bit petty of me to point that out. He didn't nearly get swallowed though, seeing as how he was apparently able to just dig his claws into the concrete like it was sodden earth.

It isn't Meph who answers. 'He kept me safe.' Gil's voice is surprisingly strident. 'And he finished that fucker off once and for all. That gets my vote of thanks.'

The young man's next to Faust, who has a burly arm wrapped around his trembling shoulders. Last I remember is Nith acting as a blocker for him, but it's true that once I lost my grip, my concentration was fully taken up by what was happening in front of me rather than behind, apart from when he screamed. Looks like Mephistopheles kept him safe, as well as Johannes.

'Yeah, that's right, mano. I knew you had it under

control.' Mephy doesn't look even vaguely bothered by my apparently unfounded s. 'I was ready to do the hard work to finish things off. The hard jaw work – nom nom!'

The demon hound spins around in a circle like that dog from the Magic Roundabout and then presses his nose to the floor. His hackles rise up again. 'Course that fucking cowardly custard piece of shit Caacrinolaas wasn't here either. I mean, he was, but then he wasn't when we got here.'

'Wasn't he? Thank fuck you told us that, Meph. I thought I'd just developed a real particular blind spot in my peripheral vision.' Sorry. I can't help myself.

'No, you didn't and also shut up, mano. He was here and then left.' Mephy's voice is a half-snarl. 'This was a fucking trap.'

I, once again, can't help feeling like this is pointing out the obvious. However, as Mephy's own points – those in his mouth – are on obvious display, his lips pulled back, I decide against mentioning it this time.

'Can you find him still?' Faust's voice is calm, measured. Though whether to get through to Meph or so as not to disturb the young man he's comforting, I'm not sure. It's a good point either way. If the scent trail led the demon dog here, perhaps it'll be too muddled for him to follow it back out.

'Nah, I've got it, Jo. No worries. Now we're here, I can see what's the freshest. Easy to see where it leads back out.' Mephy stops spinning and breaks into a loping run towards the stairs, back up out of the basement.

Once again I refrain from mentioning that it might have been useful if he'd realised that before we headed down into the basement and battled a terrifying monster unnecessarily. Truly, I am the embodiment of zen, the Mister Spock of our away team in this particular moment. Which makes a change from my usual role as an instantly disposable Red Shirt at least.

Meph hammers his way up and out. We dart up the steps, our footfalls echoing back like a cup rattling along a set of prison cell bars, back out into the strange silent wasteland that was until recently my city. The roads are still worryingly empty. If I were a homicidal demon maniac with little care for human life, I'd be flinging the inhabitants of Toulouse at us like so much cannon fodder. Either we'd have to kill them or waste a lot of time and *talent* subduing them, which would wear us down. I know I pulled off a miracle with the remnants of Clarent before, but there's no guarantee I'll be able to manage that again. Then again, there's no guarantee I won't. Perhaps that's what's making him keep them away from us, unsure of what we might be able to make them do next time.

Or perhaps we're hurtling head first into another trap. That sure seems a lot more likely.

The bridge spans out over the roar of the Garonne below us, its flow not stifled by the corpses I can still see bobbing around, straggled on the quays or coming dislodged from where they were jammed against the support columns. That cordite acrid smell that speaks of fire and desolation in an urban area hangs in the breeze, and smoke funnels claw up skywards all over the central part of the city proper.

Toulouse burns. And my heart burns with it.

Again, my mind is racing, fear and panic coursing underneath. This is hellishly exposed. All the bastard has to do is blow up the columns and struts under our feet and... Well, actually between Nithael and Mephistopheles, not to mention the rest of our combined magical might, we'd probably come up with a solution, but it would *hinder us*. I don't get why he isn't trying to do that at the very least.

Then I look back to the road in front of us and screech to a halt. I throw up a barrier across the path. 'Shield your eyes!' I roar even as I hear Mephy give a muffled curse, having crashed into my wall of *talent*.

But I don't care. It might hurt, but it'll keep him alive. A trumpeted honking of amusement echoes over the expanse between us and the other side.

The Karnabo advances towards us.

'Did I say we'd meet again? Yes. Will you enjoy it, have answers for us? No.' There's a squawking scornful joy in his gargled syllables, and by the Good God, it makes the horrendous little fuckbungle even more unbearable.

He's still a few metres away from my hastily erected barrier, but he'll be on us soon. My erected shield will only stand up to so many direct strikes from his magical proboscis. Recalling we've made a deal, that if we can tell him the reason for Caacrinolaas' whole scheme, then he'll be forced to stop and tell us why he's thrown his lot in with team World Demolition Dickheads, thus buying us some time to figure out a way to beat him, I shout, 'Caacrinolaas wants war!'

The advancing footsteps still, stop. A moment passes. Then the Karnabo speaks. 'Is it a part? Yes. But are there enough details? No.'

Damn it. I don't really know which way to go. Because my gut says that a throwdown with Nith isn't reason enough. But at the same time, I trust Mephy, so I shout out, 'A war with the angels!'

The Karnabo stops again. He's almost close enough I can hear his breathing. Mind you, as he sounds like an asthmatic bugler having a heart attack after having swallowed his instrument, that's not entirely surprising.

'Does he know it all, does he?' The tone is pondering, deliberating. 'No. But is it enough to answer our question asked?'

Again that silence stretches out, far longer than the distance separating us. Finally he speaks once more.

'Yes.'

Chapter Eighteen

I'll find out what he has to tell us, and after that? The dicknose can Karna-blow me.

Well, slap my thigh and call me Daisy Duke; we've bought ourselves some time.

'So tell us then!' I speak up brightly, loudly, making the challenge clear in my voice. 'Why are you siding with some demonic fuckscuttle who wants to destroy the world by fighting the angels?'

'Does our master want to destroy the world, last Cathar? No.' The Karnabo's gargling trumpet of a tone is so condescendingly amused, it'd make me want to kick him even harder in the nuts than I already do if that were possible. 'Would that be silly? Yes. Would we want that? No.'

'So what does he want, you idiot? Because it seems to me like a demon versus angel throwdown isn't going to end with our reality left in box-fresh condition.'

'To destroy the world? No.' Now the Karnabo sounds

triumphant, gloating. It's so hard not to look up to see if the expression matches. I really don't want to get stoned though. Not like that at least. Not until I have to honour my date with Craig – the constantly stoned Hob King from Blackburn, England, who I promised a night out with after he saved us during the De Montfort debacle. At the time, I was wearing the Fae Queen Maeve's body, so it was fully understandable. What caught me off guard was that he doesn't mind which body I'm wearing. He's an easy-going fella, is Craig.

The Karnabo's not done speaking. 'To remake the world? Yessssssssssss.'

The last word is a hissed challenge, and as it steps forward again, another quicker thud follows, telling me the creature's about to break into a run now that he's satisfied his promise to share info with us, at least to his own satisfaction.

Luckily, though, that information stalled the Karnabo long enough.

Long enough that whatever Faust has been doing, when he dropped to a crouch behind me and Isaac, is complete.

Johannes pushes past me, raising his hand as he goes. I don't see what's in it properly, only a flashing gleam as it streaks past my eyeline, but whatever it is seems to halt the Karnabo mid-stride. Another noise, like an elephant playing a snake-charming flute, tells me the cock-nosed wanker isn't best pleased by whatever Faust's pulled on him.

'A soul mirror — is it powerful? Yes.' The Karnabo sounds strained, and it's no surprise. A soul mirror isn't a joke. Frankly, I'd no idea that Faust was capable of pulling something like that off. Nor that he would be prepared to do such a thing.

A soul mirror is exactly what it sounds like – a mirror

made out of the fragment of a soul. Making one – or manifesting it rather because it is a metaphysical part of us pulled into the physical plane that involves dividing that part of our own self away from the rest and turning it to a perfectly reflective surface – is incredibly difficult. And costly.

Because it means removing the imperfections, the blemishes. Polishing them away to leave a mirror that only shows that which looks into it. Locking their own soul in place, trapped by the reflection.

Deleting all those things that make us who we are. Giving them up forever. Losing a part of our very being.

'But as powerful as me? No.' The Karnabo sounds strained, panting between the syllables. But he also sounds sure.

At least at first.

'Not a normal soul mirror, no.' Faust's own voice sounds strained too, but there's a confidence there. A surety. I've never known him to go all in on a bet unless he knows he's stacked the odds in his favour. 'But a soul mirror made of a demon?' Now the real triumph is there. 'Yes!'

I gasp. Can't help it. I look down to see Mephy lying on the cobbles. He looks up at me and grins weakly, his tongue hanging out the side. 'Don't worry, mano. Not permanent with me. Not with my bond with Faust. He's holding on to some bits of my personality until he can give me the bit of my soul back.'

Fucking hell. Now my concern's for Faust. 'Johannes, are you okay?' Holding on to demonic essence is no easy thing. Just look at Isaac's recent experiences. He only managed to hold back that working with Nith's help and even then only temporarily. Faust and Mephy might be bonded, but it's a whole different thing to take a part of his being into his own. I'm worried it might be too much for a human soul, that it might just erase him away, overwriting his being with the more evolved demon like an old, worn-out cassette tape.

'Yes, my friend, don't worry.' There's a wry tone to his words. 'Apart from a peculiar fascination with our opponent's lower extremities, I'm holding up just fine.'

I can't help it; I burst out laughing. 'Mephy lent you the part of his soul obsessed with shagging legs?'

'Hey!' Mephistopheles' voice rings out, wounded. 'It has to be a precious part of ourselves, doesn't it? Not a decision I took lightly, mano, I can tell you.'

The Karnabo's honking breathing hitches as he fights against the mirror. But it's working. A stroke of brilliance from Johannes, and one I should have thought of. This, of course, was how the original Gorgons were finally captured back in ancient Greece. It's ridiculous, the story saying Medusa's own stare turned her to stone. Sure, it fits with how magic works – turn the creature's *talent* against them. See our recent encounter with the Warabouc. But a bit of shiny metal isn't enough to reverse their sort of working. We'd have got rid of every single creature with a petrifying gaze long ago if that were the case. No, Athena didn't give Perseus a polished, mirrored shield. She gave him something far more rare, far more precious. She gave him a portable soul mirror to keep him safe.

But something isn't right, and Isaac voices it first. 'Shouldn't he be... shutting up?'

Shit. The whole idea is that the soul mirror, being empty, should slowly absorb the one presented to it, swallowing them in until all that's left facing it is an empty husk. The Karnabo should be weakening, quieting as he becomes absorbed. Instead, his trumpeted rage is the same, the sound of his straining still unchanged.

Mephy lifts his head and stares across. I've no idea if he's immune to the Karnabo's power as a demon or if it's safe now that Faust has the creature ensnared.

'Can we all do that, Meph? Have you got him locked down?' That'd make what's coming next a whole lot easier.

'Not if you value being able to dance the fandango, mano.' The words carry that usual biting humour of Mephy's, but there's something else there. A terrible weight to what he's saying. 'He's already staring into my soul. That's why I can look at him with my eyes. It's nothing compared to what he's already looking at. But if you catch his gaze – even with him looking at the mirror – it'll be enough to petrify you. Me? I can see him. See him clearly. And not just him either.'

Which is a majorly cryptic comment to finish a sentence on, and I'm about to point that out to him when the edge of the bridge right next to my leg explodes, transforming into a cloud of semi-vapourised brick dust in an instant.

'Fuck!' It's a fair response to such instant-heart-attack material. Especially when it's followed by another, more accurately thrown magical explosive. It's only Nith's wingtip intercepting, neon-blue crackling just in front of me, that keeps it from slamming into my face. A second later, I clock it.

The Karnabo's flinging magic about with his face-grafted penis extension of a trunk.

It's one of his specialties because of course being able to turn people to stone with your stare isn't powerful enough. He can fling spells – elemental magic by the looks of it – or at least that's his choice for the moment, without having to perform any kind of working.

I throw up a shield, wiping away the first blood tears forming in the corner of my eyes from having stared at Nith's wing, grateful he pulled off the save, glad when it disappears back behind me. 'I thought you had him under control!' I hiss at the duo.

'Oh, I'm sorry, mano. Holding him in place isn't enough for you?' Again the sarcastic response seems forced somehow. 'I've got him fixed in space. Give me time, I'll drain his *talent* down to zero, even if it does the same to us. Got to get through his protections first though. It'll take time for him to use them up, for the working to burn them away. Forever.'

I dodge sidewards, dropping my shield. The Karnabo's hurled two more crosses between a fireball and an RPG shell, but these ones have been aimed straight at Faust, at the soul mirror he's holding in his hand. Nith intercepts each of them, the explosive energy dispersing in a rippling luminescent wave over his trailing edge feathers, but I'd rather the ele-cunt concentrates on me rather than them.

'Oi, you cock-faced spunkmonkey! Over here!'

It works, enough at least that I have to hurl myself rightwards, an explosive projectile passing close enough through the air overhead as to have singed my hair if I didn't keep it so close clipped to my skull. Even so, it's a close matter.

'Get your shield up, my friend.' Faust sounds calm, if slightly strained. 'We can take what he might throw at us. Keep yourself safe.'

Good enough for me. I pull it back up into place, happy to take a moment's breather. 'So what do you mean, protections, Meph?'

'He's protected by demonic energy, mano.' The words are a half-growl, tired. It can't be easy to operate while missing a shard of your soul, even as a demon. 'My mirror can hold him, but the essence he's carrying is the distillation of one of my own who's been destroyed.'

'What the fuck?' This is a major revelation. 'What the hell do you mean?'

'That's how he managed it.' The sadness isn't gone, but there's something else there, below the sorrow. Shock, sure. But building anger too. 'How he made a weapon strong enough to allow him to level the playing field, to fight the angelicos themselves. He killed one of us. He killed a fellow demon.'

The shock splashes across us in rhythm with the magic thrown by the Karnabo, exploding uselessly against our shields, taking our breath away, stealing our words.

It's Isaac who recovers first. 'But... how? I thought you couldn't be killed? That you're all immortal, like the angels? Isn't that the whole point?'

'We are. And that's why it's so blasted powerful.' Meph hacks, spitting out some gargled phlegm from the back of his throat. 'Somehow he pulled off the impossible. Broke one of us. Distilled everything that made them up – their *talent*, sure, but their personality, their loves and joys and furies, their *soul* – and extracted it from them. Et voila. One anti-angel weapon, coming right up. Fuck me, what a price, mano. What a fucking price.'

What a price indeed. Destroying an immortal soul of a higher being, something not far off a god compared to us, just to let him throw down with Nithael and his compadres. If any further proof were needed as to just what an evil cockstride the fucker we're fighting against is, surely this serves well enough.

'The moment he gazed into my soul, I felt it.' Meph sounds wrung-out, though whether from his magical exertions or this terrible realisation, I couldn't say. 'The essence he's wearing was so like mine. The way it's trying to counter my own power, just like another demon. But it's not Caacrinolaas himself. It's far too much for him to manage. I felt the touch of another demon soul against mine. Only one that's been emptied out. Hollowed. Weaponised. Nothing else could even try to undo a soul mirror, the way it is.'

'So what? He'll break free?' The panic is rising. Honestly, I'm not sure the four of us will be able to take him while he's draped in demonic energy. Not with Mephistopheles half-drained and Faust having just pulled off a major working and Nithael having been almost eaten by a... well, by whatever the fuck Mister Fuzzy Butt was before Caacrinolaas popped him into a hamster's body.

'No.' Faust's voice is firm. 'It won't break the mirror. It'll burn away eventually. He won't escape. But I can't move. Can't leave. Neither of us can. Not if we want to hold him.'

Okay. They hold him. I slice him the fuck up. Definition of teamwork.

Works for me.

Chapter Nineteen

I'm going to make a Halloween pumpkin out of his stupid trunk-wielding face. Turn him into a Carve-abo.

I huddle over, bent low behind my shield. It's soaking up the damage so far, but Nith's just behind me, and the Karnabo's attacking all of us, a disperse stream of magical fireballs hurled in all our directions, hit and hope style. What I'm about to do will bring all his attention to bear on me. All his attention and all of his considerable *talent*.

Deep breath, Paul. Let's do this.

I keep my head down, my eyes fixed on the bitumen just in front of the Karnabo. Close enough to be confident I'll see anything he throws at me coming, low enough that I can't accidentally end up gazing into his sparkly disco-ball eyes. Another fireball whips towards me, screaming through the air. I'm tracking the way it moves though. Then I drop my shoulder, roll underneath it, and the explosive passes harmlessly overhead. Ha, parkour, Motherfucker!

The Karnabo realises what's up, and his gargling trumpeting noises increase, a bugle-call of panicked notes as I close the distance. More explosive magic hammers towards me, one then another, crackling forces that send shivers through my system each time one hits. But it doesn't hurt me. Nothing gets through. My shield's holding up. For the moment, at least.

A savage grin breaks across my face because now I'm sure. It'll be long enough. The speed I'm closing in on the mothertrunker, the way I'm crossing the distance even with the constant bobbing and weaving, means I'll make it before he breaks through my protections. A manic laugh bubbles up in my throat as his noises step up in pitch and volume, half-strangled screams as he knows I'm coming, getting closer, but he can't turn to fight me, can't flee away from my oncoming blade. Can't do anything except keep flinging magic my way, but it won't be enough, not nearly enough to stop me from stabbing him straight in his stupid fucking cocknosed face.

Then my smile falls away. Because there's a noise like the Good God decided to shake her duvet out, snapping it overhead. In a beat of heavy weighted wings that sends clouds of crumbled brick dust into the air and up my nose, stinging my eyes and my lungs till I'm coughing and spluttering as it fills my air pipe…

Caacrinolaas arrives.

The bridge shakes as his paws crunch into the pavement, his wide-spread wings huge enough they seem to spread the whole width of the road. He's no less terrifying now than when I first saw him in the mountains of the Pyrenees. If you asked me to draw what a demon dog might look like, this is what I'd come up with. Well, actually I'd come up with a shitty stick figure because I'm rubbish at drawing, but if I asked an AI prompt to generate an image of a demonic hound, this is what it might well spit out. With too many toes, probably an extra leg or two, but still pretty close.

Dark-black fur ripples, stretched taut over muscles that'd give a weight-lifting bulldog on steroids a complex. His head is flat, squashed, no elongated snout like Mephy's; his ears drop down. And he's twice the size of our demon hound at least. His eyes are glowing red rubies – coal embers, so as you can understand why anyone who summons him might come to believe in hellfire. They'd see it, after all, burning in his regard.

'Now, angelico! Now I'll have my piece of you!' The words are punctuated by wing downbeats. The fucker stares past me, through me even, his eyes fixed on the angel-bearer behind me. The bastard who's done all of this, who's brought such misery and suffering to me and my friends, such madness and slaughter to the streets of Toulouse, puffs up his chest proudly at his barking challenge.

'Will he help me? Yes. Let the other demon get me? No.' The Karnabo's voice is still a sibilant gurgle, but there's an additional whine in there now. A plea for help.

Caacrinolaas deflates slightly, taking in the scene properly for the first time. 'Haven't you dealt with them yet?'

'No, he hasn't, you fucking jumped up chihuahua.' Mephy's voice betrays none of the fatigue it held last time he spoke. Instead, there's a hungry readiness, a fury just itching to express itself physically. 'I'm right here, and the moment I've dealt with your lickspittle lackey, I'm coming over there, and I'm going to fuck. You. Right. Up.'

I can't help noticing that Caacrinolaas flinches ever so

slightly as Mephy emphasises each of those words, but he shakes it off, the resultant air currents as his wings steady him pushing me back half a step. 'Bah. I've no interest in you, traitor. The fight I want is with the winged ones, not a lowly earth crawling demonico like yourself. I'll let the Karnabo deal with you, then I'll have my fun with the angelico.'

As he speaks, his wing beats increase, the radius of the downdraught growing, forcing me backwards, one hand thrown up in front of my face. Then the monstrous hound lifts up into the air, wheeling away over the bridge's parapet.

Fuck me. Mephy was right. For all his wanting to fight an angel, he's terrified of throwing down with Meph.

The coward's running away.

Meph realises it too. 'No. No! Don't let him get away. Oi, feather-face! Stop him! Stop the yellow-bellied fucker! Please, angelico! Please!'

There's something in Mephy's tone. A begging but not like the Karnabo had talking to his master. No. Mephy's hurting inside. Badly too. Seeing what Caacrinolaas did to one of their fellow demons has cut him up. He's hungry for blood, for revenge, and doesn't care who metes out justice on the arsehole as long as someone does. So he's pleading. Pleading with Nithael to take the fucker down in his place.

Nithael responds. I know this. Because a second later I'm plucked from my feet.

The stained white brickwork of the bridge's parapet dangles momentarily just below my toes and then I can see the churning grey-blue of the Garonne spread out beneath me. I don't look up. Don't want to see Nithael spread out in all his glory because I need to keep my wits about me, not end up angel-struck. So I concentrate on keeping my sight from *seeing*. I check to the side, making sure Isaac and Gil are both with me.

They are. Thank fuck.

I didn't doubt Isaac would be here, but I'm relieved for Gil. Not that I think for a moment that Faust and Mephy will fail against the Karnabo, but if they do... I failed Gil once. Brushed him off, gave him the cold shoulder. It cost him dearly. And he still forgave me.

I feel happier keeping him safe myself. Or as safe as anyone can be when going to tangle head-on with a demon lord, of course.

Now the quay is there, a couple of metres below me. 'Brace for impact!' Isaac's voice rings out to my left right before Nith releases his grip on me and Gil. I grab the young man, pulling him close enough I can count his ribs through the back of his T-shirt, and wrap us in a cushion of air. A second later, we collide with the ground. My teeth still rattle despite the protective cushioning, but I'm easily able to spring to my feet as I let it disperse. No breakages, not even any major bruises. Isaac steps off thin air a second later, walking down a laser-beam of angelic neon. Positioning Gil behind me, I take in the sight facing us.

I understand immediately why Nith chose to drop us like hot potatoes on the Quai De La Daurade instead of landing with us. He's still wheeling overhead, controlling the skies. Aerial dominance, to ensure the creature in front of us doesn't make the same form of escape he's made thus far, turning tail on his massive wings. But he doesn't. He gives us the once-over, then grins, double-rowed razors on display in that hideous mouth, no doubt relieved Mephistopheles isn't with us.

He isn't. Our demon dog is back there, still battling the

Karnabo. We're here. Just us and our angel. Exactly what he always wanted.

Throwing back his muzzle, he howls.

Let me be clear, I've been around howling. I've heard the howls of werewolves and wraiths. Never trembled when the Bean Sidhe screamed. Faced off against the Coin Sidhe, the giant fairy dogs whose sound is supposed to be enough to freeze the blood and stop the heart. I've even heard recordings of myself after I've stubbed my toe. Aicha made them and insisted on playing them. At full volume. Directly into my ear. When I was asleep.

This is something else entirely. It's an aural tidal wave, a tsunami of sound that smashes into me so hard it drives me to take a knee, my head bowed against it. It's joined in harmony by a higher pitched amplified tinkling as glass smashes all around us, in every shop and flat window I can see. The noise batters against us, awful, painful. The only reason I'm sure my eardrums haven't popped is that the sound doesn't get any quieter, any less awful.

Until it suddenly does. Caacrinolaas snaps his jaws shut, biting off the unbearable ululation. As he does so, he steps forward. But this time he comes alone. Because as he puts a paw in front of him, the black opal-like flesh ripples, and a human arm tears out of the back of it. The next paw-fall causes the same effect, and then the next. Then the demon dog shakes himself, as though shedding water after a plunge into an icy river, and steps free from his human partner, leaving the man prone, on all fours, behind him.

De Monteguard crumples, collapsing as the demon steps forward. I can still *see* the connection between them though, a thin tether of energy running from one to the other. Judging by how motionless De Monteguard is, he's out for the count.

As Caacrinolaas advances towards us, his form grows larger. His wings stretch out, first ten metres, now twenty, now reaching from one side of the square to the other. His head is as high as the promenade surrounding the lower part where we stand, and his foot comes crunching down on the wooden pirate ship playground to the right side of the square, pulverising it into a mass of beams and sawdust. He stops, looks behind him, and whines. For a moment I feel hope. Maybe some more cavalry's riding to the rescue. Perhaps some of the useless sods who totally failed to turn up and save the day when we faced off against De Montfort at Bugarach might have decided to roll up and be of some actual bloody assistance this time.

Sadly not. The giant demon dog raises his back paw, bringing it swooping round to his enormous jaw. Then, with canines that are now the size of me at full stretch, Caacrinolaas worries at a supporting beam of the former pirate boat playhouse, mast-shaped, that has got stuck in his pad. He pulls it loose triumphantly and then proceeds to spit it out, launching it in our direction. Grabbing Gil, I roll us to the side as it lands just in front. It skids towards us at bone-crunching speed. It misses – just. But Caacrinolaas doesn't seem to mind. He starts chuffing with laughter, obviously finding it hilarious.

I look at the huge round worked stake of wood that could have broken my legs if it had hit. The end of it's slickened with what looks like thick oil. At least at first glance. Then I realise what it is.

'If it bleeds, we can kill it!' I shout in my best Schwarzenegger voice. Isaac looks across at me from the other side of the pole of wood, a look of polite bemusement on his face. Gil catches his eye, looks at me, then back at him, and shrugs. I sigh. Yet another moment where I miss Aicha.

Plus, it'd be really, really handy to have her here in this fight. Particularly as I have no idea how we're going to beat a giant demon incarnate on our plane.

No idea whatsoever.

Chapter Twenty

Trying not to remember that only Arnie survived the battle with the Predator. And we don't have a chopper to get to.

We've our backs to the Garonne; the Pont Neuf is behind my right shoulder. The green space was previously dotted with birch trees, although most of those have been uprooted by Caacrinolaas' growth spurt, either knocked aside as he expanded or kicked out of his path as he advanced. The high walls of the Place de la Daurade box us in on the other three sides – not that we could have skirted past him otherwise. The gigantic demon occupies a good half of the square, and he's tall enough to blot out even the timber-decked top of the Café Des Artistes' fourth floor. Plus, I suspect if we try to slide past him, we'll find an over-sized paw doing the same thing to us as he did to the kid's playground, the absolute arsehole.

The three of us close up instinctively. I do my best not to look over my shoulder at Pont Neuf, at the two people I really wish were huddling in with us now. Stopping a demonically supercharged Karnabo in his tracks was damnably impressive, and I'm glad we don't have to worry about that gargle-hissing chucklefucker turning up at our back, but I know nothing – or next to nothing – about fighting actual demons. The plus side is I haven't felt like doing the reverse of Glossolalia, the speaking in tongues, that happens when I see Nithael or Nanael become incarnate – singing death metal lyrics or something, probably. I'm also not weeping tears of blood, which is useful because I really want to keep my eyes on what this demonic red-rocket rocker is up to.

Then again, dying blindly and without knowledge of what's to come might be preferable. Because Caacrinolaas has bunched himself back onto his hind haunches, his muscles coiled spring-like, and now he launches himself into the air right at us. If staring down the mouth of Mister Fuzzy Butt earlier was daunting, this is on a whole other level because I can see deep down a throat large enough to swallow an ocean liner in a single bite. I hold my ground but only because there's nowhere else to go. Wherever I turn, he'll reach me when he lands, and there's nothing I can do, not a single thing I can think of that'll stop him gulping me into his gullet and grinding me to a broken flesh bag on those wicked double-rowed teeth.

Then Nithael surges down to meet him.

The sky above us electrifies, a crackling neon storm, and I feel the whoosh as our angel passes overhead and pushes into our world. His outline solidifies, blue lightning cutting the chisel of musculature onto the skyline, and my tongue starts babbling gibberish in praise of his perfection. My eyes streak red on blue as blood bubbles from my tear ducts.

Isaac's hand wraps around mine as he mutters some

words in a language that's almost Hebraic but is somehow even older, and my burbling and blood-bubbling eases, subsides, then stops. Looking around, I can see he has his other hand on Gil's bicep.

'That's a fucking handy trick *that would have been useful plenty of times before!*' I hiss through gritted teeth.

'Never been worth using that bit of our combined magic before. But we're all needed for the fight ahead. Now hush your trap, lad, and eyes on the prize.'

A howl that hurts my ears, that almost seems to harm my very soul rips through the air, and my head swivels without even conscious thought to see what the hell is going on.

Now that my vision isn't streaked with blood, and my brain isn't fixated on the angelic glory, I can do just that. Nithael's intercepted Caacrinolaas mid-launch, so that the gigantic demonic hound is now reared up on his back legs, his huge feathered wings beating at the air, throwing cars and bikes on the upper level of the surrounding carparks aside, using them to keep himself steady in the awkward position. His paws are up on Nith's shoulders, and his head's thrown back to issue that guttural, horrible howl because our angel's just delivered a haymaker of a punch to his gut. It's probably a good thing for Caacrinolaas that he's only just fully manifested. If he'd eaten lunch, he'd have deposited it back up onto the quay below. Mind you, as we'd be directly in the path for that and I've no desire to see what demonic stomach acid would do to our feeble human frames, it's probably pretty damn lucky for us too.

Caacrinolaas doesn't spend long in his howling. His head whips forward, and those wickedly sharp teeth sink deep into angelic flesh as he bites down hard on Nith's shoulder. Next to me, Isaac stiffens, his hand tightening in mine. I don't know if he's seeking reassurance or whether there's some sort of transfer of pain back through their tethered connection. Or whether it's just the agony of seeing someone he loves suffer. Either way, my oldest, dearest friend is suffering.

I squeeze his hand back, then drop it. I pull Joyeuse from the scabbard. If the demon wanted this sword, maybe giving it to him pointy end first will help ruin his day.

'Right. Let's go help our friend,' I say. I step forward once, twice. Picking up speed, I break into a run towards the gigantic paw larger than my whole body and let out a yell, a war cry, a scream of existence as I go. Just behind me, following my lead and backing my play, I can feel my friends running in my wake. I let my voice ring out all the louder, strengthened by their presence. It doesn't feel like sneak attacking an actual demon, even one distracted by wrestling an angel, would have worked anyway. Might as well give voice to all that jumbling mix of emotions: fear, fury, determination, and love for those beside me.

Fuck it. Time to dance with the devil in the pale moonlight.

Chapter Twenty-One

To be fair, a clown-faced Jack Nicholson rocking up with a parade of poison-filled blimps would be precisely what I would need to make this day even shittier.

Shoving my free hand through reality, into my etheric storage, I wrap my fingers around the hilt I want. I pull out a weapon that's halfway between a dagger and a short sword and all the way to being razor-sharp and extremely deadly. It's a lovely bit of steel work – wonderfully worked, simple but excellent for doing precisely what it was made for – going pointy end first into flesh and doing plenty of damage in the process.

I'll make sure it serves its purpose.

As we get level with the footpad, the razor claws are the first thing we see – hardened keratin that puts the sharp edge of either of the weapons I'm currently wielding to shame. For a moment, I consider trying to smash Joyeuse down on one, to shatter one of the killing blades. Problem is, Caacrinolaas would still have nine more, all of them in reach of me.

So I sprint on past the claws and draw level with the main paw itself. Long black fur strands dangle down shaggily around the bottom, like a slightly more groomed and dramatically oversized version of a shire horse's hooves.

Perfect.

When I'm almost next to the dewclaw, I twist at the waist and pull back my left hand until the dagger-sword is over my shoulder. Then I plunge it as hard as I can and as high as I can reach into the demon dog's calf.

But the blade hits whatever Caacrinolaas' skin is like beneath his thick fur and slows. His flesh is clearly seriously tough, which, considering he just manifested it by will alone, isn't incredibly surprising. But I *push*, adding my *talent* to the momentum, and finally, I feel it penetrate, sinking in until the crossguard almost lies flush against his skin. Only some strands of hair caught between the hilt keep it from hitting all the way home. The muscles quiver, spasming underneath, and Caacrinolaas half-growls, half-whines overhead.

I don't look up though, don't check to see what his reaction to me pricking his heel like I think he's the doggy form of Achilles is. Because whatever his initial reaction, I'm fairly confident his secondary one is going to be to try to stomp me into Bonhomme jam with his foot. So I need to be out of stomping range and pronto.

Luckily, that's all part of the plan.

Sliding Joyeuse back into its sheath, I seize a handful of the lank fur and pull. It's a strain, both on the hairs and my muscles. I push with my leg, shoving myself skywards, with my other hand outstretched. I wrap it around a higher handful of fur. Using all my muscles, I drag myself up because now the leg is moving, his musculature bunching in a way that tells me Caacrinolaas clearly thinks it's clobbering time. For a second, I don't think I'm going to make it. My feet are dangling, flailing in empty air, and as strong as I am, as magically enhanced as that strength is, there's only going to be a limited amount of time I can maintain this hold once the demon dog goes full Buckin' Bronco with his forepaw.

Then my foot finds it. The dagger handle I shoved into his leg. And it's enough.

One foot on the dagger hilt. One hand curled up into the silken fur. Poised like I'm about to do an eagle dive out of *Assassin's Creed*, I shove my hand through empty space and pull out another of my own swords.

Film version of Legolas, eat your heart out. That's some movie Tolkein-elf manoeuvre I just pulled off. Aicha would be proud. And it isn't done yet.

This isn't just a Tolkein effort.

No, because I really do go full *Assassin's Creed* and launch myself out into space. Of course, there's nowhere near as far to fall as there is in those games and I'm not heading towards a waiting hay bale. Instead, I'm aiming at the paw that's lifting off the ground with the sole purpose of dislodging and ideally obliterating whatever irritant is trying to distract him while he wrestles with an angel. I wrap my second hand around my first and hit the top of the paw blade-first, applying all my force and fury to the strike, adding weight and momentum to make it sink in deep.

Based on the howling whine that echoes from above me, now I've really upset him. The raised paw starts shaking rapidly, and I'm suddenly on the equivalent of a mechanical bull ride. Except one where I'm going to get a lot more than bruised pride if I let go.

When I let go.

Yeehaw. Ride 'em, cowboy.

Chapter Twenty-Two

I'd love to say this isn't my first rodeo. But it totally is. And I don't think going for a gigantic demon dog is a sensible choice for the first time you saddle up.

For as long as I can hold on to the sword handle, I'll be out of his stomping range. So I wrap a tendril of my *talent* around it and tie myself to the blade, hoping to the Good God it's enough.

Drawing Joyeuse, I take a moment. Mainly because it's not only my brain getting violently rattled. My eyes are too, making seeing a blurry challenge, and my teeth are slamming against each other so painfully, if I've not cracked a molar or two, I'll be astounded. So I take a second to acclimatise to the rhythm of the slamming shakes of Caacrinolaas and hope he doesn't dare tear his attention away from his grappling match with Nithael to drop a paw down and flick me flying like a spit wad.

Once I'm feeling confident about the general direction

137

I'm facing, I swing the blade right above his little toe. The flesh parts, resistance folding before the keenness of the cutting edge as Joyeuse carries on through. All the way to the other side.

Caacrinolaas' little toe —about the size of a family sedan— comes clean away from the rest of his foot.

The demon's scream would be a joy to hear if I wasn't convinced it just ran sprinting down my ear canals and did some sort of Jet Li flying kick through the centre of my eardrum. My face screws up as if were I to scrunch it hard enough, it'd close my earholes up too, but I hold on to the sword handle sticking up out of the gigantic paw somehow.

Even more impressively, I still manage it when Caacrinolaas slams his paw down hard onto the grassy bank below. My feet give way under me, slipping out and sending my body sprawling sideways, but the tether of *talent* holds.

Joyeuse tumbles from my grasp though, dropping onto the previously neatly tended greenery below, now a churned-up mixture of mud and grass and black demon blood.

Bugger. There goes my plan to trim the rest of his toes away. And now it's made my position here entirely useless.

The muscles beneath me bunch and release, making the whole of the top of his paw feel like the world's most terrifying bouncy castle as the demon dog struggles to get his balance.

But, of course, he does. Because he's a dog, in form at least. So what I cut off isn't really the little toe. It's the smallest forward facing one. But he has the rear one, the dewclaw, to allow him to keep standing where many humans would've fallen straight over.

And there's something else unnerving me. Something I can't put my finger on at first. Then I realise what it is. The muscular movements underfoot have stilled. And so have the vibrations that were travelling through the hound's body. The ones caused by his wrestling match.

My eyes swivel upwards slowly.

Caacrinolaas is still reared up onto his back paws. Still balanced against Nithael.

But Nithael isn't grappling with his front paws anymore. No. One of the demon dog's huge, downy feathered wings is wrapped around the angel's crackling form, and it's against that appendage that Nith is now wrestling.

Which, apparently, makes him a lot less distracting for Caacrinolaas, allowing him to dedicate a lot more attention in my direction.

Shit.

This might well be the moment where my tiny, little human brain gets mushed together with my torso, legs, and feet, and we find out if I get another incarnation after this one or not.

But then my mentor steps forward and... coughs. Politely.

'Stop. Right now.' The words are measured but calm. Unruffled.

Caacrinolaas, amazingly, does just that. Pausing for a moment, he looks down. I think it's sheer amazement at the ballsiness of the tiny figure in front of him. The Good God knows I'm equally astounded.

'What?' The demon growls at him, a fetid warm wave of canine breath washing over my mentor, strong enough it rolls back towards me, enough to almost make me gag.

'You are a vile individual.' Isaac lifts his hands. 'A villain. A monster. A ruinous blight who brings nought but misery where you walk. Unwelcome and unwanted.'

'Oh no!' Caacrinolaas laughs in absolute delight, the

139

rumbling almost dislodging me from my tenuous grip. 'The mano's unhappy with me! Except I've already got your angelico. What are you gonna do?'

Isaac stares up at him, sets his jaw. 'This.'

Talent pours out of him.

It's so easy to forget that Isaac is a Talented powerhouse. That there's a reason he and Jak alone were able to bring Bene Elohim to this plane, able to bind them to their bodies without exploding. Just because he chooses to stay in the theoretical field generally and let Nithael do the unpleasant heavy lifting in combat doesn't mean anyone should ever underestimate him.

In exactly the way Caacrinolaas just did.

A white-light beam of pure *power* punches into Caacrinolaas' pug-like nose, and he screams, rocking backwards in a howl of agony. The smell of singed flesh, mixed with roasted hair fills the square, like a charnel pit barbecue, and in the weight of that noise, in the depth of the agony behind that scream, for a moment I think this is it. That Isaac has turned the tide.

The next second, I think my world is ending once again. Because Caacrinolaas roars and drops his head, greased lightning, hammering it into the ground below him. It's enough to knock my oldest friend off balance, shaking him. His hands lose focus, failing to track the demon's movement. Caacrinolaas shoots forward, his jaws snapping, and seizes Isaac between those gigantic menhir-sized incisors before shaking him viciously back and forth.

Then he tosses him high up into the sky like a tumbling rag doll.

All of reality narrows down to me watching the man I love like a father flying through the empty air, limp and looking entirely lifeless.

Chapter Twenty-Three

This cannot be happening. By the Good God, it cannot.

There are moments when everything goes so horribly, terribly wrong that no one watching can really process what's going on. That the terrible instant is so much, far too much, that the brain overloads temporarily, and existence outside of what we're standing witness to seems to grind to a complete halt.

Watching Isaac sail through the heavens, a man better than any I've ever known, get reduced to his composite form, a bag of flesh and blood hurled like a water balloon ready to splash open on contact, is just such a moment. I can't comprehend it. Can't believe it's happening. Maybe I should. Perhaps it's precisely what I should have expected when I brought my scholarly friend along to fight a murderous, amoral demon. But Isaac is a real magician, a Miracle Max, a man who couldn't even work out how to walk when he was asked to be surreptitious but still provided the knock-out blow to the most infamous assassin of all time and with style and panache too. He's the man who's stood witness to my endlessly rash stupidity, yet still looks at me with pride and delight. He could bring out the best in each and every occasion by seeing the good with such determined single-mindedness as to make it manifest by sheer force of will. And he's a major Talented force. When he pulled out the magical big guns, I thought he might have won it for us there and then. But he wasn't ready for a real brawl, for the street tactics of a down-and-dirty fighter like Caacrinolaas.

He wasn't. But Caacrinolaas was.

I dash forward, finally unfrozen, freed, moving. I try to manoeuvre around the bulk of this monstrous fuckwad who's just launched the best man I've ever known into the air, and I'm trying to draw power from the ground, trying to pull *talent* from a place that should be mine but stubbornly refuses to acknowledge me. My hands are thrown out in front of me, and I'm pulling on everything left inside of me to grab him from the air, to pull him safe into my arms or to cushion his landing, to do anything to keep him safe, and please, please, please let him be safe – let him be alive and safe; it's not fair if he's not alive and safe; it wouldn't be right. *It isn't right…*

Which is when the rear claw of Caacrinolaas' rear paw catches me, cutting deep into my side, and sends me sprawling.

The floor becomes a mess. Rapidly. There's blood all around me. A pool that's formed damnably quick, which means I'm bleeding a lot. Not fatal on its own – not yet at least, but it's taken the wind from my sails. And it's broken my concentration as pain is liable to do, the demanding, attention-hungry bitch. The slice is sharp enough and deep enough that there's no option but to crumple in a heap on the floor and watch Isaac continue his trajectory, completely outside of my control.

The worst of it is that it wasn't even deliberate. The cut wasn't even the sort of bitch move the fucking Tarrasque would've pulled off – let me try to help, then stab me in the back while sniggering about it. No, the humongous demon dog wasn't even paying me attention. He was just shifting back a step in his tussle with Nithael and by chance caught me a glancing blow.

So all I can do is watch Isaac continue in his flight. Though he's not flying anymore. No. Now the angle's altering, the trajectory changing from upwards to downwards. He's losing momentum, losing altitude. I'm terrified that when he lands, I'll lose him. So I'm pushing all that *talent* I gathered into my wound, trying to heal it enough to allow me to concentrate properly, to allow me to move and save him somehow. But it's not going to be fast enough. Not even close. There's no way I'm going to regain my feet before he regains the ground.

But I'm not alone. Thank the Good God I'm not alone. There's another here who loves Isaac almost as much as I do. Perhaps more – or at least more intimately, having spent centuries tied together, to his soul. Nithael may be tied up, wrapped in wrestling with the demonic wing that's enrobing him. But he knows what's happening, and the demon isn't the only one with wings.

Nith turns in Caacrinolaas' grasp, the desperate momentum a slight pivot that opens the tiniest of spaces in the demon's wrapped wing. Through it, he unfurls his own, stretching it out, a crackling blue, a shimmering presence in our reality. He angles the tips of his feathers underneath Isaac's path so they become like a ramp, a slide. I will him to level it out, to stop Isaac's movement, but his fight with the demon is pushing him to the limit, the giant hound's teeth pressing him hard. Even an angel has his limits, and all he can do is reduce Isaac's speed. He can't pluck him from the air. Just try to cushion his fall.

But Isaac's still moving so quickly, carrying so much velocity. Nith's slowed him, brought him back from a speed where impact with *anything* would probably be instantly fatal. But he can't change his direction entirely. Isaac's moving at a clip, and though he's no longer moving straight down, the change in direction means he's now rocketing towards the snapped wooden stakes that poke up where the pirate ship kids' playground once stood. He's moving more than fast enough to impale himself on any one of them.

As my flesh knits back together, I scream, air thrown out in howls at the idea that we might be so close, yet still it might not be enough, that even an angel risking his own self in a fight against a mortal enemy could be useless simply because of physics. Tears stream down my face, but I'm up again, my feet regained, my hands once more outstretched. There's little in the tanks though, too little to pull off anything spectacular, and I'm fumbling to break through the shell of the acorn I took from home and buried in my chest, the one that was once a tree turned young again by wyrd hag magic. I'm trying to dig my way inside it, to bond with the magic there and draw it into myself, enough to do my own miracle and save the man who's saved me from the start, who I could save a million times and still be in his debt.

I know there's no time. No matter how much the scene seems to be running in slow motion, each frame clipping as he closes with the ground, I know I can't do it. Can't crack the nut and imbibe what it carries in time to perform what is necessary if I'm to keep him alive.

But there's still one more in our party. One last soul who doesn't have magic that crackles at his fingertips. Who isn't an angel, an other-dimensional being of neon and pure soulfire who burns through our petty reality's rules without a care in the world. No. He's just a man, still little more than a boy. A kid, cut adrift of everything – family, the *talent* he gave up, the safety and sort-of-love he found with Franc. A human and nothing more.

And yet, nothing less either. Because Gil's been moving this whole time, on the other side of Caacrinolaas. He must have been since Isaac got launched sideways. He's standing spectator to a supernal battle on a scale never witnessed in tens of thousands of years, and yet when he saw his friend get thrown, he didn't hesitate. Gil's *moved*, ran just like I did, except without trying to pull on *talent*, distracting himself and getting sucker punched because of it. if Nithael hadn't stretched out that wing, hadn't broken Isaac's fall and softened it by shaping the trajectory, he never would have reached him in time. But still he would've tried. And because he tried? Because he made that impossible effort in the face of impossible odds when he should have been insignificant?

He makes a difference once again. Gil is there, throwing himself forward, slamming into Isaac sideways, wrapping his arms around him to cushion the blow, so that as they connect, they're sent sprawling, away from the lethal palisade. The two of them roll, tumbling for several metres before ending up in a tangled heap near the stairs that lead back up to the street above, near the also still form of De Monteguard.

For a moment, I can't breathe. I can only mimic the utter stillness of the two forms where they've come to rest. Then a second later, that moment feels like several lifetimes

– proper ones, not the brief instances I've often experienced before dying again either. Gil's head comes up. There's a wooziness to his movement, but he shakes it off, and I see his head duck back down to press against Isaac's chest. A hand wavers into view. The thumb comes up, and suddenly, I can draw in that precious air because Isaac's alive. The Good God bless them both. Isaac's alive, and I am so grateful to Gil, to Nith, to the universe for not being the usual uncaring, malicious fucker it so often is and giving me this, keeping Isaac safe one more time.

The ground rumbles underneath me, drawing me back to what is going on above our heads. It's not good news. Caacrinolaas is still reared up, but his forepaws are closer to the ground now. Nithael's more ensnared than ever. The twist he made to force his wing through wasn't a good one for him, and he's being forced backwards, damn near pushed horizontal. Caacrinolaas seizes that outstretched wing between his gigantic incisors and buries them deep into the neon frame packed full of electric blue feathers.

For the first time ever, I get to hear an angel scream.

Chapter Twenty-Four

I'd love to make some sort of joke about Bene Elo-scream if I didn't feel like it was cracking my soul like an empty eggshell.

If you're from a Christian background or if you've grown up in a culture where Christianity was dominant for a sufficient period of time, you probably have some ideas about angelic voices. That they prefer singing ensemble pieces as part of the heavenly choir, and that a lot of the time, the lyrics are probably going to be "hosanna". Which strikes me as vaguely boring. Switch it up a bit from time to time, get yourself a solo section where you throw down some heavy-duty rhymes instead. But then, I've always found myself far more tempted by Mephy's vision of a dimension beyond our own than Nithael's.

You might expect that after eight hundred years, I'd be quite the expert on what angels sound like. But I never heard Nithael speak until our recent confrontation with the fucking Tarrasque. Which speaks of just how irritating a knobscrobber he is, that he can break an angel's apparent vow of silence out of sheer frustration and anger, but it also means I can't tell you what Nith sounds like most of the time. The only one who can is Isaac, and right now he's in a crumpled heap behind Caacrinolaas, presumably unconscious, albeit thankfully alive.

And right now? I'm glad he's out cold. Because the sound I'm hearing is horrendous for me. I suspect it'd break his heart in two.

Nithael lets out a singular tone of pure agony, but just as angels are supposed to do, it's harmonising with itself, different notes contained alongside. Ones that express shock, disbelief, horror. Disgust even. I suspect that last part is at the sullying nature of our physical world. It strikes me how dirtied it must make an angel feel, to force themselves down onto our level. It's like making someone with chronic OCD and germophobia play in a tiny, little sandpit that's full of dirt and rusty toys and what you desperately hope are wrinkled brown rocks but know perfectly well are going to go squish if you touch them. Just being in our reality must be a form of torture for him.

Now, not only is he manifest, dragged down to our level, but he's tied up in a physical brawl, wrestling with what he probably views as his hillbilly cousin who he detests so much he doesn't even send a card to at Christmas, and to make matters worse...

He's losing. I wonder which hurts more. The physical pain. Or the mental.

But while that's an intriguing mental exercise –you're hurting an angel; decide whether you're wounding their shoulder or their pride the worst– it doesn't help Nith. He's been there for me more than a few times. But more importantly, he's always been there for 'Zac. Even when I wasn't. Even when I got lost up in my own misery and suffering or disappeared off chasing after whatever latest obsession grabbed my fancy, Nithael was always there, sharing a life with him. Saving him when necessary. I owe him. Big time.

I'm at a loss though. Sure I've done Caacrinolaas some damage already. He's a toe down, although the wounds have already stopped bleeding, and it didn't have the toppling-tower effect on his equilibrium I hoped for.

But we still have Joyeuse – somewhere. It's sharp enough to cut straight through demons. It makes me wonder if that's why he was after it – to try to stop us from getting our hands on it and using it against him. Except that doesn't quite make sense because if he was afraid of it, then why wouldn't he have tried harder to take it from us?

But there's no time to unravel that particular mystery. I need to find the blade I dropped when Caarcinolaas had his hissy fit after I lopped off his toe. It isn't easy. One thing you never think about when you're watching a Godzilla-style fight is how much dust and dirt gets thrown up into the air. Nithael's wriggling around as he screams, squirming and hammering his fists and wings into Caacrinolaas whenever he can get a clean shot, and of course, it's making the demon dog shift about as well, moving and replanting his paws to maintain dominance, to keep control of the fight. Each time one moves, whether shuffling sidewards to keep up the momentum or lifting off momentarily to hammer back into a stronger stance, it's throwing up clouds of the churned-up earth around their feet. Which is only a low disturbance for the behemoths slugging it out above us, but that low level is head height for me.

I duck around the side of Caacrinolaas' paw, keeping a wary half-eye on that rear claw. I'm well aware of just how much damage he can do to me without even meaning to. If he puts some thought into it, I could easily be sliced in two. The air's so rich with the smell of loam, like a field after the tractor's pulled the rotary tiller through, trenches dug for the season's harvest, that it almost masks the smell of "burned caramel" that lingers around the black fur of the bastard we're fighting.

I pull on the *talent* I still have, drawing in some of the cleaner air from higher up, and sweep away the thrown-up muck so I can see a cone of vision straight ahead.

No sword. Panic starts to rise, only accentuated by the awful harmonic keening going on overhead. Nithael's losing. Nithael's losing, and I'm doing nothing. *Come on, Paul. Keep it together. Find Joyeuse. Save Nithael. Keep it simple, you stupid shit-head simpleton.* If there's one thing that'll help me keep calm, it's being insulted. There's a comfort in that. As there's no one else around though, I berate myself mentally. *C'mon, you cuntbungling pricknose. Find the sword. Find it!*

Somehow, implausibly, it works. My breathing calms. The blood pumping quiets down so I can hear myself think again. I keep the air currents swirling in, clearing a path ahead of me, then *there!*

A glint. The smallest momentary reflection. Pretty much squarely in the middle, between Caacrinolaas' two back paws.

Of course, now I still have to get to it. No easy task with the gargantuan paws seeming to practice a tap dance of death on the ground. Just keeping my feet over the ensuing tremors is a challenge. If one of them lands on me, I'm done, no questions asked. Mainly because it's hard to ask questions when you've been crushed so firmly you've turned two-dimensional.

Timing's the answer. If Aicha was here —oh, and by the

Good God, how I wish Aicha was here– she wouldn't even hesitate. She'd dance her way around the paws as they pounded the ground without even a pause. No paws pause, so to speak. A second later, she'd have Joyeuse in hand and would then promptly feed Caacrinolaas his own intestines. Probably through his arsehole.

I am not Aicha. Don't get me wrong, I'm a dab hand at fighting, but I'm not about to pirouette through the field of rapidly descending death without catching a scratch. I've always relied on just popping back to life if I died and having another shot at it. Pop another coin in the machine, hit the Ready Player One button, and have at it all over again.

Can't do that. So I have to try to time it. Feel when the feet shift. Notice how Caacrinolaas scrambles to keep the upper hand, how his paws scrape back and to each side, splaying to grip the ground. Hear the change, the agonising, terrible change, in Nithael's note as the demon's teeth bite deeper. The muffled grunt as the angel responds enough to slightly wind the demon dog, so as his bite must ease up.

Caacrinolaas lifts his right paw and slams it back down. Sets it in place. I know it won't move. Not for a moment, at least.

I hope.

Even through the shaggy black fur, I can see the set of the demon's musculature up along the back of his hind legs. Physically speaking, dogs aren't made to stay up on two legs for long, and his calves are bulging.

But that allows me to read them. They're extended right now, locked to try to maintain this unnatural, ungainly posture, and I'm flicking my eyes back and forth between them and the left paw. The plan is that the muscles changing shape will tell me he's lifting up, that the paw's about to become all the more lethal. I'm also looking out for it moving anyhow in case that plan turns out to be bollocks, and Caacrinolaas can shift enough to gut me without his calf muscles budging.

Then I stop thinking. Stop hesitating. And lunge for that single gleam of metal that I hope beyond all hope is the legendary blade of Charlemagne, half-buried in this muddied Toulousain green.

Chapter Twenty-Five

I don't know about 'Give Me Joy In My Heart'. I'd settle for 'Give Me Joyeuse In My Hand'. Then sticking it in Caacrinolaas' heart.

Time is not my friend here. I may not be Aicha – assessing everything in a heartbeat, picking out a path, and following it through the chaos like some Busby choreography – but once I make that decision, it's go time.

I half-spring, half-tumble towards the bit of metal, pushing off turned-up divots with my rear foot, my body leaning almost horizontal, the momentum carrying me next to it. I land, my left knee tucked in ready to springboard me back up.

And I could weep for joy. Because it *is* the glittering jewelled hilt of Joyeuse itself. I wrap my hand around the handle and pump upwards to spring to my feet, the blade in hand...

Only to promptly crash back to earth face-first, the

rocky compacted ground grazing half of my face up in the process. The sword hasn't moved.

Now, lying between the feet of your gigantic enemy, prone and winded, is not the ideal place to find yourself during any battle. Panic starts setting in pretty quickly. What's happened? Is it magic Caacrinolaas has cast on the blade? A working to keep it fixed in place, like the Sword in the Stone, only I'm definitely not the anointed King of Albion in waiting?

But I push that all down too, focus on trying to see what is actually going on. I breathe a huge sigh of relief. It's not the Sword in the Stone, but it is a sword in stone – or pretty much. There's no magic at work, just the power of geology.

So take two. I push myself back up, wrap my hand around the pommel once more, press my other hand against the compressed soil, and push some *talent* into my muscles to yank the blade free. To my enormous relief, after initial, clinging resistance, it moves, slowly sliding begrudgingly out of the earth-formed sheath.

Now I'm back up, and I've Joyeuse once again. I just still don't have a fucking clue what to do. I'm looking at Caacrinolaas' ankle itself, wondering if the legendary blade might let me lop off the whole foot. But it's multiple metres thick. I got lucky when it came to separating his toe from the rest of his foot. Razor-sharp and effective against demons it might be, but there's a limit.

The heel, mind… If it worked against Achilles, maybe it'll do a similar number on Caacrinolaas. If I slice through the tendon, he's going to find standing up on those hind legs a helluva lot harder. I don't doubt he'll be able to heal up, but it'll buy Nithael some breathing space, at least.

I dash back towards the rear paw. I'm running in a wide

circle, aiming to get behind it and deliver the severing blow when Caacrinolaas finally drags Nithael to the ground.

The collision of them – Nithael's manifested body and the heavy landing of Caacrinolaas' full weight on top sets up a miniature earthquake, the ground shifting underfoot, cracking open. I stumble, fall forward, my left hand thrown out in front to check myself, somehow still maintaining my grip on Joyeuse. But my wrist can't take all of the collision, not with me being so off-balance, so I start to roll to the left. Only to find myself checked in the process, a scream torn from my lips as pain shoots up my leg.

Looking down, it's a relief to see I haven't actually torn my leg off completely. But seeing the angle I'm at comparative to it? I've dislocated it. Badly. My foot went into a crevice that opened up and then closed again in the chaos of a second ago, trapping me around the ankle. I'm like a fox with its foot in a snare. Now my whole plan's gone to shit.

Because, of course, hamstringing Caacrinolaas while he was reared up would have been a game changer. Startle effect combined with gravity could have really swung the odds in Nith's favour. Now he's back on all four paws, taking one out of operation will hamper the demon, no question. But not enough. He'll be able to maintain his dominant position over the fallen angel unless we get really lucky.

Still, I've nothing else. So I'll stick with the plan. Hope it startles him enough to allow Nith to pull off something spectacular. Only problem is, I'm now a good couple of metres away from the nearest rear paw. And my own lower limb is effectively trapped.

First thing is to put the leg back into operation. I force the ball joint back into place, muffling a repeated scream, and use a little *talent* to heal the surrounding area. Now that

I can pull on it without passing out instantly, I set to, planting the other foot, its knee bent, before yanking on the trapped leg.

To no effect. I'm completely jammed.

Nithael's still screaming, harmonious terrified pain, and I'm about ready to gnaw my own leg off if it means I can get free and help him. Luckily, I don't need to. Instead, I plant my left hand on the floor again, readying myself to use my *talent* to yank it out of this unintended trap when I hear it. A sharp, quick whistle. A demand for attention if ever I heard one.

Snapping my head up, I see who's called for me like that. Between the rear paws, I see Gil, his eyes on me. When he sees he has my attention, he jabs a finger towards the sword, then swings around and points frantically at Isaac and De Monteguard.

I don't get it. What does he want? To stab De Monteguard? No. He's almost an innocent, a man duped his whole life.

Gil turns back, shaking an exasperated head. He narrows his eyes at me deliberately, like a charade, then turns, flicking his fingers back and forth from his eyes to the two prone forms. The mime is clear. *Look* at them.

So I do. I narrow my own eyes and open my *sight*. I gasp involuntarily as I clock what it is Gil has already realised.

The fighters are both tied to their prospective hosts by a cord.

And Joyeuse can cut through demon energy.

A thrill runs through me. I can't keep back a grin. Gil's done it again. Once more, this Talentless young lad has stepped up to save his supposed betters. He really is something else.

I grab Joyeuse by the handle, reverse the grip, and pull it

back over my shoulder. Shades of our fight with Melusine flash through my head. I threw my sword at her sceptre lying on the ground to knock it out of her reach. The sceptre ending up in reach of Gil instead was simple good fortune.

This time, I'm not targeting anything with the sword I'm hurling, other than a clear path through the oversized scrabbling legs. But there's a lot of things I'm *not* aiming for. The prone bodies of Isaac and De Monteguard, for one. Gil himself, for two, as impaling him with the thrown blade would probably put a damper on his brilliant plan. So I take a second, draw in a deep breath, and hold it. Steady myself as I aim.

Then I launch the sword through the gap towards Gil.

It bites into the earth less than a metre from his left-hand side. There's no reaction above me, no earthquake shake as Caacrinolaas whips himself around to address the threat.

The demon dog doesn't know. Gil's in the clear.

I could whoop with delight as the young lad gives me his happy, charming grin and a thumbs up. Then he turns and wraps his hand around Joyeuse's handle.

And that is when everything goes spectacularly to shit.

Chapter Twenty-Six

We've been outplayed. Again. And considering we're
bringing our A Team each time, I'm sick of it. Perhaps I
better give Howlin' Mad Murdoch a call. I'm certainly
ready to take his nickname. I feel ready to howl my fury at
the sky.

I see it. A second before it all goes wrong. A millisecond
before Gil makes contact with the blade, before he wraps
the pommel in his grip.

His hand. It isn't his. It isn't that greyish pink it
normally would be in the washed-out sunlight.

It's gleaming, glittering obsidian black.

'No!' I yell, my hand outstretched as if I can deny this,
as if that simple demand might turn back the tide, might
undo this moment and bring the sword back into my own
grip.

It doesn't.

The inky black spreads up Gil's arm, over his body,

158

covering him, consuming him within it, and hardening as it goes. Then the colour lightens, glowing, gleaming like burnished armour on a castle rampart. The liquid courses over his head and flings backwards. Finger-like locs of demonic energy come forth and turn golden, waving behind an elongated face, the mouth and nose having fused into a snout. I yank furiously on my trapped leg as whiskers spring off each side of the forming muzzle. If Mephy and Caacrinolaas wear the forms of canines, this is entirely feline, the golden strands thrown back into a tousled mane.

Leonine. But clearly not actually a lion for the body remains bipedal, its arms and legs still humanlike, just oversized and bulging, all rippling muscle underneath what looks like strawberry-blond fur.

No. Not entirely lionesque. Big cat energy, sure. But a demonic big cat.

Another demon. Caacrinolaas wasn't on his own. There's been another demon all along.

The demon cat looks at me, its pupils slitted, and raises Joyeuse in two hands, tapping the flat of the blade against his forehead as if in salute. His eyes close for a moment, and if I didn't know better, I'd swear he's murmuring a prayer. Perhaps it's a spell or incantation instead because Joyeuse lights up, glowing a white-blue, the colour of freshly frozen ice. Above me Caacrinolaas starts to chuckle, rumbling huffs of amusement vibrating down from his enormous straggle-haired belly.

A thought suddenly hits me that all he has to do is lie down or roll over, and I'd be turned into Paul paste, plastered across the remaining grass. I don't doubt Caacrinolaas knows I'm here, and even if he doesn't, the moment his demonic partner-in-crime lets him know, I'm done. So I place my hands back into the dirt and brace myself to pull out, to get clear before I become collateral damage.

Before I can though, the lion-headed kibblesniffer snaps open his eyes again, and they're ink black. The fucker's lips peel back in what might be a snarl, what might be a smile, but which clearly isn't good news for us. Then he swings the blade.

Straight through the tether connecting Isaac to Nithael.

The blade carries on beyond the thin energetic connection without any resistance, and I swear I hear the *snick* – a momentary lull in the chaotic soundtrack of the brawl overhead. Isaac sits bolt upright, his face chalk-white. His mouth cracks open, and he screams, the pitch high, and it's like my heart is made of glass because that sound sends cracks straight through it.

But the lion demon doesn't stop there. What he does next doesn't hurt my heart though, but it does catch me even more off guard than what he did to Nith and 'Zac.

Because he reverses the swing. The tether connecting up to Nithael still clings weblike to the blade. He slices through the demonic connection between De Monteguard and Caacrinolaas.

Overhead, the muffled guffaws change to a whine, a half-howl packed with incomprehension and outrage. Whatever is happening's hurting him and deeply so based on that buzzsaw whining coming from his throat. To which I would normally say, 'Good, fuck him,' but I'm not entirely sure what's happening now is going to be good news for any of us.

The lion-headed fucker twirls the blade, almost like he's running through a series of martial arts katas because there's a definite purpose and rhythm to his movements. I yank at my leg, trying to get myself free as fast as I can because now... now I see what he's doing. He's weaving together the tethers of *talent* he severed, turning the blade like a stick in a candyfloss machine, drawing them closer, bundling them around in the air above him. And the air is being rent by the sounds of unearthly screams as both demon and angel howl their pain and fury and utter incomprehension out into an uncaring sky. Only I care −Gil's gone, possessed by this fucker; Isaac looks catatonic; and De Monteguard hasn't even moved− and I do, I really do because the noise is unbearable, so loud I don't understand how my eardrums are still intact, and yet at the same time, it's so quiet, so intimate, a tiny noise down in the bottom of my soul that makes me want to sob because no human should have to feel that, not now, not ever. These noises aren't made for our ears, their notes not designed for our world. It's too much, and I want it to stop, want their suffering to stop.

My leg's free now, enough that I'm stumbling forward, fighting the urge to clap my hands over my ears, trying to focus enough to force my hand between the atoms and pull free another sword from my etheric storage, desperate to *make it stop*.

Then it does. But I wish it didn't. Because the sword's light grows, glowing with the burning heat of arctic winter. It's so bright, I can't keep my eyes open, can't even squint, but still I'm running blindly forward...

Then it's gone. The world is dull daylight again, mere shadow compared to the blade's blinding illumination.

The sword is gone. So is the demon.

And Caacrinolaas and Nithael are too.

Chapter Twenty-Seven

What just happened? I've no problem with having lost
Caacrinolaas –a Caacrinoloss, if you will– but Nithael? I
didn't even think that was possible.

For a moment, I just stand here, enrobed in the
monochrome, my eyes readjusting to a reality filled only
with the mundane. All the other-dimensional strangeness
has just disappeared, like an infection purged from reality's
system, and as shock knocks me senseless for a moment, the
only rational thought that seems to penetrate my shook-up
brain is how dull the world is without Nithael shining
brightly in it.

A primordial noise starts up. Low at first, a guttural
keen. It builds rapidly in volume and pitch, rising into a wail
of such raw anguish that it is salt in all the wounds of the
world, all the hurts of my soul. And it is a knife driven deep
into each as well because I know who that sound is coming
from, which mouth is shaping all that incomprehensible

pain into a sound, expelling it from a mind that is submerged in it, seeking to drain away the tiniest drop so as not to be completely drowned.

It's coming from my father in all but blood.

Now I'm running again, my feet flying, hardly seeming to touch the ground. Closing the distance until I'm right up next to him. He's sitting bolt upright, but his eyes aren't seeing anything. He's just staring ahead, screaming, seemingly catatonic, and maybe I'm too late or at least too little. Perhaps this has broken his mind, this severance, and I can't save him. Can't take the place of the creature he's been soul-bonded to for nearly a thousand years. If he's not gone mad, I don't know how he isn't. I would be.

'Zac!' There's a pleading to my voice. 'Zac, man, please! Isaac, come back to me!'

I wrap my arms around him, coddling him, pulling him to my chest. 'We'll get him back. 'Zac, we'll get him back. But you've got to come back first.'

Nothing. Not even a variance in the tone. No change. Tears stream down my cheeks, their wetness speaking to how much this hurts. To see the best of us broken. It shouldn't happen.

No. I should be the broken one. That's my job, my role in this endless messed-up melodrama that is life. He's the one who helps put me back together, who pulls me back from the brink. He has my back. Is always there, never changing, never wavering. And now I'm just crouched, half-kneeling as I rock him in my arms. He's this close, but I can't reach him, can't get through, can't bring him back like he's always managed with me.

I don't know what to do. I feel more helpless than I ever have in my life, more adrift, more useless, pointless. So I accept that. Perhaps I am useless in this situation. Perhaps my approach is pointless, that this outpouring of emotion isn't helping. Instead, I think about how another might handle it, how Aicha, the Druze Queen, might deal with me were I similarly snapped. When life made a glow stick out of me yet again, the big raving bastard, and she came along to pick up the pieces.

I think about it. Think about her approach. Taking a deep breath, I calm myself and clear my mind. Then I let go of Isaac, rock back on my heels, and look at his vacant, screaming face. Check him over once, physically, magically, make sure there're no injuries inflicted on him from having been shaken and flung by Caacrinolaas –Nithael, the Good God bless him, must have healed him if there were– or from the sword having severed the tether, other than the terrible cost to his soul. I nod, reassured.

Then I slap him. Hard.

The noise is almost as shocking as the action. It's a whip crack that echoes off the ruined buildings around us, growing in the echo even as it fades away. It certainly seems to linger in my ears, a high-pitched hum like a half-forgotten tinnitus tone. Isaac's mouth is so agape that I'm worried by how hard I hit him, whether I've dislocated his jaw. I was channelling raw Aicha energy, and let me tell you, she doesn't pull her punches.

But I've committed now. I'm fixed on a course of action, and the Good God be damned if I ruin it by stammering apologies or looking contrite. That'd undo the whole thing.

So I firm up my jaw, my lips thinning as they pull taut, and look at the man who's never shown me anything but kindness and compassion with contempt. 'Is that going to save him?'

'Wh…what?' Isaac's stammer is clear enough to let me know I've not actually snapped his jawbone. That's good news because I've just realised that I really should have regulated my slap more considering he doesn't have the usual angelic protection in place right now.

'Is that going to save him? Screaming your lungs out?'

'He… He's *not here*, Paul!' Isaac's hand hovers, almost to point towards his head, then clenches and pounds on his chest instead. 'He's not here with me, Paul. He's always here with me!'

'No, he's not.' I keep that tone cold, workman's-hands-calloused, even as I feel every single heartstring being plucked to breaking point simultaneously. 'He's not here, Zac. Which means he's somewhere else. In the hands of some super-malicious, overly cunning demon who, I should point out, might somehow be Demon Fart come back in demonic form, and that this was all part of his cunning plan, in which case, I'm going to be *pissed*. Either way, Nithael's alone, confused, and probably scared.'

What I want right now is to get Isaac's empathy going. Get his fear for his angelic partner overriding his pain and terror at being alone.

'What if he's dead though?' Isaac's voice is little more than a whisper, syllables floating out only to be snatched away by the wind before such a blasphemy can be heard by another living soul.

'What if he's not?' I press on regardless of my oldest friend's fear and pain, hating myself for it, knowing it's the only way. 'What if he's alive and alone and scared, and you're just standing here shrieking?' Oh Good God, I don't want to say the next bit, but I need to. I need him to be ready just in case, to not fall apart if it happens. 'And what if he is? What do you think that demonic smegcheddar stands to gain by his death? Do you think it'll be anything Nithael would approve of? If he is dead – and I don't believe he is, not yet, but if he is, don't you want to take revenge on the absolute cockstride who dared take him from you? Don't you want to make him pay?'

Isaac's eyes widen a little, and his mouth works soundlessly, as though whatever he's thinking is as much as he can bear to say. Perhaps it is because when his lips stop moving, he doesn't speak. Just gives a small nod, almost imperceptible. And I don't want to think about it, but apparently my brain didn't get the memo because all I can think behind this cold veneer I'm wearing is, *How much? How much must that have cost him, of all men, to acknowledge he'd want revenge?* Hell, he even felt proud of his brother forgiving and freeing the bastard who'd kept him trapped in a skull for centuries. Vengeance is not an appetite that comes readily to Isaac. Nor is it one he wishes for.

But right now, he knows he wants it. If Nithael is dead – if Nith is even damaged, which is the real unspoken elephant in the room – then he'll want to see the impish cuntknuckle fry once and for all for doing it. Even after centuries – lifetimes spent seeking peaceful, non-confrontational resolutions – there are always lines that, once crossed, will make us keen for the taste of blood.

It's a horrible thing to realise you're human after all. It's a terrible gift to give to someone you love.

'I just don't understand.' Isaac's back. The fact he's questioning, searching for answers, tells me that. He's not the same man he was before this incident, sure, but he's still here. Still Isaac. I hope. 'Why bother with all this subterfuge? If he could hur...'

His voice hitches, and he turns away, burying his head in his jacket, the grief too much to bear. He doesn't need to finish the sentence though. I know what he's asking. *If he could hurt Nithael, kill him maybe with Joyeuse, why did he wait until now to do it?* He's right. Apparently, Gil's been carrying a demonic hitchhiker around all this time, since we rescued him from Auch, when Isaac sacrificed the alp's hat to save him.

Instead of the demon being driven out by the hat, he'd hidden inside Gil somewhere. But why go through all the hue and cry rather than simply stealing the sword from me and making up some angel sushi with a quick slice'n'dice?

'It wasn't just the angel he wanted.' The croaky tones of the unexpected voice nearly make me need a clean pair of underwear. Swinging around, I see De Monteguard propping himself up on his elbows, his face pale, albeit looking considerably better than Isaac. Mind you, considering his soulbound companion just hijacked his body and overrode his free will, I can't imagine it was such a painful parting. Although, thinking about it, as it was his first ever friend betraying him totally and utterly, perhaps it hurt more than I'm giving it credit for. That makes me realise what he means seconds before he says it.

'The demon. He wanted a demon as well.'

Oh, shit. Of course he did. Holding the strings –literally– of both an angel and a demon? Cannot be good news. No way, no how.

Chapter Twenty-Eight

Not content with getting a Bene Elohim, he was angel-ing
for a demon as well.

De Monteguard pushes himself unsteadily to his feet. He
sways for a moment, so that I think he'll have to listen to
his legs telling him what a terrible idea that was and flop
back down, but he stays upright and staggers over before
plopping down next to us. Isaac's still sitting, his face pale
and drawn, still not even close to a hundred percent, but
his eyes are fixed on the man who's just come over, and
there's something starting to show emotion wise. Not
something good though. There's a tightness to Isaac's face,
his skin taut as every muscle tenses like his face wants to
ball itself up into a fist and punch the fucker into next
week.

Good. Isaac's angry. Better that than catatonic. Now I
just have to make sure it's aimed in the right direction.
Easier said than done because my own ire, mostly composed

of the fermenting self-hatred and guilt from how I've just treated 'Zac, is coming to the fore.

But I know De Monteguard isn't our target. He was suckered, played in the ultimate long con from the day of his birth, and I can't find it in me to hate him just for his father's blood.

'Are you all right, man?' Don't get me wrong, I want the information he's carrying, and ideally I would've had it yesterday, before we stumbled into this stupid fucking trap and got ourselves regally shafted in the process.

De Monteguard nods. 'I am. And I'm sorry.'

It's heartfelt, genuine. That Isaac doesn't hear that – doesn't want to hear it – speaks to just how deeply he's hurting right now. 'Oh, you're sorry? You're sorry, are you? Well, wonderful, lad; that solves everything, doesn't it? Remedies all of our bloody problems and means we can just tap dance off down the bloody yellow brick road with a spoonful of sugar, hey? Well, you can take your sorry and shove it up your ar–'

'Isaac!' The shock is real. No pretending. And something in my voice pulls him back, reminds him of who he is as his attention returns to me. Enough so that his expression is half-hangdog, half-petulance incarnate in the face of me having spoiled his rant.

'What, Paul?' The words are cut off, brittle, as if his tongue's chipped them off the block of all his repressed emotions, and they aren't sure if they're angry or sorry or both.

'The yellow brick road is the *Wizard of Oz*. A spoonful of sugar is *Mary Poppins*. That's a terrible mixed pop culture metaphor. Awful.'

I look him in the eyes, my facial expression still, my eyes wide, shock writ into my visage. He stares back, disbelief on his, as if trying to comprehend how I can possibly manage to be just such a massive twat. Although I'm sure his thoughts are more charitable than that.

'Paul,' he says slowly, thoughtfully, when he regains his powers of speech a few seconds later. 'I love you dearly, but you are a massive vagina.'

See? Knew he wouldn't be calling me a twat. Another win for Bonhomme.

We need answers, but we also need to move. Regardless of what's happened – or even because of it – we need the rest of the team. Right now. So I head in the direction of the stone steps leading up to the Quai De La Daurade, whose curves lead round to the Pont Neuf. Seeing as how Isaac's attention is now on me, his rage mollified at least for the moment, I seize control of the questions. 'What happened, Phillipe? And what do you mean about him needing a demon?'

His eyes look away, heated and ashamed, unable to hold my gaze. 'I saw it. I saw... the truth once Caacrinolaas seized hold of me. About papa. About what he did. What he would... have done. To me. To you. To the world. Everything you said. I saw it all.'

Now the main tone is bitterness, and I wonder what it's for. Whether it's because of the lies he's suffered since he was born or what he's just gone through, being completely subsumed in Caacrinolaas' will.

I press on. 'Okay. And?' It's not that I'm not sympathetic. But one of ours has been stolen. I'm glad he's out from under the evil demon's influence. Now I'd like to be able to say the same for our own.

'Well, that's not all. Once Caacrinolaas seized hold of me, he didn't bother keeping himself separate. He had me, held me, body and mind. Soul too. All part of the agreement dear old papa signed me up to.' He shrugs. 'Don't think he expected me to ever get free. I wouldn't have if Sabnock hadn't double-crossed him.'

Sabnock. So now we have a name to go with the kitty-faced prick. I look over at Isaac, who beats Wikipedia as a go-to reference resource every time.

Isaac frowns, thinking. 'Sabnock. Hmm. He's listed in the *Ars Goetia*, of course. I always wondered where they got hold of all those names, actually...'

Good. Intellectual problems can still distract him. He's not entirely broken. Not yet, anyhow. 'What did it say about him?'

Isaac purses his lips. 'I seem to remember he's credited with the title of Grand Marquis of Hell. The rest of the details escape me for the moment.'

That'll do for now. There's a pair of demonic experts who can fill in any other gaps. We just need to get them back off the benches, back in the game.

Not that this is a game. Not in the slightest. I don't want to play. I just want to make the fuckers pay for what they've done to me and mine.

The struggle is still in evidence at the midpoint of the Pont Neuf. The Karnabo's killing gaze is caught in the mirrored surface. Johannes and Mephy are stuck in place to keep him there. I pace towards them, prowling almost, each footfall light but determined, my absolute outrage at what has been perpetrated on us a fiery ball packed down tight in my stomach. It might consume me eventually, but for now it's a power source, pushing me forward, keeping me focused on my next goal.

At this moment, there's a certain thought that's leading the consumption. A certain sound still ringing in my ear. Not the slap, no. Though the memory of that will make me wince each time I remember it. My stomach will churn and give a little hop of shame up into my chest for that split second of recall.

No, the sound driving me forward is the sound of Isaac's soul tearing in two. Of realising he lost his other half, literally sliced from him, sundered. To hear that howl of uncomprehending loneliness from him is something I'll never forget. Never forgive that fur-faced fucker Sabnock for either.

But Sabnock isn't here.

The Karnabo is.

So I don't break stride. Don't slow as I get closer to the trunk-nosed arsehole who's thrown his lot in with the forces arrayed against us. Don't even falter as I see the muscles in his weird-shaped neck bunch and strain as he tries to drag himself out of the stalemate he's trapped in, facing off against my friends. Don't even glory in seeing the sweat beading on his forehead at the effort. There's no delight in it. No.

There'll be little pleasure in anything again until I right the wrong done to Isaac. But in the meantime, there's still revenge.

As I close with the Karnabo, my hand goes through the space between the atoms and closes on a handle. Not Clarent this time. There's no peace now. This is war.

My hand comes free, and a detached part of me is coldly amused to see I'm not holding one of my broadswords, the traditional-style weapon used by knights since medieval times across France. No, it's one of Aicha's katanas. A sole blade, one of the spare sets I carry for her in my etheric storage should anything befall her main set. Not my weapon of choice normally.

At this precise moment though, it seems entirely appropriate.

So I pull it free, my hand level with my shoulder, its edge parallel with the floor. I power up the blade so it's crackling emerald green with *talent*. I should be running on empty, and the fact I'm not should concern me; it suggests I might be burning something more precious than stored up magic, something not so easily replaced by being on the territory you hold or a good night's sleep. A part of my soul perhaps…

Except it isn't. And I suddenly realise why. Because it wasn't this Sab-cock who stole Toulouse from me, subverting the wards. It was Caacrinolaas. And with him being severed from his connection to our plane, even if he hasn't gone rushing back down the dimensional escalator to the demon realm, his link to the wards is gone.

Which means Toulouse is no longer held.

While it might not be mine precisely anymore –prior to Caacrinolaas' dick move of stealing it, Isaac had been holding the wards for several months, after all– the city still recognises me. Still knows the echo of my feet slapping down on the bridge's concrete, recognises that connection of where I walked my magic into the roots of the land time after time over the centuries. So it may not be mine. But it knows me. Acknowledges me.

It feeds me magic up through my feet, topping my *talent* back up, giving me precisely the boost I need.

I'll never know what my expression looks like. There's no mirror for me, and I'm in no hurry to glance into the one Johannes has made, to get caught up in the Karnabo's reflected gaze, which is probably exactly what he'd love for me to do. Perhaps I'm almost expressionless, unchanged by the revelation of *talent* restored. Perhaps my lip does curl back, and all I look like is a toddler with colic, full of trapped wind.

But maybe I look like how I feel. And I feel *savage*.

I take three more strides –left, right, left– closing on the bastard who trumpeted his delight at the idea of our downfall. Picking up speed, I bend, push, and launch myself upwards into the air. Then with all my force behind it, I slam the point of the blade downward with all my strength, all my *talent*.

The Karnabo doesn't stand a chance. I half-hope to hear a warbling sad trumpet noise *–wah wah wah waaaah–* when he realises his time is up.

But it's hard to do that when there's half a foot of cold steel protruding through your face, pinning your trunk to your upper lip.

Chapter Twenty-Nine

Half a metre of cold steel sticking out of the front of your face? Doesn't Karna-bode well for your chances of survival.

Perhaps it seems anticlimactic to you. That this terrible monster, this cross between the Gorgon and Saruman of Many Colours, with a dash of Nellie the fucking Elephant thrown in just to mess with your head, goes down without a final struggle, a last desperate moment when all seems lost before the forces of good – or at least the forces of not-actually-evil – triumph once more.

Tell you what. You go battling monsters. Then tell me you won't settle for stabbing one in the back of the head every now and then. Cheap victories for the win, every time.

Although, the Karnabo's not dead yet. Not fully, at least in the clinical sense. His oversized body is still jerking on the end of my blade, weird truncated –trunk-cated, heh– noises still warbling and hissing from his mouth. But the blade's gone through his brain and straight out the other side. He's not coming back from that.

I give the sword a good few twists just to be sure, feeling the grate of bone rather than the squidging grey matter as the blade scrapes against the harder substance. Then I set my foot to his posterior, kick him off, and watch him drop. Face first. Eyes down. I doubt they'll do the same job now he's dead. Then again, Perseus managed to fuck up old Polydectes with the "gorgon's head in a bag" trick. Briefly, the idea of chopping off the dicknosed twat's head and stuffing it in a sack to throw at the demonic arsehole who set this all up crosses my mind. But considering the Karnabo was swathed in that black demonic essence that's evaporating off his corpse at a rate of knots, I'd lay money this Sabnock knows he's dead, so he'd be expecting it.

And on top of that, if I was a demonic mastermind, putting some hellishly –pun intended– complicated plan into operation, I'd certainly be planning on the possibility of a double-cross from Trunky McDeadephant over here. So I have no doubt he'll have something up his sleeve to counter it.

Long story short, the Karnabo's a useless sack of shit, whether dead or alive. At least he's not in our way anymore. One less thing stacked against us.

'Paul, are you all right? Did we win?' Faust's panting, his chest giving those little lifting heaves that speak of serious, continuous exertion, but he's not about to be distracted by exhaustion. He nods at De Monteguard, then his eyes scan over us, spotting who's missing straight away. One of those missing anyhow. 'Wait. Where's Gil?'

It's Mephy who picks up the other missing team member. He's not looking as wiped out as Johannes, and he raises his muzzle, scenting the air. His eyes bead, and he dashes over in a lurching run to Isaac. Loping in circles around my oldest friend, he's led by his nose, snuffling at Isaac's feet. He doesn't see the despair that's painted across 'Zac's face, the misery that's engraving itself there. Seeing it makes me want to bring the Karnabo back to stab him to death all over again.

Mephy's face comes up, and I've never seen a hound look so grim. There's nothing joyful or playful or horny or any of the other expressions I'm used to seeing in that doggy demeanour. No. Mephy's totally, one hundred percent serious.

'How?' Mephy's getting beyond agitated now, whirling round and round 'Zac's feet, sniffing at him, trying to understand the impossible with a sense more reliable than his eyes.

'Joyeuse,' I answer for Isaac even though Mephy's looking at him. I don't think 'Zac's ready to talk about it. I'm not sure he ever will be.

Mephy makes a strange noise at the back of his throat. It's halfway to what a growl might sound like if you'd just been punched mid-note clean in the Adam's apple and halfway to something else – a dark rumbling that vibrates inside my skull at such an unpleasant frequency, I'm half afraid my brain might leap out of my nose to get away from it. He spits two strange barking syllables that seem to hang in the air as visible sound before dissipating. Then he turns that ferocious attention on me once more.

'Caacrinolaas?' Apparently we're in the realm of one word questions. Which considering how verbose Mephy usually is –takes one to know one– suggests either how seriously he's taking this or how overwhelmingly pissed off he is right now. Or, of course, both.

'Nope. We had him on the ropes –'

There's a noise that comes from behind Isaac, a coughing snort that is nowhere near as forbiddingly terrifying as whatever Mephistopheles just did with his vocal cords, but it is more insulting.

'Although apparently, his former soul-buddy-turned-slave thinks differently. How did the fight go down from your armchair seat of being *tied up in eternal bondage*?'

That I don't get a crack out of Mephy about bondage and whips and chains speaks volumes to just how seriously he's taking this. The muttered, 'Never mind,' from De Monteguard suggests he's been suitably cowed as to quit the post-match commentary.

I carry on, 'Anyhow, either way, the problem wasn't Caacrinolaas. There was another demon.'

Mephy's head whips around so fast, I'm surprised I don't hear a little mini sonic boom. 'What did you say?'

'There was another demon. Gil was still possessed.'

Now the demon dog doesn't look angry. He looks poleaxed by that revelation. 'But... What? Who? How?'

Apparently, we're back to single word questions, even if he's now delivering a multitude of them at a time. 'Another demon. I'm not sure how —'

'The essence.' This time, De Monteguard speaks up clearly rather than scoffing from the back. All eyes turn in his direction. He blushes slightly, his eyes dropping but then coming back up, apparently by force of will.

My own eyes narrow. 'Go on.'

'The demonic essence.' De Monteguard waves an encircling hand at Isaac. 'Same as him. Gil's "possession" still left him with the taint of demonic essence clinging to him, just as with your other friend here. They both still reek of demons to anyone with the ability to smell it.'

Which is why it was a hassle to get into mine with Isaac

and Gil. The front door wards didn't like the taste of either of them due to the lingering demonic energy. I swing my attention across to the one of our party who definitely falls into that category. 'Demon reek? Damn, well it's a shame we don't have a *demon who can tell such things apart!*'

'I told you, mano!' Mephy's practically whining now. 'Told you I could smell the residual energy on them, even if I couldn't tell much more about it. Plus I was looking for Caacrinolaas. Confirmed he wasn't still there.'

'You didn't tell us there was another fucking demon in him!' Okay, I'm doing more than my fair share of shouting here, and Meph's catching it in the neck. But Gil's gone, and Isaac's looking on the verge of collapse. All of this could have been avoided if we'd been able to pick this up before we got caught up in the battle with Caacrinolaas.

'Sabnock hid himself away under that smell.' De Monteguard waves a tired hand at me, a calming motion, one telling me – in the kindest possible manner – that it's not Mephy's fault and I am, once more, being a dick. 'He tidied himself into a tiny secret section of Gil's soul until it was time for him to seize control.'

My thoughts go back to Benedict, my best friend from my first life, who turned resentful monster. He trapped Isaac's brother, Jakob, and his angel-half, Nanael, inside a skull for centuries. He'd sealed his soul away in an object outside of himself so Nan couldn't recognise him after he reincarnated, couldn't realise that all of Jakob's lovers were the same person who was manipulating him, his plan of being an utter shit-sucking scumbucket having taken multiple life cycles.

With the lingering demonic traces hanging around on Gil, Mephy and Nithael would have been focused on making sure that the fuckwankle we knew about wasn't still in him. They wouldn't have been looking for another. In fact, Mephy specifically said he'd looked for the demon's signature when he bit Gil, as well as the weird weaponized essence that's apparently a distilled dead demon. Fuck, that was genius, which is shit because I'd much rather face off against a fucking imbecile. Just for a change.

Mephy, however, has fixated on something entirely different. 'Sabnock?' The word is a half-bark of disbelief and disdain. 'Did you say Sabnock?'

De Monteguard looks at him directly for the first time. And with surprisingly little amounts of fear considering Mephy's hackles are up, and he's swollen in size slightly to go with it so that now he's like an uber-Dobermann, all bristling fur and bulging bunched-up muscles. Topped off with glowing red eyes, of course. Then again, he's been soul sharing with Caacrinolaas for a minute. Maybe he's used to this sort of behaviour from gigantic demonic hounds.

'That's right,' he says without even a shake to his voice, which is astounding considering the warning rumble of a growl coming from Mephy.

'Do you know him?'

Mephy doesn't even respond to me, just barks loudly enough I'm pretty sure the whole of Pont Neuf shakes, then slinks back and slumps down behind Faust's legs.

I'm about to go over to have a pop at him for having a sulk in the middle of a vital conversation when Nithael's safety is on the line, but Johannes saves me from having my head bit off –possibly literally– by crouching down for a brief murmured conversation. I can't hear what they're saying, but Faust's tone is gentle, low, soothing, and eventually, Mephy's growl modulates enough I'm sure he's speaking back even while maintaining that noise. Then the growling eases, and Mephy buries his head under his paws, covering his ears and eyes in the process, really committing fully to the whole "if I can't see or hear you, then I'm invisible" routine.

Meanwhile, Faust heads on over to us and sighs. 'He's embarrassed,' he says, nodding his head backwards towards the demon dog.

I scratch the back of my head. 'Embarrassed because he didn't spot Sabnock?'

Faust nods. 'Yes, Paul. The lack of noticing, this is sure, but also the other signs. Your friend Gil, for starters.'

I frown. 'That's what I just said.'

'No.' Johannes shakes his head. 'Not just the hidden presence within him. Also for how he was possessed.'

I'm wracking my brains, trying to work out what he means, but Isaac, half-dazed and distraught as he is, still gets there first. 'The worms?'

'Right!' Johannes nods emphatically. 'That. That is not a sign of Caacrinolaas.' He sighs. 'To be fair to Mephy, it's been a very long time – a very, very long time since any of the demons have interacted with humans so directly. If anyone should have spotted it, it should've been me. I'm far more familiar with the *Ars Goetia* than he is.'

'Of course!' Isaac slams his fist into his hand. 'Sabnock! Let me see…'

I can see him searching inside the incredible repository of information that is his brain. 'Ah, yes! *He can afflict men for several days, making their wounds gangrenous or filling them up with worms.* That totally fits the bill, lad.'

'He's had an affliction for a lot longer than several days, mano.' Apparently, the paws aren't completely blocking Mephy from hearing our conversation. 'That filling wounds with grubs and worms is his idea of a party trick should tell you everything you need to know about the mangy cur.'

'I take it you're not a fan of him, then Meph?' I ask wryly.

'Not at all! He's absolutely the worst of the worst.'

The worst of the worst of the demons. Fucking hell. This is bad news. 'In what way? How powerful is he? A sadistic nature? An all-consuming megalomania for dimensional control? What?'

'Worse than that!' Mephy's up now, pacing towards us, then away again, back and forth. 'Far, far worse than that! He's *sad*, mano!'

I blink, run that one back through the short-term memory tape deck to make sure I heard it right. 'Sad? As in, the opposite of happy?'

'Oh, sure!' Mephy's not stopped with his ranging up and down, and it's starting to set my teeth on edge. 'Sounds like nothing to you, does it? Someone being a bit sad? But we went to *hell*, mano! The best place in the whole of existence! All anyone could ever dream of. And he spends an eternity *sad*. "Oi, Sabnock, come fight to the death, then we'll get back up and go fuck some legs together." "Ohhh noooooooeehh."' Mephistopheles puts on a drawlingly morose voice. '"You go ahead, chapos. I will sit here, alone and miserable, for no happiness deserve I, not now or ever." Fucking hell, mano, it was like spending eternity with a Christopher Marlowe portrayal of a demon, and it was bad enough seeing that with my name on it once – *The Tragical History of Doctor Faustus,*' indeed just fucking tragic, full stop– let alone having to live with such melodrama for all of eternity. He's like a goth without a sense of humour. He's worse than fucking Morrisey. Fucking Sabnock!'

Well, apparently, it would seem that our enemy is the demonic equivalent of an overly serious New Romantic.

Chapter Thirty

TOULOUSE, 30 OCTOBER, PRESENT DAY

Sabnock? More Sadcock, according to Mephy.

It's eerily quiet in the streets. The interruption stirs a thought, one that makes me feel incredibly guilty for not having thought of it before. I stop dead, then turn to look at Phillipe. 'What about the unTalented? The residents of Toulouse? Who possessed them? Where are they now?' Because the Good God knows that would be just the sort of bullshit I'd expect the fucker to do. He already sacrificed his ally in the fight, stabbing him in the back – or stabbing him in the tether, but you know what I mean. Killing a fuckload of humans wouldn't even have given him pause.

'That wasn't Sabnock.' De Monteguard winces, his cheek muscles tensing, his jaw clenching as though the words themselves delivered an uppercut, slamming it shut. Then I remember. Caacrinolaas was his first ever friend. Then he got ring side seats to see what his so-called "friend" was prepared to do to the rest of his species just to slow us down a little. Or maybe not even that. Maybe just for shits and giggles. I've no idea.

It takes him a moment to get himself together, back under control. 'His connection to them would have been severed. I think they're back to being themselves.'

That's a great relief. For a moment. Then all the other questions start to hit. Do they remember what's been happening? To them? By them? Images of the citizens of my city coming to, blood-stained, broken, all those terrible traumas burning into their brain, the weight of the things they did, even if they'd no control whilst they did them?

There's no relief to be found in that.

There's also nothing I can do to save them right now. Nothing that will keep them safe except stopping the fucker who did this to them – or the mastermind behind it at least – and making sure he can never do anything so terrible to anyone ever again. Because there's no safety on offer – not for anyone, anywhere – while his plans are in motion.

Mephy's not been paying any attention to this conversation. Instead, he's still muttering rude names and growling about what a wanker Sabnock is over and over again.

I sigh. 'Okay, Meph, I think we get the picture. You don't like the guy.'

'No, you don't! You don't get it at all! Millenia of him whining incessantly. Never doing anything fun like killing people or torturing us until we screamed. No kinky sex or even any dirty fantasies uploaded into the collective wank bank –'

'You have a…' I shake my head, force my mouth closed. It'd be too easy to get distracted. 'Never mind.'

Mephy carries on like he was never even interrupted. 'There was this one time I caught him whipping himself. Giving his back a right good thrashing all the way down to the bone. I could see the white glistening in between the rasher-stripped flesh. Fantastic work. Really top notch.'

I've no idea where this story is going. Whether it's a punch line or a kick phrase or a headbutt of an onomatopoeia, but either way, I'm lost. 'I thought you said he didn't get kinky?'

'He didn't! It wasn't a sexual thing at all. He... He...' The huge demonic canine shudders as though a ghost has just given him a spinal massage with an ice cube. 'He *didn't enjoy it*.'

Mephy sounds utterly aghast, genuinely horrified. I'm even more confused than before. 'So why did he do it?'

'*Exactly*!' Meph nods emphatically, as if we're in complete agreement, which we may well be, but I'd still like to understand what the Good God we're agreeing on.

De Monteguard comes to the rescue. 'I think I can explain. It's very simple. Sabnock made the wrong choice.'

Oh. *Ohhh*. Now it makes sense. I turn towards the young man, who's still holding himself up in impeccable posture, even if his business suit's looking somewhat rumpled and dishevelled after his time possessed. 'Go on.' Best to get the details direct from the horse's mouth. And De Monteguard was ridden hard by Caacrinolaas.

He sighs, shaking his head. 'When the treaties were put in place between the angels and demons, everyone had to pick which way to go. Up' –he points a finger skywards, then swivels it down– 'or down.'

Oh. 'And he chose wrong, didn't he?'

'Yep,' Mephy says. 'He chose to head down with the demons. And about a second after we started our wild rumpus, he instantly regretted the choice. Flipping weirdo.'

I turn my attention back to De Monteguard. 'So what's with the team-up between him and Caacrinolaas?'

He smooths away at his suit lapel, although I can't help feeling it's more to feel the comforting physical presence of the high-quality material than from a hope of it becoming unrumpled. 'I really just got a jumble of emotions from Caacrinolaas towards Sabnock. He doesn't like him, not one bit, but it seems that Sabnock went recruiting among those he thought might join him. Those who felt they'd like another crack at their feathered rivals.'

'The fucking idiots of demon society, in other words, mano.' Mephy's voice is strange. You can hear he's trying for jovial, but it's forced, strained. I decide to come back to it later though.

'Anyhow, somehow he persuaded them he had a plan for getting to fight the angels. That thanks to your friends' actions' —he nods towards Isaac, who startles and blushes, obviously not having expected to become part of the story— 'an agent would be sent here, to our world, but that there was room to manoeuvre. That if contact could be made with a certain someone, which, apparently, meant my dearest father, then two others of their number could come here and attempt what he has planned.'

Now we're getting to the heart of the matter. 'Which is what?'

De Monteguard shrugs helplessly. 'I've no real idea. All I know is that it involves using an angel and a demon, binding them together with the sword. That's why he needs Joyeuse. Caacrinolaas expected him to use it on your two friends. Apparently, when you only showed up to fight with your angel, he decided to use Caacrinolaas instead.'

Mephistopheles' skin pales under that jet-black fur, and his eyes become so wide, he's lucky it's not night-time; else there'd be lost bugs flying straight into them, thinking they'd got lucky with some localised lunar guidance.

'He got them both? Nithael and Caacrinolaas? You didn't scare the coward off?'

Oh shit. Of course. We told them Sabnock grabbed Nithael. We didn't mention he'd double-crossed Caacrinolaas as well. I shake my head, then nod, then pause, not sure which question to answer first. But it doesn't matter because his gaze swings wildly from me to Faust, to Isaac, a whimpering whine escaping from between gritted teeth, his eyes wild. 'This is bad, manos. Really, really bad.'

Well, duh, Meph. We didn't realise that at all until you said it.

Chapter Thirty-One

TOULOUSE, 30 OCTOBER, PRESENT DAY

Just for once, could someone respond to a bit of unexpected news with, 'Oh brilliant, well that's super easy, barely an inconvenience'? That's how it works in the movies, after all.

'Okay,' I say slowly, trying not to let Mephy's panic infect me despite the fact that transmission is ridiculously easy –no need for sneeze-borne water droplets in this case– because whatever the situation is, it's enough to give a *demon the heebie-jeebies*. 'Why is it really bad that he's got both of them? Because, honestly, I wasn't thinking it was good to start with, but you're starting to freak me the fuck out right about now.'

Mephy spins in circles, his paws moving like some sort of quadruped Fred Astaire routine – if Fred had been hitting the old moonshine bottle a little hard. Possibly to the point where the homebrew had blinded him. 'It's worse than really bad, mano. Way worse! Way, way worse!'

'I don't need to do some sort of comparison to a

summer's day and count all the fucking ways right now, Mephy! What I need to know is why it's worse than really bad.' I hold up my hand to stall his next panicked diatribe. 'And in *specific ways*, please. Not just general portents of doom and despair if it's all the same to you.'

'Okay, so you've gleaned that we're not supposed to be here, right, Paul?' Oh shit. Mephy's not slowed down. He's still spinning, which is his whirligig equivalent of pacing the room, I reckon. But he never calls me Paul. Not directly. It's always "mano". If he's using my name, I'm not going to like what he has to say. 'Neither me nor Sabnock nor Caacrinolaas nor your angelicos either, mano.'

'We've been over all this before, Meph! Just get to the point!' By the Good God, I wish Aicha was here. She'd smack him upside the head and force him to get on with it.

'The *point* is that before their arrival, we could only pop down in a little visitation without breaking the accord the angels wrote up. Pop up for a few seconds in a puff of incorporeal smoke to fuck with some manos, then pop off back home. Impart a little forbidden knowledge. Send people off in a certain direction –'

'Directing the action!' My anger increases on behalf of my whole species for the longest of times. 'You told me it was like TV. That you only watched for enjoyment. But you're telling me you all come here to get the scene moving in the direction you want it to?'

'You're right, mano.' Mephy sounds totally done in. 'We gave you fire so you'd hurry up and light the pyrotechnics. The angelicos were the same. They'll just never admit it. They'll say they were doing their best for the species. Trying to get them to enlightenment, to elevation so you, too, could break these physical, dimensional shackles. But the point is...'

Mephy manages to give a weak grin that'd be enough to scare a rabid Rottweiler into sitting calmly and shaking paws with a trainer. 'Nobody else wants to stay here. Want to watch this dump for a laugh? Sure. But live here? No fear!'

I can feel my confusion-fuelled ire rising once again, but a hand rests on my shoulder, soothing me slightly. I look back to see Isaac shake his head and point a finger at Johannes, who's whispering something softly into Mephy's ear. And I realise the demon dog is shaking, shivering uncontrollably.

Mephistopheles is terrified.

'That's the problem, mano,' he says through chattering teeth. 'None of them want to be here. But what if we're forced to be?'

Oh, fuck me. Fuck me very, very much.

Chapter Thirty-Two

This doesn't just sound ominous. It sounds omino-everyone.
And omino-everything. Omino-ever.

'Forced to be?' Isaac's hand squeezes my shoulder. Glancing
over, I see he's no longer full of that wonderful, gentle kindness that let him spot Mephy's fear. It's being driven out by
his own, by an uncomprehending panic. He looks at me, his
eyes pleading for an answer that'll soothe it. 'How can
anyone force all the angels and demons to be here, lad?'

I know what he really means. He means "has what I did
all those years ago doomed us all?" He wants me to tell him
it'll be okay, that his academic curiosity isn't the reason the
world is going to get fucked over by a Sadcock, but I've no
more clue than he does. So I look helplessly over at Mephy.
'How?'

'Look!' The hound's up and pace-spinning again, his
agitation clear. 'Before you make a major change to your

system on your computer, like putting in a new hard drive or something, what do you do?'

'Give it to a PC technician at a shop?' I am good at many things. A man of wide and varied skills and capabilities. I still know better than to meddle in the dark arts of IT.

'You back it up,' says the quiet voice at my shoulder, probably just in time to stop Mephistopheles from exploding into a cloud of frustrated demon dust at my utter pigheaded, obstinate ignorance. 'Make a copy to keep it safe.'

'Thank you!' The relief in Mephy's voice is palpable. 'You copy all the data so you can restore it if it all goes tits up during the new installation.'

'So, what...' I scratch my head, the metaphor slowly starting to penetrate my thick skull. 'They have a recovery copy of reality?'

'Yes!' Mephy nods so hard, it's amazing he doesn't give himself whiplash. 'What we were trying... Well, it was theoretically perfect, absolutely one hundred percent certain to work. But we all know how theory is, don't we? So we wanted an undo if it all turned to shit when we hit execute.'

An idea strikes me. 'And the undo button is if you combine together an angel and a demon?' It seems pretty dramatic, but there you go. Then again, we're dealing with beings who consider human evolution as a bit of light evening entertainment.

'No, not quite.' Mephy stops, then looks at me. 'But you can only get to the undo button by doing that – metaphorically speaking, of course. It's not actually going to be a big red button marked "undo" that appears in the sky. Stop looking at me like that, mano. I know that's precisely what you thought was going to happen.'

'Shit.' De Monteguard's tone is grim. He's discovering

that solving puzzles when rolling around in the Mystery Machine with the Bonhomme Gang doesn't lead to happy endings, just further horrible fuckeries to deal with. And no hilarious rubber faces to rip off in the big reveal. Just, you know, actual faces getting ripped off.

'That's it.' Mephy nods emphatically again and plumps back on his haunches. Apparently, sheer terror makes him alternate between frenetic exercise and utter exhausted collapse. 'I can't imagine how he'll manage to get them to bond willingly or if he's come up with a clever way to do it against their will. But if he manages it?'

I can fill in the rest. 'He can bring all three realities back here. Combine the three dimensions and fill our world with angels and demons all over again.'

'And then the battle starts up again. Fancy joining one of our armies, mano? Ha, jokes on you. There's no choice. Everyone's going to get conscripted. Every single being, whether they want to or no.'

I'm trying to get my head around this. Which, to be fair, isn't my usual approach, which is more to headbutt a problem straight on until I get my head through it instead. 'But why would it mean everyone has to start fighting again? Surely none of the angels or demons *want* to be here? So just, you know...go back?'

'You want us to make carbon dimensional copies and then readjust them to our own specific preferences again, mano?' It's a shame that Mephy doesn't have eyebrows because considering how devastatingly sardonic his tone is, it really merits a single raised, pointed eyebrow to go with it. 'Do you know how long that took? How much energy and effort we had to put in? Plus, do you think anyone is going to be pleased to find out their own personal nirvana just got smooshed together with their idea of hell – which, of course, is heaven for us, but you know what I mean – and purgatory, which is where you live –sorry, but it's true– all at the same time?'

'People are going to be right upset, lad.' Isaac's sounding more worried now and ironically more focused with it. When he was just hurting for himself, he could afford to be lost in his pain. Now, this is bigger than his own individual suffering. There's too much at risk for him not to be razor-sharp. 'And people are going to blame us. Me and Nithael.'

'And your brother and his angelico, but yes, effectively.'

'But it was Sabnock who made it happen!' This all seems damnably unfair to me.

'Right. But he could only stay because the angelicos added in their little bit of cheat code so they could stick about. You're right though. That'll be the answering accusa-tion from the other side.'

'And then everyone starts pointing fingers and blaming the others.' De Monteguard shakes his head before looking at the panicked demon dog. 'Are you sure you actually evolved to a higher state of existence than humanity? Because all of this is painfully familiar.'

Possibly literally in his case, considering his dad spent his entire life weaponizing him. Mephy doesn't take it personally. 'A lower state, in our case, but yeah, it's debat-able at times. Point is, we found our own ways of living with what we love and avoiding what we don't. We demonicos created a realm where we could indulge our every desire and whim and live within it for eternity without ever any consequences… and without ever any contemplation. The angelicos created a place of pure thought and conscious-ness… by cutting themselves off from anything that might make them feel, letting their emotions wither and die. If you force us each to confront those things we detest about existence more closely, the chances are we might try to wipe each other off the map. We're more evolved than you. It doesn't mean we're better than you. Just better adapted. More powerful. And even more dangerous.'

The hound pauses, his head swivelling to look us each in the eye. 'Now imagine us all confused and angry and running amok in your reality.'

I consider his offer and then decide not to on the grounds that I'd like to be able to sleep again at some point in the future without waking up screaming in a cold sweat. 'Right, fascinating as this all is, I think we've got enough to go on for now. So what's the next step?'

'Time is of the essence.' Faust straightens up, brushing down his trousers as he does so, a determined look in his eyes. 'I doubt Sabnock would have revealed himself unless he felt confident in his timeframe, especially with us still in the mix.'

'Agreed. But where in the Good God's name do we start looking? He could be anywhere!' I can feel my frustration bubbling away, threatening to boil over. 'Fuck my life. Just once it'd be useful if we could just get a sign. Something to lead us to where we need to go.'

'Paul, my lad…' Isaac's voice quavers, but this time I don't think it's from grief. 'Since when was Minas Morgul a tourist attraction in Toulouse?'

I turn to see him pointing a shaking finger, but he doesn't need to. I can see it. A huge cylindrical tower marked by gothic window frames, like a straightened *Through-The-Looking-Glass* version of the Tower of Pisa, now stands, as far as I can tell, smack bang in the centre of the city. It's enormous, skyscraper height, the top lost in cloud swathes, greyed sky fabric that only adds to the ominous sense of it.

'*His office is to build high towers, castles, and cities...*' Faust's voice is little more than a whisper, and I know he's just as shocked as I am. Though without the same thrill of horror that runs through my veins at seeing more open magic worked, more damage wrought on our secret long kept from the Talentless, combined with the scarring of the place I call my own. Toulouse is being marked, harmed, possibly irreversibly. And the same might be said about the rest of the world too.

I recognise the quote as well. I'd have pretty much wasted my time studying under history's greatest demonologist and the only actual manifest demon ever if I couldn't spot a line from the *Ars Goetia*, after all, even if I severely doubt that Solomon ever did anything close to capturing and taming one demon, let alone seventy-two of them.

I remember the next line too though. 'And to furnish them with armour, et cetera.'

So to get to Sabnock and rescue Nithael, we're going to have to fight our way through a magically-created, heavily fortified tower. And I'm betting Sabnock's set himself up right at the top, like some sort of video game villain, happy to watch us fight our way up to him through all the armoured defences.

But it's not the armour that worries me most. It's the et cetera. Because I've no idea what such a worryingly non-specific term might be hiding.

I'm simply prepared to bet it's not a golden ticket and a tour round a chocolate factory. Though it might be just as potentially fatal.

Chapter Thirty-Three

*Magical towers sprouting up in the centre of the city? Sadly,
I don't think it's because someone's been selling the town
planners a bag of concrete magic beans.*

The streets are quiet as we pick our way off the bridge and
up towards Esquirol. It's the same route we took when we
went to look for Franc after having visited the shizzard's
house, which seems so long ago. At least until we reach it
and turn up towards the Capitole, using the looming tower
as a navigation point. Even when the roads narrow, the
crowded overhangs of the Regency-period architecture
can't blot it out completely.

I give Isaac my phone, tell him to ring around to all our
allies, the ones who were supposed to show up for the battle
back at Bugarach but got stalled by the demonic barrier. I'm
getting him to do it for two reasons. One, because I think it's
good to give him something to focus on, to feel useful and
productive right now. And two, because I've a sinking

feeling in the pit of my stomach, one that only seems to be getting heavier, dragging at my spirits each time I catch sight of that impossible tower. A feeling that turns out to be entirely justified.

'No joy, lad.' I am utterly unsurprised to hear those words. It somehow doesn't make them any easier to hear.

'What? Why?'

Isaac sighs. 'The Sistren have been waylaid. Bordeaux is under attack by some sort of huge sea dragon that's just reared up off the coast. It's taking all their power to keep it from being noticed by a very jittery French navy. The Mother said she thinks it might be an isabit.'

An isabit – or the Isabit as I think there is only one, is a massive medieval serpentine, a ravenously hungry water-dragon thing from the Pyrenees, over by Isaby. Supposedly, the lake there was formed when it was made to swallow a white-hot metal barrel, and it exploded after having drained a nearby river. So either the myth is exaggerated –often the case– or there's more than one isabit out there, and they can live in both freshwater and saltwater.

'Leandre?' I ask grimly.

'Can't or won't come. He says he's trying to control the media. Stop all those images of Toulouse getting out. Especially now the demon barrier is down and the news crews can get in. All his resources are in play as damage control. Including Al-Ruhban.'

Fat lot of good that'll do us if the world gets destroyed in the meantime. But I get it. If the world doesn't get destroyed – and so far, that's how it's played out each time – then the Talented world not getting revealed might avoid the next cataclysmic event happening. A Talented vs Talentless war. At least for a little while longer.

'Gwendolyne?' I can't help it. My gut might have expected this, but the desperation is creeping into my voice.

'The Cagot...' His voice falters. He takes a breath and tries again. 'The Cagot are dying.'

'What?' Fucking hell. I didn't expect that. The Cagot may have mistreated me in many ways, but they're still, thanks to my short-lived marriage to Susane, the closest living thing I have to family. I'm surprised by how much the news hurts. 'Is it... is it connected? Or is it Oberon?'

Part of me thinks that's what it is. And that it's probably my fault. After all, I hijacked a Cagot body to follow Susane through their portal to Faerie before threatening Oberon and all the Summer Court with a homemade explosive jacket. I very much doubt I'm his favourite person right now. And Gwendolyne told me the time of the Cagot – or at least the time as them being the eyes of Oberon in our world – is drawing to a close. Perhaps as a spiteful move, he's just cut them off dead. Literally.

'Connected, lad.' It's a shit thing that the thought relieves some of the pressure on my heart. Although I then remember that this current situation is because of my actual family – Isaac, my father in all but blood. So the mess still lands on our doorstep. 'Unless an evil Basque spirit attacking the primary group by Bilbao is a coincidence. She thinks it's Gaizkiñ, but she's not tracked the creature down yet. Right now, she's too busy trying to keep those afflicted alive.'

I wrack my brains, but I can't remember anything about Gaizkiñ other than that it's supposed to be like a djinn, invisible to see, a maleficent creature that spreads diseases for shits and giggles. Not that we need to know much else right now. Gwen's not coming. One more down.

'The Caliburc?'

'Didn't even answer. I'll keep trying.'

My blood runs cold. I don't even want to know what might be powerful enough to take the Caliburc out of the game. There's a part of me that's hoping it's just because he's forgotten his phone or left it on silent or something. But not a very big part. I've never been brilliant at optimism.

'Craig?' I'm running out of ideas.

'He…'

Oh, Good God. Now I'm really worried. The Magus of Blackburnshire, in England, doesn't deserve to be caught up in my mess, doesn't merit whatever ill has befallen him for our paths having crossed and him having taken a fancy to me.

'He saw the news. Wanted to come and help. But he… he fell asleep at the airport. Apparently, he "smoked a proper large doobie" –whatever that means– passed out while waiting, and missed his flight. Said to say, "Sorry, like, lass," and that he'll make it up to you "big time" apparently. I think he's planning to catch the next flight, but I've no idea when that'll be.'

I breathe more easily again. My feelings might not be quite the same towards Craig as his are towards me, but he's a genuinely lovely bloke, and I'd have hated to see anything horrible happen to him. Part of me's glad he's missed the plane, glad he's clear of this absolute shitshow. Plus, I doubt there'll be many planes landing in Toulouse Blagnac right now with all the chaos going on in the city.

And that's it. All the list of allies I can think of. All the people I might reach out to who might've reached us in time. But it doesn't matter. Because after winding our way through the narrow streets, we finally break out into the widening space of Rue Léon Gambetta, and now I know where we're going. Because I can see the destination, stretching skywards from behind the bright white-and-blue boards, the history of the College Pierre De Fermat written on them just in front of us.

Sabnock didn't take the Capitole as I thought he might. No.

He's taken the Couvent Des Jacobins. The ancient Jacobean Convent. He's dragged it off into the clouds atop a tower that looks, now that I'm closer to it, like it might be made of ancient polished ivory. Or that it might be made of newly bleached bone, although what creature you'd need to kill to hollow out one of their bones and punch pointed, glassless, gothic window holes into it, I don't know. I also don't know which I'd rather meet less. Said creature. Or the being capable of killing it.

There's a doorway in front of us. No actual door. That'd ruin the whole creepy gigantic skeleton tower aesthetic the fucknubble at the top is clearly going for. I mean, don't get me wrong, it's very metal, but I'm not about to award style points to the arsehole who's kidnapped my friend. Perhaps you might argue whether Nithael *is* my friend – it's not like we hang out and chat while sinking a few pints. But in a way, we do. Because he's always with Isaac. He's a part of him; two became one in a way that a certain shitty British girl band from the nineties would be in hysterics over. And there's no one more important to me than Isaac. Not even myself. In fact, definitely not myself. I come a long way down that particular list. But Isaac is sitting at the top.

Through the wide-open arched doorway —and by the Good God, the heating bill for this place must be a *nightmare*— a stairway curves up out of sight, looking like it's made of the same polished, bone-like material. I wonder if he has an army of lesser demons whose sole purpose is to keep the place spick and span and how much polish they must get through on a daily basis. Then I hope desperately that he doesn't have any help because battling through an army of lesser demons is going to be next to impossible even if they're only armed with cleaning spray and Brillo pads.

'So...' I peer into the structure, which, thanks to the plenitude of window holes and the off-white colour of the material, is surprisingly bright and breezy for a terrifying, evil villain's HQ. 'What do we reckon?'

'Steps all the way up, with a continuous curve based on the structure's external curvature,' Faust says, stroking at his beard.

Mephy sniffs at the entrance. 'The place is fucking with my sense of smell, mano, but there are scents. I just can't identify them. Nor am I likely to be able to use them to spot threats ahead of time.'

'Okay, so he's accounted for your form in this realm. And there's probably threats waiting for us on the way up.' I curse mentally but keep it inside. We're all enough on edge, and really, I shouldn't be surprised he's taken steps to nullify our capabilities. He hasn't pursued us through the centuries in an endless hate-fuelled vendetta like De Montfort did, but he's still a mind-fuckingly powerful being from another dimension who's had access to all of De Montfort's, no doubt, meticulous notes and research. He'll have been ready for us since the get-go. Plus, the allies of his that we've already encountered: the Warabouc, the simiots, the Karn-abo, tells us just what sort of calibre of beings he's been recruiting.

This is going to get messy.

Chapter Thirty-Four

TOULOUSE, 30 OCTOBER, PRESENT DAY

'Sabnock, Sabnock, let down your hair.' Not because I trust myself to clamber up the outside of the tower more than I do to climb the steps, but because then it'd hurt like fuck for you every step I took, yanking on your roots.

I'd love to say that inspiration strikes me, that a moment of genius comes like a bolt from the blue, and I see through all of Sabnock's plans – the way we can walk that'll bring us safely past his defences and into his inner sanctum.

But I've no idea. Not a scooby. I'm at a total loss. And looking at the faces in front of me, I'd be surprised if it isn't the same for them.

Before we go up though, there's something I need to do. I turn to De Monteguard. 'Go.'

He screws up his eyes, one of those elongated blinks when it's like we're trying to squeeze our brains into working. The equivalent of a thump on the side of the machine. 'What? Why?'

A half-chuckle escapes my lips despite my sense of humour having gone on possibly permanent hiatus. Possibly permanent because I might not be living for very much longer. 'Listen, this wasn't your fault. You tried to make it right. You've given us all the information you can. But that's it. We're square. You don't owe us anything, and there's nothing you can do here that will help.' I pause. 'Except die.' I pause again. 'Which wouldn't actually be very helpful, so scratch that interjection I just made to myself. The original point still stands.'

De Monteguard doesn't budge. In fact, if anything, he looks more resolute. 'No. He is… he was my friend. My responsibility. I've enabled what happened even if I didn't really understand that at the time. I'll see this through to the end.'

I want to argue, but I don't have time. Besides, he made his choice. Unlike the demons and the angels, I'm not going to direct him into doing something he doesn't want to do.

Even if he is being an idiot choosing to come with us.

So I turn back to the tower. There might not be a door in the doorway, no solid oaken planks to block our passage, but it doesn't mean we can just saunter in, of course. The whole place pulses with demon *talent*, and there's a ward across the doorway. I've no idea if it's just the equivalent of a doorbell or if it'll zap us into our component atoms the moment we step over it. But before I can say anything, Mephy and Faust begin their investigation. It's more their area of expertise than mine, so I sink down onto my haunches, my head down, and stare at the large cobble in front of me. I take a second to breathe, to try to get my head back in the game.

'Are you all right, lad?' Isaac's voice is as gentle as ever, albeit wavering more. He sits down next to me slowly, folding his legs under himself.

'I'm fine, 'Zac.' I'm not, of course. There's no way anyone could possibly be fine. We're walking into what may well be our doom. What may be the end of our species or at least of our freedom. If we don't get this right, the whole of humanity and every other sentient *talented* being on the planet is going to become the frontline cannon fodder of a war that'll make the imagery of the book of *Revelations* look tame in comparison. This first skirmish in Toulouse – the whole mind-controlled madness we saw unleashed through the streets of my city – will be repeated globally. Free will eradicated. Just fight and die for our new other-dimensional overlords in a meaningless war. Hope that in a few millennia, they draw a truce once more and fuck off back to their own planes of existence, and there's enough of us left to start over with making a society. It'll take us right back to the Dark Ages. If we survive. If the planet survives.

'A climb ahead. An enemy who's waiting for us. Threats along the way.' Isaac's words are low in volume but tremulous. I wonder if his thoughts are mirroring mine. It does seem reminiscent of arriving at the foot of Bugarach, knowing De Montfort wanted us to go to him, having no other choice but to fight our way up to face him.

Isaac's hand wraps around my bicep and pulls down so I look across. He's leaning on me, and I can feel the heat of his hand through my jacket. He's pale, sweat beading on his forehead, his lips whitening even as he fixes me with an intense gaze. 'Poor Jak. It's so hard... so hard for him. Don't make him go. Don't make him climb up there. It's too high... too high a price to pay, lad. My boy, my lad, the paths aren't for him. He can't... can't carry that burden. Don't make Jak go, lad, please.'

His lips keep moving, but his words stop. Isaac continues pleading with me through his wide staring eyes.

Then he topples forward into my arms.

Chapter Thirty-Five

No. Good God, no. Take me but not him. He's the one
worthy of life. I'm the one who deserves to die.

'Faust! Mephy!' My voice cracks on the last syllable, panic
pitching my voice up. The two of them stop whatever
they're doing regarding the wards and are by my side in a
second. Not that I see what they're up to. My eyes are fixed
on the man in my arms.

'He's burning up!' Isaac's eyes are closed. Sweat's
cascading down him now. His lips are still moving soundlessly. And the heat is pouring off him, radiating so that I
don't even need to put my hand to his forehead to feel it.

Faust does though, laying his hand there. I look up at
him. He has his eyes closed, and I know he's trying to help,
so I bite back my urge to scream at him to *help faster*, to *do
more* because I know he'll do everything he can, that he's
going as fast as is possible, but I'm on the verge of panicking
properly, of completely losing it, and only the frail form

cradled in my arms whose chest still heaves up and down erratically keeps me from breaking completely. *He's not dying; he's not dying; he's not dying,* keeps going over and over in my mind, a soundtrack on forced repeat to stopper the screams bubbling up in my throat.

I see Johannes push a little of his *talent* into Isaac, and it's a good thing it is Johannes because if it were anyone I didn't trust implicitly with my life who was interfering magically with 'Zac? Right now, in my panicked and hyper-stressed state, I'd be likely to explode their head on instinct. Whatever it is he's doing – and I'm way too distracted to focus on the intricacies of whatever working he's pulling off – seems to work, at least a little. Isaac's lips still, and some of the strain in his face eases.

His eyes don't open though.

Faust wipes at his own brow as he turns to me. His face has none of that custom joviality to it as he sighs. I can't help noticing he's looking at me but not in my eyes, which only ratchets my panic up another notch.

'I was afraid of this, Paul.' That I do not grab him and shake him until his eyeballs rattle inside his skull at the vagueness of *'this'* is fortunate for both of us as it stops him having his eyeballs rattled inside his skull and me from getting my hands bitten off by Mephy.

Somehow, summoning every drop of patience I've ever neglected when I've gone charging in like a bull in a china shop, I wait and let him speak.

'The severing of the cord. It is… wearing on him.'

'But...' I start, searching for a hole in his logic. I wave a hand at De Monteguard. 'He's okay! He doesn't look like he's about to keel over any second! Why not?'

Why 'Zac? is the inference, of course. I may have forgiven De Monteguard for having the bad luck to be his father's son, but it doesn't mean I wouldn't switch him into Isaac's place in a single heartbeat if it meant I'd have the man, pale and drawn and fragile, laid out on the pavement back on his feet.

'Because it hasn't been the same investment. The same time. The same love.' Faust sighs again, scratching absent-mindedly at his sable sideburns. 'Our friend here may have bonded, but those two have grown to be something much more over the centuries. They have become very much one being in many ways. Trust me, I understand.'

Mephy nudges up against Faust's leg, and without think-ing, Faust drops his hand to him, scratching behind his ears. I can see the reassurance both of them draw from the act. And they don't even share a body. Isaac and Nith were soul-bound for nearly a millennium. Now they've been sundered, divided into half. And half of anything doesn't live for very long. Unless they're earthworms, of course. Well, certain types of worms. In most, the head end dies while the tail regenerates. Isaac told me that...

A second later, the tears are pouring down my face, and I'm not sure if I'm crying at the memory of all the knowl-edge Isaac has given me or at wondering whether he's the head or the tail here.

Faust pulls me in, an arm around mine, dragging me to his barrel of a chest and wrapping me in his embrace, letting me sob against him. Even in centuries of life, there are few men I've trusted enough to be able to cry in their arms. Three perhaps. One of them holds me. One died before I became immortal; I can't even remember his face anymore. And one took his place in my next life as Father and lies unmoving on the floor at my feet.

I pull myself back and wipe at my eyes with the back of my sleeve. 'Is he going to die, Jo...?'

'I don't know.' Faust doesn't lie to me. He never would. It's one of the reasons I trust him. 'He's dying. That much I know. How long he has is not clear. If we were to get him to his angel, reattach the tether between them...' He shrugs again, not unkindly, and this time he does keep eye contact, lets me see his sympathy, lets me see he's sorry. 'Perhaps. Perhaps it will save him.'

Perhaps. Not a lot. Not from a scholar like Johannes Faust. I can hear the doubt in his voice. He fears it's already too late, that the damage has been done. But it's enough for me. Enough to let me pull myself back together, to stop the terror that's already setting in, choking the air in my throat, crushing my chest, making a night hag of grief as it wraps its legs around me, threatening to never let go. I can fight it back, push it down. Get myself together enough to go on, to not collapse next to the man who's given me everything of value since my first death. Education. Purpose. Understanding. A place. Love.

I can give him this much.

'Mephy.' My voice croaks, but the word is audible, steady. I'll take that. 'Where are you with the ward?'

'Neutralised, mano.' I concentrate on the words, on what they mean. I ignore that undercurrent of sympathy that's agonising to hear, that might just bring me to my knees if I let myself hear it. 'He knows we're coming, of course, but they'll not fry us on entry. We can go whenever you're ready.'

'Now.' I'm ready. I stoop to cradle the still form to my chest, to lift him gently in my arms, but a hand on my arm stops me.

'Allow me, Paul.' Faust's close enough I can smell that sweet aniseed tang to his breath, and I want to shake my head hard, to shout at him that this is my job, my honour, but he's clearly not finished speaking, and I'll do him the service of hearing him out. 'I am not so much use when it comes to the fighting, and you know this to be true. My part? Is lending what strength I have to my dear Mephy should he need it. When the battle meets, and meet it will, my friend, it is better if you have your hands free than me. You two –' He breaks off on seeing De Monteguard draw his own sword, a cutlass-style blade that I have no doubt he got from his father. If he'll use it to fight by my side now though, for Isaac's sake, I'll not turn it down.

Faust nods, continues, 'You *three* will be far more effective than I, who will need time and space for anything I might manage to perform. Allow me to aid in this way. Give us the best chance we can.'

He's right, of course. The Good God damn it, he's right. So against my every instinct, my every desire to carry that limp, frail form myself, I nod. Step back. Turn away so I can't see another stand stead for me in my duty. I fix my eyes on the bleached gothic monstrosity that's taken root in my city.

I don't say anything more. Just reach between reality and draw my own blade from my etheric storage. Then I walk towards the doorway.

There's an answer up there. An answer for Isaac. The world can burn, but there's a way to save him up those steps…

The Good God help anyone who gets in our way.

Chapter Thirty-Six

TOULOUSE, 30 OCTOBER, PRESENT DAY

> I feel like I've wandered into a Jeff Smith comic. But I'm
> not sure this is Phoney Bone I'm walking on.

Bone. It only takes me a few steps to be sure that we're
definitely walking on bone.

There's something deeply disturbing about bone being
in shapes it shouldn't be. Trust me here. After my recent
escapades involving the not one but two *talent*-infused skele-
tons, I know magical bones. This is something else.

The closest thing I can compare it to is the pedestal Ben
made for the skull he trapped Jakob and Nanael in, right
back when all this recent bullshit kicked off, with the
enforced quest for the Veil of Veronica. Those looked like
they'd been steam-bent, the bones treated till they could be
woven around each other.

If you took one of those twisted femurs, supersized it
with one of Rick Moranis' inventions, then somehow

replaced the marrow inside with more bone, which you painstakingly carved into an elegant staircase, really digging it out to make the enormous vaulted ceilings overhead before getting into the fiddly bits like the ornate pointed window frames and the interior walls that gleam under the daylight, which you somehow get to chill on entry and seemingly congeal and pool on the whitened surface? Then you might get something that looks not entirely unlike where we are.

Of course, I don't really care how Sabnock made it. I only care about what might be waiting for us. In the tower. And at the top.

I take point, leading, my blade raised, my eyes scanning the half-gloom ahead. Isaac's words ring in my ears. The last ones before he went, his half-muttered ravings about his brother Jakob. But also the others just before, when he pointed out the similarity between this and our climb up Bugarach. A cunning, uber-powerful enemy waited for us at the pinnacle, knowing we were on our way while unknown threats lurked on the way up to waylay us, to slow us down at best. To kill us at worst.

I don't want to die. Don't want to slow down either. I want to be at the top already, Sabnock dispatched, Isaac back in peak form, smiles and hugs all round before we retire back to the pub for a few swift bottles of whatever spirits we can lay our hands on. Then maybe I can even dream about getting back to the hunt. About looking for those we lost on that last climb.

This climb we can't lose anyone. We can't. Not again. Please, not again.

I'm so focused on what's ahead, I almost miss what's at my feet, but just as I'm about to walk past it, to climb over that particular step, something catches in the sunlight. My hand shoots up, my palm out flat, and everyone screeches to a halt.

Bending over, I realise almost immediately what it is. A small circular band of metal, silver maybe, white gold or platinum possibly though, sits nestled in the corner of the stairs, almost camouflaged by the off-white background. It doesn't take much *looking* at it to see the *talent* radiating from it either.

I beckon Mephy forward, and we bend over it.

'Demon origin?' I hiss as quietly as I can.

He shakes his head, and I curse. For a moment I dared to hope we'd stumbled into *Lord Of The Rings* territory and this would be the source of his power, slipped somehow from his finger, but that would be too much to ask, really.

There's another pressing question. 'Is it dangerous?' I can see that it's magical, but what that magic does, I've no idea whatsoever.

Mephy snuffles at it, using some sense that doesn't normally exist in our world. Or perhaps it does. Perhaps all dogs can smell magic. We've just never trained them to show us they can.

Eventually, he lifts his muzzle. 'Not that I can tell. Not immediately anyhow. You can pick it up without it rotting your hand with necrotic plague or it making your balls burst a second later, put it that way.'

I kind of wish he hadn't put it that way because it fills my head with the images of something causing those exact things to happen, neither of which are things I ever want to experience, especially when I don't know if I can swap this body out for a new model if it all goes tits up. But I get his meaning, and there's one thing I'm sure of. There's no way I'm leaving a magic ring that's been dropped accidentally for someone else −like one of our enemies− to come and pick up instead. And if Mephy tells me it's safe, even if he tells it to me in the most distressingly vivid way possible, then I believe him.

So I pick it up, albeit using a hankie I pull from my storage. The mental images Mephy's infected my brain with insist on me not touching it with my skin. To my delight, no bits of me rot or explode, so I wrap it up in the handkerchief and stuff it in my pocket. I'm not sticking it in my etheric storage until we work out what it does. In the meantime, I want it in easy reach. Plus, I've no time to get into what it might do right now. Getting to the top is the priority.

'Any other ideas about it, Meph?' He shakes his head, and that's enough for me. We can poke and prod at the weird magical item later. Right now, there's a demonic cumbubbler to put an end to. I wave my hand forward, and we start back up the stairs one at a time.

It takes a while to climb. After about ten minutes, I'm wheezing, and it's only sheer bloody-mindedness and the terrible fear about the still form being carried behind me that keeps me moving. Apparently, I've been skipping on my cardio sessions. One to resolve when life stops kicking me in the nuts for shits and giggles every five seconds.

A moment later though, I throw up the 'stop' hand gesture again. Because just around the curve of the bend is something new.

There's a doorway leading into a room, with the very faintest view of the same slightly yellowed material walls inside.

My first instinct is to go on myself, to have a sneaky peek. But I promised I'd give up being reckless and suicidal for Lent, what with only having one body left maybe, possibly, so instead, I send the one who can slink silently, close to the floor, and who has the best senses. Oh, and also with demon magic a million times more powerful than mine. Which helps as well.

Mephy edges his way up, his belly pressed against the stairs, and peers around the doorframe. I lean back against the wall, glad to take a breather even if I'm simultaneously frustrated by the delay. A few moments later, he's back, descending in the same manner.

'Okay, it's a mostly empty room,' he says.

'Oh good,' I reply and then my mind replays what he just said. '*Mostly* empty?'

'Oh, yep,' he says breezily, 'mostly empty. Apart from the fuck-off, great, big blind cyclops sitting in there, covered in crackling black demonic energy.'

'Okay, Mephy, we need to work on where you put your priority in terms of information. That's slightly more important than the *rest of the room being empty*.'

Then I replay the rest of what he said. *A great, big blind cyclops.*

Well, slap me with an amphora and make me run a marathon in the nude.

Apparently, Sabnock's somehow summoned up Polyphemus for us to fight.

Chapter Thirty-Seven

Wondering if I can snap off both his legs and kill him with the two main bones. Death by Polyfemurs.

'Okay, I'm assuming nobody wants to fight Polyphemus?' I look around at the blank faces. 'Seriously? Nobody? Fucking hell, I make a classics joke for once, and it goes straight over the scholars' heads.'

'It didn't go over anybody's head, mano. It was just shit.' Mephy huffs in delight at his own twist of humour —mine was definitely better– but then turns serious. 'Anyhow, that's not Polyphemus.'

'Oh. Good.' I mean, that absolutely is good news. In the legends, Polyphemus was the son of Poseidon who ate those who strayed into his cave. Odysseus, a warrior explorer who got captured with his men, ended up persuading the cyclops that he was called Nobody, so that if his dad ever asked who did this, Polyphemus would say Nobody (see, I told you my joke was funnier!). But then Odysseus made the uncharacteristically stupid decision to shout his actual name as a parting jibe during his escape, and so he got fucked over for the best part of a decade by the god as revenge. I have no idea if the Greek gods exist —my guess is yes, probably, although they're not true gods, and I hope they've gone on to Tartarus for all eternity or whatever dimension they originally came from if they're real— but I don't need one of them pissing in my cornflakes every time my back's turned. I've Mephistopheles around for that.

That does still leave one important question though. 'If it's not Polyphemus, who is it?'

'Tartalo,' is the answer.

'Well, he should make sure he brushes between his bottom teeth as well!' Look, I know it's not the time to be making jokes. But centuries of using humour as a defence mechanism doesn't disappear overnight. The exasperated expressions tell me nobody's feeling my standup routine right now. Although, as they're not slapping me round the back of the head, they do at least understand why I'm doing it. That only makes me feel worse though because if Aicha was here, she'd understand *and* slap me round the back of the head. Does the fact I miss her physically beating me up make me a masochist?

'Seriously though,' I say once the painful silence dies down to only normal levels of lack of noise. 'Who's that?'

'Really, Paul? Between Isaac and me, we've really failed so badly in your education.' Faust tuts and shakes his head, which, considering how exhausted he must be after hauling an unconscious magician up hundreds of stairs, really shows how much fitter than me he is. And how dedicated he is to his sense of disapproval.

'Yep. Totally your faults.' Make it light. Make it a joke.

If I'm referring to them both, it means they're both still here.

'To be fair to you, Paul, the story is very similar. Tartalo is a story from Basque legend, a one-eyed cyclops who liked to kidnap passing humans to consume them as an alternative to his staple diet of sheep's milk and flesh.'

'So what you're saying is he was a criminal type? Presumably on the lamb?' I stare at them desperately. 'Look, I know, I get it. I'm sorry. I can't help it. Just ignore me, and I'll try to keep quiet.'

'*As I was saying*' –Faust's apparently taking my words to heart– 'he liked to kidnap and eat humans whenever he could. One day, he got his hands on two brothers who'd wandered into his cave. The older one he killed and ate the first night, but he kept the younger one as a tasty titbit for the following day. Well, this turned out to be unwise, for during the night, the boy drove a stake into his eye, blinding but not killing him.'

'So far, so very like the *Odyssey*.' My mind goes back to what Mephy said about recurring stories and the strange origins of them.

'Well yes,' Faust sounds distracted. 'But there were some distinct differences from thereon in. Paul, why did you put that ring on?'

'I didn't –' I start to say and then look down at my own hand. Apparently, the ring is more like the One Ring than we thought, and it slipped itself onto my finger at some point. 'Oh, would you look at that? Sneaky little pocketses. Let's...'

I go to pull it off, and my adrenaline spikes when it doesn't move. The definitely pensive look on Faust's face doesn't help either. 'What? What was the major difference?'

'Ah. Well. Yes. You see, the younger brother stole Tartalo's ring before blinding him and foolishly put it on…'

Hearing 'foolishly put it on' as a punchline for the story when I have just inadvertently, foolishly put on a strange ring we found is not good for my already panicking heart rate.

'And what,' I ask slowly, 'was it that then happened to this poor fucking idiot because of the ring he'd put on?'

Faust is about to answer when he's rudely interrupted. By a voice on my finger.

'Oy, you great, big lazy dunnyhead,' the ring shrieks at a volume loud enough to set a nearby church bell ringing in my head. 'I've gone and been nicked again, ain't I, you absolute waste of ownership! Stolen! Thieved away! And you just dozing like a useless dungmucker. Lawks!'

It's been several centuries since I heard anyone say 'lawks' in real life – or heard any *thing* say, I guess in the ring's case. But I don't have time to marvel at that strange bit of antiquated vocabulary. Because from a few feet above us, a rumbling roar, the bass tone to the ring's shrieking falsetto, starts up.

Looks like Tartalo's awake.

Gee, thanks, ring.

Chapter Thirty-Eight

In Middle Earth, does the existence of Sauron imply the
opposing existence of Sweetoff?

There're two options where this now entirely certain
combat can go down. One is in the room where Tartalo
currently is. The second is in the stairwell.

There are advantages and disadvantages to both. The
main disadvantage to the room is that we've no idea what it
looks like, apart from Mephy. He's told us it's empty –
discounting the ginormous man-eating cyclops, of course–
so it doesn't sound like a terrible option. The only other
problem is getting in there without getting squished in the
process.

The disadvantage with the stairs as a whole is they're
narrow, comparatively. Wide enough that Mephy and I can
stand and fight, but we'd be hampering any efforts from the
other two. Although that can also be an advantage
regarding Faust, keeping him and my unconscious mentor

safe. But the biggest disadvantage of the stairs for us is that we're below the doorway. Tartalo's going to have the high ground, which considering he's already going to be considerably taller than us to start with, is definitely bad news.

Mephy and I both reach the same conclusion about a millisecond after the ring shrieks and dash forward. It's only about twenty steps to the open doorway. We're splitting the party —I don't expect the same reactions from the others, and Faust's not about to dash anywhere, lumbered with dead weight— but De Monteguard can defend him if needs be. And I'm fairly certain, as the ring-bearer, that Tartalo's attention is going to be fixed on me.

Lucky me.

I'm thundering up the stairs, not even trying for subtlety. There's no point anyhow, considering the ring keeps hollering a series of insults, alternating between the cyclops ('you great blind stubtoe') and us ('thieving cockaninnies') at a volume and pitch close to making my ears bleed. The steps get eaten up as I pump my legs. I'm almost at the doorway. Five steps. Three. I'm taking them two at a time.

Luckily, I'm on the odd numbers because as I hit one, a billy club, knobbled and whorled in a way that suggests carving might not be Tartalo's main skill, slams out of the doorway, close enough as to almost take the tip of my nose off. I can't slow fully, so I twist my body, take the impact of the collision on my shoulder, and get my first view of the room and Tartalo in the process.

The room itself just carries on the "bare bones" motif, the same material leading up on all sides to the vaunted ceiling, a good ten metres above our heads. A huge window frame, the edges worked with gothic twiddly patterning, stretches almost the whole height. And in the middle of the room stands Tartalo.

He's not the biggest giant I've ever seen. But that's still subjective as he's more than twice my height, closer to three times, I'd reckon, maybe five or six metres tall. He's wearing a pair of shaggy woollen shorts that I'd bet are just sheepskin sewn together and is rocking the traditional giant fashion chic of a bare chest, although considering the rug of curly hair on there that's almost as thick as the shorts, I'd bet he doesn't feel the cold. Although perhaps the swirling demon essence he seems liberally painted in keeps him warm. He's not in shape, tending towards portly rather than ripped, but there's enough muscle underneath the fat to do plenty of ripping. Like our torsos from our pelvises. He's bald in a way that makes me suspect he's naturally hairless on his head, a gleaming pate in evidence. I can't imagine he shaves it daily, which'd be the only other method to get it so perfectly hairless. Considering the ruinous mess of an eye socket in the centre of his forehead – a blackened wound that tunnels inward, with fragments of the socket visible through the charred remains of his eye – that'd seem a recipe for disaster.

Mind you, maybe he has other senses to replace the lost one. The cyclops version of Daredevil. As opposed to an acrobatic defender of Hell's Kitchen with laser eyes. For that would be the Daredevil version of Cyclops.

Sadly, I don't think Tartalo's in the mood for a discussion about a *Defenders/X-Men* crossover. Nor is he as easily distracted as I am.

His club whips up as he rears back from the bent-over position he assumed after having slammed it down, nearly catching me on the backswing. I only survive it through my own senses screaming blue murder at me, enough so that I hurl myself to the left at the last second. The cunning bastard angles it as he comes back, and the club, thicker than my torso, whistles past my ear by mere centimetres.

He definitely knows where I am. Although I'm not surprised by that as the ring has taken full voice again and is screaming weirdly antiquated insults at both of us, like an X-rated version of a Statler and Waldorf commentary across the fight. Tartalo swings for the fences, his club aimed low ('Put your back into it, Blowsabella!'), trying to take advantage of me being off balance, but I'm ready for it. It's what I'd have done, after all. So I harden the air ('Call that magic, you addlepate?') just in front of me, two blocks a half-metre high each. I scramble up them and jump the swinging club like Mario. I feel the collision though as the bat hits what my *talent* made, and my creations collapse instantly.

Oh good. The cyclops's club seems to dispel magic. Fan-fucking-tastic.

I'm inside his aim now and expect him to pull off the same manoeuvre as last time, bringing the club back and wiping me out on the back stroke. Having gone left last time, I go right, and luckily so. Not because he does what I thought. No. He releases his double grip on the trunk-like weapon and slams his right fist down where I was standing a moment previous. The room shakes. Hell, the whole tower probably shakes. I'm astonished not to see stress fractures spreading ivy-like up all the walls. A scraping echo starting up is enough to warn me the club's coming back into play. Not as fast as when he held it in a two-handed grip, but based on the noise, I guess he's aiming to use it to squish me against the floor. I'm off-balance, with one knee down, and it's coming at a rate of knots, so I twist desperately and roll to the side, my blade up.

And that saves me. The club catches the edge of my

sword. The impact sends my arm numb instantly, changing an ordered spin into a flying sprawl. I can feel what it does to the metal even if I can't see it. The sword doesn't break, though I'm almost certain it's been ruined, bent by the glancing blow. But it's enough. ('You wave your prick like an unlicked cub!') The club might have crushed my sword, but it hasn't done the same to my internal organs. I have backup blades. Less so for my hearts and lungs.

A dark furred bolt shoots in, an almost blur that latches onto the fist on the ground. Tartalo cries out in pain and surprise and starts to pull his fist back. As he does so though, Mephy grows... for a moment. Then his shape wavers as he collapses back to his normal size. He lets go and lands by my side, spitting furiously.

'Fucking hell, mano,' he says in between attempts to apparently rid his mouth of all the saliva within it. 'That tastes *foul*!'

'I can buy that. He's a cyclops.'

'No, not him.' Mephy stops his spitting. 'Well, him too. But the stuff all over him. I could taste her. Eisheth. She was a friend of mine. Can taste the memories. The ending. Fucking hell, mano. I'm going to kill him for this!'

I'm pretty sure the "him" in question isn't Tartalo. But we're going to have to get past this challenge before we worry about the cuntstubble who did this to Mephy's friend, who harvested a fellow demon into this essence. We don't have time to discuss it any further because the cyclops has recovered from the shock of Mephy's bite and has taken up a two-handed stance on his club once again. The ring is still screaming abuse at all and sundry ('Cockscomb! Whoreson! You pair of mouldy rogues!'), so I've absolutely zero doubt which way it's going to be coming next.

But I'm sick of this. Sick of going on the defensive.

Sure, Tartalo's a big lad. But I've taken on bigger and uglier than him. For the Good God's sake, I fought the possible creator of the universe to a standstill. So I'm not going out on the end of a badly carved tree trunk to a blind cyclops. That's for chumps and Ithacan sailors. Me?

I'm ready to fight back.

Hardening the air above the club, I work to keep it out of commission by pinning it to the floor. Right now it's stationary, which means there's no momentum I need to stop at the same time. It might be able to dispel magic, but I'm hoping it needs force to do so.

Tartalo pulls up, and I can feel the working weakening the moment it touches the knobbled wood, but it holds, causing the cyclops to nearly fall over, which would be funny if I wasn't terrified he might fall on me, rendering the moment distinctly less amusing. His brow furrows, but he does what any self-respecting giant would do when finding their physical efforts thwarted; he doubles down.

The effort of keeping the surrounding barrier intact is immense, and I'm either going to burn through all my *talent* rapidly, or it'll crumble in seconds. But seconds are all I need.

Because, of course, as part of his effort to get his club back off the ground, he's wrapped both hands around the shaft and is heaving backwards like some oversized version of the sword in the stone, his muscles bulging... and both hands occupied. Plus, he's knees bent, leaning backwards, pushing against the floor, making it far harder for him to try to stamp on my head. Basically all four limbs are engaged.

And I'm a free agent.

The bent-up sword drops with a *clang*, and even as I'm closing the gap, my hand's passing through the world and out into my etheric storage, pulling out another. And you'd better believe I charge it the fuck up, crackling green *talent* running up and down the blade's edges, a localised firestorm covering every inch of the metal.

I close the distance as fast as I can, dipping right, keeping away from the club. I have an early warning system, sure. But when the magic gives, that club's going to be hammering my way like a guided missile. I mean, I might get lucky. Maybe it'll be like one of those old Warner Bros cartoons, where Tom steps on a rake, and Tartalo'll smash himself clean in the face with his club thanks to the momentum. But I'm not banking on it. Knowing my luck, he'll be like some sort of blind cyclops ninja, reverse the direction with a quick twist of the wrist, and bingo! One smushed Paul a second later.

So I keep clear and keep moving. Time's not on my side. Luckily, I don't have that far to go. Three metres. Two, and the sword is out and clear. Tartalo hears me coming, starts to let go of the club with his left hand, and I know there's a swinging backhand coming my way any second. But he's not quick enough. My sword's out straight in front of me, magic like a swirling furnace blazing off it, and I launch the blade straight at Tartalo's chest.

Then watch the blade crumple like paper on contact, the magic extinguishing as it does.

Looks like it's not only Tartalo's club that's magic-proof.

Fuck my life.

Chapter Thirty-Nine

Magic-proof giants? A Tarta-lo blow.

What I want to do right now is howl. Scream and yell at the unfairness of it all. I'm already facing the loss of my oldest friend, already facing off against a fucking demon. I outwitted a creature capable of deflecting all magic back on the caster. Hell, I just stabbed the fucking Karnabo through the back of his John Merrick face a few minutes ago. It doesn't seem unreasonable that I catch a break. But apparently, I now need to fight a magic-retardant cyclops who's also impervious to Mephy's attacks based on what happened last time my demonic friend sank his teeth in.

That's what I want to do. Howl. But I also want to live, so I don't.

I'm already off balance. I put all my weight behind that strike, really threw myself at Tartalo, and the momentum's still carrying me forward. Checking myself isn't easy. The only thing that helps me is the crumpling of the blade; it acts as a buffer, dispersing a part of the energy, allowing me to push myself back. Then it's a game of chance. Will the giant kick out at me? Swing that meaty fist back? Get his club free and go for a wider arc? Do I throw myself backwards? Dodge right? Any direction might mean safety or might mean a swift death. You pays your money, you takes your chances.

Being unpredictable seems to be the best chance of survival, so I do what I hope is the last thing he'll expect. I check myself _−hard−_ with the sword handle, wedging it against my abs in a way that's going to leave some beautiful bruises painted across it come morning, then dip left in towards the cyclops's arm. It's what I hope he'll consider the least likely direction for me to have taken but actually makes sense. He can't swing the club close enough nor backhand me easily. So my eyes are up as far as possible. A fist from above seems the most likely response.

It works. And I'm right. I see his hand shoot up not far above me. Now I duck left again, drop one knee, and lead with my shoulder. It's a risk, sure. I still have the ring calling everyone in the room 'bull's pizzles', and I'm pretty confident Tartalo's reactions are well honed based on his hearing. Hell, even without the ring, he'd have heard me drop and roll. But I'm relying on him being committed to his movement.

Based on the tremors flowing up through the floor to my teeth, I guessed right. A second later, I'm back on my feet and grabbing another sword out of my storage. Not that it'll do very much based on my last attempt, but at least it makes me feel better. Plus, now I'm back by Mephy, who's stopped trying to empty all the liquid out of his mouth onto the floor, although he still looks like he's been sucking lemons by the string-bag load.

'You okay?' Mephy's voice is little more than a whisper, not enough to draw Tartalo's attention our way. I'm glad it's him who's asking me. I came close to asking him based on his expression, but as he's not the one who's been dancing around clubs – and sadly not in the "hands up in the air and throw some shapes in the church of dance" sense – I feel it's reasonable that it's the other way around.

'Just about.' Whew, I'm panting. The ring's fallen mercifully quiet for a moment. Tartalo's balanced again, with his head swivelling straight towards us. Fuck.

'What now, mano?' It's a good question. Because frankly, I'm low on ideas.

"You knot-patted fat guts! Squish their lily-livers out of their pock-marked backsides already!" the voice screams from my finger, and I am more than fed up with the ring and its shitty encouragements to murderise us as swiftly as possible. Tartalo turns to face us while the little ring won't shut the fuck up…

Oh.

Oh bollocks. We're here again.

'Open your mouth, Mephy.' The urgency's clear in my words, and to his credit, for once, he doesn't sass me. He opens it quick sharp.

And the teeth inside? Capable of cutting to the quick. Which is the entire idea as I stick my finger inside the demon dog's viciously arrayed muzzle.

'Bite. Don't swallow!' Fuck, I'm not going to enjoy this at all.

Mephy gargles something that sounds suspiciously like, 'That's what he said,' but I might be imagining it. He has the plan though and is fully on board with it.

The teeth slam together, and there is the terribly familiar sound of bone and cartilage splintering, the finger being crunched through and severed. Pain ruptures through me, but I hold it back. Now would be a spectacularly poor moment to lose it, and hell, I've had worse. Done worse to myself. Many times. So the pain can fuck right off.

Instead, I pump my *talent* into the stump on my left hand, sealing up the bleeding. Then I hold my right hand out to Mephy. He obligingly spits my now severed digit into my palm, complete with a sodden, deeply aggravated –and vocal– white metal ring.

'You whimpering cur! You snot-nosed knave! You clappered flap-mouuuuuuuuttttttttttthhhhhhhhhhhhhh….'

There is something deeply, deeply satisfying about that sound. The trailing off of the incessant abuse which has only been haranguing me for about five minutes but has already set my teeth so far on edge it feels like if they teeter even slightly, they're going to fall out of my mouth. Of course, it being attached to my actual finger slightly dulls the pleasure, but I concentrate on the positive. Especially when I get my aim absolutely bang on, and the ring sails past Tartalo's hip and straight out of the cathedral-sized window holes behind him.

Now there is a certain reputation that is carried by those of a gigantesque stature. One that haunts them regardless of their temperament, their kindness, or cruelty. They can be man-eaters or gentle friends, but there seems to be some common assumption in fairytales that when you supersize a person, their intelligence moves in an inverse direction.

What I'm trying to say is that giants in tales have a tendency to be dumb.

Now this isn't always the case. I've met some extremely smart, extremely large people. Teryiel, the ogre-slash-goddess I once battled in the caves below the city of Nice was anything but stupid. And let's not forget Andre the Giant and his incredible gift for rhyming.

Tartalo is not doing the giant stereotypes any favours though.

I don't know about you, but if I heard the ring that was giving me directions to Murderville suddenly come screaming past me and then drop rapidly downwards, I'd be hesitant. Perhaps think it through. Have a really good listen. See if I could hear any breathing or heartbeats in the room. Decide if I think it's likely that the creature I've been fighting just decided to hurl themselves at high speed out of the window, and whether if they did, if I really need to follow them just to make sure they are dead.

Tartalo's clearly not built for rational thought. Instead, one meaty hand comes up, snatching at the air as the ring whistles past but missing by a country mile. Then he turns and, without a moment's hesitation, lumbers forward. Picking up speed, he raises his enormous club over his shoulder horizontally, lowers his head bull-like, and with a mighty roar charges...

Straight out of the window.

The roar becomes a baffled howl, echoing back up to us for a few seconds before the wind whips it away. I might be imagining it, but there seems to be another small tremor a few seconds later. It certainly seems about right time-wise for him to be getting an up-close-and-personal introduction to the pavement outside.

Mephy rushes to the windowsill and leans out over the edge. 'Can't see anything, mano. Too much cloud.'

'I'm pretty sure he went straight down, Meph. The scream gave us that much.'

'True. Plus, he didn't seem smart enough to think of shape-shifting or something on the way down.' The demon hound spins around and barks gleefully. 'Genius idea, mano. Cut the ring off and hurl it out of the window.'

He lopes back over, his tongue hanging out of his doggy grin. 'That turned out to be far easier than I expected in the end.'

'Yeah…' I trail off. Stop. Freeze, but my thoughts are rushing like a freight train down the tracks, with a car stuck at the lights, between the barriers. The car being my short feeling of victory, of course.

Fuck.

Running out the doorway, ignoring Mephy's look of confusion, I turn to Isaac on instinct. Except Isaac isn't standing, patient expression ready to stoically soak up whatever idiocy I spout in his direction. He's slumped, broken on Faust's shoulders. But I can't focus on that right now. There's an important question that needs answering. 'Faust –'

'What happened to your finger?'

'I threw it and the ring out the window. Not important. How did the captured boy get rid of Tartalo in the legend?' I'm pretty sure I already know, fairly certain I've either heard the story or a similar version with a similar cyclops at some point.

Johannes frowns, his brow creasing. 'He threw the ring off a cliff and Tartalo followed. Like your Jack and Jill, eh? Tumbling after.'

'Right, let's move. Now,' I say, heading up the stairs at a quick pace.

'What is the rush, Paul?' Faust looks both puzzled and concerned. The fact he's following shows that, even if he doesn't get why, he trusts me enough to react to my unsteady panic.

'Tartalo may not be dead.' De Monteguard and Faust

pick up the pace, but I know my answer won't be enough to really satisfy him, so I force some deeper breaths in. Enough to clear my head, allowing me to regain some strength and my own feet and stop being an encumbrance.

I start again. 'He may not be dead. Look, the kid in the legend pulled the same trick, right? Dashed the ring off the side of a cliff. *And Tartalo still came back*. And sure, I get it. A lot of myths involve people who've run into legendary monsters and then inflated their own actions, turning, "I ran away screaming and somehow got lucky," into, "I slew them, the vile beast, so now please throw gold coins and nubile maidens at me". But my *talent*-infused sword crumpled like a Robin Reliant doing a high-speed collision with a brick wall. So would him base jumping without his parachute have killed him? I doubt it. Maybe the fall's shaken him up. Broken some bones. Perhaps it'll take him some time to get back to top form. Could be days, could be weeks…'

'Could be no time at all.' Johannes finishes my sentence grimly.

'Quite. Let's hurry, shall we?'

And hurry we do. Straight up the stairs. Heading for whatever is waiting for us at the top.

Hoping we'll survive it. All of us, this time.

Chapter Forty

I'd say making us climb endless stairs to fight Sabnock was him adding insult to injury if I wasn't fairly sure, based on the agonising pain in my legs and side, it was actually adding injury to injury. The insult is just an added bonus.

It is a long, arduous, and frankly terrifying ascent up the tower of bone.

The stairs twist constantly, and the patter of our own footsteps echo, seized and amplified by the curvature of the walls and hurled back at us with arrogant force so as we're constantly looking over our shoulders, constantly trying to peer around the bend ahead, wondering if an enraged blind cyclops is racing up behind us.

Wondering what horrors might still lie in wait.

I don't know how many steps there are. At one point, I decide to count, that sort of half-action you do to distract yourself from the pained grind of both physically straining and mentally boring actions. Where you attempt to enter an almost meditative state, the pattern of counting drawing you in, sucking your attention away from the unending aching, from the complaining stretches of ligaments and tendons as you lift that foot again, put it down, and repeat with the other side.

It can work when you're just dealing with the mundane reality of overcoming a body's moaning. When it's combined with sheer terror, like you've somehow stumbled through your TV screen into a slasher film and you know the next jump scare is due any moment now though...

It leaves your concentration somewhat shot.

But wait. Was that three thousand five hundred and fifty-nine or three thousand five hundred and sixty-nine? Well, we'll take the higher number; that's the most fair. Hold on, no. That means I'm claiming to have climbed more than I was supposed to. So better go for the lower one. But by now I've climbed a further seven steps, and although I'm pretty good normally at mental arithmetic, at this precise moment, I can't add nine and seven together. So I decide to take the higher number and call it even.

I manage about ten more steps before losing count again. And at that point I give up before I start screaming in frustration. Which will probably lead to me screaming in real life when the noise brings unnamed terrors raining down on our heads.

We're not talking, of course. The horrible acoustics in here – and not in the sense of "half the live music venues I've ever been in" either, more in the "creeping susurra-tions that whisper of our imminent demise interspersed with nerve jangling reverberating thuds that might be us or equally might not be" sense mean the very idea of adding more noise into the mix is just ludicrous. No one wants to do it. Not even Mephy, who normally seems oblivious to things like fear, social norms, or other people's feelings.

It's lighter the higher we go. We poked up above the clouds some time ago, and so the sky from inside is bright blue, and the walls are lit up a brilliant white by the sunshine streaming in. It does little to cheer the mood. Instead, it feels more like being caught by a spotlight, as if someone might start barking commands at us in a foreign language before cutting us down with strafing machine gun fire.

I feel horribly exposed.

But there's not much we can do. Just keep pushing upwards. Force our feet on, keep our mouths clamped shut, hold our shattered nerves by grim resolve and possibly a bit of sticky tape and some pipe cleaners.

Then an unfamiliar noise starts up. It takes me a moment to notice it. A split second where I'm not sure if it's something in my ear, like when you have a bit of wax wedged halfway down and some water in it. Or the faint half-ringing you can get when you were at a loud concert or rave till the early hours and are now lying in bed, almost vertiginous, your inner ear baffled by the abuse it suffered over the previous evening.

But then it gets louder. A detuned buzzing, like a swarm of gigantic angry bees – and me without a balloon to float under and pretend I'm a cloud.

Not that that would help. Because they aren't bees. Oh no. I see exactly what they are a second later when one comes whipping round the corner just as another dives through the open window frame on our right.

Tiny little creatures, their wings battering so rapidly they'd give a hummingbird a migraine. Human shaped, with pointy ear tips sticking out from the wild, matted strands of their hair. What most humans, used to Disneyfied stories, would think a fairy might look like. Naked as the day they were born apart from the black demonic essence goo that coats them liberally all over.

'Pillywiggins!' Faust breathes in shock.

'Motherfucker.' I'm not sure if I'm swearing at myself for not having thought of them being used again or at Sabnock for his audacity to do so. I've no idea where King Oberon ranks against a single demon in a fight, but I'd fancy his chances. And I know perfectly well that if he ever hears that some of his denizens have been possessed – even if they've been a long time in our world, away from the Summer Court – he'll be coming for Sabnock. Taking away a fae's free will is a huge no-no. Which might sound ironic, considering what their favourite pastimes are concerning the treatment of humans, but only an idiot ever believes that the Fair Folk are in any way *fair*.

Sadly, I've no way of bringing the situation to Oberon's attention. And considering the last time our paths crossed, I threatened him and his entire Court with a homemade explosive vest packed full of iron, I don't think I'd survive long enough to explain the problem to him if I did.

Plus, right now, I've bigger problems. Well, smaller problems, but when they're all packing razor-sharp nails and wickedly filed teeth, those smaller problems are plenty big enough.

Then there's the other issue. Which is that they're possessed. So I swat at them with my hands, whirling about like when I've been exhausted on a summer's night and I couldn't, despite my best efforts, track down that last fucking mosquito who kept dive-bombing my face the moment I turned the lights off. But with them, I connect. I knock some down so as their bodies bounce off the cold, hard floor, or I send them reeling out the window. When Mephy crunches some of those prone in his jaws, I don't say anything because I'm also aware of all the tiny cuts opening up all over me, the instant stings like paper cuts but deeper. Enough to bleed. To weaken me over time.

But I don't bring my feet down to snuff them out. My brain is racing, trying to come up with a better solution. A way to keep them from killing us without us killing them even as their numbers increase, as the air thickens with arriving pillywiggins, all their teeth bared and ready to tear our flesh from the bone.

Because I'm thinking of the man unconscious over Faust's shoulder. The one who can't tell me what's the right thing to do. Not this time.

But who's still the one who has always had faith in me. The one who I'll need to tell this story to later. If he survives.

If we all survive.

Chapter Forty-One

When I say these creatures aren't bright even when not possessed, your average pillywiggin's middle name could be Ralph.

I really don't know what to do. These little fairies don't deserve to die. As far as fae go, they're as harmless as is imaginable. But the damage they're doing to us all shows that remains relative. If I don't come up with something soon, killing them is going to be the only option left. Time is against us. Both in terms of how long before the injuries we're sustaining turn the tide against us and also in that we're now stationary, our backs up against the stairwell wall. If Tartalo is picking himself up off the pavement and racing back up for round two, he'll be closing on us every second.

Nothing's coming to me though. All I can do is keep waving my hands at them, almost ineffectually. Knocking some down. Stunning one or two. But the air is thick with the creatures, and I'm bleeding from all over. My face feels like I got a shave by a blind five year old, and their nails are making a mess of my arms.

A red-hot pain shoots up from my left hand. Glancing down, I see one of the little creatures has fixed their teeth into the stump of my missing finger. I clamp my right hand around them and yank them off, which elicits a little whimper of pain as they take another chunk of flesh with them, setting the wound bleeding liberally again. By the Good God, I'm tempted to end them. To squeeze them till their eyes pop out like one of those weird mass-manufactured stress toys. Or to just bash their brains out against the nearby wall.

But that thought brings my mind back to the story of Polyphemus, of him doing that exact thing to the terrified Ithacan sailors before gobbling them down. I might not be about to chow down on the remains of the pillywiggins if I kill them, but I'm still a giant, an ogre in comparison to them. And they're not in control of their actions.

So somehow, despite my pain and rage, I manage to hurl the creature out of the window instead of against the rock-hard floor. I think to myself that, at least, if we don't find a solution without killing them all, I can tell Isaac I tried. That I spared this one when I really wanted to kill it instead.

But then I realise something. As I'm waving my hand around at the stinging pain, shaking it like I can somehow use centrifugal force to hurl the stinging burn from my body instead of just showering splatters of blood about, no more are attacking me. The crowd's eased up, the biting, stinging scratches have stopped, at least for now. Then I realise why. De Monteguard has stepped in front of me.

They're not attacking him. And he's looking as puzzled about it as I am.

'What's going on?' I scream at him over the deafening buzz surrounding us.

'I've no idea!' is the incredibly useful response.

But that gets me thinking. 'Who possessed them originally?'

'Caacrinolaas!'

Well, that is weird. Because as far as we can tell, once Caacrinolaas was severed from his connection, the wards of the city dropped, and his mass possession ended. Which means one of two things. Either Sabnock's somehow using his control of Caacrinolaas' tether to leverage his power, or he's copied his ability and seized the pillywiggins' reins. Seeing as how the pillywiggins aren't attacking De Monte-guard? My money is on the former. Somehow they're recognising the link to their master even though it's been severed.

So I plunge my hand into my etheric storage and come out with the remnant of Clarent, Arthur's first sword, the Sword of Peace. And sure enough, it works. A little. A small cone of clear air forms around us, almost like a ward. I step immediately across, in front of Faust, who's using the wall to help support Isaac, keeping him trapped against it so he can use both his hands to drive away the little creatures. Mephy huddles in, and suddenly, we have some breathing space.

'Okay, mano, what's the plan?' I try to ignore how bloody Mephy's lips are. He's done the right thing, the sensible thing. My morals are my own. I can't expect him to follow them just because I do.

I'm about to reply that I've no idea when suddenly one strikes me. A memory from a few centuries back, when I passed a stormy autumn on the coast of Gdansk. While there I did a favour for a brooding alkonost, a woman from

242

the waist up, a fabulous bird, phoenix-like in her riotous feather colours, from there down. She's not like the legendary sirens, even if she sings to make men forget everything but her beautiful trilling notes and to never seek to do anything else ever again. Because her songs are a defence mechanism to protect her offspring, those who replace her as she dies, as she sheds her bitter tears in a single tree in the Polish forest for her own demise, then laughs her joy at those taking her place before flying off to wherever alkonosts go to die. A limited species, so fragile, so easily lost forever. Which is why I retrieved her lost clutch of eggs from the hands of a hungry collector.

A certain wizard, not much of a Talent but with a cunning and an avarice that could counterbalance his mediocre abilities, had copied old Odysseus by jamming up his ears with wax. Then he'd walked in, waving fire to drive back her furious talons, and had taken her babies from her.

I have little time for those who steal children. And he didn't have the cunning, the avarice, or the *talent* to go toe to toe with me.

When I brought her the eggs back and laid them down gently, still warm, in her violated nest, she sang to me. Not a song of forgetfulness, no. A song of truth. The truth of her own *talent*, of what she was, of who she was. It was a form of communion, the only way she could think of to really express her gratitude. She let me see the song of her soul, and it was beyond beautiful.

But I am also a product of my education by Isaac and am just as curious as he is in many ways. Even if my curiosity is more in the Indiana Jones, crow-like form of "ooh, grab the shiny thing" rather than "meticulously preserve and study these ancient artefacts" sense. So when I saw her laid bare, I couldn't help but study her workings, the way her music held the key to enchantment. Her song took the hot, hungry desire of man and turned it back to the most basic of wants. Our hearts are ensnared, our souls soothed from the earliest days by rhythm, by our mothers' murmured cooings and soft hums. It takes us back to our simplest form and removes all those complexities we layer on top by pretending to be anything more than soft, frightened babes seeking reassurance from the terrors of the dark.

But I'm not about to sing them a song. My vocal cords aren't built like the alkonost's. No one is about to be enchanted by my attempt at a lullaby. But what I do want to do is take them back to the basics. And I remember the form of her *talent*, enough that I can shape a suitable working.

I think.

Reaching down inside myself, Clarent's hilt still held aloft, I search for that sensation. The feeling I had when her first notes hit. That moment of clarity, of connection. Because that, of course, is how the alkonost clears human minds. By forming a bridge and taking it into herself.

I can make the same connection. That's not the problem.

The problem is what I'll be taking.

I need something to work as the bridge. The alkonost obviously used her own emotional state – her love for her eggs, her own desire of safety and protection to find the harmonics with those of the thieves. I can't do that for what's driving the pillywiggins. But there's someone else who can.

'Bite me, Mephy!'

By the Good God, I'm getting sick of saying that.

Chapter Forty-Two

I'd love it if next time I tell someone to bite me, I mean it in the metaphorical sense rather than actually wanting them to take a pound of flesh like a savage-toothed Shylock.

Once again, Mephistopheles doesn't hesitate. His teeth sink into my outstretched hand. My blood flows down his maw, and it's child's play to send my *talent* along with it, to make a link. Of course, if he wanted to, he could snap my magic in a heartbeat. But he trusts me. He lets me make the connection.

Then I reach outwards, my magic a questing, probing finger, and it touches the nearest pillywiggin. The darkness in the creature's mind is... terrible. Terrifying. I've said it before, and I'll say it again. Mind magic is fucking evil shit. I don't care who you are, what dimension you call home, if you're hijacking living creatures and making them puppets for your own fucked-up desires, there's something seriously wrong with you.

245

Not that I imagine Sabnock gives two flying fucks – a breeding pair, for when you've no fucks to give – about what I think.

It's hard not to jerk away at the sensation. Even harder knowing what I have to do. Because now I'm going to have to take some of the demonic life-force coating them.

Not much. By the Good God, no. I don't want to end up like them. But that's why I'm not taking it into myself. Instead I funnel it, pushing it rapidly through me and into the acorn, the heart of the seed of a once-tree that I hold in my chest. At the same time, I *push* outwards. Giving up a part of myself, that carnal element. Memories of moments lost in bed with Susane, of those all-consuming instances where we held each other and screamed our love and lust in sighs to the echoing walls, and nothing mattered or existed but us.

And that? That is the song of a pillywiggin's heart.

But this is burning through the *talent* I've stored in the acorn. Replacing all that battery power I can still put to use when I need it, and I'm not ready to let that go. Not if I can help it.

'Can you take it, Mephy?' We're linked, so I don't need to specify what *it* is. He knows instantly what I mean, can see what's happening inside of me. He doesn't reply, of course – that'd be hard with a mouthful of my flesh. But he jerks his head down and up, yanking my hand with it. So I push a little bit of this demonic life-force, woven from a friend the monster upstairs harvested, out of me. Into him.

Sorry, Mephy. It's a terrible thing to do to anyone.

To his credit, he doesn't complain, doesn't refuse it, even if a tiny buzzsaw whine starts up in the back of his throat. I'm taking the least I can from the pillywiggins. I'm not looking to drain all the poison from them. Just looking to reduce it enough that their own nature can kick back in. One that the demonic essence would normally promote.

Horniness.

Pillywiggins aren't really fighters; they're much more natural born McLovins. Ready to get their groove on any time, any place. And I feel it. One of the pillywiggins spins in the air, their eyes devouring the flying flesh all around them, a veritable smorgasbord of bodies. Then they seize hold of the nearest one.

They grab other pillywiggins nearby, pulling them into their love circle. There're passionate kisses and all sorts of inappropriate touching that I'd really rather ignore, but I can't because I'm linked to them, and each time they kiss, a drop of the essence flows through the chain and into me.

Then I dump those drops of his dead friend down Mephy's throat.

Within a tiny amount of time, we're no longer under threat. Unless you count the risk of being coated liberally in tiny bodily fluids a threat. Which I do. Once I'm sure the working has spread throughout all the pillywiggins, who are now bumping uglies mid-air left, right, and centre, I gently shake my hand free from Mephy's jaw. The demon dog huffs, whines loudly, and then vomits. A steaming pile of black ooze spreads across the floor, then dissolves, evaporating away into nothingness as it goes.

'A last taste, Eisheth,' he whispers. 'A final goodbye.'

I wonder if anyone else sees the single tear that rolls down the demon's blinking red eye before it too hisses and evaporates off his cheek.

I lay my bleeding hand on the nape of his neck. That he leans into it rather than bites my hand off speaks volumes. I let him take a moment amid an airborne orgy to grieve for his lost demon.

But we can't wait too long. Time presses hard, so eventually I duck and make my way through the air dark with wriggling forms.

Once we eventually half-stoop, half-crawl our way under the shimmery gang bang going on above us, we straighten up and take a moment. I'm not the only one who's bleeding profusely. Mephy's coat was a mess even before I put my own bloodied hand on it, and Faust's beard is matted with dark sticky patches clumping the strands together. I try not to look at the state of Isaac because it won't be the multitude of tiny cuts that worry me. Faust's looking after him. I have to trust him and try not to worry any more about him than I already am. Only De Monteguard is unscathed.

Together, we start to climb.

Chapter Forty-Three

And so we reach the summit. Time to save our people. And our angel.

The Couvent Des Jacobins. The Jacobean Convent. Usually a tourist attraction for the visitors to Toulouse who are hungry for a taste of the medieval history that permeates the city. Now our final destination, a once-church pushed skyward atop a tower of bone. At last, we're at the top.

The advantage of how well lit the stairwell has been is that we don't emerge, blinking, out into the daylight. The vaulted ceilings of the church we're now in are impressive, and the sight of the sandy shading of the stone and the coloured brick detailing of the arches brings a sense of hope back somehow to my heart. Normality still exists. The world hasn't been subsumed in one demon's madness. Not yet.

Light streams in through the stained glass, painting the columns in a rainbow of refractions. I'm not religious –not even meeting what might be my actual god has shifted that– but there's a serenity here, a peacefulness. The Catholic Church and I may have our differences, what with them exterminating my entire creed eight hundred years ago, but they've always known how to build an impressive building.

Right now, that does my heart good. And I'll take that. Before I go face another ending. And this time, there's no Aicha to save me. No Jakob ready to mark his soul to save mine. Isaac is dying. Nithael is stolen. Gil is possessed.

But I have a rag-tag band standing at my back, friends old and new. I may be walking into the lion's den – or the lion-headed arsehole's den – but I'm not alone. There're people I trust ready to back my play.

That, as much as their *talent* and power, might just tip the scales in our favour.

Or maybe I'm just clinging onto that last drop of optimism in the face of certain doom.

One or the other.

But as huge as the roof is inside the convent, it isn't close to being large enough to hold what's waiting for us when we press out into the waiting cloisters.

The convent is built around the central square, a wonderful patch of green inside a wondrous antiquity. Toulouse really takes advantage of it too. In the summer, sometimes they have pop-up restaurants, Michelin star chefs offering culinary discoveries inside its walls. Other times they have DJs set up, deckchairs arrayed out so people can take their lunch break there, listening to music and sharing time with their friends. Or it becomes an extension of the museum, with armoured knights and tour guides dressed as peasants, giving demonstrations and information to wide-eyed children and their equally entertained adults. It's a vibrant, lively, happy place.

It's not lively now though. No. It's drenched in silence. Drowning in it.

An oppressive load pushing down on us from all directions.

And a terrible sight to behold.

In the middle stands Sabnock. He's taller than I am, two metres or more, but he seems larger still because of the huge tasselled mane that crowns his face like a fiery halo, the sun set burning behind his head.

He's dressed in armour. His arm is raised aloft, his sword mirroring the gothic points of the bell-tower behind, locked in place. Which, let me tell you, is unbelievably difficult to maintain for any period of time for a normal human despite what all the films show you. But he's not moving; not even a muscle trembles in place. But the other hand moves rapidly, clawed fingers poking out from the half-gauntlets' ridges. He carves sigils into the air, ones that threaten to make everything in our world cease to exist.

Then, of course, there's what's tied to the sword.

Because he's not just striking a pose. No. The sword is wreathed in a mixture of smoke and electric neon, each wrapped around the other, intertwining around the blade and exploding off it like some messed up version of Prince Adam calling for the power of Greyskull. Except it's not the power to transform the sword's wielder into a superhuman.

It's the power to transform the world.

Above us he weaves a halfway existence between Nithael and Caacrinolaas.

Inside that broiling, miasmic cloud, sometimes crackling neon wings will emerge, hands pawing at the sky. Then they'll change to actual paws, and a muzzle will pull free, stretched in a silent howl before being subsumed again.

It is so terrible, I cannot bear to watch.

Sabnock sees us and sighs as he stops carving his weirded version of Enochian symbols into the fabric of reality. He shakes out his mane, his vertical-slit pupils blinking.

'Fine –' he starts, but that's as far as he gets. Because if there's one thing Bugarach taught me? It's that letting the villain monologue while he's doing something capable of tearing holes in reality is a bad idea.

So I hit him. Hard.

Fireballs are up first. Not that I'm expecting them to work. Him just bursting into flames upon first contact with a lobbed magical firestorm would be too convenient. No. The idea is they keep him busy. Plus, it's a fitting tribute. *Magictov cocktails, Aicha*. She might not be here to help. Doesn't mean I don't carry her with me in my heart.

The distraction isn't much. Sabnock waves a lazy hand, never wavering from his sword-aloft pose as he bats the magical fireballs out of the sky with a casual paw. As he touches them, the workings dissolve, dissipating on contact.

But they've allowed me to close the gap.

I run towards him, my sword crackling to life, green balefire licking and dancing along the blade's edges. Elemental magic might not be my forte, but swordplay is. I've an idea that forcing him to defend himself will make him bring Joyeuse down from that ridiculous posture, and that might… Well, it might not break the working, but it might slow it down. Buy us some time. So I charge in, whipping my sword up to slice a diagonal strike across his chest, designed to carve open that shiny breastplate.

Sabnock hardly moves. His torso stays in the same place. But that same free paw/hand combo dances across in front, half-rotated, so that the metal plating on the back of it blocks my strike. It shouldn't work, of course. My charged-up weapon should just slice his hand clean off at the wrist. Instead it bounces off, a ringing clang that sends vibrations through my hands, an echoing ache of numbness battling against my clenched muscles.

A ringing clang that doesn't seem to affect him at all.

He twists his wrist, batting my blade aside, then swipes a casual backhand at my face. I lean backwards, and his paw passes close enough that I feel the whistling air, the centrifugal drag at my skin as it misses me by inches. If it had connected, it would have done more than dragged at it. It would have ripped my face clean off.

Turning my backwards lean into a half tumble, I pull myself out of range for a follow up strike. As I fall, dropping my shoulder, I see Mephy is tearing across the cloister. Johannes is behind him, gently depositing Isaac on the floor, and De Monteguard helping him. A grin forms on my face. Let's see what Sadcock can do against a properly motivated war-mode demon. *Fucking A.*

Chapter Forty-Four

It may not be easy. I may not manage it. But if I can try to punch the Evil God in the face? You best believe, if I can get through his defences, this arsehole is getting Sab-knocked out.

Sabnock sighs, shakes his head, and raises a hand, crackling black ooze around his fingers, perhaps aiming to throw up another of those barriers, like at Bugarach, the ones laced with the last drops of another demon's soul. But he doesn't get it all the way up. His hand freezes, locked in place, and now his eyes go wide, those vertical slits blinking frantically. I get the feeling this isn't part of the plan.

'Hard to move when the air's turned fucking solid, isn't it, you shitheap excuse for a demonico?' Mephy's words are barks of glee, full of his disdain for the chucklefuck in front of him, his readiness to tear him a new arsehole or three clear in every syllable as he closes the distance between them.

Sabnock mewls, a tiny frightened sound, but then he shakes himself, his fur bristling. His pace speeds up, the movement becoming *more*, faster, a vibration practically. Then the next second I realise that, though I can still see him, I can also see *through* him. He's paled, becoming wraithlike. Even the sword seems to have become transparent, although it's had no effect on the world-ending working happening overhead.

And now his other hand is travelling upwards all over again.

'Hard to hold a gas in place with a trick like that, *hound*.' Oof. I get the feeling that's a serious insult the twatpuss just dropped on Mephy. In his opinion, at least. 'I can easily move between even those tight-bound atoms.' He looks up, utterly nonchalant. 'My turn.'

He waves his hand, a casual gesture, towards the floor beneath him, and the stones start rolling together. Growing. Splitting. Multiplying.

Then I realise they're not stone-coloured. Because they're not stones.

They're white. Rolled up tight, fat grubs. Just like the ones I saw burrowing in and out of Gil's flesh. They're still increasing in numbers, shuddering, tearing themselves in half, forming a glistening white carpet of gigantic maggot-worms, swirling under Sabnock.

Then this living, wriggling, chittering rug of hundreds of thousands of hungry sounding invertebrates – judging by how the air is rent by the echoing high pitched gnashing of miniature incisors – come rolling towards Mephistopheles. An unstoppable train of killer demonic grubs.

The demon dog comes screeching to a stop, his tongue lolling, his teeth bared in an entirely humourless grin. 'And *that* is exactly what I was hoping you'd do, you predictable twat.'

Then he leaps forward, apparently straight towards this locust-plague grub army, as though he'll land straight in the middle.

Except he doesn't come down. He keeps going up. Paws stretching towards the sky. As he does I realise they are literally stretching, elongating. His hairs do too. Bulking out. Becoming flatter, diffusing. Becoming feathers.

Mephy's transforming into a bird. A gigantic one. The sort that'd make the Roc shit the nest and decide to retire to a quiet mountain far away. Possibly on the dark side of the Moon.

'Michael Keaton eat your fucking heart out!' He swoops a wing across his face. 'I'm Bird-dog!' He drops the wing out and grins. 'We'll do this in one take, too.'

Then he dives, floorward. His grin stretches further back, widening ever farther, Cheshire Cat like, broadening until his jaw seems to become disconnected from his head, his mouth a gaping black hole.

I always knew Mephy was a bit unhinged, but this is something else. The gap between his two sets of teeth is impossible in a way that hurts my eyes and makes my brain ache. It would make MC Escher pick up the sketch pad straight away, even as he started gibbering at the sight.

His bottom jaw hits the floor and the scuttering insects go tumbling down his Charybdis of a throat, a sucking whirlpool. He lifts away for a second to look at a stunned looking Sabnock.

'Birds love grubs! The early bird gets the worm, and you're the grubbiest fucking worm I ever did see!'

As he speaks he gets bigger, and now Sabnock turns, panicking, trying to get away. But Mephy's too big now. He's

imPerfect Demons

blotting out the sky. And the two sides of his beak-muzzle come snapping down around Sabnock. Then, with one enormous gulp, he swallows him whole.

Clever Mephistopheles. He actually got the fucker.

Or so I think. Because then Meph starts shrinking, rolling in the air, doing half-corkscrews before he comes crashing back to the floor, once more in his demon Dobermann shape. He rolls over, pawing at his belly, then, as he gives a tiny, piteous whine, a glowing silvered tip pushes out from his stomach. An instant after, the blade slides fully free from his chest. I'm so horrified, I can't move, can't react even though my brain's screaming at me that I should try to seize it while Sabnock's not holding it.

Except a moment later, I realise he is. Because there's a buzzing noise, like an enraged hornet's nest just got smashed on top of something –possibly my head– and I realise there are thousands, hundreds of thousands perhaps, of tiny Sabnocks clinging to the blade, carrying it free.

Mephy's still grunting and whining, but he shakes his muzzle. 'Biting… biting Beelzebub's style now, are you, you unoriginal bitch? This… this is my favourite game.'

I remember what he said at the Trials, about having swallowed other demons when playing their twisted version of Hide and Seek. He chewed them down, and they would reform in his stomach before bursting out from under his rib cage as an encore.

Mephy howls, shakes his head again… and comes to pieces.

I don't mean he collapses into a crying, sobbing mess on the floor. I'd understand if he did –after all, that's what I want to do right now– but he's totally committed to this demon showdown. No, he literally comes to pieces, separating first into sections – limbs, chest, head – all flopping

257

away from each other, then further still. His claws come off, his pointed ears go flying, and his teeth spray across the courtyard. But he's not self-destructed. Each of those pieces transform, reshaping into a new form. All of them the same. One with vicious teeth and claws and a furious look in their miniature red eyes.

All of them have changed into teeny, weeny Mephistopheleses.

They keep separating, breaking apart and multiplying. Now the air is just thick with swarms of the two animalistic demons, the air rent with tiny high-pitched yowls and barks, and the multitude of Mephys go tearing through the air, hunting the miniature Sabnocks as growling howls buzz around our ears.

I spin around, trying to work out how to help, to think of a working I can throw up to corral the tiny, little demonic moggies into one single place to make Mephistopheles' job simpler. A second later though, it's taken out of my hands.

The swarming myriad hound-flies suddenly come shooting back together, coalescing, swirling around each other faster and faster. A dancing cloud of miniscule dogs, whipping in and out of each other, their twisting loops tightening until one moment, there's those uncountable numbers of Mephys, a pirouetting ensemble, and the next it's the one demon Dobermann vibrating at an incredible speed. Then he slows, steadies. Comes to a panting halt. While out of his mouth comes a horrible whine.

Which is when I see it. Mephistopheles' stomach is still ripped open, leaking goo, a sable snail-trail between his feet.

'What... what is this, you fucking wannabee angelico pretentious... wanker?' Mephy's words may come out as gasps of pain, but it's not limiting his desire to verbally lacerate the other demon. Sabnock also reforms, his sword once more raised, smug as the cat who got the cream.

Blood-curdled cream in this case.

'What "this" are you referring to, you pathetic thing?' There's a vibration to the bastard's tone, a weird undernote, and it takes me a second to realise what it is. The arsehole is *purring*. 'The fact that your stomach wound is healing so slowly? Or that you couldn't snatch me out of the air however hard you tried?'

Sabnock takes a step towards Mephy, and to my dismay I see the hound take a limping step backwards, a needle-scratch whine pushing through his bared teeth.

'Both answers are the same, of course. The sword. The binding of an angelico and demonico. Did you really think I'd just pull the dimensions back together without giving myself protection from those who might be peeved by such an action? Once you're all back on this world, you'll vibrate at the same frequency, meaning you can hurt each other.'

He takes another step towards Mephy. 'But *I won't* be. The energy of the binding moves me to another energetic frequency, one neither side can harm, as long as I hold their spirits, twined around Joyeuse. However much they try. Sure' —he shrugs— 'if both sides work together for centuries, millennia, perhaps you'll find a way to get through it. But...'

His grin widens, his canines gleaming in the light reflected from the sword's shimmering blade. 'Do you really think the peace will last a day? War will be waged.'

Mephy whimpers again, and I can't help noticing the ground under him is soaked black as he retreats on trembling legs. Sabnock's smile becomes even broader, even sharper.

'Of course,' he says, 'you won't be here to see that. I know you'll heal from that wound eventually. But if the sword did that to your stomach, what do you think it'll do when I sever your head?'

Sabnock advances on my downed friend, his blade glimmering, his chest rumbling with his self-satisfied purr, ready to end the demon who dared stand against him.

Mephy's direct attack didn't work, and he's about to pay for it. Time to distract Sabnock. Draw his attention back to me. Try to knock him off balance.

'Oi! Don't just look at him! There's others of us ready to fuck you up. Do you know who the last person to underestimate me and mine was?' It's a yell, words hurled out that reverberate around the echoing cloisters.

Sabnock pauses, stops. Looks at me, a lazily dismissive glance. 'Simon De Montfort?'

'Simon De M… Yes.' Damn it, he's good at getting me ruffled. 'He was sure he'd got the better of me too. That everything was going according to plan. Right until that all blew up in his face spectacularly.'

'Yes. I know.' The whisker-faced cockstride doesn't seem at all concerned. 'I was there. Well, of sorts. Keeping an eye on the proceedings.'

There. *There.* Right at this moment, right there, I see a thing, a tiny little thing that gives me my first glimmer of hope. But it needs me to keep the fucker talking. I can do that. I'm good at that. I can keep the conversation going off on random illogical tangents long after the fight should have restarted.

'Well, um,' I say. 'And how were you there? Because I'd remember kicking your furry little arse back to the lower dimensions if I'd done so.'

'Because you didn't, little mano. You did nothing to me. And I did nothing to you apart from lending what I harvested from back home to De Montfort's amusing efforts.'

'Why, you fucking shithead?' Now it's Mephy who interrupts. His voice is low, but his eyes blaze red, and I can see he wants to leap on Sabnock, to tear his throat out. The wound to his stomach's the only thing stopping him, but it's also a prominent reminder of what the arsehole did to one of their own, to someone Mephistopheles considered a friend. 'You killed her! Brought an ending to what should have been eternal!' His voice lowers. 'Who should have been... should have been eternal.'

'What do I care?' Sabnock waves his hand lazily, but I don't miss the tensing of his neck muscles. That one scored closer to home than he wants to admit. 'Why should I be bothered by the survival or otherwise of any of *our kind*? When did any of you filthy animals ever care for me?'

'Aww, diddums. Did everyone stop coming round and asking you out to play, Sabby?' Mephy's obviously spotted the reaction too, and he's not hesitating to exploit it. 'That's because you're an unbearable, miserable, whiny fuckhole. A bore. A millstone round the neck of anyone you've ever been near.'

'Because you didn't appreciate me!' Now Sabnock's voice is a hiss, and his anger is clear, the fur on his face bristling. 'Didn't recognise that I was right.'

'Right about what?' I ask. *Keep him talking, Paul. Keep him focused on what he's saying, on you. Anything but the thing he's not noticed.*

'Right that we were wrong! We should never have created that other reality. It wasn't a wondrous discovery, not some playground paradise.'

'What was it then?'

'Base. Primal. Animalistic.' I can't help noticing that for

someone who has a literal lion's head, he doesn't seem to like animal-like characteristics very much. 'All that rutting, fighting. Games and laughter. A waste. A waste of our collective abilities.'

'So what would you have had us do, Sabby?' Mephy growls.

'Grow up. Evolve. We could have been gods. Understanding so much more than this petty, imprisoning physical form. And we took our chance to make a world. Except all we did was shape a prison.'

'We never found it a prison. We all loved it. Seems like you're the unhappy one, Sabby.' I can't help noticing Mephy's tone. There's a touch of ridicule, and it's good, it's distracting, but I don't want him to spill over into open anger. Not yet.

So I interrupt. Steer the conversation in another direction. 'Sounds like you made the wrong choice. Like you'd have been happier going up instead of down.'

'Oh, I did!' Sabnock stares at me intently, his jaw working, chewing over his words, his expression screwed up like they're bitter in his mouth. 'I had to make a choice. Didn't want to, of course. Millenia of war between our kind, and suddenly it's, "We're done with this reality. Make your choice. Which way are you going to go?" And… and I was in love. There was one. She held my heart. And she had made her choice. So I made the same one. I followed her down.'

He blinks, chokes for a moment, then swallows. Regains some of his composure. 'She wasn't interested. Didn't understand what I offered her. Said a single, monogamous partnership was "limiting". Said I was "basic". Me! Basic!'

Oof. Sabnock has really decided to undo reality because

the girl he loved called him a basic bitch. Damn. That's a hell of a response to a savage burn.

Thankfully, he's still focused on his story. 'So I tried to change, to go back. To make the choice I should have done. To head to the realm of the Elohim.' He shakes his head, giving a bitter laugh. 'But it was sealed. The deal made, the splitting off of reality had locked the way. I was stuck. For eternity. In a world full of pleasure-seeking idiots.

'So I decided to break the lock by smashing the deal. When your angel friends got called through, tethering themselves and our dimensions to this reality in the process? I finally had the opportunity to do just that.'

His gaze trails up his arm, to his sword held triumphantly aloft. Then his eyes widen when he finally sees what I've been trying to keep him from seeing. His golden fur can be seen through the joints of his armour. It covers his biceps, curves down his forearm, and swathes his hand…

Except for the knuckles. Because where his knuckles are, the fur has parted, miniature Red Seas of hair peeling away. Pushed back, so that underneath, the human skin peeks through, just visible.

'Now, Gil!' I shout. As Sabnock roars, a full-throated shout of denial, Gil seizes back control of his joints, forcing him to crack his fingers open just the tiniest bit…

So Joyeuse tumbles from the demon's hand and lands point first into the grassy ground below.

Chapter Forty-Five

TOULOUSE, 30 OCTOBER, PRESENT DAY

Gil catching this shithead off guard? Definitely a Joyeuse occasion.

There's a brief moment. When Sabnock is caught off guard, stunned in disbelief. When I pump my fist in glee, Napoleon Dynamite style, and the movement catches his eye, distracting him further. So that he doesn't react before Mephy does. The demon dog's stomach wound must have healed – enough at least – because he tears across the lawn and launches himself right at him, his teeth bared, growling fiercely. Faust is just behind him. He tumbles Isaac roughly onto the grass next to the sword. I'm not upset by his treatment of Isaac. Because if he's risking himself, making himself a viable target, then that means he must feel the risk has to be taken.

Which means Isaac must be about to die.

Mephy's enraged growl turns into a hacking whine.

Mephy hasn't reached his target – no doubt tearing the

264

bastard's throat out now he's not protected by the sword. No. He's gone slamming at high speed into a barrier of viscous black onyx. Like the one I saw dangling over my head when De Monteguard was trying to get me to hear him out. Only this one isn't made from Caacrinolaas' essence, no, nor Sabnock himself's. Those wouldn't have stopped Mephy; they would have got torn to shreds as he barrelled into them. They wouldn't have knocked him back onto his haunches, half-retching and shaking his head, a piteous almost-screech coming out over his spluttering attempts to clear his mouth.

That barrier isn't made from the demon's manifest. It's made from the drained essence of Mephistopheles' dead friend. Apparently it's as effective against him as it is against the angels. Sabnock obviously learnt after the last time he couldn't get it up, when Mephy froze his arm in place, had it ready in reserve if something went wrong. Mephy may not be bleeding out still – though he looks far from well, only his anger keeping him upright – but he still can't get his teeth into the fucker. Not only that but he's got a mouthful of the distilled essence of a dead friend, sending him reeling backwards, close to vomiting.

Meph is out of the game, for a moment at least, and there's no way I can see for him to get to Sabnock, even if he's not got the sword anymore.

Good God I wish Aicha was here. I don't care who we're facing, how prepared this bastard seems to be, she'd gut the fucker and wear his intestines as a fetching necklace while she introduced him to real hellfire, burning him alive.

Which is when the thought strikes me. Fire didn't work before. But that's when he had the sword. The barrier he's made might stop demons and angels, might hurt like *fuck* if it touches a human.

But it's only surrounding him in the air. Plus he's not likely to be on the lookout for human *talent*. What threat is that to a demon?

Well, if they're suddenly back on our vibrational plane because they've not got their demon-angel combo sword then the answer is *plenty*. Hopefully.

So I send my talent out, through the floor, letting it lance through the stone flags, racing under the barrier, and up into the air inside Sabnock's shield. At which point I connect to the atoms around his mane and persuade them that they'd like to heat up now, immediately. A lot.

Then I get the immense satisfaction of watching his mane spontaneously combust.

The demon yowls, a strangled cry of horror and pain as the heat starts licking around the back of his cranium. He might think himself better than all the animals –and I don't doubt he includes humans in that category– but it's enough to make him leap forward, instinct telling him to put distance between himself and any potential threat, unsure as to where it came from. His hands come up, beating at the flames, and I'm not surprised, even if I'm slightly disappointed, to see them start going out. He looks around wildly, but when his gaze catches mine, his eyes narrow.

Good. He's pissed. And he's pissed at me. It's quite the talent I have. Now let's make sure it stays that way.

'Oh, you silly puddytat,' I say in my best Tweety Pie impression. 'What is it with you otherworldly beings and your tendency to entirely underestimate the human spirit? Don't get me wrong.' I hold up my hand to stall his interruption, as though he was seriously about to debate me instead of try to disintegrate me. 'There's a huge proportion of humanity that are basically arseholes. And even the good ones have their arsehole moments. Look at me!'

I beam as though I've just made the final killer point that will see me lifting this year's Debating Champion trophy, crowned as the best orator, for all to admire and applaud with aplomb. 'I'm an arsehole most of the time, but there's been a few good moments that have balanced them out. Enough so that even when I've fucked up spectacularly – and you can ask the incredible human you've decided to hijack, you absolute kittenfiddler. I basically got his brother killed…' I pause, force myself to be honest. 'I *did* get his brother killed, and he still trusted me enough that once I turned up on the scene, he used all his determination and grit to push you back enough to drop Joyeuse. Because you bodyjacked the wrong man.'

I grin again and take a step forward as if I'm about to engage him in single unarmed combat. Which, let me be clear, I am absolutely not about to do because he would tear me limb from limb with those claws. But if he *thinks* I'm going to, that I am that suicidally deranged, it'll keep him off balance. Or that's the hope anyhow. Though, let's face it. The only reason he hasn't just turned me inside out with his *talent* is he finds me amusing. Or perhaps it's because Mephy has worn him out. But I'm going to go with the former so I feel like I'm actually doing something in this fight.

'You see, Gil's used to being possessed. He made a deal with a psychic monster. Let him share his head. Of all the humans you could have grabbed…' I chuckle. 'You choose one with years of experience of letting out his mental leasehold.'

I take another step forward. And then instantly regret it.

Because I've overplayed my hand. The first step worked. Did just what I wanted. Threw Sabnock for a loop. Kept him off balance.

But the second one is a step too far. It's brought me closer, almost into combat range. And he doesn't fall back. No. Now he suddenly remembers what he's up against. A measly human. Sure, one with *talent*. But compared to a manifest demon? That's like turning up to the OK Corral with a BB gun. And I just challenged him to a quick draw.

This is about to get ugly. Fast.

Chapter Forty-Six

Damn it. And it was all going so well. Sort of.

Sabnock's tongue darts out, licking around his lips like the cat who's got the cream. Although he probably doesn't drink cream. Probably considers it entirely too self-indulgent and pleasure-seeking for an ascetic arsehole like him.

His eyes dart across to where Mephy's shaking himself, steadying back on his four legs, snarl-twisted muzzle swinging back towards our enemy.

'Yes, very good, little mano.' He claps his hands briefly, indolently. Twice. 'Well done. The indomitable human spirit. Fighting back against a full-powered demon and winning. For a split second. All because he has faith in you. Wonderful. Touching.'

He pauses. Then leans forward, his eyes narrowing. 'Useless.'

A bellowing roar echoes through the cloistered square, bouncing off the stone pillars and reverberating up into the exposed sky. Then, through the same entrance we came from, his head lowered to allow passage, Tartalo emerges. His face is reddened, sweat-glistened from both exertion and, judging from his expression, furious anger. Sadly, apart from having given him a good cardio workout climbing back up, he seems unharmed from his considerable plunging fall. He straightens out, his head swinging left and right, searching around.

Sabnock waves a metal-ridged finger, and I hear a, 'Lawks, puddenhead!' shriek. My heart sinks when I realise where it's coming from. Where my stricken, prone mentor lies, Faust huddled over him, the sword in hand as he weaves *talented* workings furiously. I can't tell how −or on who− but by my reckoning, somehow Sabnock's put the ring on one of their fingers.

It's enough for Tartalo. His head lowers once more, and he breaks into a leaning, enraged charge, bull-like, straight towards the group. Mephy spins to face the new threat, snarling at the cyclops, but the being's swathed in that sticky black essence, distilled from his murdered demon friend, and I've no idea how my friend is going to stop this challenge, how he'll keep himself safe, let alone the other two, so vulnerable while Faust tries desperately to save Isaac's life.

I want to spring forward, to leap into the fray, to help Mephy and the others, but Sabnock steps towards me, and I've no choice but to fall back. He grins with delight as I do so. 'All of that investment, that one chance your captive boyo had, used up on a pathetic little thing like you. All because he believes in you. It won't work a second time. Not that there will be a second time. Once I've dealt with you, I can return to more pressing matters and resolve this whole ridiculous affair. Bring the worlds back together.' Now the smile is wild, and cold fear settles into my very marrow, freezing me to the core.

Because I know something without any doubt. Sabnock is totally, utterly, completely insane. I've seen smiles like that too many times, up close and personal over the centuries.

That is the smile of a zealot.

'I'll bring them back,' he repeats, that terrifying smile still pinned on his face, 'and make them take me back. Wipe out the demons, the humans. All these stupid physical annoyances. Remake the world in pure thought, pure order. No more of this unbridled, unrestrained, unclean *chaos*!'

I take another step back, and now I'm in trouble because I can feel the low wall separating the garden from the covered cloisters right behind me.

'Oh dear!' he purrs. By the Good God, I really wish he'd stop smiling like that. This is already bad enough, and that goosebump-raising grin is just the cherry on the shit-cake. 'Is there nowhere else to go? Guess it's just you and me.' He pauses. 'Except, of course, it's not.'

Which is when someone slams into the side of me like a linebacker at full tilt.

It doesn't just take me by surprise. The impact literally lifts me off my feet, carrying me up, my feet splaying out to the side, my body twisting from the force of it. Then gravity remembers that it's supposed to be doing its job, not having a fag break round the back of the office building, and I hammer into the ground, the shoulder of my assailant driving in under my ribs, the sharp stab of pain suggesting a part of said ribs might have caved in at the same time.

We roll together, tumbling, but my attacker comes out on top.

De Monteguard. And his eyes are ink-stained. He's possessed.

'Oh, yes.' Ah. Apparently, for all his talk of not indulging in earthly or demonic vices, Sabnock still enjoys a bit of gloating when his schedule allows. 'Your friend there made a deal. A *bargain* as your stories ascribe signing up in servitude to us. He made a deal with Caacrinolaas. I hold the idiot's leash now. Which means I own his deals. Which means the little mano is mine to command!'

I'd love to make some sort of cutting comeback. Something about how if he's going to get kinky, we should at least sort out safe words first. Problem is, that would require me to be able to speak. Which would require me to be able to breathe. Neither of which, between De Monteguard's combined weight and what feels like a punctured lung, are particularly easy to do.

Then De Monteguard wraps his fingers around my throat, and it becomes even harder. To do anything. Especially breathe.

I'm thrashing around, beached-fish style, trying to buck him off, my hands scrabbling at his, desperately, weakly, wanting to catch a single sip of air, one cool gasp of oxygen to soothe my burning throat and lungs. I can't think, can't focus to dislodge him, can't summon my *talent* to come up with some clever trick. In a moment, panic's really going to set in, and it'll go one of two ways.

Either I'll do something instinctive – wreathe him in fire and charbroil him, killing a man who doesn't deserve to die. Or else it'll be me doing the dying.

Already my vision's turning red, the edges fading to that familiar black that tells me I don't have much longer to make the decision.

'Please,' I manage to croak out. 'Please.'

'No use, this time, little mano.' Oh, yep. He really likes to gloat. 'He's used to his demon deal, that one, but he doesn't stand a chance of countering it. Not like your special little boyo who's serving me so well again.'

My hands finally find De Monteguard's wrists, and I start trying to pull his hands apart. But he has his knees pressed on my shoulders, and I can't get proper purchase. Can't get that precious air in.

'Please,' I try to say again, but I make no sound, just mouthing the shape. *Please. Please don't make me do this. I don't want to do this.*

But I know I'm going to, and I'd cry in shame and self-disgust if I'd the time or air to do so. But I don't. So my fingers tighten, pressing against the skin of his inner arms. Readying.

Then the world explodes, into blinding white light, and everything seems to cease to exist.

For a moment, I think it's me. Think that I've done what I didn't want to do. Exploded De Monteguard into component starlight.

But his hands are still wrapped around my throat, albeit his grip seems a little looser. I push against it, and sure enough, he moves. Just a tiny bit, just enough to let some cool, precious air slip down my parched trachea, an unimaginable boon to my broken body.

As the air gets in, my head clears and my spirit soars. Because the vista above us is full of crackling blue neon, wings covering all the sky I can see, cutting through between the air's atoms.

Somehow Faust and Mephy have done it. Nithael is free.

And boy, does he look *pissed*.

Chapter Forty-Seven

It's time for an Angel versus Demon rematch. Ding ding.
Round two.

Honestly, in this moment, I don't know which is more
glorious. That tiny, little slip of air that I'm managing to sup
on through the slightly cracked grip or the Bene Elohim
unfolding into our reality, becoming manifest.

I pull against De Monteguard's hands, and they come
away with the tiniest of efforts. I quickly realise why. An
angelic wingtip is wrapped around his own exposed throat,
a gentle caress lifting him irresistibly backwards. Not only
that, but as I'm staring at the crackling starlight feathers, I
don't get the urge to start screaming in tongues or weeping
bloody tears of awe. I'm protected from the effect of Nith
manifesting. Which can only mean one thing.

Isaac is alive. And that is the most glorious thing of all.

I buck my knees, heaving De Monteguard off me.
Rolling over, I push back up to a shaky standing. My throat

is on fire, and my left hand screams where the finger is missing when I put my weight on it.

The world weaves and wavers a little as I get upright. Still, I try to focus, try not to get distracted by the ethereal light show going on overhead.

It's a hell of a sight though.

Nithael isn't so much blotting out the sun as highlighting it, turning the sky into a crackling, sizzling backdrop. It's like being inside the heart of an invisible thunderstorm, and I am in awe. He's towering over the square, and all his attention is bent towards one, singular being.

Sabnock.

I'd say, 'The poor bastard,' except I don't feel sorry for him in the slightest. I should do, maybe. Normally I can find it in my heart to feel sorry for anyone. Hell, I even managed to forgive the Evil God eventually. But this fucker? Nope, fuck that, fuck him. I'm ready to see him catch an angelic ass whooping.

Except…

Except Sabnock doesn't look very worried. And that is deeply, deeply concerning.

'A perfect example,' he says, sighing once again, and I think he's probably wishing he needed glasses just so he could take them off and clean them in a bored, nonchalant manner, 'of why I must be rid of this accursed physical form. Look! Me! Distracted by revenge! Taken by emotion, distracted by their presence.'

He stops, pops his fingers in his mouth, and mimes a whistle. Or, at first, I think it's a mime, but a weird pressure build-up happens at the base of my skull, a horribly unpleasant reverberation that makes me think he's using some frequency below subsonic.

Then he stops. 'Of course,' he says, 'I did consider the

possibility that you might get free, *Bene* Nithael. And I brought along an old friend who said they wanted to play if you did.'

A rumbling shake, ominous and low carries up through every blade of grass, the lawn itself aquiver. A pounding sound grows louder; something is approaching, closing the distance. The noise is too loud to be even another giant, with too many strikes to be bipedal. Closer and closer, louder and louder until it's directly behind the wall to my right. Then two huge flippers slam down on the roof, crumbling the ancient stonework, pulverising it. Through the thrown-up dust storm, a face emerges. One I've seen in many a nightmare.

A grinning disfigured maw smiles at me, like some ingenious kid has taken a blow torch to a toy tiger's face, melting one side of it to dribble down to the jawline. Sharp spears of teeth jut out in every direction, unidentifiable lumps of worryingly large meat wedged between them, green and putrid to the degree I'd be able to smell them from here if they weren't masked by the unmistakable odour of the repellent creature's own breath. Even swathed as he is in black demon essence, coating him from head to foot, there's no mistaking exactly who it is.

Oh, by the Good God herself, no. Anything but that. I close my eyes, screw them up tight, then open them again, hoping I'm wrong.

'Hello, you poofters!' He roars with glee. 'I've heard there's a chance for a fair rematch with a certain gaylord Bene Elo-her!

No, I'm not.

It's the fucking Tarrasque.

Chapter Forty-Eight

I just wanted an easier win for once. Was that really too
much tarr-ask?

'Hello, Poo-aul!' He waves a flipper at me. 'Ready to be
eaten? You failed our deal. You belong to me!' He glances
about. 'Ooh, new friends! I see you've still got the Jew-el of
your collection!' He sniggers like the nasty little racist,
homophobic, sexist schoolboy he resembles. 'And who else?
Oh a Dopey-mann demon and... is that a German?' He
gasps in mock horror. 'After how they acted in the war! I
never thought you'd be seen... Kraut and about with one!'

He laughs so hard, slapping a flipper down on the messy
rubble that for a minute I think he's going to take me out
here and now by embedding a shard of tile into my brain as
effectively as popping a cap in my ass. And oh, Good God, I
don't know what is worse. His breath, his threat level, or
these terrible, horrible racist jokes he insists on polluting my
eardrums with.

'So Cathar-ine.' The wheezing squeal that accompanies him as he makes a woman's name out of my previous faith really isn't merited. 'This time I get to eat you.'

His eyes narrow, staring at the angel in the air above us, and his voice drops to a growl. 'Last time, you cheated. The angel was never part of the deal.'

'Neither was you lying down, blocking our way out of the city!' We made an agreement with the fucking Tarrasque. If we could get the Jack of Blades out of Lyon, the city the Tarrasque holds, before midnight on a certain date, he was ours to keep. If not, I'd serve as the Tarrasque's boon companion and insta-snack for a year. We were home and dry... until the fucking Tarrasque blocked our route. Only Nithael didn't take kindly to his cheating, so he seized him by the scrag of his neck and hurled him over the horizon.

'It wasn't not part of the deal, Poo-aul!' His shit-eating grin is so slappable, so very slappable, it makes me want to build some sort of giant fighting robot, a kaiju or gundam, just to have a hand big enough to slap it the fuck off his face.

'Well, neither was us seeing you take a flying lesson!' I don't even know why I'm bothering. There's bigger fish to fry than getting into a bitching session with the fucking Tarrasque. But he just pushes my buttons. Same as he pushes everyone's buttons, every time. If he wasn't at least notionally immortal and indestructible, he'd have been wiped off the face of the earth long ago. He knows it too. Revels in it. The absolute fucking cuntmonkey.

'Anyhow, I'm not here to argue with you, the last Catarrh.' He does an appalling impression of someone coughing with a chest infection, then hawks up a huge loogie that he spits at me. I only just have time to dive out of the way before it reaches me. Splashing across the ancient stonework behind, it dissolves it like hydrofluoric acid, accompanied by an odour like a million rotting eggs cracking open simultaneously.

By the time I'm back on my feet, I've been dismissed from his attention. He's staring at the angel in the air above us. And if I didn't like his grin before, I like it even less now.

'Last time wasn't fair, Elo-her.' A petulance creeps into his voice. I don't think the Tarrasque is used to losing. 'I've evened the odds. Now? I don't think you've got... bene... chance!'

Fucking hell, I like word play, but that is, as with most of the fucking Tarrasque's attempts at quips, stretching the point. Not that he cares. He launches himself up into the air, his flippers out front, a Troma Studios vision of a gigantic teenage racist mutant turtle. Wrapping around Nith, he crashes into the angel and carries the pair of them through the solid stone wall and into the chapel beyond. Part of me recognises I should be sad, disturbed by the destruction of the beautiful structure. But I'm more worried for Nithael, newly freed, now at the hands – or the flippers – of the fucking Tarrasque.

'What are you gonna do now, pussycat?' I ask, my attention back on Sabnock. I was aiming for low and threatening, hoping the damage to my strangled vocal cords would add a gravelly, menacing tone. Instead, I just sound like a bored secretary in their sixties who's smoked three packets of cigarettes a day for the past four decades. Probably somebody's kink out there but still not exactly what I was going for.

'What do you mean?' He's still not looking worried, but I reckon he's trying to cover it. The odds have definitely swung in our favour.

'Well, now it's just you versus me, Mephy, Faust, and

Isaac. I don't fancy your chances.' Maybe I'm over-egging it a bit, but the fact remains that with another actual manifest demon, the world's foremost demonologist, the inventor of Kabbalah, plus me bringing my chaotic good energy to the party, surely we have the upper hand.

'Oh. Really?' He doesn't sound worried. Fuck. 'And have you seen your elite team?'

Which is the precise moment I realise I haven't even looked at them. My attention's been entirely focused on my back-and-forth with the fucking Tarrasque after Nithael's appearance, then trying to intimidate Sabnock. But now as I look across, my heart sinks.

Because I don't have an elite team ready to back me up. Not anymore.

Chapter Forty-Nine

With all these twists, the odds are swinging more than a bored middle-aged couple after the kids have left home.

They're not dead, thank the Good God. If they were, I don't think I could summon the energy to even try to stop Sabnock. Not that I have the first clue how I'm going to do that without them by my side.

There's no sign of Tartalo and no shrieking bawdy screams from the ring either. Somehow they got rid of the two-for-one duo, whether before or after freeing Nith, I can't say. Either way I'm grateful they got it done because they don't look like they'd be able to fight him now. Actually, they don't look like they'd be able to roll out of the way before he stamped them underfoot.

Faust's lying on the floor, his skin pale, with huge black rings under his eyes. Mephy lies on his lap. The demon dog's chest is heaving up and down, so he's not dead, but that's the only way I know he isn't. Isaac looks peaceful, at least. Not chalky-skinned, drawn as he looked the whole time Faust carried him up here. But not in peak form. Not awake.

All of my MVPs are out for the count. And I don't have any subs left on the bench.

I rush over to them. Sabnock doesn't try to stop me; he seems to find it all very amusing. I drop to my knees next to Mephy and run my hand along his fur.

'Is he dying?' I whisper to Faust, hardly daring to even verbalise such an impossibility.

'Course… course I'm not dying, you… stupid, fucking… mano.' Mephy's voice is weak, struggling, but the fact he took the time to throw in some insults eases a certain pressure in my chest.

'Time was running out for Isaac, so he took a risk.' Faust's eyes are drained, dimmed. He doesn't look far from death's door himself. But as long as Mephy's going to survive, I have to believe he will too. 'Bit through Isaac's finger. Took the ring. Spat it over the roof. That strange, not very smart – albeit very dangerous – cyclops lumbered off after it. Was betting the angel would heal your friend once free.'

So Sabnock did manifest the ring on Isaac's finger. Clever work by Mephistopheles under pressure. But that alone – chomping free a digit and projectile spitting it out into the blue yonder – doesn't explain why the demon hound looks almost at death's door.

'What did you do?'

'I… bit… through the tether. The one tying the two of them to the sword.' Mephy coughs, one of those ones where it seems like it'll just be a single hack, but it carries on, another, then another, his chest heaving each time. Slowly, though, he settles. 'Well… most of it.'

'He couldn't destroy it, my friend. It was built of the ones they'd made when striking the deals with their respective partners.' Faust strokes the fur of the demon dog who is half his heart. 'It would have killed their links, killed Isaac entirely, possibly De Monteguard too. But he needed to weaken it. Reduce it to the point where Nith could break free. Especially with a strong enough motivation. Bringing them back from the brink of their ending provided plenty of that.'

Brought *them* back from the brink. Which means that Nithael was close to going too, not just Isaac. And suddenly I'm even more worried for him in his fight with the fucking Tarrasque than I already was.

'Took... took all our... strength, mano.' Mephy cracks an eye open, fixing it on me. 'Couldn't... couldn't wait. Had to... trust... you could do... this. On your own.'

He manages to get the last words out before his eye closes. For a second, I think he's gone to sleep, but then it cracks blearily open once more, just a fraction.

'Don't... don't fuck this up, mano.'

Then his eye rolls back in his head as he passes out. Glancing up, I see Faust's eyes are also closed. Whatever Mephy pulled in desperation to save Isaac has taken every last drop of both of their reserves.

Leaving me on my own. To battle a manifest demon.

Don't fuck this up, mano.

Easier said than done.

Chapter Fifty

'Don't fuck this up, mano.' Could a different mano have a go at not fucking it up instead, please? Actively fucking things up is more my style.

I can feel Sabnock. Can't see him. Not yet. My eyes are taking in the remnants of my team. Drawing in on the strange mix of emotions. Despair that they're all out of the game. Relief that they're all still alive.

Determination not to let them down.

'So I think...' Oh, fuck me. No wonder he teamed up with the Fucking Tarrasque. He can fit the same amount of conceited self-satisfaction into three words as that over-grown hairball. I can't help thinking maybe it's the feline connection. Maybe all cats would be smug arseholes if they could talk.

What am I thinking? There's no maybe about it. And no need for them to be able to talk.

'I think the advantage is not with you after all, little mano.'

Oh, you don't say. Thank you, Captain Obvious. You mean that you, as a super evolved being from another plane, have the advantage over me, an exhausted, wounded, spent excuse for a human being?

Of course I don't say that. Not even the Captain Obvious bit, tempted as I am. I'm too exhausted for small talk. Too broken to try to bait the demon with my stinging words.

No, I don't really have any options. No secret Hail Mary like I had up on Bugarach, burning my reincarnation magic to throw death itself at the evil being incarnating on top of the mountain. Maybe I could try for the Cailleach's wand in my pocket, try to hit Sabnock with that. But I suspect if I try to reach for it, I'll get magically gunned down, dead before I can even draw. I'm a nine-fingered wreck, my throat burning, my limbs on fire with bruises and aches, still covered in tiny cuts from our showdown with the pillywiggins.

A bloody mess. Luckily, if there's one thing I'm used to being when faced with insurmountable odds? It's a bloody mess.

I go to push myself back up to standing, and my hand touches something hard and cold that Mephy's lying on. A small smile starts to creep across my face.

Guess, just maybe, it might be Hot Mess Summer after all.

Slowly, painfully slowly, I get to my knees. Sabnock's come closer; he is now standing over me, watching me struggle to stand. I'm so glad for the arrogance that all sentient beings seem to be capable of displaying – or perhaps the ones who do better know well enough to avoid our corner of the galaxy, and who can blame them? But

Sabnock's so sure of victory now, he's happy to let me get back to my feet. He's enjoying watching me struggle. Of course he is. The feline fuckface is toying with me.

Well, this little mouse still has one claw left.

I don't often use martial arts, and there's a good reason for that. Because as a general rule of thumb, the creatures I'm facing are armed with claws or magic or rock-hard skin or razor-sharp teeth, and anything that involves me getting within striking range is probably going to result in me getting the striking appendage torn off at the root. I've learned that the hard way and more than once. Using a bladed weapon or a mace or a quarterstaff or even a piece of two by four increases my chances of not getting the Stretch Armstrong treatment by whoever I'm facing off against.

That doesn't mean I don't appreciate them. Or that I haven't studied them.

Now, if you asked Aicha, she'd tell you I've two left feet on the dance floor. And, you know, if we're talking about throwing some shapes in the house of a rave, then yeah, I'm not exactly grace incarnate. But I'm not Isaac either, thank the Good God. I do know how to move.

I also know capoeira.

There was a summer I spent over in Brazil, that was, if I'm honest, mostly spent tripping balls with a *curandero*, a healer. But I also spent several weeks training in the Brazilian martial arts, hidden inside dance, in the favelas of Rio De Janeiro.

What that incredible time taught me was how to transition from the floor to standing quickly. And how to strike as I do.

The pivot up from my knee isn't easy when I don't have the momentum of the *ginga*, the back and forth swaying dance that constitutes the basic standing movement. But I've a lot of experience and a lot of determination. My knee comes off the ground so I'm sitting back on my haunches, and I twist around, my right leg straightening, my arm touching the floor, a variation of the *martelo no chão*, the hammer from the ground.

I have the immense satisfaction of feeling my right foot hammer into the oversized pussy's jaw, taking him completely by surprise.

Oh, there are moments. Moments that, even as they happen, you know you're going to treasure. When a plan comes together better than even Hannibal Smith could have imagined. When it all slots into place beautifully, and you know –you just know– that this is one of the instances that each time you think of it, you'll get the warm, fuzzy feeling of a job well done.

Snap-kicking a demon lion in the face hard enough to spin him like a wooden top definitely rates as one of those moments.

Now I need to make it count. And I know exactly how.

Because I was very deliberate in where I put my hand to steady myself in the capoeira manoeuvre. Precise in the placement so that I could turn my flat palm into a closed fist as I come up.

Bringing Joyeuse with me.

And as I stand, facing Sabnock's back, I *look* as hard as I can, studying the giant man-lion-demon thing while his attention is taken up by putting his dislocated jaw back in place. I've only seconds. I know it. Once he gets over the shock, those armoured claws are going to be scritch-scratching my skin into pretty little flesh ribbons.

I look at the glowing mass of *talent* that makes up the incarnate demon, and I see the thinnest wisp. A tiny lining trail glowing ever so slightly differently, just between his shoulder blades. One that isn't just a trail.

It's a tether.

And this sword can sever them. Make him useless on this plane.

So drawing a fraction back, I thrust Joyeuse with all my strength at that one spot, the base where the magic of the tether fades, disappearing into what it's tied to below. Something without magic.

Someone whose magic got eaten up in a deal long ago.

As my sword whips through that single point in Sabnock's back, the darkened thread wraps around it like a lonely string of candy floss. I pull back, twirling the blade as I do. Weaving it around the edge. Pulling Sabnock clean away from the body he's inhabiting.

Ripping him from Gil.

'Well, look at that,' I say, a savage grin on my face. 'You got what you wanted! You hate the physical world so much? Ta da! No more body, you absolute wankshaft, prickfaced, cheap Lion-O knockoff.'

He turns towards me, pulled closer by the blade's spin.

The grin on his face matches mine.

He doesn't look scared. He looks delighted.

Shit.

Chapter Fifty-One

TOULOUSE, 30 OCTOBER, PRESENT DAY

Honestly? Without Aicha, Isaac, Nith, Jakob, Nan, Faust, Mephy, and Gil? There's no way I'm the A-Team. The O-Team, perhaps, or the P-Team. Certainly feels like I'm about to P myself.

It would be fair to say that when I cut Sabnock's tether to Gil, who's slumped to the ground but is mercifully still alive based on the groans emanating from him, I didn't expect him to look *happy* about it.

'Erm,' I say, showing just how erudite I can be in a crisis. 'Now, er, now you're in trouble.'

Good God, if I ever find Aicha and bring her back, you'd better believe I'm going to come up with some better repartee to insert in the telling of this tale.

Always assuming I survive to tell it, of course.

'Oh, am I?' Fuck me. How can he still be so smug? The fucker yawns that ridiculously impossible opening that only felines can manage and grins back at me.

Through his opaque head, I see Nithael come smashing through the already structurally challenged wall, the roof section of the building collapsing in behind them. The fucking Tarrasque springs clear before it does, lands on the stricken angel, and he starts tearing at Nith with those horrible, disfigured teeth. That unbearable sound rises again – one no human should ever hear, of an angel crying out in pain. It hurts me in the heart of my soul. It should not exist, and every part of my being knows it too.

Sabnock's insufferable smile widens further.

'It doesn't look like I am the one in trouble, little mano. Do you know how long it's been since I heard that sound?' The tether continues to wind about the blade even though I've stopped turning it, and each loop brings Sabnock floating closer to me. I want to back up, to drop the blade, but my feet feel rooted to the floor, the blade stuck to my hand.

'Do you know,' he says as he expands to cover my vision so that the world narrows down once again to him and me, 'how long it has been since I heard an angel *die*?'

'You'll die next!' I try to fill the words with a confidence I'm really not feeling. 'You're tied to the blade now! I control you!'

'Oh no, little mano.' Closer again, edging towards me. The prick's milking it, enjoying the moment. 'Did you think it was just a case of cut the string and control the demon? I have spent centuries, millennia preparing for this. Working out precisely what to do to bind a manifested angel and a demon together, to tie them up in their own bonds they've thrown into this pathetic little world. Bonds that they have made, bargains struck, partnerships formed.'

He laughs again, that smug, satisfied noise of someone who knows they've already won. 'I didn't form a partnership. I possessed your friend. You might have exorcised me, but you just broke a single strand, one sole spell. And I'm still free. This tether is the one I tied onto the blade in the first place, the working I cast to combine your angel friend and poor, stupid Caacrinolaas. Just as I will again once I've dealt with you. And what better way than to let you see everything that happens? From now until the end of your world? Your friends will be the first to go, of course. Or perhaps I'll let the Tarrasque keep them as playthings. A small thank you. We must appreciate our employees, mustn't we? I think I'm going to enjoy looking out from your eyes, little mano. Are you looking forward to all I'm going to show you?'

Oh, shit. By the Good God, the fucker's not tied to the blade. The blade's tied to him. Now he's going to seize control of me. Possess me. Use me as his puppet. Make me watch him destroy everyone I love one by one. And next?

Who knows what will happen when the other dimensions come crashing together with ours? One thing is sure. The world as humans know it will be over. Humanity might just follow along with it.

I don't see any way out.

I can still move. My arms at least. My legs seem to have been turned to stone, and the release mechanisms in my hands seem to have permanently malfunctioned. So all I can do is swing the blade around, shake it, like I can somehow dislodge the evil demonic spirit crawling up it towards me.

My mind's blank. Completely shut down. Just blind panic, all my senses screaming over the top of each other, a cacophonous riot of sensory input that's overloading me. I can feel the terror scaling my spine, crawling up inch by inch, freezing it as it goes.

Because what I've always done is died. Only once, in a cave under a hill in Faerie, did I see what might happen if I didn't. If I could be kept captive in the nameless dark. Now the dark's taken a name, taken form, and come for me, and it's going to take me too. This time it won't ever let me go. Not ever. Not until the end of time itself.

I don't want that. I can't do that. Can't go back there. Not now. Not ever.

But that's easily said. It does nothing to stop my prison creeping closer, Sabnock edging along the blade in time to the wind of that thread of essence, his smile all-consuming.

Ready to swallow me whole.

Chapter Fifty-Two

'Oh, we can populate the dark with horrors, even we who
think ourselves informed and sure, believing nothing we
cannot measure or weigh.' – John Steinbeck

It's a strange thing, not knowing what will happen when
I die.

I've lived so long with the certainty of popping back up
like the proverbial bad penny, whatever happened. A bit like
one of those weighted Bozo The Clown punching bags,
springing back up as soon as you knock it down.

You and me, Bozo. You and me.

But now, I've no idea. Maybe I'll get another do-over. A
coin popped into the slot for me by the Good God.

Or maybe I'll be done. Will the Good God think I did
what I needed to with the extra life she gave me? Or will I
be the eternal disappointment? Another credit squandered?
Another waste of time?

I've no idea. But I know what's waiting for me if I don't

die. What's coming to wear me like an oversized overcoat. To make me watch it destroy everything I love.

That, I can't have.

So I may not know what will happen when I die. But compared to the alternative?

I'm happy to find out.

Sabnock's done something so I can't drop the sword, can't run away. Maybe it's him or maybe it's part of the workings he's cast with the blade. Either way, the effect is the same.

But I can still move my arms, stretch them straight out. And I can still rotate the blade. Spin it straight round.

Aim it straight at my chest.

The movement pulls Sabnock with it, and he sees what I'm doing. Snarling, he accelerates, closing the distance.

But there's a lag. He's a fraction behind the blade. He won't be quick enough.

I plunge the sword straight into my chest. Directly between the appropriate ribs. A clean strike for the heart with nothing in the way.

Except there is. I hit something.

I don't know if there really are invisible muses, the equivalent of the urluthes whispering words we need at just the right moment. But if there are, one's sitting on my shoulder right now. Because a flash of inspiration strikes me like a lightning bolt from the blue, and I do something I never thought I'd get to do again.

I smile.

Then I twist and drive the blade into the heart of the once-tree acorn rather than the heart of me.

Oh, by all that's holy, it hurts. Just that crack is enough. Parts of the radiant power within it starts leaking out, flooding through my cells, and it's like a nuclear bomb just went off in my chest. But I keep myself together, grit my teeth against the pain. It won't beat me. We're old friends, pain and I. Go way back, the pair of us. Pain's been my constant companion throughout the centuries. Pain means I'm alive.

Good to see you again, old friend.

It feels like my chest is swelling, like a face-hugger gave me a French kiss when my back was turned, and I'm about to have a little, itty-bitty alien burst out at any second. Except nothing's getting out.

Sabnock's going in.

Oh, it's glorious. Not the pain, of course, even if I do welcome it compared to the alternatives. Nor the feeling that my atoms are getting stretched, that I'm surely swelling up like Violet Bauregarde after having taken an ill-chosen piece of chewing gum in a health and safety nightmare of a chocolate factory.

But the look on Sabnock's face? Makes it all worth it.

Now that self-conceited, self-satisfied smugpuss expression isn't there. Nope. Now he's looking confused, thrown. He's felt the change and is trying to pull back, trying to work out what's happening. Only to find he can't. No, now I'm controlling the process. Dragging him in, reeling in the line like I've gone fishing and caught the world's ugliest demon catfish in the process.

Come to papa. Come on, you twatfish. Now I've got you. Now you're mine.

'What's happening?' Fear's starting to appear on Sabnock's face now. This isn't what's supposed to be happening. Not in the slightest, and he's *terrified*.

Good. Fuck you, Sabnock. Fuck *you*.

'I once made a tree into an acorn.' The words are effort. My lungs seem to be climbing up into my throat, trying to get out of the way of the expanding spot in my chest because surely that once-tree's now bigger than I am. It feels larger than Toulouse, let alone my chest cavity right now. But still I carry on. 'Not just me. Me and a hag. And I... I was wearing the body of a former fae queen. A... a triple threat, if you will. Hag, fae, and human magic. Wound together.'

My breathing's not getting any easier, but I'm finding my stride in getting to tell this fucknugget exactly what I think of him. 'I thought of it as a battery.' I laugh at the ridiculous idea. 'Embedded in my chest as something to draw on in an emergency, with Toulouse being cut off from me.'

I grunt as a jolt of the demonic energy being sucked in shockwaves through my frame. Sweat's pouring down my forehead. It's not going to stop me though. 'But I sacrificed some of it. Not for me. Not even for my friends. But for the pillywiggins. To save them. To drain some of that demonic essence from them before we had to kill them all.'

People will try to convince you in this life over and over that only the strong prevail. That selfishness and greed are the way to win. That you should only ever look after number one, and anyone who can't do the same should be allowed to falter and fail.

It's a lie. Always has been. There's no greater strength than a selfless act.

It's amazing how often it pays dividends.

'When I did, it changed.' The pain is excruciating now. I don't think I'm going to survive this. But I want him to know what happened. Why he's going to be trapped inside a tiny little acorn. Hopefully for all eternity. 'It became a reservoir for the demonic essence. A storage spot. The three magics combined, learning how to keep it in place until I could move it on.'

I grin up at the terrified feline face drawing closer towards me against his will, so happy to share something that I worked out as I tried to kill myself, when I got lucky for once, a realisation that hit me like a tonne of bricks and changed *everything* about this fight. 'Making it the perfect prison for a disembodied demon.'

Sabnock yowls, panic stretching his vocal cords, the note rising as it does. He turns, clawing at the air, trying to pull himself away, helplessly trying to grasp at the nothing in front of him. I laugh at his feeble, useless efforts.

Until he suddenly gets purchase.

His claws tear into the space between the atoms, the one between the worlds, and he starts scrabbling at the thin air, digging it apart, widening it. As I start to whimper at the unbearable burning spreading through every fibre of my being, I can see what he's making.

A portal. He's opening a way through to another world.

I've no idea where it is. Whether it's back to where he came from or somewhere else entirely. Perhaps in his own panic, he doesn't know either. But wherever it is, I can see the shimmering appearing in the space between his hands. He wraps his metal-covered claws around the edges of the portal and heaves.

He pulls himself inch by inch over the lip, over the rim of reality and into another one.

By the Good God, it hurts. It hurts so much, and trust me, I am a pain connoisseur, the sommelier of agony. I can feel it. Exactly what's going to happen. The grip I have is slipping, and he's going to tear the acorn from my chest. Rip it out and take the light from my eyes in the process. Leave me dead, my body broken, and then he'll be free. He can close the portal and carry on with his wicked plans, and I'll be helpless to stop him, whether I come back or not.

I have to pull him back. Have to win this tug of war we're playing with that strand of his being.

But I'm not winning.

After all this. After that one stroke of unimaginable luck. After turning the impossible tide, of King Canute finally getting the victory...

I'm going to lose.

I'm going to die.

Chapter Fifty-Three

Please no. Don't let me fail now. Not when I've come so close. Please don't let me let them down. Let them all down. Let everyone down.

The pain just carries on building, layer after layer, a temple to pain, a pyramid built of bricks of suffering constructed inside my chest. There's no space, no more room in the inn. I can't take anymore. There's just too much of it. Too much of the screaming in my atoms, too much of the essence wound up in my chest. Too much. It's all too much.

And then. A touch.

It's tiny, at first. Barely a whispering breeze on the scalding burning. But it grows, strengthens until it's whistling through my body, a veritable cooling gale that blows through every part of me.

A crackling, cooling, neon gale.

Nithael.

It's the tether. That tiny strand Mephy couldn't sever.

He can feel my pain. But it goes both ways. I can feel his too. Can feel the fucking Tarrasque tearing chunks out of his side, feel the electric starlight pouring from his wounds.

He doesn't care. He's here to help me.

And he does. He creates a relay, linking himself to me just like Mephy did with the poison coating the pillywiggins. He starts drawing some of that to himself. Lets the Tarrasque do his worst while he helps me do my best.

The pressure eases. Just a touch. Just to the point where I feel like a body again rather than a breaking dam, a barrage at bursting point. I'm still wracked with excruciating agony.

But I will not break.

Sabnock howls his fury and frustration and redoubles his efforts, heaving himself towards the door he's made in the very air. But now we're back to a stalemate. He's not about to tear my chest open anymore. He's not going anywhere.

Then I feel another touch. This one's burning as Caacrinolaas' unbridled fury pours through me. It burns out the pain. How could any agony stand in close proximity to such radiant anger? The demon hooks himself into the prison I've made. And starts to draw off some of that excess energy.

Sabnock looks backwards, and I can tell the panic in him is really setting in. Because he sees what he's made. A union between an angel and a demon, all right.

But not just that. One between an angel, a demon, and a human. With the touch of a hag and the taste of the fae thrown in for good measure.

He's made a chimera of power, and he's tied himself to it.

Yet, it's still not enough. Because the problem is, he

made it. The ties are his, the power bound to him. It ebbs and flows, back and forth along the taut, tied line. Sometimes I'll feel my soul swell with a purity of hedonistic rage, self-indulging fury, and one of Sabnock's fingers will come free, pulled from the frame. But then I'll sense his own self-hating righteousness flood back down, and he'll tighten his grip, strengthening his hold on an impossible window out of our world, even as a logic balm smoothes away his advantage, and we come back to a struggle that's stuck, locked in balance.

It's not enough. Even our three forces combined aren't enough to dislodge him. They might all be immortal, beings of pure thought or emotion, outside of the rules and whims of our reality.

But I'm not. And I can't survive this forever.

It doesn't seem fair. Doesn't seem right. I've stared down the Evil God who might've made our world. Threw everything I had at him. Made a sacrifice of myself then, and it worked thanks to the Good God. Here I am making a sacrifice of myself again, but it isn't enough. Demon, angel, hag, fae, human, and life magic combined aren't enough to reel him in like the utter cuntfish he is.

Then I remember. One other thing I tried on Bugarach. One other thing that didn't work then, that I've been sure wouldn't work now.

But it's the only element missing. And while it might not work on Sabnock, it might just work.

On me.

My arms are outstretched, pulled in each direction by the opposing angelic and demonic forces flooding through me. But I can move them. Enough. Slowly, like I'm chest-pressing reality itself —and in a way I am— I pull my two hands together. I send a message back through the connection, telling them to *trust me*. Nithael does, of course, so my left hand moves faster. Caacrinolaas is warier, but we're bound, and he can tell I'm not trying to screw him over, so the right hand comes too. Then it's a difficult fumble in my pocket, my trousers soak-slicked with blood from my chest, my fingers weakened, stretched, but I find it. I pull out a thin twig-like stick, hardly even a branch. I feel Caacrinolaas' intrigue and Nithael's instinctive disgust.

I don't care. It's not for them. This curse is meant for me.

Last time, the first time in my existence that I ever used death magic, I burnt my reincarnation *talent*. I threw it as a ball of anti-life at Papa Nicetas, the Evil God's representative on this plane. He laughed and swallowed it whole, showing how useless it was against higher beings.

This time, I take the Cailleach's stick, charged to the brim with that filthy form of spell-working, and shove it straight into the gaping gap in my chest, following along the blade's edge until it touches the acorn inside.

Then with it deep inside my being, I release the death magic, turning it on my own soul.

With that extra element combined – that of true death, of final death, not simply the ending of life but the dissolution of it entirely, Sabnock's will is beaten. The stalemate is broken.

He's screeching now. Spitting. Yowling. Screaming wordless noises of sheer terror. Scrabbling, his left hand slips; it tries to grab on again, but it can't. He can't. No. The portal's out of reach of his left hand; his body is pulled taut. The fingers of his right hand are stretched to breaking point, and one by one, like Sylvester in a Warner Bros cartoon having them lifted off by Tweety Pie, they pop loose until he only has one single claw-point still dug into the nothingness he's made in the very air itself.

Then that slips, and Sabnock comes flying towards us.

He slams into me at a rate of knots faster than the speed of light. No, he's moving at the speed of *life*, the speed with which an empty universe fills, a myriad prism of points resisting an endless, uncaring void that unifies us all.

I shout. Because, of course, I'm dying.

Actually, I may already be dead.

Because suddenly I realise I'm seeing all of this from above, from overhead. The death magic's not eaten up my soul – or not yet, at any rate. That's what I expected to happen. That I would sacrifice myself, dissolve away finally into nothingness, the eventual promise I accepted as mine when I broke my Perfection all those long centuries ago. That this was why the Good God sent me back. Gave me one last chance to do good before I ceased to exist.

Instead, it seems to have evicted me from my body and given me ringside seats.

Sabnock strikes the hilt of Joyeuse and starts being channelled into it, following along the blade's blood gutter, back into my own guts and guttering heart. He's screaming, wailing in disbelief, but he can't escape. His very essence is being compressed, sucked down into the groove, and fed away into the acorn's heart. As he hits, he gets forced into the trap we've made of our combined beings, and the acorn starts to seal. Nithael is wrapping swathes of his essence around it, and Caacrinolaas is following with bands of his own. Closing it up. Making it impregnable.

The energy of an angel and a demon combined. What beautiful poetic justice.

A moment later it's done. He's been swaddled in the

magic of all the dimensions. Locked away from any of the worlds.

And who'd have thought it? That I'm still not done. Though I'm not quite sure what I'm supposed to do now.

The body – my body that I got driven out of by the death magic doesn't look, well, *dead*. I mean, it doesn't look well. There's a blade hilt sticking out of it, not to mention the Cailleach's wand I jammed in, and there's a lot of blood coating my lower extremities.

But my chest is still moving, still heaving half-broken, ragged breaths. Which is weird when I don't seem to be occupying it. Deeply peculiar.

I'm not sure what happens now. Will I move on? Am I going to get another audience with the Good God, a last beaker of that divine whisky to say job well done, now bugger off to whatever comes next?

But then I see it. The portal. It's still here.

Everything slows down, freezes. The swirling plumes of brick dust come to a halt in mid-air. Then I see the White Lady, the Guardian to the Portals.

She's standing there, a column of pure light, of pure love, her featureless expression invisibly creased in amused joy at my actions, like a love-struck mother at her beloved offspring's antics. She's holding the portal open, keeping the way for me, giving me the time to see that everyone here is okay, that it's all going to be all right.

As she looks at me, the memory of what Mephy and Isaac said about the angels and the demons being able to come to our plane of existence comes back to me.

The angels and demons used to be able to see all the different realities from their own dimensions, but that all changed when Nith and Nan got called down to our reality.

After that? The only plane they can now see, the only

plane they can come to is this one because it's the only one an angel is tied to.

Except the Good God told me that they had all survived. So if Nanael is still alive, there are now two realities the higher planes are tied to.

And only one other reality Sabnock could open a portal to.

No...

The White Lady's non-existent features form a delicate invisible frown, which still messes with my head however many times I see it without seeing it. Then her voice speaks, pure rung crystal inside my brain, where my grey matter is the aforementioned ringing crystal.

'The portal will only lead to the two other realities for the demons. They're tethered there. There are many places it could lead to for you.'

'But that's where he opened it to! I mean, surely that's how this works, right?'

She nods without moving. 'He did. But as is normally the case with moving from one place to another, you must pass through many other places to get there.'

Shit. The fact she said *normally* means I suspect it doesn't apply to her. But I also suspect she isn't willing – or isn't able – to help me further than she already is.

'If I go through,' I think it at her as hard as I can, 'if I pass through that doorway, will I find them?'

I don't need to specify who *they* are, of course. It's been the thing driving me forward. Has always been the thing driving me forward. Save the ones I love. Whatever the cost to me, save the ones I love. The thing I've failed at so many times no matter how hard I've tried.

So what if I get it wrong this time too?

'You might.' I can feel her benevolent non-smile at me.

'It isn't for me to say. Isn't possible for me to say. But know this – if you don't, they won't suffer. They are well, Aicha and Jakob. But they will be lost to you. Just like your friends here will all be fine if you go. All will be as well as can be. But you may be lost to them, with all the weight that will carry in their hearts.'

Oof. That's a hell of a choice. Sounds like this is a one-time deal – a choice to make. But it isn't about saving them. Not really. It's about bringing them home.

'There is more to know,' she says.

Isn't there always? Yet, it's amazing how often it's stuff I don't really want to know.

Chapter Fifty-Four

TOULOUSE, 30 OCTOBER, PRESENT DAY

The problem with there always being more to know? It's like the Mother always says. There's always a price to pay.

It'd be fair to say I'm waiting with some pretty hefty amounts of trepidation to find out what bombshell the White Lady's going to drop on me.

'I can see something inside you. Deep buried, where you can't make it burn. Your reincarnation magic is still there.'

Okay. Wow. I was expecting her to come with some, "if you go through there, you'll doom the world" sort of heavy-weight load thrown on my shoulders. Not the good news that the Good God came through fully for me. After I used it up on Bugarach, burned it as fuel in the useless death magic I threw at Papa Nicetas, and then got sent back, I've never known if I'd get a do-over if I died. Now I find out that, yep, I have some more 1-Ups in the arcade machine coin slot, after all.

That's good news.

Isn't it?

Ha. Of course that isn't going to be the case. Not for me. It never works that way.

Waves of sympathetic understanding wash over my cortex. She gets me. Knows I'm waiting for the other foot to drop, know she's about to stick that boot in. 'It means you can't die. Not now. Not until you're Perfect. And if you go through there – if you don't find your way to them? You'll never achieve Perfection. And you'll never find your way out.'

Oh. So if I go through that doorway, I could fail. I could get lost and not just for a lifetime but for all lifetimes, forever. In the same form as I am now, disembodied, unable to interact with anything or anyone. I think back to Ben, my best friend from my first life, how he became twisted, ruined by his endless rebirth, the helplessness of being stuck, aware in a newly formed foetus, imprisoned in the womb for nine months each time he died. It broke him, destroyed his morals, his mind.

That was for nine months out of every lifetime. For me it'd be for all time, for all lives until reality itself came to an end.

No one – none of us who bear the title of "immortal" are really that or would really want to be. None of us saw the world form nor expect to be here to see the universe reach heat death and wither away. Maybe the Good God, who I met outside of life itself, but even with her, I'm not sure.

And none of us would want it anyway. Certainly not in the form I'm being offered now.

So I could end up living forever, observing but never being part of life, always stuck on the outside. I think back to the Evil God, to his desperate attempt to force his way back into our world. Is that what happened to him? Was that why he was so full of anger, so consumed by hate?

Is that what I'll become?

But there's more than that too. Because I think back to Isaac's desperate tears as he broke down on the mount of Bugarach when I came back, to his words. *I thought we were the only ones left.* Even with Nithael, an angel who's made a home in his soul, he was near broken by the idea of being left alone. That's the true fear of every immortal. That those we love will die.

That we won't.

To be the last remaining being when everyone else has ceased to exist, and yet to keep on going with no ending in sight. No ending possible. If there's a worse horror, I can't imagine it. Because I don't have an angel in my soul. I've nothing but me. And I've often found myself lacking. Being stuck with just myself for eternity isn't just my definition of hell. It's my own personalised one, my punishment in Tartarus for having insulted the gods. Give me having my innards torn out by an eagle every day, any time. At least it'd be company.

At least I wouldn't end up on my own.

So that's the choice. I can try. Take a step through that portal. Try to find our missing family and bring them home. But they're… *well*, she said. Not happy. Not glad to be there. But *well*. They aren't at risk. Aren't suffering. They won't die if I don't go after them.

But if I do, and I mess it up? I'll be lost for eternity.

So bring my sister home or suffer forever. How I can I make a choice like that? I can't. Nobody can be asked to make such a decision. It's not possible.

It's not fair.

But neither's life. Neither were Susane's two deaths, first

in a pool of flooded out blood drenched through our wedding bed, second by the son she loved enough to suffer his abuse, or perhaps it was guilt that tied her to him. Either way, she suffered, and that wasn't fair. Neither was Ben's suffering for having been touched by the Grail's energy, by the deaths of those Perfects whose souls were lost inside it. Not Esclarmonde, a beautiful soul who walked into the fire as the Cathars fell for the final time on Montsegur.

Not poor Lou Carcoilh, dying alone in the dark till I reached him, under Hastingues' hollowed-out hill.

Nor all the other tragedies I don't know of. Haven't lived through. All the endless miseries and sufferings and longings and losses that humanity lives through, writ big and small through all the tapestries of their days and all the cut threads of their coming nights.

None of it is fair. It's all just choices made that weave those threads together and make them into something more. Into something with meaning. Into something beautiful.

They're what gives life shape and worth and purpose.

I know my purpose. Know those I've failed. Know the times I've taken the easy choices, picked the way out that hurt less, that stopped the pain for a short period of time. I've let others pick up the bill for my actions and inactions. Let them suffer in my stead.

This time, it's on me.

The White Lady nods without moving, her featureless smile beatific, a blessing on me and my course of action.

And without a second's further thought, I dive headlong into the portal.

It's a peculiar sensation, moving without any body. A bit like using one of those virtual reality headsets, where you point and click to your next destination while your inner ear screams blue murder at you because you physically don't move from where you are. I change location, but there's no sense of the change, and I'm pretty sure I'd be feeling nauseous as all hell right now if I had a stomach and bile ducts still attached to me.

But however it happens, I zip across the space and through the gap, through the window that's not just through the world, like my etheric storage, no...

It's a window through all the worlds.

I can see them. Snatches. Mere smidgens. Images I can't process, not properly; my brain can't move that fast. But subconsciously, I clock them, and they play me like a fiddle made of strings of emotion. One second I'm laughing with joy, the next gibbering with uncontrollable terror, then weeping tears that can't fall from my bodiless eyes at the unbearable, unknowable sadness, at the grief that I don't know, unable to tell you what I see but which shreds my metaphorical heart to shreds.

But even that – even the range of emotions painting themselves across my mindscape like Bob Ross got loose with a multidimensional paintbrush after dropping two tabs of acid and snorting some werewolf testosterone – it all seems almost exterior to me. Because what I am – the core of me, the central part to my being is boiled down to a single, simple mission.

To find it. That other world.

To find them.

'Paul! What are you doing?' There's a voice in my head once more. But not the brain-ringing words of the White Lady this time. Rather, it's a voice I know better than my own because it's one that I've listened to more than any other, that's guided me through this strange second chance

– and third, fourth, five hundredth, six thousandth chance I've had since my first death.

Isaac.

I can feel him. The tether, created from the shared effort of Nithael and Caacrinolaas, stretches backwards from me through impossible non-distances where I've not moved and yet am farther away than the whole expanse of a universe. It's being pulled tauter, thinner. Made fragile by passing through impossibilities. Places where demons and angels aren't supposed to pass. Where humans certainly aren't supposed to venture.

'Paul!' The voice comes again, insistent, worried. No, not worried. *Terrified*.

'It's okay, 'Zac. I can do this. I'm going to bring them back.' I want to add, 'or die trying,' but that's a lie. That'd be a far better alternative. The truth is "or live trying", and that is a horror so vast, so unbearable that if I think about it, I'll lose my nerve and yank on the safety cord leading back to them, bailing on this one chance to bring back our family.

No. I'd rather doom myself. I keep that thought from the other end of the line though.

'Paul, you can't do this! You mustn't! Nith is telling me the line, it's stretching too far. They can't hold it, can't… can't hold you. You'll be lost, lad!'

For a moment, I can feel everything through the line. His fear for me. His guilt; did he fail me? His shame at his deep-seated terror. That I'll not come back. That those terrors he suffered through on Bugarach are coming true, and he'll be the last one left, just him and his soul-bonded Elohim throughout the ages. Without Jakob. Without Aicha. But most of all, without me. I feel how much he's suffering right now, how many times he's suffered like this. Watching me head into the unknown, where he can't know if I'll ever come back. Where I've walked down paths he can't walk beside me, holding death's hand, and all he could ever do was hope, pray to his god that I'd turn up again. Never sure I would, not with all the risks I take, the danger I just waltz into willingly.

I can't reassure him. Can't promise him it'll be okay. The signal's weakening, breaking up like crackling distortion bursts breaking up a telephone call. So I don't try to give him words. Instead I send back what he gave me. An honest view into my heart. Allow him to feel my determination, to do the right thing for him but also for me. To get my sister-soul back, to get his brother back. I make all my pride flow back through the tether. The honour it's been to be his student. That being his son has made life a pleasure. I let the love and admiration I feel for him every single day go flooding back for him to experience so that if this is the last time, he knows that it is him who's made time itself surviv-able. Without him there to keep me centred, to be my moral compass, I'd have gone the route of Ben or De Montfort long ago, lost into villainy, doubtless believing myself a hero every step I walked into the darkness.

Isaac kept me safe. *Love you, old man.* The connection wavers, chops, cuts. The tether's still there but immeasur-ably thin; I can't understand how it even counts as a link. *Quantum probably,* I think to myself and concentrate on what lies ahead.

Because Isaac kept me human. But after the death of Susane, after my heart shattered, it was all automatic exist-ing. I was nothing but a golem, animated clay, acting in the way I did only so as not to disappoint Rabbi Isaac even if it was all just dust and ashes in my mouth.

Aicha Kandicha taught me how to live again.

Isaac kept me safe. Aicha saved me.

So this one is for Jakob. It's for Isaac. For Nith and Nan, to reunite the Bene Brothers. But this one is also for me. Truly for me. Because I need her back. Maybe if I'm lost in here, I'll live as a phantom, bodiless, meaningless, tearing through the multiverse forever, a terrible fate to suffer. But if I stayed back there, in a world without her, I'd be little more than a ghost haunting an immortal shell.

What difference is there in that choice that really matters?

I push on, picking up speed, trying to find a sense of direction as I move through a million worlds without shifting a single inch. The signal's gone, and the tether's too stretched, too pulled between too many realities. There's a second when it's there and then a moment later – a multi-verse later, it's gone.

I'm on my own.

314

Chapter Fifty-Five

A lost spark among myriad lights. Somehow still forever
alone in the dark.

The snatches I'm seeing are growing now, moments caught
of other worlds. Realities that seem familiar yet fundamentally different, where the laws of physics aren't laid down in
the same way. Cities where the glass structures hold panes
of metal that run trickling spatters down under the purple
sun's intense radiance. A town of bubbling waterways that
hiss and spit as the people glide along the surface, multi-
coloured trails left behind matching their *talent*. Fields and
farms flicker up for a second. Another, more close to my
own but not mine. A wooded scene suddenly fills with blood
as a giant wyrm smashes through what looks like a group of
warriors, tearing them apart, painting the greenery a vivid,
shocking red. Screams fill my ears, and my hands flex
instinctively, searching for a sword.

But this isn't my battle. Isn't my world. Isn't even

anything I can touch. I'm unable to save myself, let alone anyone else.

I'm lost. There's no way home, no ruby red shoes to click three times and get back to Kansas. The tether's gone. But still I press forward, bullish and determined not to think about it too deeply. Because if I am lost, then let me be lost watching over her. Cheering her victories, weeping for her losses. If I have to live forever alone, then I'll live vicariously through her.

If only I can find her.

Suddenly, I see it. Something different from the myriad shifts. Something other but familiar in its otherness. A glinting, glittering chrome over the ever-changing horizon, a flipbook made of stills of a million different movies made of a million different versions of worlds, realities, of me, myself. *There*.

And impossibly, the silver sees me too. Then it's traveling towards me. Coming to meet me across the multiversional planes.

It reaches me, and I hear once more an angel sing a song of peace and joy. Nan hands something to me, something he's been cradling as though it were the most precious thing in existence.

Aicha.

The person in my arms looks up and gives me a smile that makes every single second since I last saw her worthwhile.

'Hello, dickhead,' Aicha Kandicha says. 'About fucking time.'

About fucking time indeed.

I can't see her properly. It's an impossibility as is, that I'm holding her physical being in my incorporeal arms, but I guess that's what happens when other-dimensional beings decide to play about in our sandbox. Somehow the angel has handed me her essence. But even if she hadn't spoken – words forming inside my brain– even if she'd been mute, just a simple glowing ball of energy clasped between my disembodied fingers, I'd have known. Known it was her.

There's no way I could fail to recognise her soul. It's the part of my own that's been missing for far too long.

But that thought – about what's been lost and about being missing kicks my panic levels back up. 'No! *Laguna*, no!'

I feel her own confusion radiating back up at me. 'What is it, *saabi*?'

'I'm lost! You can't come with me!' Nan's presence is still there, a towering luminescence seeming to stretch across myriad realities. I start trying to push the tight-clutched essence in my grip back towards the Bene Elohim. As is, I'm delighted. If I must be a lost soul for all of time left still to come, then let it be here. Let me stand spectator to her doings and actions, to all her triumphs still to come. She'll know I'm watching, cheering her on from the sidelines. That's enough for me, more than I could have possibly hoped for when I felt the tether snap. But she can't be lost too. I can't take her down into the void with me. That's too terrible a price to pay, too much for me to bear. I can't allow that. I'm trying to push her back into his arms, trying to make him understand. *No, I can't. I'm doomed. Don't entrust me with anything. You mustn't.*

There're no words, but I feel his question, his demand to know *why*? So I show him. The snapped tether. The lost way home. Back to our world. Back to my body. How there's nothing for me now but an eternity of suffering, wandering as a restless ghost.

And I feel Nanael, a Bene Elohim, an angel from

another realm, *smile*. He leans forward and presses crackling neon lips to my forehead, and I could weep because I feel them, feel the touch of another being. I never thought I'd have that ever again, have that sense of anything outside of me.

Great rolling tears, drops of my spirit essence, spill from my incorporeal eyes. Because from that touch, I feel his *talent* infuse me. The power of an angel boils through my soul, charging my being. It's as though I just shoved a fork in the universe's power socket. Impossible lightning crackles between what I can't help thinking of as my atoms, although I reckon you need to have a physical form to be made up of matter. The ghosts of atoms, perhaps. A molecule's dream. Either way, whatever they are, they're vibrating, electrified by the unimaginable power hammering through them.

A millisecond later, I'm full, loaded up with all of it until it feels like surely it's too much, I have to burst, and I'm wondering if perhaps that's it. Maybe this is the mercy that Nan can offer me. Extinguishing me, burning my being to ashes with his incredible power. An out from an eternity alone.

Then his *talent* finds its own out, a way to escape my overloaded soul, and I'm struck dumb with wonder and joy. Because I can feel what it is.

The tether. He's fixed the tether.

Except, now it's there, I realise it isn't that he fixed it. He recharged it, reinforced it. Strengthened it enough for me to feel. It was always there, just too diffuse, stretched too thin to sense. Certainly too difficult to locate for me to use to find my way home.

At least until an angel powered up the link again from this side too.

Nan breaks contact, pulling his lips away from my fore-head, but the tether doesn't waver. The power crackling through my ethereal form is enough to maintain the link. I reach out a hand towards him for him to take. I assume that he's linked to Jak, that if he grabs hold of me, we can follow that tether all the way back to our world. But the angel smiles, his neon electric lips spread wide, and shakes his head. Then he pulls back, disappearing through the whip-ping whirl of worlds, back to where he came from.

I want to go after him, to pull him back for Nithael and Isaac, but he made his choice clear. I have to respect it.

So I reach back. Tug on my tether, giving them the signal that this deep dive is done. I'm ready. Pull me up.

And pull me up they do.

All of those realities I saw whistle past me in reverse, but this time they don't touch me, don't play me like an emotional wreck. Because I can't see them. All I see is what I'm holding in my arms. That's enough to make me laugh and cry over and over.

That's worth everything.

Because when, a second later, a million lifetimes later, we crash backwards out of that invisible, impossible window, back out into the trashed atrium that was once a monastery before it was raised up as an enemy's tower of power in the heart of my city, I'm not alone.

Aicha Kandicha, the Druze Queen, Slayer of Men, and my best friend, is clutched tight in my arms.

Her face twists, her siyala tattoo dancing as she gives me that lopsided half-grin, the one I don't see very often. The one reserved for when I get things totally, completely right. When my boldness bordering on idiocy has paid off, well and truly for once, just for once.

'Knew you'd make it eventually, *saabi*.' She gives a seal-bark laugh. 'Kept expecting you to just fall out of the fucking sky, to be honest. That you'd blunder your way across and get stranded.' She thinks about this for a moment. 'Which is, actually, pretty much what fucking happened. You idiot.'

The words are harsh but the tone's gentle. She's right – she'd never have expected anything else from me. This time? It's paid off. It's all paid off.

There's a cry of joy from behind me, and I put Aicha back on her feet, standing her upright just before Isaac barrels into her, wrapping her in a lion's embrace, his emotions overflowing, a mixture of laughing and crying emanating from his frame as he enfolds her in his.

'All right, old man,' she says when she can eventually pull free. Both of them laugh at that, considering she's his senior by some centuries. 'Good to see you too. Sterling work, keeping this dickhead alive. I'd have thought it impossible without me about.'

Isaac mock frowns. 'I managed to keep him alive against all imaginable odds, for several centuries before you turned up, young lady.'

She stares back at him, disbelievingly. 'No, you didn't.'

'No, I really didn't. Some things are beyond the capabilities of any mere human.' He nods sagely, wisely, and the two of them collapse into cackling fits of laughter.

'Erm, excuse me? Still actually here?' The two of them look up at me, at my peeved expression, and crack up all over again. But it's good to see the tears streaming down Isaac's face being from joy instead of fear and pain for once. I'll let them have their joke at my expense.

Doesn't mean I'm not already plotting my terrible prank-based revenge, believe you me.

There's a polite cough from behind them, and I see Gil

scuffing his shoe against the rubble scattered from the destructive conflict.

'Hello, Ms Aicha. Glad you're back.' He blushes slightly, a reddening to his pale cheeks. I know Gil doesn't fancy girls, but I think he has a bit of a hero-crush on my best friend. Then the colour fades as he looks seriously at me and Isaac. 'Thank you for saving me. Again. Sorry. I... I didn't know he... didn't know he was there... guiding... controlling... not until he —'

'Enough, Gil.' I cut him off. He's deep into beating himself up for Sabnock having managed to use him as a hidey-hole, as a way to slip past our defences. That needs to stop. 'You wrestled control of your body back from a fucking demon manifest in our dimension. That is beyond impressive. And it saved us all. Again. So thank you, my man. Thank you.'

I give him a nod, heartfelt, appreciative, and the kid blushes once again. Guess he's not used to people giving him praise, earned or otherwise. We'll have to see what we can do about that.

Aicha's eyes widen. 'Is that Faust and Mephy?'

'It is! I put the band back together!' I say, treating her to that trademark, million-watt, Bonhomme grin.

'You're not Joliet Jake, *saabi*. Less Elwood, more El Wouldn't.' She stares at me for a moment, poker-faced, then we break into sniggering laughter, like a pair of naughty schoolkids, an analogy only further added to by the tutting sighs of a headmaster-like Isaac.

I fling my arm around Aicha's shoulder and, for once, she doesn't threaten to slice it off and feed it to me for invading her personal space. Miracles will never cease. But as I've been granted the best, most impossible, most wonderful miracle imaginable and got my sister-soul back, it's clearly the day for them.

We look at each other, and she bows her head slightly. '*Shukran.*'

I shake mine. 'No need to thank me, *laguna*. How about what you did to need rescuing? Sacrificing yourself to save us all on Bugarach? So no need for that at all.'

She tilts her head bird-like, thinks for a minute, then nods. 'Fair enough, dickhead. Now let's go see the others. Who's the suit with them?'

Oh, this is going to be fun. 'That? That's De Montfort's son.' I watch her eyes widen, her hand going for one of the doubtless innumerable blades stashed around her body. 'Chill out. He's on our side.'

Now Isaac's beside her too, his arm wrapped around her from the other side, with his other hand resting on my bicep, a communal moment, a deep delight drawn from just being here, together, in this place, at this time. Gil steps away, starts to pull back, desperate not to intrude, but I grab him and pull him in on the other side. I throw my other arm across his shoulder, eliciting a squawk of surprise and delight from the shy young man. He's earned his place in this line-up.

Then arm in arm, we walk back towards the rest of our team, unified once more, ready to take on whatever this strange and wonderful existence might choose to throw at us next.

As long as we're together? Bring it on.

Chapter Fifty-Six

TOULOUSE, 30 OCTOBER, PRESENT DAY

There's a whole lot of nothingness in between those tiny bright motes of life. Always has been, in every direction. It's what makes them all the more precious.

The scene is chaotic, of course. But measured chaos, one where we've our fingers on the chaos. Our chaos. Chaotic good, perhaps, just for once.

Apparently, according to Isaac, as soon as Sabnock was contained, the demonic essence working he distilled from that other poor demon dissipated, leaving those previously on Team Twatfish totally vulnerable. The Tarrasque fled like the little bitch he is. We'll track him down later. I'm sure Nithael, who's over with Mephy, would like a few words. Plus a possible rematch. The fucking Tarrasque is fucking fucked if you ask me.

The tower of bone is sinking, slowly, being consumed back into the bowels of the earth, now that Sabnock's been locked down. Not just dissolving into nothingness, leaving us hanging in mid-air Wil-E Coyote style which would have been shit but totally on brand for our luck. Instead it's a sedate ride back downwards, giving us time to start putting things right. Or, at the very least, less FUBAR wrong.

As we walk back over, De Monteguard is having a heated discussion, although not with our other friends. No, it's with his once-more tethered higher being, who's outside his body in his dog form. Nithael is also demonstrating his displeasure on Phillip's back-stabbing buddy. He may have been briefly joined with Caacrinolaas – and I can only imagine just how much the haughty Bene Elohim enjoyed that – but now that he's free, the demon dog's locked up tight in a crackling neon headlock that suggests Nith might be moonlighting for the higher dimensional equivalent of the WWE in his spare time. Guess he's still feeling a little sore from the rigged tussle back on the Quai by the Pont Neuf. Either way, the hound's not even trying to fight back. He's just hanging in mid-air, a woebegone expression painted across his pug-like face.

Which makes me suddenly realise that Nith is fully manifest. 'Cover your eyes!' I shout at Gil and Aicha, waving my hands downwards at them. I don't need them to be lost in gibbering rapturous nonsense for the next few days. There's serious drinking to do.

Gil's head shoots around in all directions. 'What? What is it? The Karnabo?' He's nervous, clearly. Understandably so, considering what he's just been through.

'The fucking angel!' I hiss back, twisting to look at them both, trying to position my body between them and the impossible crackling lightning shape picked out across several metres of sky behind me. Which is precisely as useless a gesture as it sounds, but, hey, I have to try something.

Isaac chuckles. 'Don't worry, lad. I gave Gil a touch of the same working you got at the bottom of the tower. Lad's been through enough of recent not to start crying blood now we've blooming won.'

Okay, phew. Which explains why he looks startled by my weird shrieking but unaffected by the sight behind me. It doesn't explain why Aicha is looking at me with a quirked eyebrow that manages to ask me both what on earth I think I'm doing and whether I was born this much of a dickhead or if I had to put in a significant amount of work to achieve it, both at the same time.

I narrow my eyes at my newly returned friend. 'How are you not weeping great drops of O Negative that brings all the vamps to the yard?'

'Firstly, you twat, damn right, my blood's better than yours.' She gives me a duh gesture, spreading her hands wide. 'Second, who do you think's had Jak and Nan riding shotgun for the last few months? Gives me a bit of natural immunity to it. Although I'm running low on resistance to your bullshit. Need to build that back up.'

'Are you, Aicha Kandicha, saying you find me irresistible?' I can't help grinning at that particular win, crafted from what she said.

For about a second. Until the slap around the back of my head sets my brain ringing like Notre Dame. 'My hand finds your skull irresistible. Almost magnetic.'

'You could have just said it without demonstrating it!' There's a slight petulant whine to my voice.

'And disgrace the scientific method? Fuck me, *saabi*, you've really let things slide in my absence, haven't you?' Oh. Aich. More than you know. More than you know.

'What about Nan? Where is he?' Isaac's voice hitches, panicking and his neck flushes, purpling. In the unexpected delight of getting me back – and the twofer of me having Aich in tow – he hadn't pressed about his own brother, but now the mixture of worry and shame are heavily present in his words.

Aicha stops, turns to him, and puts her arm back around his shoulders. 'He's fine, 'Zac. Promise. A choice. He chose to stay there. Where he can make a real difference. Where they both can. Where they can do what they always wanted to do.'

Isaac gasps, then bites his lip, his eyes misting up at her words, but I'm confused. 'What he always wanted to do? Meaning what?'

'Protect people. Keep them safe.' Isaac, my oldest friend's voice is low, still trembling, though this time with the weight of emotion. 'Stop them from being hurt by those who hold the power.'

'Precisely.' Aicha nods. 'What they set out to do before. What Ben guided them towards. What got them trapped in that fucking skull.'

What started all of this. Good intentions that led them into their own personal hell but which they passed through. Perhaps not unscathed but unchanged. Still fundamentally pure of intent.

Aicha lifts her chin, looks Isaac straight in the eye. 'Sharing my head with them? A privilege. I couldn't have done it with anyone else. But Jak is the best of us.'

'He really is,' Isaac says at the same time as I say 'What, not even me?'

My sister by choice turns her head from 'Zac to me slowly, a dragging motion, as though forced against her will. 'Have you inside my noggin?' She shudders. 'Are you trying to turn me into a world-destroying supervillain? That's Ben levels of horrible suffering.'

326

Of course, talking about the world where Jak's elected to stay gets Isaac's scholarly curiosity up. 'What was the place like where you were, lass? Was it terrible?'

That's right. The world Papa Nicetas originally meant to send us to when he tore open the portal was some nightmarish reality, a terrible world of unending pain. Aicha shakes her head though. 'It was our world. Pretty much, anyhow. Some fundamental differences.'

Now my own catlike curiosity is being piqued. 'Like what?'

'No magic for humans.' Wow, that's a pretty big difference. 'Means the magical beings ran the world. People were chattel, little more than slaves most of the time.'

I can't help noticing she's using past tense. There's no world I can imagine where any of that would sit well with Aicha Kandicha or Jakob.

'Tell you about it later.' She grins. 'Will tell you one thing though. Guess who I found as the Mayor of Toulouse?'

My mouth goes goldfish wide. 'Me? I was the mayor?'

The scorching look of disbelief she gives me is withering. I can feel myself wilting in the face of its blistering heat. 'Are you a fucking idiot, *saabi*?' She pauses, shakes her hand as if to shoo away the question. 'Forget that. No need to answer. Already know you are.' Aicha sighs. 'I just told you there's no magic for humans. How the fuck would you still be alive from the twelfth century, dickhead?'

Oops. It's a fair question. 'Winning charm and dazzling personality?' Her cold stare wilts that idea, decomposing it instantly. 'Okay, not me. So who was it?'

'Fucking Franc.' She grins savagely. 'Franc was the fucking mayor of Toulouse.'

If I gaped before, now I'm actively looking for a shovel

to pick my jaw up off the floor. Past tense once more too. I wonder whether she persuaded him to vacate the job position or whether she "persuaded" him to vacate the mortal coil. Again.

My eyes flick to Gil, but he stays silent. I wonder what he's thinking. Whether he's wishing he could be there, with the monster who became his world. Whether it'd be for him to be wrapped up in the giant's embrace, or to slide a sword through his heart for what he saw in Franc's cold storage.

Perhaps it's both, at the same time.

We carry on walking towards the rest of the team and the restrained Caacrinolaas. 'Anyone else we know or knew kicking about?'

Aicha nods. 'A few.' Then she stops, giving me that magical flashing grin. The one that eases the things constricting inside my chest that I didn't even know were there. A far more effective treatment than slicing it with a *talent*-made laser sword was. *Fuck you, knight of the Trials of Charlemagne. This would have been a much better way of achieving the same thing.*

'You know who I did meet?' Still that grin is there. 'Someone who didn't use to get out much but really loved TV and film. Someone who, over there, was a movie star.' She frowns. 'Well, who used to be anyhow, until the talkies started up.'

The talkies. How we referred to the films when we moved out of the silent era, when suddenly we could hear the actors as well as watch them in action. Fuck me. There are moments when, for all our modernities, we really show our age. But then what she said sinks in, and I clock who she was talking about.

'Lou?' I can hardly even whisper it, hardly believe it to be true.

She leans towards me and drops her voice to match mine. 'Lou *Carcoilh*, you bloody ignoramuth. Lou means –'

'The, as in The Snail,' we chorus it together, and it's just perfect, the timing exactly right. We burst into fits of laughter, leaning against one another as tears roll down both our cheeks at the memory of a certain giant gastropod's outrage. By the Good God, it does me better than any medicine I ever took, any drink I ever drunk to ease the sorrow in my heart. Our Lou – Lou Carcoilh, pardon me, might be gone, but learning there's another out there? One who got to be free, to roam the surface, to seek his fame and fortune… and to find it too?

Well that's just the icing on the cake. And –for once– not a shit cake either.

We're close enough by now that we can hear the conversation between De Monteguard and Caacrinolaas. Close enough too that they can hear ours.

'… see?' Caacrinolaas tries to nod in our direction, but chokes instead. Looks like Nithael's not about to let him get any wiggle room. 'There! He's not dead, is he? No one's really dead. Only in this world, and that's not really dead, is it?' The gigantic demon hound has the gall to look distinctly put out about being in a headlock, as though we're all being deeply unreasonable. Whereas I think we're being overly reasonable letting him still have a head to be locked, even if he did switch sides and help us out in the end.

'That's not the point, Caacky!' Oh fuck me. I've heard some terrible pet names between friends and lovers over the years. This one might just take the award for the multiverse's worst. However, considering how deeply upset and hurt Philippe De Monteguard already looks, I decide to avoid taking the piss out of him. For now. You'd better believe I'm making a mental note to do precisely that the minute he cheers up.

'What is going on?' I ask Philippe, who looks both absolutely furious and also on the verge of tears.

'He doesn't understand!' He waves a hand in the direction of the giant hound. 'Won't get it! He's being deliberately obtuse, I swear. As far as he's concerned, he's done nothing wrong.'

'Nothing wrong?' Oh, man. I fully understand why De Monteguard is looking so vexed. In fact, I'm amazed by how well he's keeping his cool. 'Nearly killing Isaac and Nith, nothing wrong? The dead of Toulouse, nothing wrong? The simiots who paid the price, nothing wrong? The *children*, the *fucking children*' —my voice rises, building up steam at the very thought— 'on that aircraft to Germany who could have died just to fuck with us, *nothing wrong*?'

'But they wouldn't really have died, would they!' The absolute arsewipe just looks bemused at why I'm so outraged. 'They'd still be *there*. And they'd probably come back *here*.'

'They aren't the same people, Caacky!' There's a pleading edge to Philippe's voice. Although I might have to plead with him not to use that nickname again because it's making it hard for me to stay righteously furious instead of sniggering like the small, immature schoolboy I am in my heart of hearts. 'Just because they are *versions* of the person doesn't mean they are that person. Those are totally different souls. We cannot break our being into fragments like demons, scatter them across multitudes. And the same with reincarnation. Maybe it's true, maybe it isn't —not talking about for you Paul, I meant more generally— but if we have lived before, *we don't remember it*. There's no surety, no certainty. Not for the person who dies. Not for all those left behind, who suffer for their loss. You have cost so many so dearly, just to have a throwdown with an angel. So many families left broken and distraught, hurting. You hurt them.' He stops, half-chokes. Takes a calming, steadying breath, then raises his head, looking the demon dog straight in the eye. 'You hurt me. So very badly. I thought you were my friend.'

Perhaps nothing else hit home –I can't read the canine expression clearly enough– but based on the sucking in-breath, that one hits the mark at least. 'I am, Phil! I am!' Well, I'll be damned. There's a begging tone there I'd not have expected from the villainous fucker. 'This – I know – Look…' Apparently, Caacrinolaas can't find his words.

Not that Phillipe is about to let him. 'You stole my body! Took me because I tried to stop you doing the wrong thing. Because you made the decisions for both of us. The wrong decisions. Decisions that if you'd discussed them with me, I could have helped you to understand. Instead you treated me like a pet. Worse! Like a slave!'

'But we borrow each others' bodies all the time down below!' Caacrinolaas rolls his eyes desperately in Mephy's direction. 'Tell them Mephy! Tell them it's normal for us!'

Mephy raises his tired head, shaking it in disbelief. 'You're a fucking idiot, *Caacky*.' The restrained demon winces at that one. *Good work, Meph*. 'Did you really think just because you could snoop on all the different dimensions before that they were all linked? Is that how you justified running the war when we fought and drove the manos in droves to their destruction for our honour? That it was all just a game? Are you really that fucking stupid, demonico?'

Now Caacrinolaas is trembling, his mouth working, shaping for words, failing for them. Finally he finds his voice. It is small, diminished as he is before their admonishments. 'I'm… I'm sorry, Phil.' It seems that's all he can manage. He quiets, his eyes downcast, unable to meet the stare powered by hurt from his tethered former friend.

'So what do we do with him?' De Monteguard asks. That's the most pressing question right now.

'Easy,' I say, remembering the frailty of Isaac in my arms. 'He wants to buddy up with Sabnock? Fine. Stick them together for eternity. Pop him in the acorn.'

Chapter Fifty-Seven

There's a quote misattributed to Satre - "Hell is eternity spent in a locked room with your friends". Caacrinolaas picked his friends. Now he gets that own, personalised form of Hell.

Now Caacrinolaas' head comes popping up; his eyes widen, panic stricken. 'No! Please no! Not with him! Not forever! He's so whiny! I'd never have tolerated a second in his company if he hadn't promised me the chance to have another crack at the angelicos! Don't put me with him! Kill me! Erase me out of existence, but don't let me spend eternity listening to him *moaning*. He's so *boring*.' He punctuates this with an agonised groan, as if the very idea is torture. I don't know; for a demon, perhaps it is. Good. Fuck him for what he did to my father.

'Lad…' Isaac says, laying a hand on my shoulder. 'Take a moment. Breathe. Let the anger go. Look at him.'

If there's one thing I don't want to do right now, it's let

my anger go. But the gentle voice in my ear is one who's never steered me wrong. It's not one I'm about to ignore now, just because it suits me. So I do. I look at the demon hound. Really look at him. See the way he's trembling, his lips quivering, his eyes wide, panic-stricken. It's a look I've seen many times. A look when someone has fucked up dramatically and they've only just realised it.

It's a look I've worn plenty of times myself.

'What would Jak do, lad? What would he want? He's not here, is he?' I twist my head, look into his dark brown eyes, full of compassion. 'Unless we hold him my boy. *Here.*' He presses a hand to his chest, then to his head. 'If we do that, then he's always with us, even worlds apart.'

'Well, we can't exactly allow him to go either, now can we?' Faust's voice is mild, but his words are steel. There's no way he's about to let the arsehole off the metaphysical leash.

'I'll make you promises! Oaths! On my power! Anything at all!' The giant hound's wings flap furiously, instinctively, though it gets him nowhere against the angel's rock-solid grip.

Mephy pushes himself to his feet wearily. He lopes slowly over to stand before the other demon. 'Do you? Promise on your power? To do whatever we tell you?'

'Yes, yes! Anything!' Caacrinolaas is whining, his voice a nasal screech.

'Witnessed.' Mephy lets out a bark that rings off the cloisters, bouncing back, echoing and amplifying, channeling inwards, striking Caacrinolaas like a thunder clap. The giant winged demon shakes his head as though the bark's still going on, building inside his head, giving him a headache. Perhaps it is. Good, fuck him some more.

Meph turns to us. 'Right. Off you go then, manos. Sort it out. Yes, Aich, nice to see you by the way – What is it?'

'What,' my returned friend says slowly, 'did I say would happen if you kept using the word *mano* for humans, Meph, you sexist shitbag?'

I have no idea what the answer is, but apparently Meph does because he suddenly looks just as stricken as Caacrinolaas did a second ago, sitting down hard on his rump, his tail pressed protectively beneath it. 'But I just helped rescue you!' he whines.

'And that's why I'm asking you instead of demonstrating it. *Humanos*, okay Meph?'

'Fine, fine.' He jumps back up and hurries over to Faust. I can hear him muttering, 'She's bloody terrifying, even for demonicos. No way she's just a man… humano. No bloody way.'

By the Good God. Even demons are scared of Aicha Kandicha. Mind you, rightly so.

Back to the business at hand. 'Right, let's start with the mess you've left below.' I realise that "below" isn't actually that far now. Judging by the fact I can see some building tops, we must be approaching ground level. 'What about the people?' The ones still alive at least. There must be plenty of dead. But that's a problem we can deal with afterwards. The living are the first priority.

'What about them?' For a moment the old Caacrinolaas is back, a cocky sneer, but then I see his eyes go across to Phillipe and it falters, fades, crumbles away. The demon dog cast his eyes downwards. 'I… I can help.' He looks back up, an eager expression on his face. 'Actually, it's no worries. I can make them forget the whole thing.'

'No!' I can't let him do that. This has been too big, too

public for something like that. It needs to be subtler. 'Find a reason in the minds of those in charge. Something plausible. A weapons leak from a research facility, perhaps.' There're a few military tech research sites around Toulouse, so it's not outside the realms of possibility. 'Someone spiking the water supply maybe. Whatever you need. But make sure you put it in the minds of those in charge that everyone affected – and I mean *everyone*, those who survived and the loved ones of those who didn't – are going to get compensated, taken care of. Make sure you correct the memories of all those who didn't die too. Make them match the scenario you're putting out there. Take away the worst of what they saw and did too.' No, hold on. *That's not the answer, Paul, and you know it.* 'Scrub that. Just make it fuzzy. Take away the sharp details.' It's not right to just strip them of their trauma. They'll know it's not their fault. Hopefully the government and those in control will provide them with the right care and counselling, thanks to Caacrinolaas' working.

'Something like that will take all my power.' The gigantic demon dog looks doubtful. 'I'll be wiped out for a while. Unable to do anything. Plus, I'll be zoned out while I do it.'

'Don't worry about that.' I give him my sharpest, most tooth filled grin. 'We'll keep you perfectly safe.' *Then make sure you never need any power again, you fucking wankpuffin.*

For a second I think he's going to argue. The subtext wasn't exactly subtle. But once more his eyes stray to his bond-mate, De Monteguard. Mine do, too, in time to see the firm nod. But I don't miss the set of Phillipe's jaw, either. I don't think he's going to be on board with my plan. I'll deal with that after, though.

Whatever he sees is enough for Caacrinolaas anyhow. He inhales, filling his enormous muscular chest, swelling it almost to bursting. His eyes roll back in his head, ink-stained sclera on view, and as he breathes out a dark miasma, a blackened mote cloud rolls out of his mouth, that same impossible black as his essence. It pours from his maw, going up and over the top of the roofs, out in every direction.

De Monteguard's eyes are fixed on his once-friend, making it easy for me to give the others a subtle signal, letting us draw away, further back where he can't hear us.

'We're going to kill him anyway, right?' Aicha's voice is low, calm, but utterly certain.

I'm in complete agreement but with only one proviso. 'I'm not sure we can. But we can lock him away in that acorn still.' There's a grim satisfaction to that. If that's his idea of hell, then I'm all for putting him there. He might not have really understood what he was doing, but that doesn't excuse the terrible things he's done, not for one second. An eternity with Sabnock seems like just the ticket to me.

But Isaac shakes his head. 'No, lad. We made a deal.'

'A deal with a demon? Since when was that worth the paper made out of skin it was written on?' I can't believe what he's saying.

'I heard that, mano, and it was deeply offensive!' Mephy's voice rises from the other side of the courtyard, followed by a panicked, 'Humano! I meant humano!'

'But it's also a deal with us.' Isaac's tone brooks no argument. 'He didn't understand. And he regretted it!'

'He regretted hurting Philippe!' That's a selfish pain, one relating to those he knows. It's nothing compared to the careless damage he wrought against those he didn't.

'But it's a start! It means he can change. With the right help. And if we keep those who are missing with us, their voices in our minds, lad, their wishes in our heart, then we can keep their presence alive. So, I'll ask you again. What would Jak want us to do if he were here?'

We stand in silence for a moment. But there's no answer to give. Even Aicha can't match his intensive glare. We drop our heads, and Isaac nods firmly. 'Right. So let me handle this, okay?'

We shrug and then wait to see what our resident genius has in mind. Although we exchange a quick glance, the message clear in it, confirming that we're both on the same page. If we're not happy with what Isaac does? Caacrinolaas is going in that acorn whether 'Zac likes it or not.

It doesn't take long. The spread-out fog cloud rolls backwards over the roof tiles, back down the demon dog's gullet, and his eyes roll forward once more. He sags, collapsing against Nith's angelic grip, going limp. The Bene Elohim deposits him ungraciously in a heap on the floor in front of us. He's shrunk, so he's little above the size of a bulldog now, although still with eagle wings poking out of his back, albeit to scale with the rest of his form.

'It's… it's done.' He gasps, his words seeming hard, his chest heaving up and down. 'No… there'll be no… questions asked.'

'Good.' Isaac steps forward, looking down at him. 'It's a start.'

Caacrinolaas lifts his head and whines. 'A start? I did… did my side of the deal.'

'No, that was the start. You swore on your power to do whatever we decided.' Isaac keeps his voice level, but there's no softness to it. This is the judge-delivering sentence, and Caacrinolaas knows it. He shrinks in on himself.

'You are tied, tethered to a good man. So here's what you will do. You will not use your power, your *talent*, in any form, not once. Not without his express permission. If you do, you will break your oath. You will do everything in your remit to keep him safe and happy-'

'Hold on.' Aicha interrupts, holds up a hand. 'That seems like a lot of power to be putting in your new friend's hands. No offence, I'm sure he's lovely, but what happens if one day he's *not*? Remember Ben, *saabi*.'

Shit. She's got a point. Benedict was my best friend in my first life, my sworn enemy determined to destroy me by the time I encountered the shit wizard, his mind bent and broken by his centuries alive. I don't think De Monteguard would go that way. But then again, I'd never have believed Ben would have either.

'I'll stand for him.' A quiet voice, from further back. I raise my head to meet a calm gaze, but one packed with hidden depths, flesh-sheathed steel. 'Give me equal responsibility if you want.'

Fucking hell. Gil is offering to be bonded. To a stranger, and another monster. One who is a demon, when he's just suffered being possessed. Twice. But the kid believes it's the right thing to do. So, of course, yet again, he's going to do it, without hesitation.

Isaac's got a better answer, or at least an easier one. 'How about this? For the time being, any time you use your *talent* Caacrinolaas, you must have it approved by both of them. You don't need to be bonded to both. Verbal permission will do. We can consider later if that will be modified, to release Gil from that pressure.' He turns to Aicha. 'Will that satisfy you, lass?'

The sharp nod he receives in response confirms it. Isaac rubs his hands together, getting back in the swing of what he was saying. 'Right, you will protect them both, keep them both alive and well. If you do not, you will break your oath. Should they one day die, and it be from any action or lack of action on your part, you will break your oath. If it is not, you will return to one of us here, one of our number gathered, and plead your case. Show us you have come to understand this world and its inhabitants. Should we judge you to have done so? You may be deemed to have kept your oath and allowed to return home. Do you understand?'

The demon hound, the President of Hell according to the *Ars Goetia*, ceremonial title or no, looks thunderstruck, entirely tongue tied. But there are no other options for him, and he knows it. Eventually his chin droops, and he nods his head, acquiescing.

'Good.' Isaac doesn't clap his hands together with glee, but it's a close-run thing. 'Phillipe, did you hear all that?'

The young man steps forward and nods far more eagerly than his bound companion. 'I did.' He grabs Isaac's hand, presses it between his two, and pumps it up and down. 'Thank you! Thank you for seeing... for seeing what I can see in him.'

'That's why I could see it.' Isaac's words are gentle, full of kindness. 'You saved him, lad. Remember that.'

'I will!' De Monteguard grins, laughs, a free clear sound, all burdens lifted. 'I will, sir, I will!'

The quiet rumble of the descending tower, so constant as to have become our new normal, ceases, shocking in its sudden absence.

'Ground floor, please look out for the closing doors.' Aicha gives me a shallow bow as she waves a hand towards the exit.

'Fucking A, let's get the hell out of Dodge.' A sudden thought strikes me. 'Shit, what about Tartalo?' The cyclops took a huge tumble from the top of the tower but we already saw that had no impression the first time he pitched out the window head first.

Isaac frowns and nods to Nithael. The angel streaks off over the balustrade. 'Nith'll find him. He seemed a simple sort despite his appetites. Mostly interested in his ring. I'm sure we can find somewhere safe to keep him, away from passing hikers he might decide to make into a protein bar.'

I groan. 'Does that mean we'll have to deal with that *before* we can start drinking?'

Isaac looks at me, shocked. 'Are you bloody kidding me, lad? What do you think I was asking Nith? If he can't keep him occupied while we get to the nearest bar, I'll boot Tartalo off to the bloody moon, him and that ring of his!'

I can just picture it, the angel pulling on his size hundred hiking boots and planting his foot up the cyclops' backside. Apparently, Isaac can too because he starts to giggle that little infectious noise where he's trying – and failing miserably – to hold it in check; it just keeps building more and more. Then he's in hysterics, and so am I, each of us with tears rolling down our cheeks.

'Imagine… imagine,' I manage, 'if NASA found… him on a… moon landing?'

'Found… found… the ring,' Isaac gasps.

'Lawks!' I shriek, and we both fall about laughing again.

Aicha shakes her head disbelievingly. 'No idea how you two chucklefucks survived without me here to wipe your arses. Fucking hell.' It doesn't even come close to hiding the upward twist of her lips. 'C'mon then, you bloody idiots. There's a fruit mocktail with my name on it.'

A mocktail? Wow, she's really pushing the boat out. I give her a grinning nod, and we head towards the exit, now level with the rest of Toulouse outside.

Epilogue

'What is so bloody important that you had to drag us both out here at…' Isaac considers for a moment. 'Far too bloody early o'clock for any reasonable human being?'

He shades his eyes from the low-slung sun, the rays managing to work their way around the concrete structures surrounding us in Arenes to strike his irises. Considering how late I kept him up last night – and how much single malt we polished off between us – I can imagine that must feel like being struck directly in the eyes with little golden hammers.

I wouldn't know though. Because I was smart enough to bring and wear sunglasses. They make me smug. Smug-glasses if you will.

At least until Aicha tears them off my face and tosses them across to my mentor. 'There you go.' She turns back to me. 'Your idea. You get to look at the sun.'

'Fucking hell, you make me sound like a vampire being executed.' I squint against the sudden assault of my eyeballs by the big yellow sky bastard. Foiled again.

342

'You're enough of a mopey, whingy twat to be one. Now. What are you up to?'

Oh ho. Clever Aicha as always. I notice she doesn't say "why are we here", because she's already worked out the why in the sense of being in this place at this time.

I grin. 'Two years.'

'Two ye... oh! Two years!' Isaac's clocked it now. Two years. Two years since I died at the hands of the shit wizard and woke up back at Purpan hospital. Two years since this whole recent shitstorm kicked off. It's only just now calming down.

I shove my hand into my etheric storage, emerge clutching two champagne flutes, passing it to the two people dearest to me in the entire world.

'Champagne for you, 'Zac, which should take the edge off your sore head.' And hopefully mean I can get my shades back. 'Champony alcohol-free kiddy drink for you, because the world isn't ready for a tipsy Aicha.'

'I can get tipsy. I could shove enough tips into you as to transform you into my new blade holder.' She rubs her chin as she accepts the glass. 'Tempting. Seriously tempting.'

'So, right, happy anniversary of you dying in a horrible manner once again, lad, but once more, why are we here?'

'Ah, well. This isn't quite where we need to be, but it'll do us good to stretch our legs a bit.'

And with that, I head off up the road at a brisk pace, towards Saint Cyprien and away before either of them can gut me for being unnecessarily enigmatic.

It does me good. So much good. Not just to walk, although of course it's always a pleasure. But to be walking here, in my streets, of my city. Stamping myself back into the pavement, writing my talent into the concrete. Reclaiming the city fully as mine.

The other two catch up with me, quickly enough. Neither of them attack me, either, which is credit to their self-restraint. I guess they must be feeling indulgent as it's my death-day anniversary. Maybe they'll bake me a cake later. Maybe it won't be poisoned, either.

'How's Phillipe getting on?' I ask Isaac. As always, he's the one keeping in touch, making sure everything's running smoothly, that everyone's okay.

'Aye, good. I spoke to Gil yesterday.' Isaac gives me a grin. 'They're settling in well.'

Brilliant. Unsurprisingly Gil wasn't in any hurry to set up again in Auch after what happened. With Caacrinolaas's demon talent at their disposal, there was no need for them to be under our purview and protection.

Eventually, the pair settled on Pau. Once home to my friend Al-Ruhban, it lay empty after the arrival of Melusine. It seems fitting that her slayer should claim that area. Plus, it turns out De Monteguard isn't just comfortably well off. He's absolutely loaded. De Montfort, his father, got him Board Member positions at all sorts of top companies, the sort of ones where he's only expected to turn up once a year for a couple of hours and gets showered with money for doing so. No doubt it was to give him easy access to an immediate fortune if he ever took over Phillipe's body, but with Simon gone forever, it means De Monteguard's never going to struggle financially.

'What's their plan?' I'm guessing they'll be aiming for a quiet life, after all the madness they've had recently. 'Retirement?'

'Does that sound like Gil to you, saabi?' Aicha shakes her head derisively. It's a fair point. 'He's looking for ways to help those like him. People who stumble enough into the

Talented world to get hurt, but without the power to keep themselves safe.'

Apparently she's been in touch with him too. Damn, I really do need to step up my game in that regard.

That does sound more like Gil, though. At least with Caacrinolaas – or Caacky as Phillipe still insists on calling him, despite me mocking him relentlessly whenever he does – at their beck and call, I don't have to worry about the messes he might get himself into. Which I realise is the pot calling the kettle black, but I've got people around to keep me safe. The Good God knows I need them. I'd probably impale myself on my shoelace tying my shoes otherwise.

Not that I'd admit that to them, of course.

Further questions will have to wait because we've got to where I wanted to be. A rolldown metal shutter, nondescript, blocks access. It's taken me a while to set this up. It's totally going to be worth it.

'A car park?' Isaac peers at the entrance as though he can see through to the other side. Mind you, with Nith on board, maybe he can. I decide to get on with it, just in case, so as to guarantee the big reveal. I've worked hard enough.

'Ta da!' I wave my hand, and the shutter retracts, rolling up with a clackety rattling, revealing behind…

'Cars?' Isaac's tone is even more confused than before.

'Brilliant. Good spot. They are indeed cars. You've passed the test, and will now be crowned King Of Albion. The Knight from the Trials is just around that corner with the paperwork if you'll step round and… for fuck's sake Isaac, not just cars.'

'Not just cars?' He wrinkles his brow. 'Are they planes as well? Transformers of some sort.'

And now I feel like I've not done a good enough fucking

job. 'No, because damn it, Jim, I'm a wizard, not a fucking sci-fi engineer. Not just cars, 'Zac. Your cars.'

His eyes go wide, running over the collection. Sleek sports models. Rugged ATVs. Shiny plastic and metal wonders in all the colours of the rainbow, every one top of the range.

'Your electric cars, 'Zac.' They're all here.

Every one that I could lay my hands on, that I think he'd like. From a super sensible, practical Volvo XC40 that I'd actually consider getting in with him only because I'd believe I might survive when he totalled it, to a Lotus Evija – two million euros worth of sports car, one of only a hundred and fifty ever made.

I give it a week before it's a flaming heap in a ditch somewhere. Thank the Good God he's got an angel on board with him. The ultimate safety accessory.

'But… But why, lad?' Isaac's like a kid in a candy shop, given free rein to go full on Charlie Bucket. He's staggering around, running a finger along each chassis.

'The keys are inside, if you want to rev one up. On your own. I'm not going anywhere near you in control of one of these.' I snigger at his aghast expression, but then sober up. 'As for why… Because I promised it.'

'When?' He doesn't remember it, of course.

'When we made our way back to Toulouse and I was worried about wrecking your Tesla. But also when… when you went down. Outside the Couvent. Before we climbed the tower.' When being severed from Nithael hit him properly, and he folded up like a petal, curling inwards.

When I'd thought he was going to die. I'd have given anything right then if it meant he didn't die.

'You promised me… a garage?' Isaac's still gobsmacked.

'I promised you a whole fleet of electric cars.'

I reckon I've come good on that promise.

Good. Even if he didn't hear it, I made it. It mattered. Just like he does. He deserves this. Plus the electric cars weren't just important to him. They mattered for Jakob. So that matters, too.

Isaac stops his awe-struck, fidgeting examination of all the vehicles, strides back over, sweeps me into an all-encompassing hug. 'Thank you lad. Thank you so much.'

I hug him back, give him a squeeze, then push him away. 'Right, enough of that, you daft old bastard. Go! Have fun! That's what they're here for!'

He doesn't need any more encouragement, and zips back away, diving into a Mercedes-Benz, I can't remember the model, although the engine doesn't start up.

'He's probably learning all the buttons first.' Aicha's entirely on my wavelength, as per usual.

'So he can ignore them and drive like a lunatic the moment he goes.' A thought strikes me. 'In fact, he's probably sat in there, rubbing the steering wheel like fucking Toad of Toad Hall right now.'

Aich looks across at me, and simultaneously we both say 'Toot, toot!' Then collapse into hysterics, strong enough to have us wheezing. When I do start getting my breath back she says "Toot... toot... motherfucker' between gasping laughs and I'm gone, lost in side-splitting, uncontrollable laughter all over again.

Once we finally manage to calm down, I reach into my etheric storage again. 'He's not the only one who gets a present.'

Then I pull them out, hand them across to her.

They're not wrapped. They don't need any covers except the sheaths the master craftsman made to house them, which are perfect. Just like the blades themselves. A katana and a wakizashi. But not just any pair. No, sirree. For once Aicha's eyes stretch, her normally stoic expression cracking as she realises what they are, taking them reverently.

'These… these are Masamune.' Her voice cracks on the second syllable.

'They are.'

'But… how?'

I can't believe it. I cannot believe it. But it's true. I've stunned Aicha Kandicha into silence. Caught her completely off guard. Which makes everything I've gone through to get these blades totally worth it.

'Leandre. We came to an… understanding.'

Which is a very shorthand way of describing the absolute shitshow I had to go through to get my hands on these one of a kind priceless antiquities but that story can wait for another time.

A honk sounds, though it's a noise far away from the strangled goose wail of most car horns. This is a blaring proud war cry. Isaac pulls up next to us, the smoked window rolling down, his enormous grin infectious.

'Come on you two. This? This merits the bloody Dalmore!'

Oh. Oh! He means the Dalmore 50 Year Old. The one he thought I didn't even know exists although I've no idea where he's hidden it. The one worth about a hundred grand.

The one we're apparently about to crack open.

Fuck it. I'll even get in a car with Isaac for that.

I pull open the door, swing myself into the back, let Aicha grab shotgun, as we pull off towards the Forest of Bouconne, back towards Isaac's now rebuilt house.

As we drive, the clouds break overhead, the sun's brilliant rays punching through, illuminating us, soaking us in a shared warmth, radiating out, fighting through the autumn chill to touch our very cores. This time, it doesn't feel like a moment's peace, to hold on tight to, that might get us through the coming storms.

It feels like when the thunder has raged out, when the hail has lashed down, when the lightning has crashed, splitting the sky with forks of pure brilliance that blind the eye and threaten to overwhelm the senses. When the world has narrowed down to the hammering fall of the tempest's fury.

But then the front has passed. Nature's rage has been mollified, for now at least. Sure, there'll be other storms, other howling gales, other times when the skies strike down upon us with all their force and might.

This time – this storm – is over. The clouds are parting. Now, for this period, however long or short it may be, now we get to bask in the sun's warmth, feel it on our faces, and raise a glass in comfort and safety, with those we've chosen to share our lives with, those who we love more than we could ever love ourselves.

This is what we do it for. This is what makes it all worthwhile.

A phenomenon. One that is phenomenal.

As are those who are in the car beside me. My family, in every way that matters.

Those who are, once more, here by my side.

Only a moment of peace perhaps.

But I'll take it.

Afterword

There it is. Done. My very first ever series, finished and completed. Nine books and three novellas, forming The imPerfect Cathar. It seems unbelievable that we've reached this point, that this whole story is now told, out there in the world, wrapped up and ended.

Not that it is ever ended, of course. Not that I think for one moment that the Bonhomme Gang are done with me. But this tale, this saga, is closed. For now, they get some well deserved rest. A chance to raise a glass and savour the moment. The Good God knows they've worked hard enough to earn it.

So, that's it for now. The end of the imPerfect Cathar series. But the imPerfectVerse is just getting warmed up. Look out for imPerfect Monsters, the first book of The imPerfect Strays series, a co-write coming with Krista Walsh, as the next project in this universe. And keep an eye out for the Bryar Hawthorne series from me, a new Urban Fantasy series, coming very soon as well. There's plenty more arriving for you all, I can promise you that!

In the meantime, you have my thanks, my endless appreciation for your company, coming this far with me.

The road ahead is gleaming bright.

But with many a twist and turn…

About the Author

C.N. Rowan is the multi award-winning author of the imPerfect Cathar and the Broken Hotel for Magical Misfits series. His books have won the Pencraft Award for Literary Excellence, the Best Indie Book Award, the American Legacy Book Award and the Audiobook Reviewer Award.

It's been a strange, unbelievable journey to arrive at the point where these books are going to be released into the wild, like rare, near-extinct animals being returned to their natural habitat, already wondering where they're going to nick cigarettes from on the plains of Africa, the way they used to from the zookeeper's overalls. C.N. Rowan ("Call me C.N., Mr. Rowan was my father") came originally from Leicester, England. Somehow escaping its terrible, terrible clutches (only joking, he's a proud Midlander really), he has wound up living in the South-West of France for his sins. Only, not for his sins. Otherwise, he'd have ended up living somewhere really dreadful. Like Leicester. (Again – joking, he really does love Leicester. He knows Leicester can take a joke. Unlike some of those other cities. Looking at you, Slough.) With multiple weird strings to his bow, all of which are made of tooth-floss and liable to snap if you tried to use them to do anything as adventurous as shooting an arrow, he's done all sorts of odd things, from running a hiphop record label (including featuring himself as rapper) to hustling disability living aids on the mean streets of Syston.

He's particularly proud of the work he's done managing and recording several French hiphop acts, and is currently awaiting confirmation of wild rumours he might get a Gold Disc for a song he recorded and mixed.

Acknowledgments

So now, to the thanks. You'll have seen – if you read the dedication – that this book is dedicated to you. To all of you. The imPs, the fans who've been there, walking beside me on this first leg of my author journey. I feel luckier than I can say to have you on my side.

I have to thank my family, who've watched me lose myself in worlds inside my head while attempting to hit little plastic buttons hard enough to pulverise them into dust. My editor, Miranda Grant, who has made these books not a little bit better, but infinitely so, even if she's dragged me through the seven stages of grief after every book. Becca, my critique partner, and Becky, my beta reader, who have helped me eliminate so much dross beforehand, allowing Miranda to concentrate on spinning what's left into gold. Heather G Harris and Catherine Webb who mentored me before the first book ever came out, and gave a novice, debut author so much encouragement. Athena, Mardie, Darin and Melody who proofread the audiobooks for me. Mel (again), Rachel and Jimmy for their work as the moderators of my Facebook reader's group, C.N. Rowan's imPerfect imPs. Also, a big thanks and congratulations to Jimmy, who came up with Mister Fuzzy Butt in a reader-voted competition I ran on Facebook for a demon's pet companion. I hope I did him proud when I brought him to life! To Perri Corbett for her wonderful work translating the series into French, and J.L. Henry for his work in beta reading that version. To my ARC readers, who come through time and again, trapping those last little errors that snuck through the net and who give me those first reviews that are essential in bringing readers in to discover the series.

To my parents, my siblings, and all the others of my huge, sprawling family who cheer me on endlessly. Steph, Sally and Dee, my Semper Eadem sisters. Craig, my other brother. All of the people who I've forgotten to mention and who deserve to have been remembered. I can only plead that, if you know me, you know I am a Bear of Little Brain and Littler Memory, and will plead brain deficiency as the cause.